Tuscan Holiday

Books by Holly Chamberlin

LIVING SINGLE

THE SUMMER OF US

BABYLAND

BACK IN THE GAME

THE FRIENDS WE KEEP

TUSCAN HOLIDAY

Published by Kensington Publishing Corporation

Tuscan Holiday

Holly Chamberlin

KENSINGTON BOOKS
http://www.kensingtonbooks.com

KENSINGTON BOOKS are published by

Kensington Publishing Corp.
850 Third Avenue
New York, NY 10022

ISBN-13: 978-0-7582-1403-4
ISBN-10: 0-7582-1403-0

First Kensington Trade Paperback Printing: September 2008
10 9 8 7 6 5 4 3 2 1

Printed in the United States of America

As always, for Stephen.
And this time, also for Virginia.

Acknowledgments

As always, I thank John Scognamiglio for his unflagging support.

I would also like to thank Becky Lee Simmons and Winnifred Moody, who do the important work of nurturing so many of us here in Portland at their wonderful restaurant, Katahdin.

Finally, I offer this book to my cousins Jean and Robert in memory of their mother, Joanne, and to Dylan, Paige, and Robert in memory of their grandmother.

1

Motherhood and prostitution have a lot more in common than one might assume. Both are largely thankless professions into which many women unwittingly fall and out of which they rarely, if ever, are able to extricate themselves. Doomed to a life of service to others, most of whom have little if any understanding of the depth of commitment involved in such service, women in these professions are never properly appreciated or decently compensated, and are doomed to be tossed aside like so much refuse once their perceived usefulness has expired.
   —The Utter Folly of a Life of Service: Women and
      the Trap of Selflessness

"You shouldn't have spent the money, Elizabeth."

My mother sniffed delicately at the bouquet of Purple Moon Carnations. They were her favorite, a fact she often mentioned in the weeks before a holiday.

"You're welcome, Mom."

"Of course I love them. Thank you, honey. But you know I don't need any gifts from you."

In spite of the frequent hints about favorite flowers, fragrant beauty creams, and scented candles?

"But I need to give you gifts, okay?" I said. "So bear with me."

"But still, they must have cost you a fortune!"

My God, I thought, you'd think I'd given her a diamond-encrusted evening bag! What ever happened to the art of gracious receiving?

"It's rude to talk about the price of a gift, Mom," I reminded.

"Oh, I'm sorry. The flowers are lovely. Thank you again, dear."

My mother—Jane Caldwell, still teaching high-school English though nearing retirement—went off to put the flowers in a vase. I glanced casually at the mantel on the far side of the living room. No Mother's Day card other than the one from me. So, Marina had forgotten or neglected to give her grandmother a card. . . . Or, a charitable thought, maybe she had a card for me and one for her grandmother in that monstrous bag she'd taken to lugging around, a metallic sack with grommets and fringe and buckles too numerous to count.

"This is a very popular style," she told me, defensively, I thought, when I asked her where she'd gotten it.

"I know that," I said. "I read *InStyle*. I read *Vogue*. I just asked where you got it."

"It wasn't expensive, if that's what you're asking."

"Uh, no. What I'm asking—for the third time—is where you bought the bag."

I swear, sometimes talking to one's child is like negotiating a minefield. You didn't ask to be in the middle of a minefield, you have no idea how you got there, and all you want to do is survive said minefield with your limbs intact.

I did finally learn that Marina had bought the bag at Marshall's. I'd taught her well when it came to bargain hunting.

The doorbell rang, interrupting the mostly critical thoughts about my daughter. "I'll get it," I said. It was Rob. He hadn't been at the graduation ceremony; Marina had been limited to three tickets.

"Where are Jotham's parents?" Rob asked when he'd taken a survey of the guests: my father, Tom; Marina; her long-time boyfriend, now fiancé, Jotham Grandin, who'd also graduated earlier that day from Graham College in Boston; my mother, back with the carnations in a cut-glass vase; and me.

"Invited," I explained, "but they said they had a previous engagement. Whatever. They took the kids out to dinner last night."

"A pricey steak house, no doubt."

"Now, Rob."

"What? So, where did they go?"

"Capitol Grille. A pricey steak house."

"Hey, it's a celebration," he said. "A time for indulgence."

"Now you're defending them?"

"What defending?"

"Anyway," I said, "you're right. This is a celebration, so I got a Carvel ice-cream cake. You know it's Marina's favorite. And considerably less expensive than a specialty cake from Patisserie Claude."

"Mmm, Carvel ice-cream cake. Gotta love the crunchy chocolate layer."

We joined the rest of the party in time to hear my father relating to a bored-looking Jotham his latest home-repair triumph, a tale involving the installation of a brand-new air conditioner in his tool room in the basement.

Rob hugged Marina and handed her a small, prettily wrapped gift.

"Oh, Rob, thank you," she said. "Should I open it now?"

Rob shrugged. "If you want. And there's a gift receipt inside in case you want to exchange it."

Marina carefully sliced one taped end and slid a plastic-encased electronic device into her palm.

"Wow, it's the new iPhone! Thanks, Rob." She gave him another hug and handed the plastic case to Jotham, who immediately set to the difficult work of opening it with his Swiss Army knife.

"What exactly does the new iPhone do?" I asked, *sotto voce*.

"I'm not entirely sure. I think it has something to do with being able to use any service, not just AT&T. Or something."

I looked hard at Rob. "You're an engineer. You're supposed to know how things work. You're even supposed to know why they work."

"True. But the world is changing awfully fast. . . ."

"Now you sound like an old man."

"I am fifty."

"Hardly old. And you can prove it to me later."

"Really?" he said, with a grin. "Ice-cream cake and sex in one day? Who's got it better than me?"

Rob Wayne and I had been together on and off for about thirteen years at that point, long enough to be comfortable with each other's flaws, foibles, and weaknesses but still, amazingly, excited by each other. When we weren't too tired or too busy or too hungry.

The buzz over Rob's gift had died down enough for me to feel that it was time to present my gift. I retrieved a rather bulky envelope from the credenza in the front hall and brought it to my daughter.

"From me," I said, struggling not to cry. Your child's graduation from college—especially a graduation capping a successful four years of study—is a very proud moment.

Marina smiled, and if she was eager to see what was inside, you couldn't tell by the way she carefully opened the envelope, barely ripping the sealed flap. With a questioning look at Jotham—what had she expected, snakes to pop out?—she extracted my present, two round-trip tickets to Florence.

"Oh my God!" she cried, turning once again to her fiancé. "We're going to Italy, Jotham, you and me!"

I was painfully aware of the awkward glances shooting among the other three adults in the room, my mother to my father to Rob and back again. None of them looked directly at me; I was thankful for the small favor.

"Um, no, Marina," I said. "Actually, you and I are going to Italy. I bought those tickets for us. You know, as . . ."

I hesitated; I was embarrassed at having to explain what I had hoped would be obvious.

"As what?" Marina asked, clearly disappointed and just as clearly trying to hide her disappointment.

"Well, you've graduated college, and you're getting married next spring, and, well, I just thought this would be my send-off present to you, you know, as you venture out into the world."

"Oh," Marina said, with about as much expression as a turnip. "Thanks, Mom."

"Yes," I said. "I mean, you're welcome."

Well, I thought, that big surprise fell flat. At least there was the Carvel cake.

"But Mom," Marina said suddenly, "I have no idea what I did with my passport!"

Was that relief I heard in her voice, or was I just projecting? "Remember I asked you to give it to me? It's in the safety-deposit box, at the bank."

"Oh," she said. "That's good. Because I know you can't get on a plane to Europe without a passport."

Jotham winked at Rob and put his arm around Marina's shoulders. "My dad knows some people. He could probably get things speeded up if you needed a passport right away."

No doubt Frank Grandin did know "some people"—i.e., the "right people"—but did his son have to be such a self-important little—

"How about we cut the cake!" my mother exclaimed.

Rob took my mother's elbow. "I'll help, Jane," he said and led her off to the kitchen. As they passed, I heard my mother say:

"I don't know why Elizabeth had to get such a big cake. I just can't imagine what she was thinking, spending all that money. Really, she can be such a spendthrift."

Over his shoulder, Rob offered a consoling little smile.

2

Dear Answer Lady:

I have this little problem. I've been married for six years now to this really nice guy (that's not the problem part), and we have two kids, a boy and a girl, five and three. See, the thing is, I'm pretty sure that if I'd thought about it before just getting pregnant because I could (being married and all), I would have decided not to have any kids. I mean, sometimes I look at them, and I think: What? Who are these people? I'd never hurt my kids or anything, I mean, I play by the rules and provide clothes and food and a place to live and all, but . . . I don't know. I just can't seem to work up any feeling for them. Am I some kind of weirdo?

Dear Latent Sociopath:

Lady, you're one kind of weirdo, all right. What sort of mother can't even work up enough emotion to hate her kids? Indifference toward one's offspring is a far more egregious and potentially poisoning stance that will no doubt cause your children endless years in therapy—and result in your being stashed away in a filthy, state-run nursing home. Do your children—and your future self—a favor and run away now. Disappear, hit the high road, leave no forwarding address, and make no effort to contact them, ever. Hopefully,

your husband will get over his grief in a timely
fashion and provide the children with a step-
mother who cares enough to loathe them.

"Marina didn't seem very happy to be going to Italy with her mother."

That was the understatement of the year. She and Jotham had made off immediately after cake and coffee, with only a "See you later, Mom" and a wave.

I tossed my bag on the hall table. Rob shut the door of my apartment behind him.

"She'll have a great time once she's there, you'll see. Plus, you know how she loves to shop. She's a professional bargain hunter. She'll get into buying clothes for the trip."

"She does love to shop, but she's so damned finicky. It takes her hours to find the perfect T-shirt. It drives me nuts. What's so special about a T-shirt?"

Rob gave me a look. "Good thing she's old enough to shop on her own."

"Okay," I said, "so I'm being grumpy. But I don't know, Rob. Maybe this trip is a stupid idea after all. Maybe I should cash in my ticket and buy one for Jotham instead."

"No, Elizabeth." Rob took me by my shoulders and looked into my eyes. "You deserve this vacation. And Marina deserves some time alone with her mother. Besides, we agreed it would do her good to spend some time away from Jotham. She's attached to that boy like white is attached to rice."

"That boy," I pointed out, "is a young man. And that young man is going to be her husband this time next year."

"Maybe."

"What do you mean by that?" I asked quickly.

Rob shrugged and stepped away. "Just that anything can happen."

"Do you know something I don't know?" I asked. "Did Marina talk to you?"

"Of course not. Look, just go to Italy and have a great time. Promise?"

"I promise to try. A glass of wine?"

"Sure."

I went off to the kitchen for the wine and glasses. When I returned to the living room, Rob was frowning in the direction of the end table. The end table, a dubious antique I'd bought at a local garage sale, was where I'd been displaying holiday cards since long before Rob and I met.

"I see there's no Mother's Day card," he said.

"She's got a lot on her mind," I replied, defending the unthankful child I'd been condemning earlier.

"She could have gotten you a card. Sorry. I know I shouldn't comment."

I handed Rob a glass of wine. "No, that's okay. After all this time, you have a right to speak up."

Honestly, it didn't much matter to me that Marina had forgotten Mother's Day, though I did feel bad on my mother's behalf. As any parent can tell you, what hurts far more than no card on a Hallmark holiday are the casual slights, the eye rolls your child thinks you don't see, the muttered "whatevers," the unasked-for-and-unwanted criticism of your clothing, your speech habits, your existence.

Rob left about an hour later—after having gotten his cake and eaten it, too—and I busied myself straightening up. I'd rushed out of the house that morning, not wanting to be late for the graduation ceremony, uncharacteristically leaving breakfast dishes in the sink and several rejected outfits strewn across my bedroom.

I didn't expect Marina to be home until much later that evening; I assumed she and Jotham would meet up with their bosom buddies, two other engaged couples who'd met during high school and who'd also graduated that day. The six of them were inseparable, a little club of eager-to-be-marrieds who were already planning how to save for their as-yet-to-be-born children's college educations.

Not that there was anything wrong with that; it was just that sometimes Marina and her crew seemed even older than Rob and me, without the sense of adventure we assume the young should possess. Of course, the flip side of my daughter's ostensible maturity was that she didn't do drugs or drive without a license or have serial abortions, all of which a mother seriously appreciates.

Teeth brushed and face washed, I settled into bed; next to me sat the stack of guidebooks I'd been studying in preparation for the trip. On the small nightstand to my right stood a framed picture of Rob and me taken a few years earlier at Old Sturbridge Village. The two of us are cheek to cheek, arms slung around each other, laughing happily into the camera, oblivious to the goat that had snuck up on us and taken a mouthful of Rob's sweater into his mouth.

I smiled, remembering Rob's response to discovering the hem of his sweater in the mouth of a mad-eyed goat. He turned around to me with a sigh. "Why didn't I wear the red sweater today?" he said. "I've never really liked that sweater."

Two of the best things about Rob are his sense of humor and even temper, traits I found appealing right from the start. He doesn't have a tendency toward frenzied action or manic speech; he doesn't need to be the center of attention. Rob is the sort who can engage in intelligent conversation without either the need to dominate or the tendency to lose ground. In short, he's mature and stable without being narrow-minded or rigid. I suspect he was pretty much always this way, though his parents are long gone, so I've no way of confirming this. It's not that Rob won't talk about himself if pressed; it's just that he's self-effacing enough not to indulge in details. This can be frustrating, but, the advice of women's magazines notwithstanding, when you really think about it, reticence is hardly a major failing in a romantic partner.

I reached for one of the guidebooks and suddenly realized

just how tired I was, too tired to read. Instead, I thought back over the day, remembered how immensely proud I'd felt when Marina had received her diploma. It had seemed a great culminating moment. I'd guided my daughter, my only child, through day care and kindergarten, through grade school, middle school, the relative hell that is high school, and, finally, through college. And through it all, Marina had thrived. You could even say that Marina's life had been charmed, to the extent that any life lived without tragedy is charmed.

Yes, it had been a good day. It had made me happy to see my daughter surrounded by the people who meant the most to her—and to me: her grandparents, Rob, Jotham. The only person of importance—if one could call him that—in Marina's life that hadn't been present for the occasion was her father.

But he'd never been present for any of Marina's important events, not even her birth. One would think I'd have been used to Peter Duncan's absence by then, his utter lack of concern. One would think, but one would be wrong.

3

You've tried cajoling. You've tried giving elaborate gifts. You've even feigned illness in an effort to get the attention, care, and respect of your adult child. But every effort has met with failure. Don't despair. Simply announce that if your son or daughter doesn't pay more attention to you, he or she summarily will be cut out of your will. Then watch your adult child come running.

— How Sharper Than a Serpent's Tooth: How to Handle the Thankless Child

After the party at my grandparents'—complete with Carvel ice-cream cake; I swear, it wouldn't have been a special occasion in my family if we didn't have that cake! I hadn't really liked it since I was about twelve, but I never had the heart to say anything to my mother—Jotham and I stopped at the Cherry Pit. It was kind of "our place." At least once a week we met our friends Allison, and her fiancé, Jordan, and Jessica, and her fiancé, Jason, there. We'd all gone to college together. And we were all planning to be married within eighteen months of graduation, first Allison and Jordan, then Jessica and Jason, and finally Jotham and me.

The Cherry Pit was nothing fancy, just a chain pub/restaurant. We liked it because of the usual things people like chain restaurants for—consistency and relatively low prices. And pretty decent food, though a lot of it wasn't exactly what you'd call diet or health food. Anyway, we knew we could always get a table or snag a place in the bar. Being sort of a family place, the bar area emptied out after nine, except for Saturday night, which was still date night in our suburb of Boston. That night, a Sunday, the bar area was almost empty. Once I'd overheard my mother call the Cherry Pit "one of those bloodless generic suburban holes", and her tone was anything but complimentary. It didn't bother me. It wasn't like Jotham and I ever asked her to hang out with us there.

We perched on high stools at a smallish, round table and ordered drinks; a basket of popcorn was already waiting.

"So, what do you think of my mom's gift?" I asked. "Pretty . . . unexpected, right?" I was a bit nervous about Jotham's reaction to my going away without him, and for two whole weeks.

"I think it's great," he said, squeezing my hand. "It's good for family to do stuff together."

I searched his face for a sign that he was fibbing, but as usual, Jotham's expression was inscrutable. He wasn't a guy to give anything away easily. "You're not upset my mother didn't invite you, too?"

"No, no," he said, dropping my hand. "It's fine. Besides, what would I do while you girls shopped and sat around in cafés, or whatever they have over there, drinking wine? I hate shopping, and I don't drink wine unless it's from California."

"You could spend time in museums," I teased.

"Yeah, that would happen. Look, you should go and enjoy and buy yourself something. I hear you can get good leather in Italy pretty cheap. Treat yourself. You only graduate from college once, right?"

I smiled and kissed his cheek as if I believed he was fine with the trip. But I didn't really believe it, not after the Paris incident. But this was different, I argued with myself. This time my mother would be with me. What possible trouble could I get into traveling with my mother?

"Let's talk about our honeymoon," he said suddenly.

"But we haven't even planned the wedding yet," I pointed out reasonably. "I haven't figured out how much the reception is going to cost, and I want to check out buying a used dress, and since we have a budget to consider—"

"Don't worry about the budget right now. Let's just talk pie in the sky. I bet I know where you want to go."

I laughed. "I bet you don't."

"If I get it right, will you share some jalapeño poppers with me, no complaining about fat and cholesterol?"

"You're on."

"Hawaii."

I laughed. "You are so totally wrong."

"I don't believe you."

"No, really," I said. "I have no interest in going to Hawaii. You really have no idea where I want to go?"

Jotham shrugged. "You got me."

"The Grand Canyon! And maybe other parts of the Southwest, too: New Mexico, the Mojave Desert, Sedona with those big red rocks. Joshua trees. All those big open skies and Indian stuff and turquoise jewelry and a totally different landscape from New England. Doesn't it sound exotic?"

Jotham looked puzzled. "Hawaii isn't exotic?"

"Well, sure," I said, "I guess. But everybody goes to a beach resort for the honeymoon. Jamaica, Bermuda, the Caribbean. I just thought we could do something a bit different, try something new."

"What, like go camping? We've never been camping," Jotham pointed out. "You know I'm not a big fan of the outdoors. And since when have you become Miss Crunchy Nature Girl?"

"Well, we wouldn't necessarily have to camp," I said, though a vision of a vast, starry night sky had come to mind. "There are spas in the Southwest, Jotham, and I'm sure there are plenty of nice hotels. Santa Fe is supposed to have some great places to stay. I'm sure we could find something within our budget." The look on Jotham's face stopped me. "What? You don't like the idea of the Southwest?"

"No, I didn't say I don't like the idea, exactly. But it is our honeymoon, Marina. Not just some silly vacation."

"I don't understand," I said.

Jotham glanced around the almost empty room and then leaned in as if he were about to impart a big, important secret. "What if I told you I've already arranged for us to spend two weeks in a five-star hotel in Maui? Award-winning restaurant, exclusive day spa, personal trainers on hand, Vegas-style shows every night. Sounds good, huh?"

I knew it was a disloyal thought, but it occurred to me that the only reason Jotham wanted us to go on an expensive, fancy honeymoon was because he could be a bit of a snob. It was just possible that he cared less about pleasing me than he did about impressing our friends.

"What do you mean you already arranged it?" I demanded. "How are we supposed to pay for that?"

"Don't worry about it. I've taken care of it," Jotham replied in that condescending way that had been getting on my nerves ever since our junior year of college, when Jotham won a big prize for the debate team. I don't know why his attitude should suddenly have started to bother me; he'd always been the same way, ever since (and probably before) I met him in sophomore year of high school.

"How have you taken care of it? What are you talking about?"

"Look, before I say anything, I want you to promise not to jump down my throat, okay?"

"Yeah, okay," I lied. "Just tell me. And you'd better not have taken out some crazy high-interest loan."

Jotham frowned. "Please, Marina."

"Okay, okay," I said. "I'm sorry." Jotham was nothing if not fiscally responsible.

"My parents are paying for our honeymoon. It's our wedding gift. Well, part of it. They'll be picking up the tab for the rehearsal dinner, of course. That's traditionally the responsibility of the groom's family."

This news stunned me. When I recovered, my voice was unusually high. "But I thought the plan was to pay for everything on our own."

I wasn't used to what I saw as charity, and I had no desire to get used to it. True, while I had been known to complain about not driving a better car and not having enough money to buy the latest Coach bag for spring, I had lived a pretty good life, and I knew it. My mother and I were not poor; we had never really suffered or done without. It wasn't as if we'd been forced to rely on food stamps or welfare; it wasn't as if my mother had had to work two or three jobs to put me through college. I was proud of what my family had achieved— we'd earned it, after all, me included—and I wasn't about to take a handout from anyone, especially not my future in-laws.

"A gift," Jotham pointed out when I'd made my big statement, "is not a handout."

"A gift," I argued, "can be inappropriate. This is just too much."

"We can't say no to them," Jotham said with maddening calm. "It would be rude."

"But it's our honeymoon, Jotham. It's our wedding and our marriage. It's supposed to be all about us. No one else can tell us what to do."

Jotham gave me the look that was meant to shame. "I can't believe you're being so ungrateful," he said. "Look, you're taking a trip to Italy with your mom. It's not like you're opposed to accepting big gifts."

"I'm not being ungrateful," I argued. "How can you say that? And the trip to Italy is not the same thing as our honeymoon. My mother isn't—interfering—with our relationship."

"How is giving us a trip to Hawaii interfering? It's not like my parents are coming with us. Come on, Marina, be reasonable."

And just like that, I caved. What was the point in arguing? In the end Jotham always got what he wanted. "All right," I said. "Fine. Your parents aren't interfering. We'll go to Hawaii. I'm sure it will be very nice."

Jotham straightened his shoulders and smiled the smile of the victor. "Good. Now, how about an order of poppers."

I didn't bother to point out that he'd lost the bet. "Sure," I said, "whatever you want."

"Ah, here comes the gang!" Jotham waved over to Allison, Jordan, Jessica, and Jason. Jason still wore his mortarboard; I cringed and at the same time wondered why this should embarrass me.

Jotham dropped me home at about eleven that night. My mother had left a light on in the kitchen and a note to say that she'd gone to bed. The next day she'd be up at six, out the door at seven-thirty, and at her desk by eight. My mother has always been a hard worker, as well as a very sound and easy sleeper.

I wish I could say the same for myself, in terms of sleep, that is. I've always had trouble sleeping, even when I was very young. Things had gotten really bad in the last months before graduation. I'd lie awake for hours before finally falling into a restless doze. And then, come morning, I'd have a terrible time waking up.

Now that the actual graduation ceremony was over, I hoped for a long and restorative rest. But that night, as had been my habit for months, I lay in my bed in my room down the hall from my mother's, staring at the ceiling, my mind unable or unwilling to let go.

I wondered if Jotham's parents would be so eager to pay for a trip to the Grand Canyon. I doubted it. With his parents, too, Jotham got what Jotham wanted. I was pretty sure his parents didn't even have a clue as to my desires. But then again, why should they?

Because they were going to be my family, and I was going

to be theirs. And family was supposed to care about each other. Anyone could tell you that.

Unless, I thought, in-laws weren't really family, not the way blood relatives were. I thought about my father's parents. From what I knew, they'd been no more accepting of my mother and me than my father had been. But maybe Mr. and Mrs. Duncan had just been showing loyalty to their own blood. Maybe they'd had no doubt whatsoever that their son was telling the truth when he told them I wasn't his child.

Because I'd always found it hard to imagine that Mr. and Mrs. Duncan wouldn't have approached my mother with an offer of financial help or maybe even just with an apology if they had doubts that their son was telling the truth. I found it hard to imagine they wouldn't have shown some concern. But they hadn't shown any concern, which, to my mind, meant that they believed in their son one hundred percent.

I'd often wondered if my mother believed in me one hundred percent, even when I disappointed her, like when I turned down that trip to France after she'd already paid for the ticket, or when I got detention that time in middle school for talking back to my history teacher. Was maternal love absolute? Was it even supposed to be? Could it be, or was that just a fiction found in silly poems and tearjerker movies?

I figured I wouldn't know for sure until I became a mother. But what I did know for sure was that love between a husband and a wife was supposed to be totally supportive. Love, honor, and cherish, in sickness and in health, forever and ever. And so, I thought, shouldn't Jotham support my choice of a honeymoon? Shouldn't he at least agree on a compromise, a third place, not Hawaii or the Grand Canyon, but someplace we would choose together?

I flipped to my right side, hoping a change of position would magically bring about a change of disposition. I wasn't happy thinking along such grumpy lines. So I set my mind to another task: counting my blessings. My grandmother had taught me to do that back when I was a kid, and though for a time in high school I'd found the exercise silly and embarrassing, once I got to college I'd taken it up again. At least for the time it takes you to list your blessings, your mind isn't dwelling on the negative.

So, my blessings. I'd graduated college with honors. I had a good job lined up. I was going to Italy for two weeks, and even though it was with my mother, I was beginning to feel oddly pleased about the prospect.

And, most importantly, I was engaged to Jotham. He was who he was, which was a pretty nice guy, and overall I felt pretty lucky to have avoided all the jerks and losers and all the messiness of falling in love with the wrong guy and having my heart broken. Since sophomore year of high school, I hadn't spent one night alone wishing I had a boyfriend or wishing my boyfriend hadn't dumped me for a cheerleader or wondering if I'd ever meet my one true love. Because since the age of fifteen, I'd been Jotham Grandin's girlfriend.

I pulled the covers up tighter around my neck, making what I hoped would be a comforting cocoon that would induce sleep. Big deal, I told myself. So we'd go to Hawaii for our honeymoon. I'd be gracious to Mr. and Mrs. Grandin, and Jotham would be happy. It could be my gift to him. That's what I told myself on that long night of lying awake, watching the moon traverse the sky, wondering what it would be like to sleep beneath the Arizona stars.

4

Dear Answer Lady:

I'm a forty-eight-year-old wreck. The skin on my neck looks like a day-old baked apple. It seems that every week a new weird growth appears somewhere on my body. My once-flat stomach is as round as a muffin top in spite of almost daily trips to the gym. You could put a sandwich in the bags under my eyes. My hair is thinning, my butt is drooping, and my bunions are causing me to walk with a limp. But the worst thing about this aging process is that I suspect my daughter, who's only twenty, sees me as a decrepit monster. Am I being paranoid?

Dear Saggy:

It's inevitable that younger people view older people, particularly those they love, as in some sense grotesque. The reasons for this are many, and I'm not being paid to illuminate the psyche of Youth Culture, so suffice it to say that you are probably correct in your assumption regarding the light in which your daughter regards you. Your aging body is to her a dismal glance into her own future (okay: I'm giving you that one bit of illumination), and, naturally, she reacts against the grim inevitability you embody. Relax. There's nothing you can do about her disgust. Still, for the sake of your husband and the public in gen-

*eral, you might want to get some of those repul-
sive skin growths lopped off.*

Friday, June 2

"You're sure you have your passport? And a copy of it in
another place in case the original gets stolen?"

"Yes," Marina said, her voice betraying not the least bit of
annoyance. "Jotham, you already asked me that three times
on the way here."

How did my daughter stand it, I wondered: the patroniz-
ing tone, the frown meant to convey responsibility.

"Just making sure. You can't be too careful these days,
what with lax airport security and these crazy stories of—"

"Now, no talk like that today," my father interrupted with
a meaningful glance at his wife, whose eyes had widened in
alarm for the third or fourth time since we'd arrived at Logan
Airport.

Rob gave me a hug and spoke softly into my ear. "Have a
wonderful time, Elizabeth. Try not to think of work or anything else stressful."

"Impossible," I said, "but thanks for the suggestion. I'll
try."

My mother took this moment to clap her hands to her face
and cry, "Oh, my two little girls going off to Italy together! I
just can't believe you're going all that way for two long weeks!"

My father put his arm around my mother's shoulders. "Now,
Jane, it's not like they're shipping off to Iraq or Afghanistan.
There are probably more Americans in Tuscany at this time
of the year than there are Italians. They won't even know
they're out of the good old U.S. of A."

"Uh, thanks, Dad," I said.

Marina laughed. "Yeah, thanks, Grandpa."

"What?" My father looked utterly perplexed, assuming as

he did that the overwhelming presence of Americans abroad was a consoling notion.

Rob spoke up before Marina and I would be forced to explain our reaction. "Let's let these women get on with their vacation, okay? And Jane, don't I have to get you home before nine so you can watch your show?"

"Those girls in Celtic Woman are something," my father said with a sudden sly smile.

There was another round of hearty farewells from my father and cautionary advice from Jotham and more tears from my mother and a secret smile from Rob to me, and then Marina and I were alone, finally, about to begin our big Italian adventure.

Once through the nightmare that is security, an experience that seems to sober even the most chatty and carefree of travelers, Marina and I walked to our gate and settled in two seats at the end of an already-crowded row.

"Why does Grandma always have to make such a big fuss?" Marina asked. "It's not like we're going away for a year. I mean, did she have to cry?"

My daughter, I thought, is too young for sentimentality, too young, or just one of those people immune to it.

"It's her generation," I said stupidly.

"Watch my bag? I'm going to buy some magazines for the flight. Do you want anything?"

I said no, having a good selection of guidebooks in my carry-on, and watched my daughter walk back down to the concourse, seemingly oblivious to the interested glances of almost all the men she passed.

Idly, I wondered if Peter would have been an overly protective father, the kind to grill his daughter's dates, to subtly threaten them with bodily harm and worse if they laid a hand on his daughter, the sort of father to spoil his little girl rotten with affection and gifts and a sense of her own true worthiness.

I doubted it. Any man who could do what Peter had done

was unlikely to have the real Daddy gene. About a month after I told him I was pregnant, he'd gone off to law school in California as planned, and even the pleas to his parents by my own parents had fallen on deaf ears. No, I decided. Peter hadn't been and maybe still wasn't real Daddy material.

My parents had suggested an abortion when it was clear that Peter was not going to accept responsibility for his child. Rather, my mother had suggested it, speaking, she assured me, on behalf of my father, too. I remember being horrified at the idea and also being terribly upset that my own parents would suggest that their daughter put an end to the burgeoning life of their grandchild.

Later, I came to understand their reasoning. First, of course, they were concerned about my future, about the life I would live as a single parent. And second, they were concerned about themselves. They knew their lives would drastically change with the arrival of a baby. After all, I wasn't "settled" with a job and a husband. I would be living in their home with my child, a continuing financial burden for some time to come, and an additional responsibility, because it would be absurd to think that they wouldn't be called upon to help me care for Marina.

Eventually, I enrolled Marina in day care, and I hired a babysitter for special occasions, but for a while it was tough on my mother, who was teaching full time, and on my father, who hadn't yet retired and would come home at the end of the day exhausted and looking forward to a quiet dinner and his favorite TV show only to be met by the cries of a cranky baby, an overworked wife, and an occasionally frantic daughter.

Sometimes I wonder if I could have done it without my parents, could have raised Marina entirely on my own, and of course I would have done it—what choice would I have had? But there's no doubt that my mother and father made it a lot easier for me and for Marina, and for that I'm forever grateful.

Well, I thought, my daughter might not have a sentimental bone in her body, but I certainly do, indulging in what amounted to nostalgia, that most distorting of states, in which we "remember," i.e., create, a false past and pine for it.

I decided to blame my mood on the situation. There's something about travel that makes one so aware of the awful possibility, always lurking, of never seeing loved ones again, of disaster, of permanent change. Travel reminds one of just how ephemeral life is; at least, travel does that for people like me who spend very little time away from home.

Maybe I would have traveled more had I not been a young, single parent. Our disposable income had never been hefty, just one of the difficulties Marina and I encountered as we pretty much grew up together. The relative lack of funds, of course, was nothing compared with an absent father and husband.

Well, I thought, and not for the first time, Peter might not have been there to read her bedtime stories and listen attentively to my work woes, but on the plus side, Marina didn't have to come home from school each afternoon to a set of feuding parents. Our home was a peaceful place, except for the usual, mostly manageable tensions that occasionally arise between any mother and daughter.

Not only did Marina have the benefit of a peaceful home, she also had the benefit of living in a sort of extended family. She'd spent time with her grandparents almost every day of her life, and that's something special. If I wasn't able to give her the specific kind of support or comfort or attention she needed, there was always Grandma or Grandpa available just upstairs—and later, just a few blocks away—to boost her confidence with a hug or soothe her anxiety with a trip to the old-fashioned ice-cream parlor (now a cell-phone store) or to encourage her reading with a visit to the library. We were three generations of family caring for each other, and though at times it felt stultifying, I was always aware of and grateful for the benefits.

I watched my daughter walking back toward me, a frown of annoyance on her pretty face.

"Can you believe there's not one copy of *People* left in any of the stands on this concourse? How insane is that?"

"That's pretty darn insane."

"Mom, please," she said, flopping down next to me.

"Well, it's not the end of the world, Marina."

"I know that. I'm fully aware of that. It's just that I had my heart set on reading *People*."

Funny thing about life. You can have your heart set on any number of things, big or small, and you can be pretty sure you're not going to get half of them.

5

It's all about the umbilical cord. Yeah, sure, it might be physically severed soon after the moment of birth, but let me assure you that it never is nor can it ever be severed psychologically. You are forever bound to the woman who bore you, and the sooner you accept that powerful truth the better able you'll be to survive this miserable life with a minimum of gnashing of teeth.

—Enduring the Tie That Binds

Settled into our coach-class seats—if you can be "settled" into cramped quarters—carry-on bags safely stowed beneath the seats in front of us, seat belts securely fastened—does anyone really need a flight attendant's instructions on how to fasten the belt? Probably not, but I feel it's rude not to pay attention—I readied a pen, a highlighter and one of my guidebooks: this one with a focus on art. I'd spent the last few months preparing for the trip; sometimes I wondered if I'd overprepared, if I'd find anything surprising and powerful once in its actual presence.

For all the money you're spending on this venture, I warned myself, you'd better be awestruck at least once.

Marina took off the light, tightly fitting sweater she'd been wearing over a form-fitting T-shirt, and I saw for the first time a gold locket on a gold chain around her neck. I recognized the locket immediately—oval, set with a tiny diamond in the middle, filigree work around the edges—as a family heirloom I'd last seen around my mother's neck some years ago.

"That locket," I said. "Where did you get it?"

Marina lifted the locket off her chest and looked down at it. "Grandma gave it to me for graduation. Didn't you know?"

"No," I said. "I had no idea." The locket had belonged to my mother's mother originally, a gift from her sisters on her wedding day. In turn, my grandmother had given it to her daughter on her wedding day.

"Grandma told me she'd thought about giving it to me on my wedding day," Marina was saying, "but something changed her mind. She just felt I should have it now." She let the locket fall back against her chest. "I wonder why she didn't tell you."

I shrugged, though I had some idea.

"I put a picture of Jotham in it. Well, of course."

"Of course."

Marina twisted in her seat to look more fully at me. "I wonder why she didn't give the locket to you. Doesn't it seem strange that she decided to skip a generation?"

Strange? Hurtful was more like it. I suppose I'd always assumed the locket would one day come to me. But I was reluctant to let Marina know how I felt and thereby taint the gift in some way.

"Strange?" I said. "No. People give gifts for all sorts of reasons. And they don't give gifts for all sorts of reasons."

"I guess." Marina twisted back to face forward again. "I wonder," she said. "I mean, well, if you had gotten married before me, then maybe she would have given the locket to you."

I thought it entirely possible. In spite of her education, even her intellectualism, my mother harbored the old-fashioned view that a woman's highest calling was marriage and motherhood—preferably in that order. Having failed to achieve marriage, I'd failed to earn the locket, the token of that achievement.

"Well, whatever Grandma's reasons for giving it to you now," I said, "wear it in good health. It's a very pretty piece."

Marina lifted the locket off her chest again and peered down at it. "Well, honestly, it's not exactly my style. It's too old-fashioned."

"But that's what makes it special," I said.

"I guess. Maybe I could have it—I don't know, changed in some way, updated."

I bit my tongue and wondered what my mother would say to that. Sure, destroy a cherished family heirloom and replace it with some trashy bling. Why not?

Marina continued to fuss and fidget in her seat, dragging her carry-on from under the seat in front of her, rummaging through it for a bottle of water, then for hand moisturizer. I pretended to flip through my guidebooks and watched her.

To this day, when I look at my five-feet-three-inches-tall, small-boned, dark-haired daughter, when I look at her from a certain angle, or see her tilt her head in a certain way or watch the way she purses her lips when concentrating, I can't help but see Peter as plain as if it's him sitting right in front of me and not his daughter, the product of us both. It's disconcerting how much she reminds me of the man I was infatuated with for the eleven months of our relationship. Marina is a constant reminder of Peter, which might sound as if she's a burden to me in some way, but she isn't. I can think of Peter now, all these years later, with almost no emotion, positive or negative.

Still, the irony isn't lost on me, how much like her father Marina looks and how little like me. The parent who denied paternity left such an obvious mark on his child; no one seeing them side by side would think they weren't father and daughter. Once, a long time ago, someone at a grammar-school event asked me if Marina was adopted. When I told her no, she said, "Oh, but she looks nothing like you!" It was a terrible thing for her to say, and I was too stunned to be angry (afterward, I was furious). I should have made no reply, but, being in a state of shock, I spoke stupidly, inviting yet another rude question. "She looks just like her father," I said. At which point, the woman—whose own daughter was a carbon copy of her mommy—scanned the room for a slight, dark-haired, thin-featured man, to no avail. "Is he here today?" she asked, turning back to me. "No," I said. "He's never here." And I finally walked away, leaving the nosy woman to jump to her own no-doubt-erroneous conclusions concerning the whereabouts of Marina's father.

"Do you want some?" Marina turned to me, holding out an allowable-size tube of moisturizer. "The air on planes is so dry. You're supposed to keep hydrated. Remember to drink a lot of water, too."

I accepted a small dollop in the palm of my hand, and Marina began to study the latest issue of *US Weekly*. Clearly, though it wasn't *People*, it was better than no celebrity-gossip magazine. Drug charges; DUI offenses; assault with a cell phone; wardrobe malfunctions; nasty divorces; paternity claims.

Now there was a topic I could relate to. In the early days, when Marina was a baby, I often thought about the old expression "love child." This was a child born out of a passionate affair, a child unplanned, unlooked for, but very real indeed. But that wasn't quite what Marina was, I realized. Because Peter hadn't been in love with me, and in the end it seemed I'd been in love with an image of my own creation, not the real man at all. What did that make my daughter, a "fantasy child?"

Marina sighed and flipped another glossy page. "I can't believe people are still interested in Paris Hilton," she murmured. "I mean, get a life."

I smiled. Whatever Marina was, she was my pearl of great

price, living and breathing evidence if not of my sin against God then of my challenge to myself. And I loved her more than anyone or anything.

Even when she was pissy about not getting the latest issue of *People* magazine.

6

Dear Answer Lady:

I'm not unnecessarily bitter. I'm not making up stories just to get attention. I have a legitimate cause for wanting to kill my mother. Really. See, after a lifetime of secrecy I finally "came out" to my mother, and believe me, it took a lot of courage, as my mother isn't what you would call a warm and fuzzy type. In fact, you could say she's a narrow-minded, generally unpleasant person who tends to fall back on the worst stereotypes of people to explain the problems of the world. Anyway, she didn't react well to my news. In fact, she burned all of my childhood stuff and told me I disgusted her and that I was out of her will. Also, I'm not "allowed" to ever speak with her again. So you can see why I want to kill her. I won't, of course. I mean, I might want to kill her, but I know that would be a horrible thing to do, so I won't. Of course. In fact, I'm not really sure why I'm writing to you. It's not like I'm asking your permission to kill my mother or anything! I would never do that. Never.

Dear Potential Matricide:

Sometimes it's best to keep your mouth shut. Really, knowing your mother as you do, why in God's name would you tell her that you're gay? I'll leave you alone to explore your deep and no

*doubt twisted motivations for opening your mouth
and deal directly with your urge to do away with
your unenviable mater. You might think you're
not asking me for permission to murder her, but
you are, and so here is what I have to say to you:
You are NOT allowed to kill your mother, not
now, not ever. Okay? Clear enough? Fantasize
about wrapping your hands around her neck if
the desire strikes, dream of smashing her head
against the pavement if you must, but under no
circumstances are you actually to take steps to
end her sorry life. If it helps, I think it's just fine
that you're gay. Okay?*

Marina smiled as she flipped to a new page of the small
scrapbook on her lap. I looked down to see a photograph of
Jotham standing with his legs wide apart, his arm draped
around my daughter's shoulders.

"So," I said, "do you want to look at one of my guidebooks? There's a very interesting chapter in this one about—"

"That's okay, Mom. Don't you love this picture of Jotham
and me? I miss him so much already."

So much for the history of the Medici family. "We've only
been off the ground for half an hour," I said. "How could
you possibly miss him?"

"I still don't know why you didn't get an international
phone," Marina said, not answering my question. "Don't
you want to check in with Rob?"

"He knows where we're staying. He'll get in touch if
something happens to Grandma or Grandpa. Otherwise, I
don't need to bother him. He's on a really big project right
now."

Marina shrugged. "Whatever."

Had it been wrong of me to feel that as mature adults Rob

and I didn't need to be pestering each other with incessant phone calls and text messages?

"Besides," I said, "if I feel the urgent need to talk to Rob, I can always borrow your phone, right?"

Marina finally looked over at me. "Well, sure. Assuming we're together at the time you want to make a call."

Assuming we're together? I'd thought this trip was all about togetherness. Did my daughter have plans to cavort on her own? I didn't ask; I was afraid of the answer I might get. Besides, I thought, maybe she just meant she'd be in the bathroom while I was sitting at a café table waiting for her to return so I could hurriedly call Rob and relate to him the latest installment of our Italian adventures.

Marina closed her scrapbook.

"You know, Mom," she said, "I'm so glad we're staying in Florence and not in some tiny little village out in the countryside. Who knows if I'd even get reception on my phone?"

And what a disaster that would be, I thought, disconnected from Jotham and his paternalistic warnings and reminders.

"Yes," I said, "reception would be a crapshoot."

Frankly, I would have preferred to stay at a lovely country villa. Instead I'd booked us into a small hotel in Florence, knowing Marina would be happier. Though when at home she wasn't in the habit of going to clubs at night (the Cherry Pit certainly didn't qualify as a hot spot) or frequenting museums by day (the closest mall had a Museum Shop, but to my mind that didn't count as a cultural center), Marina's suburban habits made her a better fit for two weeks in Florence than two weeks tucked away in a small town, inhaling the incense-like scent of a rosemary bush, plucking figs off a tree for breakfast, and strolling through olive groves.

"And who knows what the food would be like out in the country," Marina was saying. "I mean, at least in a city you have a lot of options. And if worse comes to worse, there's always a McDonald's. They do have McDonald's in Florence, don't they?"

I sighed; I couldn't help it. "I really don't know," I said. To myself I added: And I really hope not. I was not flying to another continent to eat in a fast-food joint I didn't even frequent when home.

"Well, if Jotham were coming with us, we'd need to know for sure he could get some normal food."

"Authentic Italian food isn't normal?"

"Oh, you know what I mean."

Yes, I thought, I do, and I rather wished I didn't.

"If you'll excuse me," I said, "I'm going to read more about the Galleria del Costume. That's in the Giardini di Boboli, by the way."

But Marina was no longer listening. She was back to studying the scrapbook.

7

The current crop of celebrity moms spends an awful lot of time singing the praises of motherhood. You can't open a magazine while on the treadmill or watch the E! Entertainment Channel after a long day at work without some perfectly coiffed Hollywood mom bragging about how thrilled she is every time her baby spits up. In this writer's opinion, these ladies are protesting a tad too much. Those of us in the real world—i.e., those of us without multiple nannies and thousand-dollar diaper bags—know the truth about motherhood: it's a grueling, thankless job that has nothing to do with glamour and even less to do with personal fulfillment. Get real, Hollywood! It's okay to admit to wanting to toss the tantrum-throwing monster off the balcony. (Not, of course, that any of us would ever actually do such a thing.)
—Dirty Diapers and Ill-Timed Tantrums: The
Unhappy Truth About Parenting

Flipping through my scrapbook filled with pictures of Jotham and Allison and Jessica took only a tiny part of my attention. With another part, I watched my mother as she read, underlined, and took notes as if she were doing serious research in a university library. Vacation, I'd always thought, was supposed to be about fun, not about homework. But as long as she didn't badger me to study up for my vacation, I was fine with her nose always stuck in a book.

Which was only one way in which my mother and I were different—she read at least three books a month, and I read about three books a year. Of course, the biggest, most obvious difference between us was—is—our appearance. Tall and short; light and dark; red hair versus dark brown hair; blue eyes versus brown.

I'd seen pictures of my mother from when she was just a baby and then a little girl, pictures of her taken in high school and college. And then, afterward, in most of the pictures of my mother, there was me, too, as if she was no longer just herself, which I guess, in a way, she wasn't.

My mother told me once that she got to be her full height, five feet seven inches, by the age of fifteen. Of course, she was taller than a lot of the boys in her class, including the one she had a big crush on in her sophomore year. It didn't matter to her that he was shorter, but clearly it mattered to him that my mother was taller, because he stopped talking to her at all and started dating a girl that was, in my mother's words, a shrimp.

She was always thin, my mother, not thin like models today, who look startled and knock-kneed, as if they're going to have a heart attack if you show them a pretzel. My mother was—is—thin in a good, healthy-looking way, and though ever since turning forty she can get pretty down on herself for being "fat," she wasn't—isn't—fat. She's just not twenty anymore. Sure she'd gained a few pounds over the years (haven't we all?), but in my opinion all she needed to do was tone up.

With a murmur of excitement, my mother closed one book and opened another, cross-checking some arcane historical fact she'd no doubt point out to me as we were tramping through a dusty old museum, supposedly admiring ancient works of art. Absentmindedly she tucked her hair behind her ear; I noted she was wearing a pair of earrings Rob had given her for Christmas, garnet drops set in yellow gold.

My mother's hair is lovely, what I've heard people call strawberry blond, though I think that's misleading. Her hair is more of a rich, sunset color. She's always worn it long; it really is her best feature. Which is why it drove me nuts for a time that she didn't color the gray that was beginning to show here and there. I'd point out—none too subtly—that it wasn't hard to buy a bottle of L'Oréal hair dye; the drugstore alone offered hundreds of color options. I remember thinking that I should work on Rob to help me convince her but tossed the idea when I realized that all he'd say was "I like your mother just the way she is." And the odd thing—the good thing—is that he'd mean it.

Unlike mine, my mother's eyes are blue, nothing special, as she would admit, not the intense blue of Paul Newman's eyes. But they're pretty enough, and at the time of our Tuscan holiday, her skin revealed barely a wrinkle, though she smiles so much you'd think she'd have had millions of wrinkles by the time she was thirty-five. Really, for a woman in her forties, my mother looked pretty good, even to my young and critical eyes. I mean, I'd be at a mall and see other women my mother's age, and an awful lot of them looked terrible, overweight and tired, with bad haircuts and dumpy clothes. I remember my twenty-one-year-old self vowing that I would never let myself go, that even if I had five kids and a job and a husband and a house to look after, I would make time to go to the gym and eat right and get regular facials. Needless to say, over time I've become a lot kinder about my own sex, finding that I am no more immune to the ravages of time than anyone else.

I've become a lot kinder and also a lot less naïve.

I still don't like to admit it, but for a long time I felt angry with my mother for having let some jerk get her pregnant and then leave her. What had she been thinking? How could she have been so stupid? Hadn't she ever heard of birth control? And couldn't she tell that this Peter person was a loser? Not that I thought I was perfect, but the one thing I was absolutely sure of was that I would never be so crazy about a guy that I would forget to take my pill or not use a condom or whatever it was she did or didn't do that resulted in—well, that resulted in me.

"Do what I say and not what I do"; this disconnect between my mother and me caused tension. To her credit, she taught me right from the start about protecting myself from STDs and pregnancy. And as for staying away from jerks, she didn't have to teach me how to do that. I just seemed to know a loser when I saw one, and Jotham was as far away from a loser as you could get. Of course, he wasn't perfect, but I was absolutely sure that the last thing he'd do is get a girl pregnant and walk away. Not like my father.

That summer after graduating from college, I simply assumed I had better instincts than my mother, that I was immune to the kind of mistake she'd made with the man named Peter Duncan, that I was fundamentally inured to the whims of the heart.

Well, the young can be dangerously naïve, as well as magnificently sure of the future, as I was of mine. After all, I'd spent some time making a plan, and I thought it was a very good one. Jotham and I would marry the following spring, just about a year after our college graduation. In the meantime, I'd be starting a job at a small accounting firm downtown and would spend the next few years laying the foundation of my career. Jotham would start law school in the fall, and with any luck, when he finished he'd get a good job and we'd buy our first home.

Then, the plan dictated, when we were about thirty, we'd start our family. I would stay at home with the kids (two or three, depending on Jotham's salary), and eventually do some part-time accounting from a home office. As the kids grew up, I'd expand my business—and, well, there it was, the basic plan for our life, Jotham's and mine. It wasn't a super-exciting life we were going to build, not a life full of risk and adventure, but who wanted that kind of life anyway?

Certainly I didn't.

8

Dear Answer Lady:

I am really pissed off with my mother. See, last week I told her I'm not going back to school in the fall. I would have been a junior at my local state college, but I'm just so sick of studying! I feel like I'm getting nowhere. I mean, I could make a lot of money right now if I quit and tended bar at this totally hip place in town. (A guy who works there, this really cute Brazilian, pretty much promised he could get me a job.) But my mother just won't stop pestering me about getting my degree and thinking about my future and sticking to things I start and all that garbage. Who does she think she is? Just because she went to college and has a big corporate job, she knows what's right for me? She's not the boss of me. She's, like, only my mother!

Dear Girl Teetering on the Edge of Disaster:

As much as I hesitate to acknowledge it, in some cases Mother does know best, not necessarily because she is your mother but because she is older and, one hopes, wiser than you. With experience can come wisdom, and in your particular case, your mother is demonstrating that she has indeed learned from her experience of the world. If you still won't take her advice, take mine: Go

back to school. Finish college. Follow your
mother's example before it's too late and you do
something extremely stupid like marry a really
cute Brazilian guy looking for a green card.

Marina dozed off after the meal, a decent pasta primavera
that she'd hardly touched but that I had devoured, travel of
any sort rendering me unaccountably ravenous. Whenever
Rob and I went anywhere together—a weekend on Martha's
Vineyard, an overnight to Portland—he packed what he called
"Elizabeth's emergency provisions," which usually included
a bag of cashews, a chunk of hard cheese, and a box of crack-
ers.

That's one of the beauties of the long-term relationship:
being with someone who knows and doesn't question your
quirks, habits, and foibles. But, of course, there were many
years before Rob and his kind attentions.

Scattered throughout my twenties, like the occasional rau-
cous, unpleasant thundershowers of summer, were dates with
men thoroughly wrong for me, something I had in common
with every other unmarried woman in the U.S. A few times
my mother convinced me to go out with the son of a woman
she'd met through the local food co-op, or someone she'd
spoken to at coffee hour after church. You'd think that given
my particular situation my mother would have exercised extreme caution when pushing me into the idling cars of men
she knew only through their doting maters. But there was
enough of the old-fashioned desire for her daughter to be
well married—i.e., taken care of—about my mother to over-
ride any urgent sense of caution.

The fix-up that stands out in my mind as the absolute
worst was the date with the semiprofessional wrestler. His
real name was—and he admitted this reluctantly—Todd, but

he preferred to be called by his stage name, which was—wait for it—The Caped Combatant. Not very original, but lack of creativity was only one of his many drawbacks.

The evening—drinks and dinner—was a total disaster from my point of view. Amazingly, CC (for short, he explained) called me two days later for another date, at which time I feigned the onset of a phony contagious disease (betting he wouldn't know it was phony), one that might inhibit his wrestling abilities should he catch it, and that was the end of that.

I can still recall the maddening conversation between my mother and me once I got home the night of the date with CC.

Me: "What were you thinking?"

Jane: "Wasn't there anything about him you liked?"

"Mom, he has the word 'KILL' shaved into his hair. He sucks down steroids like they're M&Ms. He has a stage name, Mom. He calls himself The Caped Combatant."

"Well, I don't understand why you're angry with me. I didn't know that when I asked Mrs. Lutz to have him call you."

"That's it, that's the last time I'm going out with one of your so-called 'nice young men.' Ugh. Look, I'm still shuddering. He asked me if I would let him carry me over his shoulder to the car after dinner. He wanted to bench press the maitre d'. He spends a small fortune in waxing his body hair. How do I know this? He told me. Just thought I might want to know."

"You can't refuse to see everyone I find for you just because of one—"

"One disaster. One disaster of major proportions. And yes, I can refuse to see everyone I want to refuse to see. And I don't even need a reason."

"Now you sound like a silly little child."

"Fine. So be it. Now, if you'll excuse me, I'm going to pour myself a stiff drink and try desperately to forget I ever laid eyes on The Caped Combatant."

"Drinking doesn't solve anything. You know that, Elizabeth."

"Maybe, but it's sure as hell worth a try."

And then, when I was thirty, I met Rob Wayne. I'd agreed—well, I'd been badgered into agreeing—to attend a charity auction with a country-western theme. At the time, I'd been at WSS & Associates, a small but successful ad agency in Cambridge, for six years and had risen from copy editor to account manager. At the time of my Tuscan holiday, I was still at WSS, and, incredibly, still loving my job. Except for the clients.

Anyway, a colleague's sister-in-law (or somebody) was organizing the event and having trouble filling the tables. Swearing I was not going to be forced to wear a cowboy hat or chew on a piece of hay, I, along with a few other badgered colleagues, took a table.

At the next table was an attractive man who had been guilted (his word) into buying a ticket to a "rubber-meal event" by his assistant, whose partner's nephew was suffering from the illness our money was supposed to help cure. (For the life of me, I can't remember the cause.)

Finished picking at tasteless chicken, bored with the auction and with our tablemates, we got to talking. At the end of the evening, he asked for my number, and I gave it to him.

Rob was thirty-seven at the time, and though he'd never been married, he had been in a long-term relationship for most of his twenties. He had no children, and when I asked him about his interest in having a family (and I asked him almost right away), he explained that he'd never had a big drive to reproduce but that he liked children, was close to his nieces and nephews, would be happy to meet Marina should things progress between us.

Things did progress between us, and Rob did meet Marina. I'm not exactly sure how he won her over, but he did. Of course, she was jealous of his increasing presence in our life, suspicious of his intent—was it to steal her mommy away? In the end I think it was Rob's very nature that accomplished what a lot of dramatics couldn't have. Rob simply was himself; he didn't insult Marina by trying too hard to impress her; he didn't try to buy her acceptance; he didn't lash out the one or two times she was unpleasant to him. He didn't roll over, either.

When we'd been together for almost three years, when both Marina and I had come to count on his presence, Rob brought up the subject of getting married. I rejected the idea out of hand for reasons both sensible (I thought) and some not so. There was, for example, the sudden and inordinate fear of Rob's leaving me, of his realizing too late that marriage wasn't for him, and the also unexpected and somewhat vague feeling that a husband would demand and deserve more than I was willing to give, owing, as I did, every ounce of my energy to my daughter.

I didn't tell Marina about Rob's proposal. I would have if I'd seriously considered accepting; I couldn't leave my daughter entirely out of a decision that would impact her life so hugely. But since marriage didn't seem—manageable—once confronted by the real possibility, I kept silent.

Of course I knew that saying no to Rob meant I was risking the relationship; he might have moved on then, but he didn't. I sometimes wondered if I was still carrying a torch for Peter, and if that was the real reason I'd rejected Rob's proposal. I wondered if a part of me was reluctant to replace the man who should have been my husband. The idea seemed so absurd and yet so oddly possible that it frightened me, and with great effort I would push it from my mind.

After another three years together—I was thirty-six, Marina almost fifteen—Rob once again suggested we tie the knot. This time I found myself unable to say either yes or no; my indecision was painful for us all, Marina included, because this time I felt she deserved a part in determining the future of our family.

The long story short is that I simply couldn't bring myself to make the leap into marriage. I can best describe my state then as one of emotional paralysis; I simply couldn't make a decision.

Rob left, and soon after he did, my mother told Marina about his earlier proposal, only one of the many times she betrayed my trust and interfered with my parenting choices. Her excuse was her anger; she was furious I'd not agreed to marry Rob and wanted an ally in her granddaughter. It was a bad period in our relationship; we hardly spoke for months, and when we did, the most mundane conversation would erupt into conflict.

As for my relationship with Marina, well, it bumped into another phase about then. She met Jotham and withdrew from me—no surprise there. Almost immediately they were inseparable, the most important person in each other's life, before, it seemed to me, they'd had much of a chance to get to know each other.

After some time I began to date again, though reluctantly, more in an attempt to reduce my mother's nagging than because I wanted to start another relationship. (See, though my mother loved Rob, in the end any good man would do. Marriage was the point, a legal union.) There was one guy, Tony, whose company I enjoyed, but not enough to accept his offer of marriage, which came unexpectedly after only three months of dating. I suppose by then I'd realized that if there were one person I would—could—ever marry, it was Rob. But for all I knew, Rob was out of my life for good.

Imagine my surprise when, about two years after our breakup, he called. We met for dinner and talked about all sorts of things; Rob was very interested in hearing about Marina. I told him briefly about the few men I'd dated, omitting only one (what I had with him didn't merit mention).

In turn, he told me about his few relationships, none of which had turned out well, though none of which had come to a disastrous end. I wasn't surprised. Rob doesn't court drama. It was impossible to imagine him on the receiving end of a violently hurled piece of crockery.

After that meeting, we stayed in touch; eventually, we were talking almost every day, and finally, we reunited. We never again mentioned the people we'd dated during our hiatus. They weren't important, and if Rob felt any jealousy, he hid it well. As for me, I didn't feel I had a right to be jealous of the other women in Rob's past. After all, I was the one who'd sent him away with my inability to make a commitment. Well, maybe I didn't have a right to feel jealous, but I did. But over time, with no fresh provocation, the feelings faded away.

There was also some initial awkwardness; I found myself doubting I knew anything about Rob at all. Did he still like marmalade on his English muffins? I'd reach for the jar of marmalade and then pull my hand back, ask Rob what he wanted, afraid to presume the daily intimacies.

This phase passed, too, and our lives settled into a pleasurable routine. Some people define happiness as the absence of pain; others say it's the presence of joy. I like to say that happiness is simply the state of being content, on an even keel, not ecstatic and yet not despairing. Happiness—contentment—best described my life with Rob the summer of Marina's graduation from college.

I might have been content with the state of our relationship, but Marina wasn't. Marina felt bad for Rob; I knew she did. Somewhere along the line, no doubt after I rejected his second proposal, she'd cast me as the aloof princess, and Rob as the suffering Prince Charming. That wasn't the way it was at all between us, of course, but Marina's experience of the world at the time of our Tuscan holiday was really quite limited—her views and opinions could be surprisingly narrow and unimaginative. Well, that was my opinion.

Marina had made it very clear that she had plans for an ordered life, a life tied up neatly in a manageable bundle. I, in my capacity as older and presumably wiser woman, couldn't help but view my daughter's determination to "keep life at bay" (my words, not hers) with a mixture of pity and disappointment. Still, I knew I had to be careful about criticizing or giving advice concerning being more "open to experiences."

So I kept to myself the fact that I would have liked to see her date other men before she settled down with the only boy she'd ever dated, the only boy—I was almost certain of this—she'd ever slept with. Which was not to say that I wanted to see Marina hurt; Jotham was basically a nice guy, and I knew I should have felt relieved she'd met someone so trustworthy. But I didn't feel relieved, most times. I felt she was being cheated of her life somehow, or that she was cheating herself; it didn't much matter, because the result would be the same.

Do you see what I'm admitting? I'm admitting to believing that I knew what was best for Marina simply because she was my daughter. I don't remember how aware I was at the time of our Tuscan holiday of being so—smug. After all, Marina wasn't me, and I had no right to expect or want her to be me. But it's a mistake, a fallacy many (most?) mothers fall into at some point or another—assuming they know best about a person who, in spite of being the human being closest in flesh and blood, is an entirely unique individual.

9

Why is it always the Mother's fault? Why is it okay to blame the Mother for an individual's every ill? Worse, why is it acceptable to blame the Mother for society's every flaw? I say it's high time we women started pointing the finger of blame at the so-called stronger sex! After all, they're the ones with the bulk of power, money, and influence in this world. Why shouldn't men shoulder the responsibility for all that's wrong with everything!

—The Movement to Reject Responsibility: Or, It's All His Fault!

Saturday, June 3

The plane landed at around seven-thirty on Saturday June 3. By eight o'clock, we were waiting at baggage claim, feeling slightly grubby after hours on a plane full of stale air, burpy babies, and coughing adults.

Grubby and, in Marina's case, anxious. My bag appeared almost immediately, causing her great alarm.

"But we checked in together," she pointed out, practically pinching my arm in her concern. "Our bags should have come out together."

I disengaged my arm from her fingers. "Marina, baggage handling is not a precise science. I'm sure your bag will be along any minute now."

"I just don't see why it hasn't come out yet," she repeated, now chewing her lip. My daughter seemed to have inherited a bit of her grandmother's penchant for unnecessary worry. It was a part of her I'd never really noticed until then. Maybe someday she would be the matriarch seeing off her family at the airport, visions of plane crashes and terrorist bombings and sick chickens and tubercular passengers dancing in her head.

Marina fretted until her bag, unused since it was bought for the Paris trip that never materialized, made its appearance on the circulating belt.

"Oh, thank God," she muttered, snatching it to her side. "I would have died if my bag was lost."

"Marina, you wouldn't have died. You would have been inconvenienced."

She didn't seem to hear me; either that or she ignored my comment.

We got a taxi from the queue outside and were soon on our way into the heart of the city. Our hotel, the Hotel Francesca (named, we were told, after the proprietor's wife), was located on Via Cavalcanti within a few blocks of the Piazza della Signoria. On our journey, Marina focused her attention on her phone.

"He's awake?" I said—who else would she be texting but Jotham? "It's the middle of the night back home."

"We promised to be in touch all the time. You know, we've never been apart for more than a day or two."

"I'm aware."

"Well, except for that one time Jotham went with his parents to Indiana for a funeral. I think it was a great-aunt or something. He was so annoyed that he had to go. I mean, he'd only met the woman once or twice."

"Yes, I'm sure it was a great inconvenience."

"It's weird knowing I won't see him for two whole weeks."

"But what are you talking about?" I asked. "I mean, what are you typing him about? You can't have made many observations of Italian culture. We've only been on the ground for an hour."

"If you must know," she said, eyes on the screen, "I just told him the food on the plane sucked."

I'd thought it was as decent as airline food could be but let it go.

"Don't you want to look around, see what the approach to the city looks like?"

Marina briefly looked up and out of the side window before turning back to her phone. So much for my career as tour guide.

We checked into our hotel and were shown to a standard room with two double beds. There was no possibility of my sharing a bed with Marina. Our sleep habits were vastly different. I wasn't even sure how we'd handle sleeping in the same room.

I walked over to the room's one window. Through its large pane I looked out at the backs of other buildings, some ugly, twentieth-century constructions, others old and beautiful but covered in soot. A broken neon sign advertising a pasta company stood on a roof directly across from our room. Pigeons had littered windowsills with excrement and pieces of feather. But I found it all perfectly acceptable. For what our hotel lacked in terms of ambience and what our room lacked in terms of view was amply made up for by a location convenient to some of the city's major attractions and a cleanliness that would have impressed my mother, a woman who'd been known to glory in the advancements of mop technology.

"I am so tired," said Marina, and yawned hugely. "I think I'll take a nap before we do anything."

"No, no naps. We should get out now and go to bed tonight at our normal time. It's supposed to be the best way to beat jet lag."

"But I'm tired!" she complained, casting a longing look at her crisply made bed.

"You slept on the plane."

"So? It's been crazy lately—finals, graduation."

"That was two weeks ago, Marina."

"Mom!"

"But there's so much to see! We're in Florence!"

Marina heaved a dramatic sigh. "Fine, fine, we'll go out. Can I at least take a shower?"

"Of course, but don't be long. I want to freshen up, too."

"I won't even blow-dry my hair. I'll put it up, okay?"

While I waited for Marina to shower and change, and after I'd unpacked the relatively small bag I'd brought—simple clothes, nothing requiring ironing, things that could be rinsed in the bathroom sink if necessary—I picked up a magazine from a stack on the small desk. It was a "what's going on around town" sort of publication, with articles (about local businesses, colorful characters, and small theatres) and ads (for jewelry stores, restaurants, and galleries) in both Italian and English. Near the back I came across an article about a beautiful young actress named Marina Mendini—she had recently stayed in the city—and it made me think again about the arrival of my own beautiful Marina.

When I was pregnant—once I'd discovered that the baby was a girl—my mother urged me to give her one of the family names: her own; my own (I was named after one of my father's sisters); or one of the other names that appeared at least once in every generation of our family. I like the notion of family, I like the notion of continuity, but when it came to choosing a name for my daughter, I wanted something special, something unique to her. I chose Marina for the music it made.

Unfortunately, I was pretty sure that my daughter didn't think her name all that special. When she was about eight, she asked me what "Marina" meant. "It's from the Latin name Marinus," I told her. (I'd looked it up.) "It means 'from the sea.' "

"I'm not from the sea," she'd replied, in some confusion.

"No. But I just liked the name. It's pretty, don't you think?"

Marina had just shrugged.

Teachers occasionally called her Marian; more than once the school paper identified her as Miriam Caldwell. I don't remember Marina caring much about these slips, but they irritated me—perhaps another indication that my daughter's name meant far more to me than to her.

Still, I didn't see Marina as the kind of person to change her first name. The paperwork alone, she'd say, just wasn't worth the effort. Interestingly, she'd already informed me that she'd be taking Jotham's last name when they got married. I know I was being overly sensitive, but it seemed to me that by taking Jotham's name she was rejecting me—a naïve young woman who got knocked up and then abandoned by her boyfriend.

Parents can be notoriously touchy. Marina had a right to do whatever she wanted to do with her life, I knew that, and not every decision she made was made in relation to me.

"I'm ready." Marina emerged from the bathroom wearing a pink and white striped wraparound sundress that celebrated not only her small but shapely figure, but also her natural olive complexion. Her damp hair, as promised, was wound into an artfully messy updo.

I tossed the magazine back onto the desk. If what I'd heard about Italian men was true, we weren't going to get to the corner before they were trailing her with cries of "*Bellisima!*"

10

Dear Answer Lady:

Here's the thing. There are more than a few bad apples clinging to the branches of my family tree. I mean, every generation, on both sides of my family, seems to produce a drug addict or a drifter or a criminal of some sort. My own brother is in prison for arson and aggravated assault. Am I doomed to repeat history by giving birth to a loser? Is biology always destiny? Can my as-yet-unborn child avoid the fate that's plagued generations of my family? Help!

Dear Doomed:

No, your as-yet-unborn child cannot avoid his family's fate. Your as-yet-unborn child should play things safe and stay that way—unborn. Hope I've been helpful!

Marina and I spent that first afternoon of our Tuscan holiday strolling the neighborhood surrounding the hotel. Marina, with the easy ability of the young to recover, seemed entirely refreshed. After about an hour, I was ready to drop, but I wasn't going to admit to my weariness, being the one who'd vetoed a restorative rest.

We stopped for a much-deserved lunch at a small trattoria. The design and décor of the place—and so many others we visited during our two-week trip—were familiar from movies and magazines: both inside and out were small round tables (some cafes eschewed tablecloths) set with white linen napkins, around which were gathered clean-lined, sometimes cane-backed chairs; on the walls, graphic posters advertised brands of olive oil and other foodstuffs; behind the bar stood rows of liqueurs such as Campari and Cinzano and bottles of vermouth; in front of the bottles sat a large, gleaming, and complicated-looking espresso machine. Invariably, the waiters, both young and old, wore white shirts or coats with black pants and an air of dignity. It was easy to see that most took their tiring work quite seriously.

I ordered a *speck e brie* panini, "speck" being, according to my research, a smoked ham from the Trentino region, and something Rob and I had bought on several trips to Boston's North End. Marina chose the more familiar *mozzarella e pomodori*. Sparkling water arrived in a tall, slender bottle. I raised my glass in a toast to our adventure, a gesture that embarrassed my daughter, though she wouldn't or couldn't say why.

When we'd finished our light but refreshing meal, Marina took a stack of postcards from her voluminous bag and set them on the table; she'd bought them at the first tourist shop we'd encountered.

"How many cards did you buy?" I asked.

"Twenty," she said. "It's a start. I promised I'd send one to Jotham every day, and there's Grandma and Grandpa and Allison and Jessica."

"You're not planning on sending a postcard every day to them, too, are you?"

"Of course not," she said, as if the idea was preposterous.

That was reassuring news. I'd imagined my daughter spending her entire two weeks in Italy—her first trip to Europe, though not my own—corresponding with the Commonwealth of Massachusetts. The Uffizi Gallery? No time, I have to write a postcard. Michelangelo's *David*? Are you kidding? I have to text my boyfriend, and what if I lose reception while crossing the Arno? Day trip to the Banfi winery? Uh, hello? I'm expecting a call from my girlfriends, and what if the reception out in the countryside sucks?

I glanced over at the card Marina had just written to Jessica. It read: "Once we're married, all six of us should come here!"

I looked through my measly "stack" of three postcards— one for Rob, one for my parents, and one for the people at work. I couldn't imagine any of them waiting eagerly for the appearance of the mail carrier.

Nevertheless, I chose a card for Rob—a photograph of Brunelleschi's Duomo—addressed it but got no further than his name before my mind went strangely blank.

Suddenly, I couldn't remember the last time I had written anything to Rob other than a dashed off e-mail to say "working late, call u when home." Here was the person I loved most in the world aside from my daughter, and I just couldn't find any words that weren't tired and old and meant for just any old person.

And it occurred to me that we treat the ones we love most so casually, that we too often take our loved ones for granted. It occurred to me that I had grown somewhat lazy in love.

The thoughts bothered me. I tucked the blank card into my bag and instead penned a quick note to my parents and one to my officemates.

> Florence is lovely. The flight was uneventful. Sitting
> in a little café, watching the people go by while
> Marina writes a tome in miniscule letters on a three-
> by-five card.

"There, that should do it for now," she said finally, tapping the postcards into strict order as one would tap a deck of playing cards. "I'll give these to the guy at the desk when we get back to the hotel. Do you want to give me yours?"

"No," I said, "that's okay. I haven't really finished. . . ."

But Marina wasn't listening. Her attention was caught by another text message from Jotham.

"What does he have to say now?" I asked, wondering why I had. I didn't care what Jotham had to say. I wished he would keep his mouth shut at least long enough so I could have an uninterrupted conversation with my daughter.

Marina smiled down at the phone and then snapped it shut. "Oh, nothing," she said. "He's just being silly."

I'd never known Jotham to be silly. More likely he was being an interfering pain in the ass. "You know," I said, "I was thinking about what you told me on the plane, about the fight you and Jotham had about where to go on your honeymoon."

"Yeah. It wasn't really a fight, though."

"Well, I think you should stand firm about going to the Southwest." Though what the quality of phone reception would be out in the desert, I had no idea. Not that it would matter; Jotham would be right there with Marina, watching her every move.

"Oh, it's no big deal," Marina replied hastily. "I shouldn't even have brought it up. I'm sure Jotham's right. Hawaii is a better honeymoon destination, more romantic and all that. We can always go to the Grand Canyon later, when we have kids. Kids love that sort of thing. Nature. History. Camping. The great outdoors."

"But if you had your heart set on the Southwest—"

"Mom," she said, "drop it. I'm fine with the decision, really."

I didn't believe her, but I wasn't stupid enough to persist. We sat for a while in companionable silence. I could feel my mind beginning to absorb the fact that my daughter and I were indeed in Florence, alone together, on the brink of all sorts of possible adventures.

Marina's thoughts, however, were still firmly planted in American soil.

"I have to get a few new suits when we get back to Boston," she said abruptly. "The ones I have are too tired looking for starting a new job. Plus, I wore the best one to the final interview at Fischbach and Gall. I don't want to look ridiculous showing up for my first day of work in my interview suit."

I doubted anyone but Marina would notice. "Let's not talk about all the stuff we have to do when we get home, okay?" I suggested. "Let's try to enjoy every moment here. Remember, we only have two weeks."

"Well," she said, "I can't completely forget about my responsibilities."

"Of course you can't completely forget. But maybe we could both try to focus on the moment. Maybe we could both try to have fun together right here and now."

"Sure," she said doubtfully. "I guess."

Marina looked back to her phone. I watched her rapidly punching keys and felt a bit deflated. Only the first afternoon of our Tuscan holiday, and already I doubted that these two weeks would be the seminal mother/daughter experience I'd hoped they would be.

That's the problem with high expectations—the reality can never live up.

I flipped open the guidebook I most recently had been reading. "Did you know," I said to no one, "that in the fourteenth century the Black Death killed half the population of Florence?"

11

There are two basic types of mothers in this world: those who believe their children can do no wrong, and those who believe their children can do no right. If you're fortunate enough to have a mother of the first sort, go ahead and rob that bank. At least you know you'll have one devoted visitor at the state penitentiary. And if you're unfortunate enough to have a mother of the second sort, go ahead and rob that bank. At least you'll be proving your mother right, and that might, just might, earn you some points.
—Identifying and Playing to Your Mother's Nature

Marina and I began the evening with a stop at the famous (and admittedly tourist-thronged) Harry's Bar for a cocktail before dinner. We each ordered the ubiquitous Bellini, a mixture of puree of white peaches and Prosecco.

"Don't tell your grandmother we came here," I said after a first sip. "She'll flip if she knew I spent so much money on what's basically a fancy wine cooler."

"It's your money, Mom. You can do anything you want with it."

"Not according to your grandmother," I said with a dry laugh. "I've never been in debt, not once, yet she always acts as if I'm on the verge of blowing every penny of my savings."

"She's just concerned. You're her daughter."

"She's just nosy and doesn't trust me."

"Mom!" Marina seemed genuinely shocked, as if a critical comment about her grandmother were a sacrilege.

"Well," I said, "it's true." I remembered my mother's recent complaint about the money I'd spent on the large-size Carvel ice-cream cake. Yeah, that purchase had really broken the bank.

"Grandma told me you always had problems with numbers. That's probably why she worries about your finances. She said you failed algebra in freshman year of high school and had to repeat the course that summer."

"She told you that?" I said, stunned. My mother had had no right to tell my daughter about my failing that course. She knew it had been a source of shame to me. What purpose could it have served, other than to bind Marina to her grandmother "against" me?

"Yup," Marina said, oblivious to my consternation. "Grandma and I are close, you know that. She tells me lots of things."

And she gives you the locket that should rightly have come to me.

My relationship with my mother was both fraught and solid. She had been the dominant parent in my childhood; at least I'd experienced her as the disciplinarian and my father as the comforter. The situation probably wasn't all that unusual; when I was a child, mothers were often saddled with the dirty jobs (which could make anyone cranky and eager to instill order) while fathers, who arrived on the doorstep each evening as if by magic, blissfully unaware of what tussles and tantrums had taken place during the afternoon, were often gifted with the pleasant jobs, like reading stories and playing monster.

I know it was difficult for my mother to refrain from interfering, criticizing, controlling (she would have said "helping") me when Marina was a child. We both struggled to negotiate our proper territories. I needed her support but also her respect; often my mother seemed to forget that she wasn't the primary person responsible for raising the child. Tension was inevitable. My mother is a very strong personality, and after all, Marina and I were living in her house.

That is until just before Marina's tenth birthday, when I was finally able to move us to our own apartment. For the first time in my life, I wasn't living "at home." It was a move that was both difficult and liberating for me. For my mother, I believe, our leaving was both a loss and the lifting of a burden. I liked to think that after this the relationship between my mother and me normalized, became more a relationship of equals. At least we'd fought a lot less after that, and I suppose that relative peace is always a sign of progress.

"Grandma thinks you should have married Rob the first time he asked you."

Where had that come from? "Yes," I said, "I know. She made no bones about telling me that I was making a big mistake when I turned him down."

"Why did you turn him down, Mom?"

"There were reasons," I said carefully. "Not on a whim, I assure you."

"Were they good reasons?"

"I thought so at the time."

"You're not going to be any more specific, are you?"

"No," I said, "I'm not."

Marina shrugged and sipped the Bellini appreciatively. "This really is delicious. I can't wait to make these for Allison and Jessica."

"Not for the guys?"

"Are you kidding? They'd never drink anything this pretty. They'd say it's a 'girly' drink."

"Their loss. Your grandfather would drink this with no problem." As, I thought, would Rob, though his preference was for Jameson.

"Well, Grandpa's different. You know, I kind of feel sorry for him, being the only man in our family. I mean, all those years he spent alone in that house with you, Grandma, and me. Don't you think it drove him crazy?"

"He loved every minute of it, trust me." My father, never entirely trusting of or comfortable around other men, found his greatest pleasure in the company of women. His respect and admiration for "the fairer sex"—an ancient term he continued to use—was absolute.

"He did?" she asked doubtfully.

"Well, on second thought," I said, "when Grandma and I fought, it was hard on him. He never said anything, but I'm sure he felt really uncomfortable, stuck in the middle. I mean, of course I loved—I love—your grandmother, but there were times when I was downright mean. And, truth be told, there were times when she was downright mean to me."

"Really? I can't picture Grandma ever being mean to anyone. She's always so nice to me."

"That's because you're not her daughter."

Marina gave me a look, but I said no more. What I'd come perilously close to saying was that mothers—all of us—have the potential to be surpassingly mean to our daughters. On the part of the mother there can be an awful sense of lost opportunities (if I hadn't had you, I could have conquered the world!), of resentment (look at all the stuff you have that I never had!), of jealousy (you're so much prettier and more confident than I was at your age, and it infuriates me!).

Feelings one might consider unworthy of the exalted Mother, but feelings that are all too real. The trick is not to act on them.

Marina looked pensive and finally said: "I wonder why Grandma and Grandpa didn't have more children. I wonder if they ever tried for a boy. I know I'd like to have a boy and a girl. Preferably in that order, too."

Ah, the secrets we hold from one another! But this one wasn't mine to tell; unlike my mother, I can keep my mouth shut. My mother had a hysterectomy a few years after I was born. There'd been "troubles," she told me when I was much older, and two miscarriages. I don't know much more than that, so I don't know if whatever "troubles" there were could today be treated without taking such a radical course. I do know that the only reason my mother told me was so that I could be forearmed; maybe, she thought, the same "troubles" would visit me.

The mysterious "troubles" did not visit me.

"Mmm," I said and let it go at that.

We left Harry's Bar—a Bellini was one thing, but an entire dinner for two was quite another—and went to a restaurant called Pezzoli for dinner. I'd read about the place in a winter issue of *Gourmet* magazine and was happy to have gotten reservations. Though I was wary of it being overrun by magazine-reading Americans, Marina and I seemed to be the only foreigners that evening.

Well, Marina, me—and Jotham.

"First thing tomorrow, I have to start the search for the perfect gift for Jotham," Marina said when we had been seated at a table in easy sight of the restaurant's cozy bar. "I have no idea what to get him."

"It would be easier if he had a hobby other than golf," I said.

"I guess. I wish he liked leather jackets. I could get him a really nice leather jacket."

"But he doesn't like leather jackets."

Rob did, but Rob had two leather jackets already, and I doubted he'd want a third.

I supposed, though, that I should get something for him. The thing is, we'd fallen out of the habit of giving each other gifts in any official way some years earlier.

No gifts. Meaningless words. When, I wondered, was the last time I'd really given of myself to this man?

We each ordered a bowl of *pappa*, a hearty tomato and bread soup (Marina looked dubious about the addition of bread to soup until I reminded her she'd eaten plenty of bowls of French onion soup with a slab of cheesy bread on top), followed by *ossibuchi alla Toscana, osso buco*, or sliced veal shank, Tuscan style. Much to our waiter's chagrin, we skipped a pasta course.

But his mood improved when, after the soup, he presented us with a bottle of Vernaccia, a delicious, light white wine.

"Compliments of the gentleman at the end of the bar," he said in very good English.

I half turned to see an older man with thick, groomed white hair, a lovely gray suit, and noticeable gold cuff links at his wrists. He raised his glass to me; I believe he was drinking champagne; at least, it was some sort of sparkling wine.

I nodded and smiled at the man in thanks. He returned the smile. He struck me as the epitome of sophistication.

"Well," I said, turning back to Marina, "I'm going to flatter myself and think he meant to include me in his gesture, not just my beautiful daughter."

"Mom," she whispered fiercely, "we can't drink this! Won't he, you know, expect something in return?"

"No," I said, wondering why her face was so grim. "This is purely pleasant flirtation, an old game. He knows the rules. In fact, from the looks of him, he's a master of the game."

It occurred to me that my daughter might not know how to flirt or be flirted with, having been with a rather jealous boyfriend from the age of fifteen. If that was the case, it was too bad.

"This is weird," she said. "I've never seen you like—like this."

"Like what?" Not rushing off to work or cooking dinner or online paying the bills?

"Like not my mother."

I resisted the urge to laugh. "Newsflash, Marina: I might be your mother, but I'm also a woman, and though I might be forty-two, I'm not immune to the charms of the opposite sex. What do you think Rob and I do all evening? Play chess?"

"Mom!"

"You are so easy to tease! Life doesn't end at twenty-five, Marina."

I became aware of someone approaching from our left. It was our older gentleman. As he reached our table, he smiled and bowed his head slightly. I saw now that he was far older than I'd first thought, definitely in his eighties.

"I hope," he said in trembling, accented English, "you beautiful ladies enjoy your meal."

"We will," I said, "and thank you again."

The man moved unhurriedly toward the door, every step deliberate, his back admirably straight. This was not a man easily succumbing to the indignities of old age.

"Oh, my, God," Marina said when she was sure he was out of earshot. "I was a nervous wreck. I so expected him to, like, you know . . ."

"Drag us off into sexual slavery?"

"No, but . . ."

Marina, I thought, needed to get out more. If flirtation sent her into a tizzy, just how short a leash had Jotham been keeping her on?

"Well," I said, "he's gone now, so you can relax and enjoy the wine. It's very good."

Marina shot a suspicious look toward the door through which our generous gentleman had exited the restaurant. Did she expect him to be lurking in the shadows, waiting to snatch us and stuff us into a limousine with blacked-out windows? Hadn't she noticed that the man could hardly walk without assistance? Ah, but maybe he employed a young and burly accomplice!

I sighed and poured more of the wine into my own glass. Youth, I thought, truly is wasted on the young.

12

Dear Answer Lady:

My parents are beginning to show signs of de-mentia. My three brothers and I called a family meeting to discuss options for our parents' care—and imagine my surprise when my brothers an-nounced they'd chosen me to be the primary caregiver. They, of course, will deal with our par-ents' finances and eventually their estate. But I'm the one who'll be bathing and feeding them and visiting them in a musty nursing home! Why can't one of my brothers take care of my par-ents? Why is it always the woman who gets the dirty jobs?

Dear Burdened Daughter:

From time immemorial women have been considered caretakers of the young, the old, and the infirm. This is nothing unusual. What is un-usual is that you seem not to be acquainted with this dynamic. While I can't say much for your brothers' style of decision making (perhaps they're unfamiliar with the notion of democracy, much as you're unfamiliar with the notion of traditional feminine roles), I can't register any surprise. My advice is to grin and bear the tortures of caring for two elderly, dementia-riddled people—and to sneak away as much cash and portable goods as possible while doing so. Boys can't be trusted

*when it comes to portioning money to a "mere
woman."*

Sunday, June 4

The first stop that morning was to the Archaeological Museum on the Via Colonna, housed, as so many museums seemed to be, in an old palace or palazzo. The collection of Egyptian and Etruscan artifacts was impressive; at least, I thought so. Only one or two items seemed to catch Marina's attention, and before I was halfway through the collection, she announced that she'd wait for me outside.

So much, I thought, for the ancients.

"What was so fascinating?" she asked when I emerged into the hot late-morning sun forty minutes later.

"History is what's so fascinating," I said.

Marina shrugged, and, after consulting our map, we headed off in the general direction of the Uffizi Gallery, according to my guidebook housed in a Medici palazzo built by Giorgio Vasari between 1560 and 1580 to house offices of the government judiciary.

I doubted that bit of information would appeal to Marina; instead I thought to further entertain us as we walked by reading aloud the colorful stories of a few local female saints.

"Glad you're not a martyr, aren't you?" I said after relating several tales of horrific torture and gruesome death, all met with a supernatural—and maddening—calm and acceptance.

Marina made a face. "Zita? Reparata? What kinds of names are those?"

"It's not the names that matter," I pointed out. "It's their actions. The point is that women are just as heroic as men, maybe more so. Well, heroic or insane, depending on your point of view."

"Uh, Mom? Doesn't your shoulder hurt from carrying around all those guidebooks?"

"Not at all." I reached into my bag for another book, flipped it open to a marked page. "Listen to this. At one point in his life, Henry James—you know who he is, right?"

"Of course. He wrote all those incredibly dense and boring novels I was forced to read in that American literature class freshman year."

"Yes, well, be that as it may, Mr. James had this to say about Florence: 'The very *sweetest* of cities,' a 'rounded pearl of cities.' Isn't that wonderful?"

Marina laughed. "How can a city be sweet? Sticky, okay, like in the middle of summer. You can feel a city, like if you step in gum or dog poop. Sour even. You can certainly smell a city! All the sewers and subways. And you can hear a city, with all the cars honking and construction and people shouting. But sweet? You can't taste a city."

My daughter, I thought, had no poetry in her soul, and I wondered if that had always been the case or was the unfortunate result of years spent with her decidedly unpoetic boyfriend.

"Oh, Mom," she said, tugging on my arm. "Let's go in here. Maybe I can find something for Jotham."

The storefront was ratty looking, with peeling paint around the grimy glass. "It doesn't look very promising," I said.

"You can wait outside if you want," she said over her shoulder, already pushing her way inside.

I dutifully followed. Marina had listened to my martyr tales; the least I could do was accompany her on her quest for souvenirs.

The place was crammed with cheap and tacky merchandise. Holographs of Jesus wearing the crown of thorns, his eyes opening toward Heaven, then, when tilted (I couldn't resist a try), closing in resignation, then, once again, beseeching his Father. There was a shelf of macabre "momento mori" pieces, plastic, of course: skulls with the Latin phrase *Tempus Fugit,* or Time Flies, circling the brow; pint-sized cadaver tombs depicting the decaying corpse of the supposed body inside; badly drawn images of the Danse Macabre, led by a frolicking Grim Reaper. (I explained to Marina that the purpose of such items was to remind a person that Life is fleeting and that Death awaits us all; her reply was "That's repulsive.") And there were shelves of countless bad reproductions of Michelangelo's *David,* some with rather interesting anatomical adjustments I doubted could actually exist in Nature.

"Marina," I whispered, mindful of the proprietor, a heavyset, stern-faced older woman who was watching us closely from behind a sort of podium just inside the entrance. "This is just a tourist trap, and a bad one at that. You're wasting your time here."

"You never know," she whispered back. "Sometimes you have to dig through some really crappy stuff to find the really great bargains."

"But you're not looking for a bargain. I thought you wanted to get Jotham something special."

She didn't answer but moved over to a shelf of architecturally disastrous plastic reproductions of famous Roman buildings—the Coliseum, the Vatican, Hadrian's Tomb, otherwise known as Castel Sant'Angelo.

The cramped quarters were making me feel uncomfortable. I checked my watch again.

"The Uffizi closes for lunch in half an hour," I said. "Come on, let's go. We'll come back to shop later, I promise."

Marina's eyes were now fixed on a rack of what looked to me like T-shirts you could find at Wal-Mart. "No, you go ahead, Mom," she said. "I want to think about these soccer shirts. Maybe Jotham would wear one, but then again I'm not sure he's ever watched a game. I'm not even sure he knows who David Beckham is."

Shopping for fancy T-shirts over art? I'd heard some people would sacrifice a moment alone with a Bernini for a sale on sneakers, but until that moment I'd thought it was all a dreadful lie, an urban myth.

"Fine," I said. "I'll take a look now and meet you outside the front entrance of the museum in forty minutes. We'll have lunch. But I'm warning you, I'm going back to the museum this afternoon, and I'm bringing you with me."

"Sure, whatever."

While Marina's attention was caught by a startlingly gory painting on velvet of a dying Jesus on the cross, I left the store.

13

Instead of being the apple of your mother's eye, you're the dog poop she wipes off the heel of her Ferragamo pump. When other mothers brag about their child's career success, your mother ostentatiously examines her manicure. When other mothers display photos of their adorable grandchildren, your mother declares she doesn't like to clutter her purse with unnecessary items. Face it: not every woman is cut out to be a mother. Sever all ties to the harridan at once, before her very presence destroys the self-esteem of your children as thoroughly as it destroyed your own.
—Estranged from Mother and Loving It

While Marina shopped, I stood in a hushed room before a painting of the Holy Family in a Renaissance landscape by an Italian artist; in the background rose sixteenth-century buildings, and the style of the characters' dress was far from ancient. A roly-poly John the Baptist, struggling from the lap of his elderly mother, Elizabeth, reached out in welcome to his equally roly-poly cousin, Jesus, who himself was seated comfortably in the lap of his young, blue-robed mother, Mary. Standing over them, as the apex of the triangle the family group comprised, was the figure of Joseph, his arms extended as if to embrace them all.

Looking at this most famous of families, I couldn't help but consider the idea of inheritance.

Of course, Jesus was a case unto himself. If God was indeed his father, and not the humble carpenter named Joseph, then his imperfections could only have come from his human mother. Poor Mary must have been the source of her son's occasional but spectacular anger and impatience, of his habit of destroying other people's property (I thought of the moneylenders in the temple), of his rabble-rousing tendencies.

Looking up at Mary's placid expression—obviously belying her vicious temper—I thought about the legacy we receive from our parents, and the legacy we in turn pass on to our children. I thought about the things we choose to give our children, and the things we wish we could prevent them from ever inheriting, things like poor physical health and mental illness.

Marina had inherited my bad vision, just as I'd inherited my bad vision from my mother. It wasn't fair that my daughter had had to wear glasses and contacts since the age of nine, but once the pregnancy was underway, there was nothing I could do to prevent this particular trait from showing up in my child. By the act of choosing to give birth, I had automatically "condemned" my child to be the recipient of any number of weaknesses and difficulties.

I noted the unusual delicacy of Mary's fingers, her left hand wrapped around the pudgy thigh of her son, supporting him. Where, I wondered, does a mother's responsibility end? She can teach her child right from wrong and thereby give her an inheritance of good values and right conduct. A mother can feel good about that. But how is she to feel about having given her child bad teeth that will require braces, or a family history of breast cancer, or a family legacy of mental illness?

Looking at that lovely painting of the Holy Family, I suddenly remembered a particular fight that took place the summer Marina was twelve. I couldn't remember what the fight was about; it took its place in my memory as one of countless tussles that adolescent summer. What distinguished this argument from the others was what Marina had yelled just before storming out of the living room: "I didn't ask to be born!"

It was a typical thing for a hormonal adolescent to say, but it had hit me particularly hard. No, Marina certainly hadn't asked to be born, and in fact there were several voices suggesting that she not be born. The fact of Marina's life was due to only one factor—my desire for her.

I moved on to the next old oil, another painting of the Holy Family by a German artist whose name I didn't recognize, working in the mid-sixteenth century. Mary's mother, St. Anne, joined her daughter, grandson, and son-in-law. The artist had portrayed Joseph with an expression of benevolence and an air of willing self-sacrifice. Though gray haired and somewhat stooped, the figure projected strength and the ability to protect his young family from harm. In short, Joseph was shown as the ideal of Father.

About as far apart from Peter Duncan as a man could get. I wondered again about Peter's legacy to our daughter. Besides the obvious physical similarity, what other genetic traits had he bestowed? Doctors had urged me to get Peter's family medical history for Marina's sake. I tried, but as the old saying goes, you can't get blood from a stone, and you can't get information from people who refuse your calls, letters, e-mails, and pleas in any other imaginable form. Well, unless you take them to court, I suppose, and for better or worse that's where I'd always drawn the line.

I wondered, too, what emotional or intellectual traits Peter had given our daughter. (Nurture is huge, but so is Nature.) I knew so little about her father, even though during our relationship I was convinced I was the only one who really understood him. The result was that whenever Marina acted selfishly or meanly, I couldn't help but wonder if I was seeing evidence of Peter in our daughter. Not that I thoroughly demonized Peter; not that I considered myself a perfect person. But still, I wondered.

After our Tuscan holiday, I wondered less. After those two weeks in Italy it became less important to assign origin to my daughter's character and personality and more important to see her as her own person, a part of me and of Peter but, more importantly, another person entirely. I suppose it was all part of the process of my letting go of my daughter—and of my daughter actively, even eagerly, letting go of me.

14

Dear Answer Lady:

Here's the thing: I hate my mother. Most times, anyway. And I feel really guilty about it. Horribly guilty. I mean, the guilt keeps me up at night. I do love her deep down. I guess. It's just—God! I can't get away from the fact that I also hate her! What can I do?

Dear Ignoramus:

Have you just arrived on this planet? Just woken from a coma that caused you to lose all knowledge of human societal norms? Ambivalence toward one's mother is a universal experience. Get over yourself. You're normal. You're nothing special. You're just like every other miserable child that ever walked this earth buying her mother chocolates and flowers while fantasizing about how to murder her without getting caught. Next question?

"Did you find anything for Jotham while I was in the museum?"

Marina and I had stopped at a small café for lunch, where we shared a salad of fresh, marinated calamari; a small plate of *funghi alla graticola*, or grilled mushrooms; several slices of the ubiquitous Tuscan bread, called *filone*, made without salt and surprisingly tasty. And for dessert, neither of us could resist *granita di limone* from the *gelateria* next door.

Marina sighed. "No. This is harder than I thought it would be."

"Olive oil," I suggested. "A bottle of really good olive oil, extra virgin."

"He doesn't like olive oil. And he hates margarine. He only eats butter."

"Balsamic vinegar," I said, just to be annoying. "There's some very fine quality balsamic vinegar available."

Marina didn't bother to respond.

It was then that I noticed a young man sauntering along the piazza, headed in our direction. He was slim, something his dark jeans and tight-fitting T-shirt accentuated, with hair the color of chestnuts worn in a studiously careless style that must have taken him at least a half hour to perfect.

He wasn't particularly handsome, but he had the appeal of a young man flush with a sense of his own importance, absolutely sure of romantic success. No doubt at some point a careless young girl would dash his hopes and trample upon his spirits; love wasn't always kind. But for now, this young man was a legend, if only in his own mind, and sometimes that's good enough.

Imagine my surprise when he stopped his predatory stroll at our table, ignored Marina entirely, looked directly down into my eyes, and said, "You would like to walk with me, yes?"

I recovered my wits quickly. "Oh," I said with a smile that was tinged with false regret, "thank you, but no."

"No? A walk around the piazza?"

I shook my head. "No, really. But thank you again. It was kind of you to ask."

The young man shrugged, smiled, his divertissement accomplished, and with a "Ciao" strolled off to chat with other feminine pastimes.

I watched him go, both amused and flattered. I wondered what it would be like to be a "cougar." Did a woman have to be rich to be a cougar? Was being a cougar a bad thing? I couldn't imagine how it could be, provided the young man didn't get hold of your bank account.

My innocent musings were interrupted by a gagging sound from Marina's throat. I'd almost forgotten that she was there.

"That was so disgusting," she said. "I can't believe he was flirting with you!"

I laughed. "Am I so hideous that a younger man should run away in terror?"

"No, of course not, but he was, like, my age!"

"So? Some men like older women. And please don't tell me that you embrace the double standard."

"Well . . ."

"So it's okay for younger women to be with older men? So if I had gone out with that older man we met last night, the man who sent us the wine, that wouldn't have bothered you? Assuming I wasn't involved with Rob, of course."

"Well," she said, "it wouldn't have seemed so—odd."

"That's just because it's so common."

"And it does seem to work out, mostly," she said. "Older men and younger women."

"Yes, well, that depends on your definition of 'work out.'" And what, I wondered, would my daughter feel about this issue when she was my age and male peers were beginning to ogle women half her age?

"So you'd go out with that young guy?" Marina asked, disbelieving. "Or some other young guy?"

"No," I admitted, "and for a lot of reasons, only some of which concern age. Besides, he was just flirting. I don't think he really wanted or expected me to take a walk with him."

"Then you should have called him on it! I would have loved to watch him squirm his way out of a 'walk.' It would have been hysterical."

"Hysterical, maybe, but also cruel. Young men—all men—can be very, very easily hurt."

"You think so?" she said. "I don't think Jotham is easily hurt. In fact, I don't think much affects him at all. He's—what's the word?"

An emotional desert, I suggested silently. Barren? An empty vessel? A shallow bowl?

"Sanguine," Marina said. "That's it."

"Yes, well, maybe he just doesn't let on when things hurt him." Why not, I thought, give the guy the benefit of the doubt?

"Maybe. But I don't think so. He's—imperturbable."

Marina's cell phone rang. Imperturbable, maybe; needy, definitely. Needy or a control freak, maybe both.

This call lasted well over five minutes, during which time I fumed. Why had I dragged my daughter all the way to Europe if she was going to spend so much time on the phone with her boring boyfriend back home? I tried not to listen to Marina's side of their banal conversation. Yes, no, I'm having a good time, I miss you, how's the weather back home, have you seen Jordan and Jason, tell Allison and Jessica I say hi. I knew my prudent daughter had included such communication in her budget, but this was ridiculous.

And didn't she think it rude to talk on the phone to someone thousands of miles away while letting her companion go neglected?

Finally, she ended the call.

"That was Jotham."

"Yes, I gathered it was him."

"He says hi."

"That's nice," I said. "You know, Marina, you might want to spend a little more time enjoying the sites and sounds of Florence and less time on the phone with Jotham."

Marina gave me such a look then, the tiniest bit pitying, the tiniest bit surprised.

"You just don't know what it's like to be getting married,"

she said. "When you make such a big commitment to some-one, he has to come first."

I felt as if I'd been slapped. And yet, there'd been no nasti-ness in her tone, no superior attitude, either. I believed Ma-rina really didn't know that she'd hurt me. I believed she thought she'd only been imparting a truth about which I had no knowledge at all.

"Yes," I said evenly, "you're right. I don't know what it's like to make such a big commitment." Other, of course, than the lifelong commitment I made to you the moment I knew you existed.

"I think I'll write Jotham a postcard," Marina said, utterly innocent of her offense.

Without reply, I opened one of my guidebooks and pre-tended to read.

15

Global warming. Nuclear threats from Iran and North Korea. A dishonest government intent upon destroying true democracy. Cancer. Random mass shootings by mentally disturbed loners. AIDS. Mothers. Terrorism. Let's face it. No matter where you turn, you're going to find a stumbling block on the road to contentment. The trick is to learn what you can change, what you can safely ignore, and what you can negotiate.
    —Overcoming Our Mothers and Other Major
        Obstacles to Happiness

There was no point in pretending that I wasn't hurt by Marina's careless and unfair comment. And sitting on my bed in our hotel room, waiting for Marina to finish getting ready for dinner, there was no point in pretending that the hurt wasn't sliding into the gooey pit of self-pity.

I was the one person who had done and would continue to do everything for Marina to ensure she had food, shelter, an education, a loving home. I was the one person who had sacrificed and would continue to sacrifice everything I could for Marina's happiness, safety, and peace of mind.

And she thought I knew nothing about commitment.

Indulging in self-pity is like eating a Cadbury Cream Egg, the ones that show up in the stores around Easter. One egg definitely goes a very long way; two eggs, and you're in a sugar-induced coma for days. I was onto the third egg, as it were, while waiting for Marina that evening, remembering the nine long months of my pregnancy.

Looking out at the grimy, mid-twentieth-century apartment building across from our hotel, I remembered how lonely I felt, suddenly thrust into a world entirely different from that of my friends. It's true they were sympathetic. Everyone roundly denounced Peter and swore oaths of loyalty to me. But once graduation took place, they were off to enjoy the final summer of their youth, without their pregnant friend in tow. While they were out at clubs dancing to Duran Duran and Culture Club, I was waddling around on swollen ankles, craving pink grapefruit smeared with anchovy paste. While they were dressing in torn fishnet stockings and slathering on black lipstick, I was putting up with the indignities of maternity clothes, which, let me assure you, were not half as attractive as they are now. While, come September, when they were going off to graduate school or starting careers that would one day afford them a home on each coast, I was learning how to diaper a squirming baby without letting her roll off the makeshift changing table my father had set up in my bedroom.

Honestly, I was lonely but not unhappy. I didn't mind not going out to nightclubs and smoking clove cigarettes and wearing dead people's clothes, as my father called the rags my friends bought at used clothing shops in Allston. I don't mean to sound like a goody-two-shoes perfect mommy, but about a month after I found out I was pregnant, a month after Peter hightailed it out of my life, something clicked—suddenly I wasn't afraid or angry or suffering the pangs of humiliation the abandoned woman is supposed to suffer. I suddenly felt—happy. Excited, too; not stupidly, not in a naïve way—I knew being a single parent would be a rough road. But suddenly everything was all right.

I got up and wandered the short distance to the dresser and stared into the mirror above it. The woman reflected there looked unhappy. And I wondered, not for the first time, how you go from this loving, contented place concerning your child to a place where you look at her and realize that you don't very much like her? That right at that particular moment, you don't very much care if you never see her again, if she takes her attitude and her ungrateful, full-of-herself, know-it-all behavior and stalks off into the sunset for good.

Marina emerged from the bathroom just then, and I looked away from the mirror. Her beauty took my breath away. I don't think Marina knew how beautiful she'd become; while she cared about her appearance, it wasn't to excess, and when someone would comment on her face or figure, no matter how carefully or respectfully, she brushed off the compliment with annoyance. Such lack of obsessive self-consciousness only, in my opinion, added to her appeal. Jotham, I'm sure, knew he was envied among his peers—among men of all ages. Unlike my daughter, he was very aware of his own power to please.

"Ready to go?" she asked.

That night we had dinner at a restaurant other travelers had highly recommended on several of the Internet travel sites I'd visited while planning our trip. The reviews proved to be accurate. The walls were hung with a fabulous collection of pottery plates and bowls painted with intricate designs in bright blue, deep yellow, brick red, with accents in aqua. The evening's meal was memorable for its roasted vegetables mix and a steak from Maremma, a region known since Etruscan times for its cattle (so my guidebook had informed me).

Though I wanted to banish Jotham from our lives, at least for the duration of our vacation, my better self decided to show remarkable maturity and generosity by introducing the all-important topic of his special gift.

"I had another idea for Jotham's gift," I said. "What about cuff links? Gold cuff links would be expensive, but he could wear them at the wedding."

Marina paused. "I think he might consider them too much like jewelry," she said finally.

"But if he wears a tuxedo for the wedding, and I'm sure he will, won't he need cuff links?"

"Yes, but he could borrow a pair from his father. I don't know, I just don't see Jotham getting excited about cuff links."

"Well, I'm not sure many people actually get excited about cuff links, but—"

"No, Mom. Cuff links are a bad idea."

"Okay," I said. "I suppose you know him best."

Marina smiled a bit. "He's not very hard to know, actually. What you see with Jotham is pretty much all there is. Wait, I didn't mean that the way it came out. I mean that he's—"

That he's not very deep or thoughtful? That he's transparent? That he's a puddle rather than a pool?

"He's not complicated," Marina said finally. "I think that's a good way to put it."

Unlike my daughter, I would be bored senseless with an uncomplicated person. That had been to my disadvantage on occasion, most memorably, of course, with Peter Duncan, a master of manipulative dramatics. In Rob, I was lucky enough to have found depth without despair.

"Actually," Marina was saying, "I find it kind of—relaxing—to be around him. There's no craziness. There's no hidden agenda. I know I can rely on Jotham because, number one, he hates change."

Because he fears it; because he dreads a loss of power. Well, I thought, begrudgingly, who doesn't? "And number two?" I asked.

"What?"

"You said number one, Jotham hates change. What's the second reason you know you can rely on him?"

"Oh." Marina paused a moment before saying, "Well, I guess it's that he's loyal. He's very close to his parents, and he's been friends with Jason and Jordan since middle school."

Certainly, loyalty was—is—a virtue to be lauded and appreciated, especially in our throwaway culture. But loyalty isn't impossible to find. You can get loyalty from a friend; for that matter, you can get it from a dog and even from the occasional cat.

I wondered if Marina really believed in her contentment, or, if by stating it so emphatically, she was trying to convince herself of it. It was hard to keep my not-so-hidden agenda from intruding and marring my opinion of Jotham and of his relationship with Marina. I was aware of my all-too-human frailty—the tendency to make unfair judgments—and at the same time, I was unable to keep that tendency entirely at bay.

"I'm glad," I said carefully, "that you feel you're doing the right thing by marrying Jotham."

"Oh, it's more than a feeling," Marina said. "I know I'm doing the right thing. I'm one hundred percent absolutely certain."

No one is one hundred percent absolutely certain about anything. The lady, I thought was protesting too much. Unless once again the lady's mother was succumbing to her particular prejudices.

"How about dessert?" I said. "I saw they have *zabaione* on the menu."

"Jotham had *zabaione* once and hated it."

"Yes," I said, "well, we just won't tell him anything about it."

16

Dear Answer Lady:

*I just don't understand what went wrong.
Since the very first, my husband and I have done
everything we could for our son. We sent him to
excellent private schools, hired tutors when he
needed more academic help, took him on fabulous vacations, supported every hobby he ever
adopted, and showered him with love and affection. Everything was just fine until he turned fifteen last fall and just went berserk. He started
cutting classes, hanging out with a rough crowd,
abusing us verbally, and has even refused to care
for his once-beloved dog. We've tried counseling,
but he either doesn't show up for his appointments
or does show up but sits there saying nothing.
Now our son is facing charges of assault with a
deadly weapon. My husband and I are heart-
broken. What did we do wrong?*

Dear Mother of Delinquent:

*Recently, I was rereading one of my favorite
novels, David Copperfield, by one Mr. Charles
Dickens, in which there is a line that pertains to
the situation you describe. The line reads as follows: "Accidents will occur in the best regulated
families." In other words, shit happens. Don't
blame yourselves for your son's choice of life as
a criminal. You gave him the proper tools, and*

he chose to use them for destructive rather than constructive ends. So be it. Now take yourselves out for a nice dinner at a fabulous restaurant and try to forget about the bum it was your misfortune to bring into this world.

Monday, June 5

I seemed to spend a good part of every day of our Tuscan holiday, at least that first week, waiting for Marina to emerge from the bathroom. That morning, slumped on my unmade bed, vaguely aware of the sound of water spilling into the bathtub, I wondered about my relationship with Rob.

Had I fallen into the habit of neglecting him? Had he fallen into the habit of neglecting me? I didn't feel neglected; but did that mean I had become used to careless treatment? Had Rob?

Marina and her obsession with Jotham—Jotham and his obsession with Marina—it had become almost an object of mockery to me, and suddenly I felt ashamed. They might not have the kind of relationship I wanted for myself, but that didn't mean I couldn't respect them for their choice.

Angry with myself—and maybe, too, at Marina—I picked up her cell phone. Rob and I had agreed only to call in an emergency, but there I was allowing myself to be shamed into being a "good girlfriend," according to my daughter's definition, which demanded virtually constant communication.

The call went to voice mail; I didn't know if I was glad or not. I left a brief, awkward message, something to the effect of "Hi, it's me, just checking in, no need to call back, hope all's well, bye."

I had no idea of what Rob would make of my call. I doubted he'd worry; Rob is not a worrier. More likely he'd raise an eyebrow and assume I'd had one glass of wine too many and was feeling sentimental. He'd never assume I was wondering

if my daughter was right, wondering if I had any real understanding of devotion and commitment, if I really knew what
it was like to put someone first and foremost.

I worked hard that morning to get past any ill feelings
about my daughter's perception of me, but I'm afraid I wasn't
entirely successful.

When Marina was finally showered and dressed, we headed
out for the Basilica di Santo Spirito, taking a deliberately cir-
cuitous route. In a nameless but charming little square, we
unexpectedly came upon a woman and boy, begging.

"It's a gypsy, Mom," Marina stage-whispered. "Don't give
her anything."

Puzzled by the lack of logic in that advice, I said "Wait
here then" and walked over to where the woman sat slumped
on the ground, surrounded by her worldly goods in various
bags and sacks.

I dropped a few coins into the woman's outstretched hand.
She didn't thank me; I hadn't expected her to. She might have
been anywhere between thirty and sixty; through the dirt, the
missing teeth, the weatherworn skin, it was impossible to tell.

I walked back to where my daughter stood waiting, a
frown of disapproval on her face. "We are very lucky, Marina," I said quietly to her. "I hope you realize that."

Marina lifted her bag under her arm and hugged it like it
was a giant squishy football. A giant squishy football covered
in sharp metal pieces. "Yeah," she said, "I do. Just so long as
the kid doesn't steal my bag. Jotham told me that gypsies are
notorious pickpockets and thieves."

I watched the child—the woman's son or not, I couldn't
know. He circled the small piazza, working independently of
his mother, his aunt, his friend. I watched as he drew closer
and approached a well-dressed couple, clearly tourists, not
American. The boy might have been eight or nine or ten and
had the distinct look of malnutrition about him, eyes glittering bright in too-deep, shadowed sockets, stick-thin limbs on
which elbows and knees appeared like lumps of fungus on a

sick tree. What torment must a mother feel, watching her child go hungry?

"Not because they choose to be thieves," I said, turning away and taking my daughter's arm, the one not engaged in maintaining a chokehold on her bag.

"Whatever. Jotham's mom got her bag snatched when she and Mr. Grandin were in Rome last year. Luckily her passport was in the hotel safe."

"Yes, luckily."

"Look, Mom." Marina nodded ahead. "There's a row of shops down that street. Maybe I can find something for Jotham in one of them."

I sighed. There was really no point in my protesting, not after Marina had so firmly put me in my place with her remark the previous afternoon. It was inevitable that several hours of each day would be spent in pursuit of the perfect souvenir for the man to whom she'd made a Big Commitment.

"Sure," I said. "Let's go."

As we walked along the narrow street, dodging the fast-walking, well-dressed Florentine businessmen and women, Marina reviewed her pressing dilemma. "He doesn't wear jewelry," she said, "so that's out."

"Yes," I said. "We covered that with the cuff link conversation."

"Except for a wedding ring. He's promised he'll wear one. I can't stand married men who don't wear a wedding ring. That's totally false advertising."

I didn't bother to inform her that I'd come across plenty of married men wearing a wedding ring who'd had no trouble whatsoever in making a pass at me. The ring might be a concession to the wife, but it didn't guarantee good behavior.

"What about a new wallet," I suggested, inspired by the leather shop we'd come upon. "I'm sure you could find him a really beautiful leather wallet."

"No. Jotham is very particular about his wallets. I know what kind he prefers, but he likes to pick them out himself."

"Okay. How about a briefcase, then? He's sure to need some kind of briefcase for law school."

Marina gave me the Are-You-Totally-from-the-Last-Century? look. "Mom, no one carries a briefcase to school anymore!"

"Well, like a backpack," I suggested. "Something youthful, like that gorgeous black one in the corner. See?"

Marina turned back to the street. "He bought a bag at the L. L. Bean outlet in Portland when we were there last fall with Allison and Jordan to see a hockey game. I think he's going to use that. It was only thirty dollars."

"Okay. How about a money clip? You could have it engraved. Or a really good pen, though I have no idea where we'd go in Florence to find one. Or—"

Marina sighed loudly. "Mom, you're not helping."

"All right, fine. I'll keep my lame ideas to myself." If my future son-in-law was so picky, I thought, he could expect cash from me for Christmas. That or a box of cheap milk chocolates he could throw into the trash, because no doubt he only ate designer dark chocolate.

Resignedly, I followed Marina down the street of small, expensive shops, fully aware of the irony of our quest for what was essentially a luxury item—books could be carried in a plastic bag if necessary; money could be carried without a wallet; notes could be taken with a pencil—after having so recently encountered the gypsies in the square. I wondered if the experience had registered with Marina, if she felt any shred of guilt or shame. I could tell nothing from her words or manner, and I was strangely reluctant to ask.

17

The inestimable Sophia Loren was once quoted as saying: "When you are a mother, you are never really alone in your thoughts. A mother always has to think twice, once for herself and once for her child." Consider carefully this mind-boggling truth before you decide to have a child. Are you willing to let your mind, once a private and inviolate space, be forever inhabited by another human being?
> —Never Really Alone: The Inevitable Loss of
> Private Selfhood with the Arrival of
> Motherhood

Later that afternoon, we found ourselves at one of the city's wonderful outdoor flea/antique markets. We wandered slowly up and down long rows of booths packed tightly side by side, taking some advantage of their awnings as a respite from the beating sun.

"It's kind of overwhelming," Marina said after about half an hour. "I'm having a hard time really seeing anything in particular, you know?"

"Yes," I agreed. "I do know. Let's stop for a bit at the end of this row and take a break."

We found ourselves facing a tiny parking lot at the edge of the market.

"Whew," Marina said. "I felt like I was suffocating. Just let me text Jotham, and I'll be okay to go back in."

"Sure," I said, doubtful that while my daughter "chatted"

with her fiancé I'd find anything of interest to stare at in an urban parking lot.

But I was wrong. A few yards away, a couple, probably in their thirties, stood against a low stone barrier separating the market from the lot. He clutched more than held her hand to his chest; their faces were mere inches apart; their murmured conversation punctuated by frequent kisses. There was an air of passionate concentration about them, an air of intensity an interested onlooker couldn't fail to miss. At least, I hadn't failed to miss it and assumed they were having an affair, a desperate couple seeking whatever odd chance they could find to kiss and talk and dream.

At home I might have turned away from such a sight with distaste, murmuring something about inappropriate public behavior. Now, in Florence, in a city far from home, I couldn't look away. I thought this couple was—beautiful.

And I thought again about how travel—how being in an unfamiliar place, surrounded by unfamiliar faces and languages not your own—changes so much about a person, at the moment and, sometimes, forever after.

It's that travel is both disconcerting and liberating, if done outside of the tightly controlled, slightly anemic tradition of planned tours. You experience a sense of dislocation, a heightened awareness of possible lives other than the one you are currently living; you live in anticipation of something unpredictable about to happen, something you both fear and desire.

Watching the couple, without, I hoped, seeming to, I thought back to my one and only other trip to Europe, the summer between my sophomore and junior years in college. I'd signed up for the school's two-week art tour of Paris and London. I was very excited at first, but only days into the trip I realized that those two weeks weren't going to be the astounding experience I'd hoped for. Bundled into and out of museums and churches and galleries, loaded onto buses and trains and ferries, eating dinners at preordained restaurants not known for their exceptional or even interesting cuisine, and with very little time to explore on my own, I felt isolated from the real cultures of France and England. The trip wasn't entirely a waste, of course—how could it have been when I got to visit the Louvre and the National Gallery—but it left me feeling that I'd missed out on a very important aspect of travel.

Now, watching the couple slip away through the crowd, I hoped that Marina and I together would have a grand and life-altering experience while in Florence, something we could recall for years and someday share with her children.

"Do you know," Marina said suddenly, obviously having ended her communication with Jotham, calling me back to the moment, "I've never seen Jotham's parents touch each other, not even hold hands. I've never even seen Mr. Grandin take Mrs. Grandin's arm, like if they're crossing a street. It's strange."

Had she, too, seen the lovers? I'd often wondered how affectionate Marina and Jotham were when alone. Often enough I'd seen Jotham touch Marina in a protective, even a possessive way—lay his arm around her shoulders, take her upper arm in his hand—but I was never sure if the gestures were romantic or undertaken solely on my behalf as some sort of proof of his importance.

"Well," I said, "every couple has their own way. Maybe the—distance—works for them."

"Maybe. But it seems odd to me, especially when you see how affectionate Grandma and Grandpa are. I mean, I used to be grossed out by it, back when I was about thirteen. Now I think it's adorable, how they're always hugging or holding hands or kissing each other on the cheek."

"They're a good couple," I agreed. "They're utterly compatible."

"Do you think they were always that way, back when they first met, when they got married?"

"I don't know," I admitted. "I suppose some of that affection came with time. Of course, maybe the Grandins' lack of affection is a result of their being together so long."

"So," she said, "are you saying that time makes or breaks a relationship?"

"It's hard to generalize about relationships, Marina. Each one is so different."

Like my relationship with Rob. It couldn't be any more different from the one I'd had with Peter if Rob were a kangaroo.

"I guess." Marina looked troubled; I wanted to reassure her somehow.

"Besides, like I said, maybe the Grandins are totally happy with each other. They are still married. Something must be working."

Or they're both too emotionally exhausted to care. Or she can't bear to lose the comfortable lifestyle she has as Mrs. Grandin. Or he won't entertain the notion of losing half of his hard-earned wealth to a woman of whom he's long since grown tired. I kept those depressing thoughts to myself.

"It just seems kind of sad," she said, "to live with someone for so long and not to even touch. It just seems so lonely. They sleep in separate beds, you know."

"No, I didn't know." And I wasn't sure I needed to know. "But, Marina—the Grandins' marriage is in no way a prediction of how your marriage to Jotham is going to turn out."

"Of course, Mom. I know that."

Marina wandered on through the aisles of the market. I followed, but my mind wasn't on the myriad of goods for sale: elaborate rusted candelabra and massive, crudely made hand tools and old rhinestone-encrusted baubles. My mind was on my future in-laws.

Mrs. Grandin—Barbara—could best be described as thoroughly uninteresting. Her conversation was limited to what new piece of furniture she'd just bought for her latest redecorating venture, what fabulously expensive resort she and

Frank had just returned from, and what Jotham was up to at school—being made president of a club and being accepted into a fraternity and scoring higher than anyone else in all of his pre-law classes. (When pressed, Mrs. Grandin never seemed to have any details about her son's achievements—the nature of the club, the name of the fraternity, the subject of the classes.)

Also, she seemed to lack any sense of humor or irony, two deficiencies that made it very difficult to spend any length of time with her. I mean, if a person doesn't get any of your witty asides and doesn't even emit a chuckle when others are laughing heartily at your boyfriend's hilarious telling of his five-year-old nephew's attempt to make breakfast for his mother on her birthday, what kind of relationship can you expect?

To make matters worse, early on Mrs. Grandin made it clear that she wasn't in the habit of reading anything other than the daily local papers; global politics, art, music—all were off-limits as topics of conversation. She didn't like going to the movies; according to her, there hadn't been a really good movie made since *Gone with the Wind*. She would only eat at the highest-end steak houses. "Foreign" food held no interest for her.

Consequently, I'd never felt jealous of Marina's relationship with Mrs. Grandin. I'd seen them together quite a few times, and it was clear that while they got along well enough, there was not a great bond. I imagined that when Marina and Jotham had children, she and Mrs. Grandin might become closer—but I wasn't banking on it.

As for Jotham's dad, Frank, well, I had no use for him whatsoever. Poor Rob could barely work up the energy to be civil to the man. Frank Grandin was straight out of central casting, the pompous, self-important, narrow-minded, big businessman, from his full head of suspiciously jet-black hair right down to the oversized gold watch on his wrist. Rob, with his graying temples and good old Timex with a fraying leather strap, was, in my eyes, almost a different breed of being. The relatively few times my parents had been in the same room with the Grandins, both Barbara and Frank, I don't think more than a pleasantry was spoken, and that only when drinks were refreshed.

And there was something else about Jotham's mother that irked me, something in addition to her coldish personality and boring conversation. It was clear from her every careful question and her every mildly pitying look that she felt the need to remind me of my status—a lower one than hers, naturally, that of Abandoned Woman, or Victim of Love.

Unfortunately, I suspected that Marina shared her future mother-in-law's opinion. I know it shouldn't have mattered, what other people thought, but when "other people" meant my daughter, then it did matter. It mattered a lot. No one respects a victim. You feel sorry for a victim, you pity her, but you don't respect her.

In my more mean-spirited moments, I wondered to what extent Barbara Grandin's opinion had informed my daughter's view of me. But that was something I'd never know.

Suffice it to say I was sure there'd be a minimum of family gatherings in our future. Barbara and I would not be sharing patterns for Baby Grandin's trousseau; Frank and Rob would not be spending long, lazy Saturday afternoons fishing at the Grandins' lakeside vacation home in Maine. And my parents would not be inviting the Grandins to their monthly card game. (For one, the beer nuts would definitely not cut it with Barbara.)

"Maybe you'll find something special for Jotham here," I suggested, catching up with Marina.

"I doubt it," she said. "He's not interested in antiques."

"Look." I stopped her by taking her arm and pointed down at the table on our right. "Look at these brass nutcrackers. He likes lobster, right? You could use these when you serve lobster. I mean, when you get your first apartment together."

"That is so lame, Mom."

"I know," I said. "I'm trying."

But I decided to stop trying. A small but exquisitely carved wooden chess set. Jotham didn't play chess, and if he did, he'd no doubt prefer a larger, more ornate set. A book of old maps. No doubt Jotham would wrinkle his nose at the almost imperceptible smell of must. A bottle of good Italian wine. No, Jotham only drank wines made in the U.S. A jar of shaved truffles. Eat something dug up by a pig?

Fussy, particular, unimaginative. Any of those terms might be used to describe my future son-in-law.

I preferred censorious, hypercritical, and prudish.

18

Dear Answer Lady:

My daughter—she's thirty-five—doesn't like me very much. I've tried to be a good mother, and I know I've never consciously done anything to hurt her. Yet she never responds to my notes and only rarely to my e-mails (with a short, curt reply), and when we're on the phone (I call her), she hardly says anything. Plus, I haven't gotten a birthday card from her in years. Is it my fault she doesn't like me? I've given up on expecting her to love me, but if only she'd like me, just a little, I'd feel so much better.

Dear Spineless Wonder:

Stop groveling and cut off all communication with the bitch—and that means no more pathetic phone calls and cute little notes and faux-jolly e-mails. It's too late now to assign blame here; maybe it is your fault your daughter doesn't like you—what of it? Move on! Got a niece who's sweet to you? A friend's daughter whose company you enjoy? Redirect your attention to her. And maybe once your daughter realizes you've stopped courting her attention, she'll start sending those birthday cards. Maybe, but I doubt it.

Dinner that evening was memorable not only for the food but also for the odd choice of music being played over the restaurant's sound system.

"Is this some sort of disco?" Marina asked, frowning in distaste.

"It's some sort of something," I said.

"Are they singing in English? I can't even tell. It's like a combination of bad seventies rock and bad eighties dance music."

"Maybe it's some sort of European pop music. At least it's not blaring."

Marina shrugged. "I can ignore it if you can. What are you having? I think I'll order the *saltimbocca*. That's veal, right?"

"Right." I glanced down at the menu and made an immediate choice. "I'm going to have the *cinghiale alla cacciatora*. That means *cinghiale* huntsman-style. I've read about it. It should be quite hearty, and I'm absolutely starved."

"What's *cinghiale*?"

"Wild boar."

"Wild boar?" Marina wrinkled her nose. "I don't think so."

"You can taste a bit of mine. Maybe you'll like it."

"Maybe. Have you ever tried it?"

"No, but I love pork. How strange could it be?"

Marina looked at me as if I'd finally gone over the edge. When had she become incurious about food? As a child, Marina was unusually receptive to new tastes and textures. But truth be told, we ate so few of our meals together anymore that I'd failed to note a change in her habits.

"And how about some fried squash blossoms," I suggested, partly to goad her, partly because I'd had them once in a wonderful little restaurant in New York's Little Italy and loved them.

"But it's a fried flower," Marina said. "And I don't know about squash. I've never been a big fan."

"You like zucchini bread."

"That's different. It's got a lot of other stuff in it. You can't really taste the zucchini."

"Oh, be a little adventurous! No *cinghiale*, no fried zucchini blossoms." You might as well, I thought, be eating at the Cherry Pit, where the major ingredient was fat and the primary seasoning was salt. "Just try one," I encouraged when the plate arrived. "How bad could anything fried be?"

"Okay, okay." Marina gingerly took a small bite, chewed, and swallowed. "Actually," she said, "that's pretty tasty. I'll never get Jotham to try one, though."

"No, I don't suppose you will. He's really a meat and potatoes kind of guy, isn't he?"

Marina laughed fondly. "The wildest thing he ever ate was a piece of turnip, and that was by mistake. He thought it was a potato."

"So I'm guessing you won't be serving tripe at your wedding?"

"Ugh, gross, of course not!"

"Marina, I was only kidding."

"Oh," she said. "Get this. Allison's mom wants them to take a trip together now."

Allison, I remembered, lived at home with her mother and her mother's third husband, who was by all accounts (Allison's) an idiot. Why, exactly, he was an idiot, I didn't know, but Marina had assured me that Allison was very good at assessing character. Maybe so, but I also knew that Allison worshipped her father, with whom she spent as much time as she could, considering he lived in Chicago and had a new wife and small child of his own. I suspected that any man her mother married, no matter how accomplished and loving, would, in Allison's estimation, come up short.

"How does Allison feel about that?" I asked.

"Are you kidding? She's freaking out. She says it's all my fault. Well, your fault, really, for planning this trip to Italy and giving her mother ideas."

Poor Mrs. Wright. I didn't know much about her other than that she had married two "idiots" in quick succession after her husband left her for another woman, but my heart did go out to her. Couldn't Allison cut her mother some slack? "Huh," I said. "Sorry. Can't Allison say no to her mother?"

Too late I realized I'd asked a loaded question. I remembered Marina's initial unhappy reaction to our proposed Tuscan holiday, and before she could reply, I said, "Well, I guess that could be difficult."

Marina shrugged. "Anyway, she's been using work as an excuse not to make plans. Can you believe she's asked for more hours at the Olive Garden this summer? She hates waiting tables."

"Maybe she makes good tips," I said lamely.

"It's not about the tips. It's about avoiding her mother. Though the extra money will come in handy. Weddings are so expensive these days."

That's because they are overindulgent displays of ridiculous self-absorption. But given that Marina and Jotham were determined to pay for as much of their wedding as was humanly possible, I wasn't anticipating the need to take out a loan.

"Jessica and her mom," Marina was saying, "go away together all the time. Mostly weekend trips to spas. Once they went to New York just to shop. Can you imagine?"

"I can imagine the bills."

"Yeah, well, they have a lot of money. Jessica's dad is a CEO. Jessica and her mom stayed in one of those incredibly hip boutique hotels in SoHo."

I felt a twinge of defensiveness and wondered if my daughter was comparing our mid-level hotel to the top-level one in which Jessica and her mother had stayed. I'd saved for almost two years for this trip to Italy; I was doing the best I could for my daughter.

"I don't know," Marina said thoughtfully. "Even if I had a ton of money, I can't see myself going for five star when three star would do nicely. It just seems wasteful."

I relaxed; the incipient frown made no appearance. Why did I work myself into a state when I knew where my daughter's priorities lay?

"Was Grandma close to her mother?" Marina asked after a moment. "All I really know about her is what she looked like, from photo albums. Grandma doesn't talk about her, at least not to me."

"Yes," I said, "from what I know, they were pretty close. I was only ten when she died. That means my mother was about thirty, thirty-one."

"Was Grandma really upset?"

"Yes. I remember her crying a lot in the weeks after my grandmother died. But I was too young to really understand what she was going through. And too young to be of much help."

"Were you upset, too?" Marina asked. "Were you close to your grandmother?"

"You know," I said, "not really. Not like you are with your grandmother."

"Why?"

I thought a moment before answering. "I guess it was because she didn't really take a lot of interest in me. That's not a complaint. I mean, she was there for holidays and birthdays. But even when she was at our house, she spent more time with my mother than with me. She had a lot of hobbies, too. She was an avid gardener. She was fanatical about her roses. You weren't allowed to touch the rose bushes, let alone bend down to smell the flowers. She spent a lot of time traveling to award-winning gardens. I do remember thinking that she preferred the company of flowers to the company of people."

Marina laughed. "And Grandma can't even grow a plant in a pot."

"Neither can I. I guess Great-Grandma's green thumb died with her."

"I never really thought about gardening," Marina admitted. "I like flowers and all, but . . . Maybe someday, when I have my own house, I'll give it a try. Who knows? Maybe there's a bit of my great-grandmother in me."

I thought for a moment about Peter's family. Had his great-grandmother been a keen gardener? Were either of his parents growers of prizewinning roses or tomatoes? There was so much Marina and I didn't know about her father's side of the family.

"Maybe you could grow your own squash and fry the blossoms for appetizers," I said.

Marina laughed. "Now you're just fantasizing, Mom."

19

Your daughter is intelligent, caring, and physically attractive. She's built a successful career and enjoys a solid marriage to a great guy. And you, her supposedly supportive mother, are sick with envy at the mere thought of your female offspring. Don't despair. You are not alone. Intense jealousy of one's daughter is actually quite normal.
        —What to Do When You Hate Your Daughter

Tuesday, June 6

The day was proving to be hazy, hot, and humid; I was annoyed with myself for not having packed lighter clothes. If the weather persisted in being so ugly, the two pairs of jeans I'd brought with me were going to stay unworn in my closet.

We stood on the Ponte Vecchio, the Old Bridge, overlooking the River Arno. At least there was an occasional breeze off the murky water below us. The bridge, once made of wood but rebuilt to be mostly of stone (so my mother informed me), was lined with shops selling gold jewelry and porcelain statues.

"Listen to this." My mother was peering down at one of her guidebooks. "It says here that the bridge was built in 1345—can you believe that?—and that it actually survived destruction by the Nazis because Hitler thought it was so beautiful."

"Wasn't he a painter or something?" I asked, a dim memory of a PBS documentary Rob had watched at our house surfacing briefly.

"A failed painter," my mother said. "A bad one."

"And what was up with that stupid moustache?"

"I think the moustache was the least of his deficiencies." My mother turned away from the water and nodded in the direction of a shop with a sign that read, in both Italian and English, FUSCO FAMILY JEWELERS, SINCE 1970. "Let's go in this shop," she said.

"Why?" I asked. "I'm not interested in buying any jewelry."

"Well, maybe I am. You can wait outside if you'd rather."

"No, I'll come in. Maybe they've got air-conditioning."

My mother walked directly to the center display case, where a nicely dressed older man immediately appeared to help her. I remained just inside the door, overwhelmed. Necklaces set with diamonds, bracelets made of glowing gold— every piece was absolutely gorgeous. I'd heard that Italian jewelry design was special; I'd seen plenty of pictures in magazines to prove it. And Mrs. Grandin had come home from Italy the year before with a stunning bracelet that weighed down my wrist when I tried it on. But being in the presence of so much beautiful jewelry and all in one small space was unlike anything I could have imagined.

Suddenly conscious of my engagement ring, I twisted it with my thumb, feeling all the hard, tiny bumps of the encrusted band. Jotham and I were supposed to have chosen it together. We'd had a plan, a reasonable one, I thought, because the ring would be a mutual investment, and any financial investment demands a plan. And I'd known just what I wanted, a platinum band with a brilliant-cut solitaire, something simple, elegant, and classic.

I'd even worked out a forecast that showed us approximately when we'd be able to "trade up," or sell the first ring and buy one with a larger center stone and two, maybe three smaller diamonds on either side. (The lack of sentimentality in this thinking appalls my adult self.)

But even the best-laid plans have a tendency to go awry, something I was just beginning to learn. I'm sure Jotham thought he was being romantic when he surprised me with a ring while we were having dinner one night at Locke-Ober, an old and famous restaurant in downtown Boston. I suppose I should have known that something was up; we spent real money on food only on special occasions, maybe once or twice a year. And this was just a regular Saturday night in March. At least, it had been just a regular Saturday night until right before dessert, when Jotham got down on one knee beside my chair and asked me to marry him. He handed me a red velvet box that I opened in a sort of trance. Still in that trance, I croaked "Yes" to enthusiastic applause from diners at nearby tables and even a few calls of "Congratulations" and "Best of luck." One man even came by to shake Jotham's hand.

Part of me had been pleased. What woman wouldn't be flattered by such a public display? It was all pretty exciting, being the center of attention. For Jotham, too. He looked— he was—very proud of himself and received the applause as very much his due.

But though part of me had been pleased and flattered, another part of me had been annoyed, even a bit angry, though of course I hadn't let on. I hated surprises, and Jotham knew that, yet he'd abandoned our plan and picked out the ring all on his own and "popped the question" in a way anyone who knew me well would have advised against. And I was sure he spent more money than he should have, money that he— we—could have better spent toward his law-school tuition or general living expenses, like rent.

It occurred to me then, standing in that jewelry store on the Ponte Vecchio full to bursting with flashing precious stones and gleaming gold, that Jotham's parents might have helped to pay for my engagement ring. I'd be furious if they had, but I doubted I'd ever know the truth.

While my mother was busy with the salesman, I walked over to a large display case of rings. One in particular caught my eye; it was very simple, just one long gold wire twisted round and round, the ends eventually forged together. I'd never seen anything quite like it, certainly not back home. It was striking, and I wanted very much to try it on, but I didn't. My budget didn't include a fanciful purchase, especially with the cost of international calls and stuff, so why even pretend?

I walked slowly on, past trays of delicate bracelets, past clusters of sparkling earrings, and then to a display of glittering, beaded minaudières. Looking down at the outrageously expensive little bags, I couldn't help but think about the other aspect of Jotham's big surprise that bothered me. The engagement ring was beautiful, but it wasn't really—me. Jotham was totally convinced he'd done a great job in choosing a ring his fiancée adored, but the fact was that he hadn't done a great job at all. The ring was simply too much for me; my hand looked weighted down. Besides that, the setting was yellow gold, not platinum as I'd hoped. The center diamond was a marquis cut, not round. And the band was encrusted with diamonds all around, which resulted in the skin on my pinky and middle finger being always a bit raw.

Still, I figured that in a few years I could upgrade as planned and this time make absolutely sure that I picked out the new ring, not Jotham and definitely not Jotham's parents. Though, of course, to upgrade from this particular ring would mean a major reworking of our financial plan.

A familiar, pleasant laugh made me join my mother at the front counter.

"What do you think?" she said, holding out her right hand. On the middle finger was a large gold ring in the shape of a rectangle. "I'm getting it."

I don't think I'd ever seen her look so excited. "I can't believe you're buying yourself a ring," I said.

"Why not?"

"I don't know," I said. "I never saw you buy yourself any-thing not strictly necessary. I mean, anything that cost more than, like, a hundred dollars."

My mother's expression hardened just a bit. "Maybe it's about time I treated myself," she said.

"Rob would buy you a ring."

"You mean an engagement ring."

"Of course."

"Well," she said, "Rob's not here right now, and I'm buy-ing this for myself."

"Relax, Mom. I think it's great that you're doing some-thing nice for yourself. It's a gorgeous ring. I've never seen anything like it."

"I show something special to the young lady?"

A second clerk had appeared, about my mother's age, I guessed, tall and smiling. He wore a beautiful dark suit, three buttoned, with a shirt the color of apricots and a silk tie the color of hyacinths. I couldn't help but stare; he was right out of a fashion magazine. Jotham, I thought, would never wear such colors, and certainly not together. He wasn't a fashion risk taker; he wasn't a risk taker at all, I thought, and for the first time, this fact didn't strike me as an entirely positive thing. Since when had I begun to think critically of my fi-ancé's general air of caution?

"Marina?" my mother nudged.

"No, no, thank you," I said to the clerk and turned swiftly away.

20

Dear Answer Lady:

My mother is, like, totally embarrassing. I
mean, every time I even think about her, I cringe.
It's really stressing me out! She insists on wearing these, like, caftan-type things, and she refuses to dye her hair (which is this disgusting drab
gray), and she won't diet, so she's, like, size bazil-
lion or something. But the worst thing about her
is that she pretends to be so freakin' happy all
the time. I mean, she's always smiling and doing
charity stuff and getting awards for her research
papers on global warming and—this is totally
weird—going out with guys! (I mean, what sort
of freaks are these guys if they find a fifty-year-
old, caftan-wearing woman hot?) What can I do?
I've tried to set her straight, but she just shakes
her head and looks at me like she pities me or
something and says, "Where did I go wrong?"
Can you believe that?!?! Help!

Dear Shallow Gal:

Better the umbilical cord had wrapped itself
around your slimy little neck and strangled you
at the moment you made your sorry appearance
in this world than that you should survive to
write me your bitchy, whining letter. If you had
half the character your mother has, you might be
worth the air you breathe. As it is, you're taking

*in precious oxygen that could be better used and
appreciated by my friend who is dying of lung
cancer caused by living in proximity to a belch-
ing chemical plant. (Remind me to talk to your
mother about that.) How about setting yourself
straight by redirecting your priorities to . . . Who
am I kidding? You're a lost cause. Don't ever
write to me again.*

I glanced down at my new ring; it was warm and glowing
in the hot midday sun. I loved it. I absolutely loved it, in spite
of or maybe because of the reasons that had prompted me to
spend a large amount of hard-earned money. (Hurt over the
locket that should have been mine; hurt over Marina's careless comment about commitment.) It felt odd not to regret an
irrational purchase, an expensive Band-Aid for an emotional
wound, but it also felt wonderful and decadent and right. I
realized I was grinning. I'd come late to retail therapy, but
late was better than never.

I was jolted out of my pleasant reverie by the sight and
sound of a young mother passing by our small café table,
dragging a squalling child of about three, snapping at him in
an undertone that spoke of the last dregs of patience. And
though I didn't understand the exact meaning of her words,
their intent was clear. I felt a rush of sympathy but caught
Marina frowning at the woman's retreating figure.

I recognized the look on my daughter's face; it was the
look of disapproving superiority the young and naïve adopt
so readily. It was the same look I used to adopt before I had
Marina. I'd see a mother scolding her child on a bus or in a
park and I'd feel quite morally superior and 100 percent sure
that if I were ever a mother I would never lose my temper
with my child, in private or in public. What's more, I was

sure a child of mine would never resort to tantrums or stubbornness to the point of irrationality.

And then I had Marina and realized the extent of my ignorance.

"Mom," Marina said suddenly, "remember that old Madonna song, the one about a girl getting pregnant?"

" 'Papa Don't Preach.' Of course I remember. It was all over the radio for a while. You couldn't get away from it if you tried."

"Well, I just heard it again the other day in some store in the mall—I think it was Macy's—and for the first time, I realized it's such a silly song. I mean, the lyrics don't make any sense."

"Really? I'm not sure I ever listened to the lyrics."

"Well, she keeps saying 'I've made up my mind I'm keeping my baby.' And then she says she needs advice from her father about what to do. Doesn't that seem contradictory?"

"Marina," I said, after a moment, "I can't believe I need to point this out, but it's a pop song, not great literature, not a symphonic piece. I don't think pop songs strive for internal consistency the way great art does."

"Whatever. I just think if she's made up her mind, then she shouldn't also be asking for advice."

Was my daughter really so unimaginative? Was this unfortunate lack of capability or willingness to "suspend disbelief" the result of Jotham's influence? The result of Peter's genes?

"Yes, well," I said, "sometimes, when it comes to the really big decisions, you want someone—you need someone—to confirm that you've made the right choice. It's hard to make big decisions in a void. Sometimes you have no choice, but if you do have a choice, it's good to get advice from someone hopefully wiser."

Marina shrugged. "I just think if you make a decision, you should stick with it and stop bothering people for their opinions."

Marina turned her attention back to her cup of hazelnut gelato, and I wondered: did my daughter really think life was so simple, so uncomplicated? Well, maybe for some people life was uncomplicated. Certainly, I'd been rightly accused of overthinking a situation. Maybe Marina's inner life was— would continue to be—a more peaceful thing than my own.

Or maybe, I thought, taking a bite of my own *gelato di fragole,* life just hadn't kicked her in the head yet.

21

The tensions and resentments that occur between generations of women, say between a mother and a daughter, are of far greater weight and cause far more destruction than any negative dynamics that exist between a man and a woman, say between a husband and a wife, a brother and a sister, or between a son and his mother. The brutal fact of the matter is that women are by nature problematic and when paired or grouped with other women of the same genetic strain inevitably create havoc.

> —Antagonism Between the Ages: It's a Woman Thing

After dinner that evening we sought out a place our waiter had recommended for dessert. It reminded me of an old-fashioned American cafeteria, but in miniature. It was very well lit, with a fair amount of formica and chrome, and paint accents in aqua and pale pink.

In addition to a variety of American favorites—classic apple pie; Red Velvet cake; even, impossibly, Ambrosia—the place offered a selection of Italian pastry, including *tortiglione,* or almond cakes, and *torta di albicocche,* or apricot tart. There was also a *budino Toscano,* or Tuscan pudding, sprinkled with vanilla sugar, and a selection of *tartufi di cioccolato,* or chocolate truffles.

After some deliberation, Marina chose the apricot tart and

I selected the Tuscan pudding. We took our desserts to a tiny table near the front window, perfect for people watching, though Marina's out-of-the-blue comment made that pleasant prospect impossible.

"Grandma told me you tried to make contact with my father for years," she said abruptly. "And that he always refused to respond. And she told me that once you even had to go to therapy, you were so obsessed with him."

I put down my spoon. I felt stunned and slightly sick. "She had no right to tell you that I went to therapy," I said. "That was my business, not hers, and certainly not hers to share. And I wasn't obsessed with Peter. It wasn't like that."

And how, I wondered, had my mother known about my attempts to contact Peter? Not all were advertised, especially after she'd made it clear she thought I was being foolish "chasing after a man who wanted nothing to do with" me. Had my mother snooped through my apartment, read my outgoing mail?

"I just can't believe you kept trying to contact a man who rejected you so totally," Marina was saying. "Didn't you have any self-esteem?"

I tried to answer calmly, though my nerves were jangling.

"It wasn't about me or my self-esteem," I said. "It was about you. It was about trying to make decisions in your best interest. And at the time, I thought that having your father in your life, even in some small way, would be the best thing for you."

Marina shrugged. I probably should have changed the subject right then, but I couldn't. I wanted my daughter to understand.

"Eventually," I said, "I changed my mind about your father's involvement. His repeated rejection of my appeals—his repeated ignoring of my appeals—made it clear that you—the both of us—were probably better off without him. If he ever relented, it was going to be grudgingly, and that, I thought, would be far more hurtful than his absence."

Marina patted her lips with a paper napkin; for the first time, the familiar gesture struck me as incredibly pretentious.

"Well," she said, "I think you were crazy to even try to get his attention in the first place. Grandma told me how horrible he was to you. She told me she never liked him, right from the start."

I struggled to remain calm; I wished my mother were right there at that table with us so that I could shake her.

"Thanks for your considered opinion," I said. "And I'll be sure to thank your grandmother when we get home."

"I'm just saying that you should have listened to your mother. She could tell when you first started dating Peter that he was no good."

"Funny, she never said a word to me about him. Not until the end, of course. Not until it was too late."

"Grandma says she did. She says—"

And I'd had it. To hell with calm. It was about time I stuck up for myself and my choices.

"You have no idea of what happened back then," I said, my voice trembling, "so don't pretend you do."

"I—"

"Let me finish. You think you know everything about life, but let me tell you, Marina, you don't. You don't know anything about what life can throw at you or about how things happen so suddenly, so unexpectedly, that your head spins and you feel sick to your stomach like you just got off an amusement park ride. Because in a way, you have, and because you're human you'll just stumble back on another stupid ride before you've fully recovered from the first. You're not immune to trouble, Marina. No one is. No one, no matter how in control they think they are, can keep life from happening to them."

I stopped, took a deep breath, embarrassed, relieved, proud.

Marina's face was expressionless; her voice calm and controlled. "I'm just saying that I know enough not to get myself in a situation that's going to ruin my life. I know enough not to lose my self-control. I learned from your mistakes."

My mistakes. So, I thought, you consider yourself a mistake. I could feel the blood pulsing through my temples. A terrible anger arose in me, and I felt a sneer come to my lips.

"Is there nothing about my life you think I've done right?" I snapped. "Wait a minute, why am I even asking such a question! It's my life, and you have no right to judge it."

Marina rolled her eyes, laughed. "Oh, please, Mom! You judge my life all the time."

"I do not. Tell me one thing I've ever said to you that was judgmental, and I don't mean telling you not to lie or cheat or steal, because those things are wrong."

"I can't think of anything right now, but all mothers judge their children; they can't help it. God," she huffed, "I am so not going to be like you when I have kids."

I didn't bother to point out the inconsistency in her statement. "Fine," I said. "I hope you're nothing like me. Because obviously I've done an incredibly lousy job raising my daughter."

Marina looked disbelieving, stricken. "Are you insulting me? Are you saying I'm a failure or something?"

"Or something. I can't have this conversation. It's making me sick."

I thrust my balled-up napkin on the table, reached for my bag still stuffed with the guidebooks my daughter thought I was a fool to carry, and stood.

Marina stared up at me, wide-eyed. "You can't just leave!" Was there a trace of panic in her voice? Good.

"Oh, yes," I said, "I can. How many times have you stormed off in the middle of an argument?"

"But—"

"But what? That's okay because you're the kid? You're supposed to be angry and rebellious? Well, guess what? I'm the mother, and I can be angry and rebellious, too. Everyone's angry and rebellious about something. Everyone hates some aspect of her life. Get used to it."

And I tossed a few euros on the table and walked off— stalked off, rather—in what used to be called "high dudgeon," hardly able to believe I'd just spoken to my daughter in such a manner.

It was only a few minutes' walk to the hotel, but the journey seemed interminable. My feet slammed the pavement in the thin, nighttime sandals I'd bought especially for our Tuscan holiday, the holiday I thought would be so wonderful.

Stupid. I knew then that Marina and I never should have come on this stupid mother/daughter trip. It was turning into a complete disaster, not the warm and fuzzy bonding experience I'd hoped it would be. Clearly, I had watched far too many movies on Lifetime and the Oxygen channel.

I reached the hotel just as the tears started to burn my eyes. Without even turning on the light, I crawled into my bed and, mercifully, was asleep within minutes.

22

Dear Answer Lady:

I'm a college-educated woman with no criminal record, no enemies, a good job, and a close, supportive family. Also, I've been in a committed relationship to an upstanding man for four years. We recently got engaged, and, as to be expected, my fiancé has introduced the subject of children. Before now, when having a family of my own was just a distant possibility, I was fine with the idea; I even looked forward to being pregnant. But now—I'm panicking! What right do I have to think I can raise a child and have him or her turn out to be normal? Who do I think I am? Why am I so special? Just because I graduated from college? Please, lots of idiots graduate from college! Just because I have a good job? Come on, lots of morons have good jobs! Am I insane not to have my tubes tied immediately or, better yet, have a radical hysterectomy??

Dear Painfully Conscious Person:

Yes, you're probably insane, but not more so than all the other women who get pregnant, give birth, and attempt to raise a nonsociopathic child. At least you're stopping to consider the enormity of the journey on which you are embarking. That, in my opinion, puts you way ahead of the game.

*Going into motherhood with a clear understanding
of the futility of your action will actually preserve
your sanity in the long run. P.S. Keep your trepi-
dations from your fiancé. Most men find women
who doubt the wisdom of motherhood oddly
sickening and strange.*

Wednesday, June 7

I knew it was morning. The sun was obvious—and hot—
through my closed eyelids. It was time to rise and face the
consequences of the previous evening. I opened my eyes,
wondering what I would find—Marina sulking, Marina texting Jotham, Marina gone.

But there she was, in her nightgown, sitting on the edge of
her bed facing mine. Her hands were folded on her lap, and
her expression was one of tense anticipation.

"Mom," she blurted immediately, "I'm sorry about last
night. I said some pretty stupid stuff. I don't know what
came over me. I don't know, maybe—"

I put my hand up to stop the flow of her words. "Thanks,"
I said, hoisting myself to a sitting position. "Apology accepted. And I hope you'll accept my apology. I shouldn't have
stormed off like that."

Marina laughed a bit awkwardly. "I have to say, Mom, it
really freaked me out. If that's what you feel every time I walk
out on you, wow, I'm really sorry. I promise I'll never do it
again. It's definitely not cool."

"No, it isn't," I agreed. "But maybe sometimes it's better
than prolonging a fight that's already gotten nasty."

"Maybe." Marina still looked chastened. I'd be lying if I
said I wasn't pleased with her apology—and with her recog-
nition of its necessity. "You're still in your clothes," she said
quietly.

I swung my legs free of the covers and stretched. "Yes, I'm aware. Let's get some breakfast," I said. "I could use a coffee."

"I could use about five. I hardly slept last night."

I didn't need to ask why. Marina had always had trouble sleeping when something was bothering her. Obviously the memory of our argument had tormented her, while it had hurled me into a deep and dream-fraught sleep. Marina being eaten by a monster (fraught; I didn't say original or especially creative); me back in college, late for class, frantically trying to remember the location of my locker, pleading with passing strangers to help; Marina and I running for a plane that was already taking off.

An hour later, anxiety dreams almost forgotten, Marina's expression of tense anticipation almost gone, we were seated at a small table at a café in a small, unspectacular piazza. The sky was overcast; the hotel clerk had advised us to bring umbrellas. For once, as I'd forced my own umbrella into my already-full, hobo-style bag, I saw the benefit of Marina's enormous Marshall's-purchased knock-off. Her umbrella slipped easily into its depths.

Our waiter, a young man of about seventeen with a thin fuzz of a moustache, brought us our coffees, smiled distractedly at my poorly pronounced thanks, and went off to serve an elderly couple—British, I thought, if her Burberry umbrella and his tweed hat (in summer!) were any indication—who'd just taken their seats.

"When you were pregnant with me," Marina asked suddenly, apropos of nothing, "did you worry about labor and giving birth? Did you think about dying?"

And my daughter accused me of being dramatic. I took a sip of cappuccino before answering. It was delicious, as always, and far superior to the overpriced designer stuff sold on every corner back home.

"Dying?" I said. "No. I mean, I wasn't exactly looking forward to labor and delivery, but Marina, in spite of the silly haircuts, excessive makeup, and massive shoulder pads, the 1980s were hardly the Dark Ages. St. Ambrose Hospital has one of the finest women's health departments in the country."

"I know. But I'd still be worried about my baby being born with some terrible problem."

"These days," I assured her, "the chances are very good that you'd know long before actually giving birth if your baby had a serious health issue. What's got you thinking about this now? Oh my God, you're not—"

Marina looked at me as if I were crazy. "Of course not. Jeez, Mom, you know me better than that."

"Whew," I said. "You scared me there for a moment. And I'm sorry. I do know you better. So, anyway, why is child-birth on your mind?"

Marina looked off in the direction of several slim, well-muscled men on bicycles in full cycling gear. We both watched them pedal smoothly out of sight. "I don't know," she said finally. "I guess it suddenly hit me that you were my age when I was born. And to go through all of that on your own, the pregnancy, the planning, labor. It must have been really hard."

"I did have Grandma and Grandpa."

"But you know what I mean," she said, turning back to me. "No husband or partner."

"Yes," I said. "I do know what you mean. You're right. It wasn't easy doing it all alone. But it was worth it."

Marina rolled her big dark eyes, a habit I found amusing that morning. "Mom, you don't have to say that."

"I know I don't have to say it, but I want to. It was worth it. Do you know how few times in life you get to say 'I absolutely made the right decision'? Not often, believe me."

"You mean that life is full of regrets."

"Well, I didn't mean it to sound quite so bleak, but—yes, I guess that is what I meant."

There was a lull in the conversation while we each sipped our coffee. Marina's next question took me by surprise.

"So," she said, "you don't regret being in love with my father?" Before I could react, Marina reached out and touched my arm. "Wait, Mom, I'm sorry. You don't have to answer that."

"No," I said. "It's okay."

But I didn't answer right away. I couldn't, even though I'd asked myself that very question many times over the years.

"If you hadn't come along," I said finally, "I probably would have regretted the relationship. If I hadn't gotten pregnant, and he'd left me for some other reason, and he would have, I see that now, yes, I would have regretted ever having set eyes on him. But because I got you out of the relationship, no, I don't regret the experience. You know what they say about experience."

Marina put up her hand in the universal signal that means *stop*. "Please, Mom, I hate that stupid saying: What doesn't kill you only makes you stronger. I just can't believe that's true. Sometimes really bad things happen, and I just can't believe that a person is happier or better because of them. What if I was in a really terrible car accident and lost both my legs, how would that make me a stronger person? I'd be handicapped and probably have nightmares about the accident for the rest of my life!"

"I know," I conceded. "It is a stupid expression, though I do believe that in some cases difficulty does challenge you to be the best person you can be."

"I guess. I remember my accounting professor in freshman year was so tough I was sure I was going to fail the course. But it turned out that I learned more from him than from any other professor that year. I guess he just made me work harder. Maybe he even inspired me."

"Maybe fear was your motivation. Maybe you were afraid to bring home a failing grade. You know what an ogre I can be."

Marina laughed. "Yeah, that's it. Anyway, Mom, I'm glad you don't regret—what happened. In spite of what stupid things I said before. I think it would be terrible to live with regret over a love affair. A relationship, I mean. Over a person who meant so much to you."

"Most people—many, at least—live with the memory of a lost love, or a relationship gone horribly wrong, or a broken heart. And some people," I ventured carefully, "live with the memory of a missed opportunity, a road not taken, a possibility not explored, a relationship not embraced. It's a rare person who doesn't carry around some big sadness."

"But all these people living their lives," she said, "going to work and the movies and eating at restaurants and going on vacations, all as if—"

This thoughtful mood was uncharacteristic of Marina. I didn't want to interfere with a prompt.

"As if everything was fine," she said after a moment.

"Yes. It's amazing what you can adjust to. The human spirit is wonderfully resilient."

"But are all those people happy?" Marina turned to me, her expression worried. "I just wonder how many people can actually say they're happy."

Unknowable. And people lie. They pretend to themselves. They put on masks, and some come to think the mask is in fact part of their skin. All survival mechanisms. All necessary. All understandable.

All I said was, "I wonder, too."

23

A grandfather who spoke only pig Latin after his fiftieth birthday. A grandmother who took an axe to her neighbor's crab apple tree because she was convinced it was mocking her. An uncle who ate only artichokes for breakfast, lunch, and dinner after he lost a bet that he could put a quarter in his mouth and make it come out of his nose. An aunt who changed her name to "Inflammation" and wore knee socks pulled up over jeans. A father who brutally murdered his best friend because he thought the man had stolen his bathing trunks. A mother who has resided in a group home for the last ten years after taking the advice to "sew her lips together" literally. Your future is clear. You are indeed doomed to madness of some form or another, and therefore, in the interests of society at large, you are in no way advised to reproduce.
—What to Do When Your Family Tree Is Rotting
from the Ground Up

"I'm so glad it's less humid today," Marina said. "I don't know why I didn't realize that Italy could be so hot."

"Well," I teased, "if you'd done some preparation before the trip, you would have known all about what to expect weather-wise."

Marina smirked at me, but it was in jest. We'd chosen to

have lunch at an unprepossessing restaurant recommended by another guest at our hotel. As he and his wife were self-described foodies, Marina and I figured his recommendation wouldn't be half bad. We were right.

We had a simple and delicious *fritto misto di mare,* or mixed fried fish, served with slices of fresh lemon for flavor. At my suggestion, we went wild and each ordered a glass of wine. I felt the need to celebrate the clearing of the air between us. Our fight, and the reconciliation that had followed, was proving to be a turning point in our relationship. Suddenly, the exchange of intimacies was something a lot easier than it ever had been: at least, easier than I could remember it having been for years. And all I'd had to do to get my daughter to be normal with me was stalk off in a huff like a petulant teenager. Well, no one ever said that parenting made sense.

When the plates had been cleared and coffee ordered, Marina folded her hands on the table, something she only did when she had to tell me something important, like when she'd decided to have sex with Jotham and wanted my help choosing birth control.

"I never asked you this, Mom," she said then, "but I've thought about it about a million times."

"Okay," I said, and my heart beat faster.

"Did you ask my father to take a paternity test?"

Well, I thought, that wasn't as bad as it could be. Besides, there was no going back now. The truth would out, and it might as well out on a lovely, if overcast, June day in Florence.

"I asked him to, of course," I said carefully, wondering if Marina already knew the answer to her question, wondering if my mother hadn't blurted the truth about this, too.

"And he refused?"

"Yes." And in no uncertain terms, I added silently.

"Then why didn't you take him to court?" Marina asked. She was trying to sound calm and collected, but there was an edge to her tone. "A judge could have forced him to take a paternity test. And then, when it was proved that he was really my father, he would have been forced to pay child support, right?"

"Yes, I suppose I could have taken Peter to court."

"Of course you could have, Mom. Didn't you even talk to a lawyer?"

"No," I said quietly. "It wasn't how I wanted to handle things."

I could feel Marina's frustration with me. But what I didn't say aloud was that the notion of forcing Peter to acknowledge Marina as his child and then legally compelling him to pay child support seemed so distasteful—and humiliating. Maybe it was pride that made me not want to take his money under such circumstances. But if I had, would Marina's life— and my own—have been substantially easier? Maybe, but there was no point in pondering such questions almost twenty-two years after the fact.

As if she'd read my mind, Marina said, in a lightly joking tone, obviously trying to get past her own annoyance over my long-ago decision, "You mean I could be driving a new car instead of the broken-down jalopy I was forced to buy?"

I smiled, appreciating her efforts. "I didn't know people your age used the word 'jalopy.' "

"Don't change the subject."

But Marina seemed to have tired of that particular line of questioning. After a moment, she said; "Back in third or fourth grade, I can't remember which, this kid in my class, a real bully, called me a bastard. I didn't even know what the word meant until another kid explained it to me."

"Oh, Marina, I'm so sorry! Why didn't you ever tell me?" I was immediately filled with sorrow for my little girl—and equally with rage for the boy who had been so cruel to her. If anyone says that you can't feel like throttling a child, he's lying.

Marina shrugged. "I don't know. I guess I didn't want to

make things worse. If I'd told you, you would have gone to the principal, and it would have become a big deal. Anyway, it only happened that once."

"But you remember it all these years later."

"I remember lots of stupid stuff," she said. "Anyway, can you believe that in this day and age someone would even use that term? It's not like there aren't thousands, millions of kids living with one parent. It's not like there's some big stigma about not having two parents or parents who aren't married."

"It does seem ridiculous," I agreed.

"Whatever. I saw him a few months ago, actually, in town. He looked awful. He looked like a street person. I think he might be on drugs."

"I hope you didn't take pleasure in that fact. Revenge isn't something that should be indulged, even in fantasies."

Marina gave me a look that plainly asked, "Was I raised in a cave?"

"Sorry," I said. "Just being obnoxious. The truth is that just a moment ago I was itching to wring his neck."

"It wouldn't take much effort. He was as thin as a rail."

We were quiet for a time. Suddenly, I recalled an article I'd read a few weeks earlier.

"Did you know," I said, "that nowadays women who opt to have a baby without a father or a partner are called SMCs—Single Mothers by Choice? If I'd only known back when I was pregnant that my lonely decision would someday be a badge of honor!"

Marina turned to me, her expression serious. "Do you think it would have made a difference? I mean, would it have made you feel less excluded, with your friends and all?"

"No," I said immediately. "At least, I don't think it would have. I don't know. It's an unanswerable question. Things change so quickly. American culture today is not what it was in the eighties. And I'm not who I was in the eighties, not entirely."

"Yeah," she said. "I suppose that's all true."

Marina began to twist her engagement ring. I'd noticed she'd been worrying at it a lot since we'd arrived in Italy.

"Is it too tight?" I asked.

"What?"

"Your ring. You've been twisting it."

Marina looked down at her left hand as if it were an alien thing.

"I have?"

"Yes. Have your fingers swollen in the heat?"

"I guess. It feels a bit uncomfortable."

"You can probably have it stretched when you get home." When you get our family's heirloom locket modernized, I thought with a twinge.

"Yeah, maybe. But with all the diamonds in the band, I'm not sure it's possible."

What I didn't suggest was that she could exchange it for a ring that looked better on her hand. I hadn't shared my honest opinion of the ring aloud, but to myself I acknowledged that it just didn't seem right for Marina. But she seemed to like it; at least, she hadn't said otherwise. Not to me, anyway.

24

Dear Answer Lady:

Am I a terrible person because I don't breast-feed my baby? Worse, because I don't want to breast-feed? I mean, I know it's supposed to be healthier than using formula and all, and they say by breast-feeding you bond better with your baby. But I just can't do it! I feed my baby the very best formula on the market, and he's very healthy—or so his doctor says. But every time I give him a bottle, the other mothers at the park or wherever we are give me dirty looks, and some have even scolded me. Am I doing my son a terrible disservice, one that will cause him all sorts of troubles later on in life?

Dear Independent Thinker:

Contrary to what the media and breast-feeding women everywhere would have you believe, there is no official Mommy Police ready to pounce on you for choosing not to breast-feed your child. And any self-appointed biddy with the audacity to scold you for not breast-feeding should receive a stinging retort or a slap across her fat face. It's a free country (sort of), and you are entitled to make your own decisions about how to feed, clothe, and educate your child (within reason, of course)—don't forget that. Besides, plenty of healthy, intelligent, happy, and successful adults

were bottle-fed (myself included), so stop worry-
ing. You are not a bad person or a neglectful
mother. Now, go warm up that formula and work
on those stinging retorts.

According to my notes from our Tuscan holiday, dinner
that evening included a *pappardelle alla lepre,* in other words,
pasta with a hare ragout. Marina surprised me by eating it
without hesitation. I'd thought for sure the notion of rab-
bit—a Thumper all fuzzy and cute, twitching nose and floppy
ears—would have put her off. My supposedly predictable
daughter was proving to be not so predictable after all.

"What's my father's middle name?" Marina asked when
the plates had been cleared and we were enjoying an espresso.
"Does he even have one? I don't remember you ever telling
me."

Why, I wondered, all the questions about her father? Months
would go by without her even mentioning him in passing.
Was it only because we were alone together—no Rob, Jotham,
or grandparents to overhear or to add an unasked-for opinion—or was something else going on in Marina's mind?

"I can't believe I'm saying this," I admitted, "but I've forgotten. If he has a middle name, I must have known it, but
for the life of me I can't remember."

"Early onset Alzheimer's?"

"Selective memory, I'd bet. Well, if I ever knew, I'm sure
it'll come to me."

"It doesn't really matter."

"No," I said, "I suppose it doesn't."

While Marina went off to the ladies' room, I thought of
how I'd spent so much time over the years wondering about
how I'd react if Peter approached me with the intention of es-
tablishing communication with his daughter. It was what I'd
wanted at first, for Peter to have a change of heart, for him to

assume some degree of responsibility for his child. But as
time passed, and especially after his rejection of the package
that contained Marina's middle-school graduation picture, I
began to dread the notion that he might want to play an active part in our family. We were doing just fine without him,
and the idea that he might expect to be an accepted presence,
that he might try to make Marina love him and reject me,
scared me deeply.

Of course, I knew I could refuse his overtures, but that
might only make someone like Peter—spoiled, self-absorbed—
more determined to claim what was his, and the thought of
his doing something drastic like seeking custody haunted me.
Any parent feels fiercely protective of her child, especially
when a threat (real or imagined) looms, but a single parent
can worry to the point of distraction.

Now Marina was legally an adult. If Peter wanted to contact his daughter, he could do so directly. A part of me hoped
he'd stay lost; a part of me hoped that Marina would never
have to make the decision to have a relationship with her father
or to turn him away like he'd turned her away. But in the end,
would his continuing silence really be the best thing for her?

I just didn't know. Anyway, the decision wasn't in my
hands. It was in Peter's, and for all I knew he was happily
married with perfect kids and in no way interested in introducing his "youthful indiscretion" into the mix.

Marina returned then from the ladies' room and, apropos
of nothing, said, "So, Mom, what was one of your most embarrassing moments?"

"What?" I said. Since our big fight, life with Marina had
become an episode of *Oprah*.

"You know, everyone remembers doing something really
stupid or saying something really ignorant. What was one of
your most embarrassing moments?"

"No hidden cameras?" I asked.

"Mom." There it was, the ubiquitous eye roll. At least it
wasn't done behind my back.

"You promise to tell me one of your most embarrassing moments?"

Marina shrugged. "Sure."

I thought for a moment and then hit on a memory I thought had been lost to my aging brain.

"I do remember an embarrassing moment," I said. "But there were no witnesses. Does that count?"

"Sure, I guess."

"Okay, it was the summer you went to that weeklong sleepaway camp, remember?"

"How could I forget?" Marina frowned. "I had to share a cabin with that awful girl who never washed. And I got poison ivy. And the food was awful. And the counselors were mean."

"So the camp thing didn't work out for us. At least we learned a lesson."

"Right. So, the embarrassing thing?"

"I remember," I began, "it was the first morning that you were gone. I came into the kitchen to make coffee, and I noticed three or four small, dark, brownish stains on the floor in a sort of uneven row. I didn't think much of it that first time, just wiped them up and went on with my day. And then the next morning I noticed another three or four stains, pretty much identical to the ones I'd seen the day before and in pretty much the same place. This time I was curious and tried to remember what I'd had for dinner the night before. I thought that maybe I'd spilled something, but then I remembered that I'd had dinner out with a woman from work. This went on for another few days, by which time I was beginning to be a nervous wreck. I started to think that maybe someone was sneaking into the apartment at night while I was asleep and dripping—blood—on the floor."

"Blood?" Marina said. "This is getting totally creepy."

"I know. Anyway, I started to think that maybe someone was stalking me, but I couldn't think of whom it might be. And I knew I had to get to the bottom of whatever was going on, because you were due home on the weekend and there was no way I'd let you stay in that apartment if I thought it was dangerous."

"What did you do, Mom? Did you call the police?"

"No," I said, "I didn't. Because the night before you were due back from camp, just when I was on the verge of calling the police and making a fool of myself, I figured out where the stains were coming from."

"Where?" she asked, sitting forward as if in anticipation of a big revelation.

"They were coming from my nightly cup of tea."

Marina sat back again. "What?"

"The stains were coming from the teabag I carried from the counter to the trash. I thought I'd been squeezing out all the excess water, but I hadn't been. I was the one leaving the mysterious stains. And the reason I didn't see them at night was because I never turned on the overhead light, only a small night-light. Money was tight, and I was fanatical about saving energy."

"I remember. The apartment was like perpetual twilight."

"Be that as it may. In the light of day the stains were obvious."

"I have to say, Mom, that's pretty—"

"Go ahead."

"That's pretty pathetic."

"I know," I admitted. "But there is a lesson to be learned."

Marina laughed. "I can't imagine what."

"Don't let your imagination run away with you. Sometimes the answer to a so-called mystery lies right before your eyes."

"I guess," Marina said dubiously. "Wow."

"Your turn."

"Well," she said after a moment, "once in middle school I realized I was wearing two different-color socks. I remember looking down in math class for some reason—probably because I was bored; that teacher was so slow!—and realizing I was wearing one plain white sock and one white sock with a design on the cuff. I think it was hearts."

"Okay. Did anyone else notice? Did anyone make fun of you?"

"No. I was wearing jeans. You couldn't really see much sock."

"That's not very embarrassing," I said. "Can you really think of nothing worse?"

"No. Maybe I just don't embarrass easily. Maybe I've just been lucky."

"So far."

"Gee, thanks, Mom."

"Marina," I said, "no one escapes embarrassment and regret and an occasional bout of stupidity. It would be great if you could, but you can't."

"You can be vigilant," she argued. "You can try not to do things you'll regret."

"Sure. And you can try to do things you won't later regret not doing. But you can't live life perfectly. It's just not possible."

Marina didn't respond at first, and when she did, there was an odd tone in her voice. Sadness? Resignation? I couldn't quite tell.

"I know," she said.

"Well, for your sake I hope the worst thing that ever happens to you is wearing mismatched socks."

"I didn't say it was the worst," she corrected. "I said it was the most embarrassing."

"Oh."

What was the worst thing that had ever happened to Marina? Her father's rejecting her? Her mother not giving her the stepfather she'd wanted? Her boyfriend persuading her to cancel a trip to Paris so that he could keep an eye on her?

"You know what felt really bad?" she said. "Back when Maggie Barry—remember her from high school? She moved away in sophomore year—anyway, back when Maggie got these really cool shoes that were in all the magazines, and I wanted them so badly, but you said I couldn't have them. That felt like the end of the world."

"Oh boy," I said, laughing, "do I remember! You ranted and raved and cried and stomped around for days."

"Let me guess. The reason you said no was the money, right?"

"Right. The shoes were outrageously expensive, absolutely out of our budget."

"Well, all I could see was that my mother was being totally unfair. Sorry about that, Mom."

"No problem," I said. "It was the only time you ever went crazy about not getting something the other kids had."

"The funny part of it is, those shoes were really ugly. Do you remember what they looked like?" she asked.

"No, I don't."

"Like shoes the Frankenstein monster would wear. In retrospect, I'm seriously glad we couldn't afford them."

"That bad, huh?"

"That bad. I don't think anyone below the age of sixteen should be allowed to dress herself."

I laughed, pleased that my daughter didn't seem to be dragging around much baggage; if not getting a pair of shoes was her deepest emotional scar, she was doing just fine.

Unless, of course, Marina was lying to protect my feelings. Unless, of course, she was lying to protect herself.

I looked keenly at Marina and tried to discern any evidence of deception in her manner or in her tone of voice but could find none. Which, of course, didn't mean it wasn't there.

And in that way lies madness. When you're a parent, you never cease to worry about your child's well-being, at least until you lose your mind to senile dementia, which, at that moment, didn't seem to me like such a bad thing.

"How about dessert?" I suggested. "We could share a *budino di Mandorle.*"

"What's that?" Marina asked.

"Almond pudding. If my food dictionary is correct."

"Do you think they have a chocolate pudding?"

I shrugged. "I don't know. But if they do, let's go crazy and order both."

25

Any intelligent woman who is capable of being honest with herself will admit that on more than one occasion in her life she has wanted to emulate the English Victorian author Mary Lamb by simply stabbing her mother to death at the dining table.
—The Ties That Bind and Gag: Mothers, Daughters, and the Inevitability of Misery

Thursday, June 8

"Sometimes I think about that trip to Paris, the one I didn't take. With that girl from school, Delphine."

I looked at my daughter in surprise. We hadn't talked about that trip once, not since I'd taken her passport and put it in the bank for safekeeping. But now, under the hot Tuscan sun, fortified by a cup of excellent coffee and a plate of assorted biscotti (almond for me, chocolate for Marina), Marina somehow felt encouraged to revisit that part of her past.

What had happened was this. Three years earlier, Marina had had the opportunity to spend a month in France with a friend whose family owned a small apartment in Paris and a farm in the southwest. An eighteen-year-old girl's dream, no? At least, it would have been for me at that age—at any age.

I'd met Marina's friend, Delphine and her parents and liked them all; they were intelligent and personable, and from what I could tell, Mr. and Mrs. Fournier were responsible people. So I encouraged the trip, and though Marina seemed excited at first, the closer the day of departure drew, the less happy she became. I asked her several times if anything was wrong, but she continually brushed aside my concern. After a while, I stopped asking. And then, at the last possible moment, Marina backed out. It seems that Jotham wasn't happy about their being apart for a month, and this clearly played into her own nervousness about being away not only from Jotham, but—I guessed—also from home.

The tickets were largely a waste of money. I was disappointed in Marina and furious with Jotham. I swear I could hardly look at him for months without wanting to shake him for ruining such a wonderful opportunity for my daughter. But of course it had been Marina's choice in the end. Instead of exploring the streets of Paris, instead of visiting the Louvre and Notre Dame and the neighborhood of Montmartre, she took a retail job at a local mall. One weekend she and Jotham went to Cape Cod. And Marina's friendship with Delphine, one I had hoped would grow, rapidly disintegrated.

"Do you regret not going?" I asked in an absolutely neutral voice.

Marina shrugged. "Yes and no. I mean, yes, I guess I do regret it; it would have been so much fun to see Paris. But—"

"But?"

Marina seemed to be intently watching two young women about her own age who were walking by, arms linked, heads together, chatting away confidentially. It was a few moments before she replied. "But Jotham really didn't want me to go, and I guess maybe I wasn't ready to be away from home for a whole month. I don't know."

"There's always the future. You can still go to Paris." And drag Jotham along with you, I thought uncharitably. He can sit in the hotel room tapping his foot and thinking about how weird the food is while you make a mad dash to the Rodin Museum.

"Yes," she said, but without enthusiasm. "Jotham never

liked Delphine. Neither did Allison or Jessica, actually, but I kind of miss her. I heard she transferred in her junior year to New York University. I wonder what she's doing now."

"You could Google her."

Marina laughed, but it wasn't happily. "I'm not sure I want to know what she's up to. Probably something glamorous. Maybe she's living in Paris. She was fluent in French, you know."

"Yes, I remember. You speak Spanish."

"Not very well. I know enough to get by, maybe. I can read the Spanish ads on the T."

"But your grades in Spanish class were always high. I'm sure you could—"

"Mom," Marina said, her tone one of controlled irritation. "Please. I know my limitations."

No, I thought, you don't. You have no idea how far you can take your life. It hurt me to see her seemingly so resigned. A parent never, ever wants her child to feel bad about herself, and not only for altruistic feelings. A child's lack of confidence, a child's misery, always reflects on the parent; the parent is forced to assume some degree of responsibility, no matter how imaginary.

Later that morning we went again to the Uffizi Gallery. I had a desire to see again Raphael's *Madonna with a Goldfinch* and da Vinci's *Annunciation*. Eventually, we found ourselves in front of *The Birth of Venus*, painted by Alessandro Botticelli some time around 1485. I'd seen countless reproductions, of course, as had Marina, I'm sure, but to see the real thing was a much richer experience.

"It never occurred to me before now how much she looks like you," Marina said.

"What? Oh, please, Marina."

"No, really. The reddish hair, the white skin, the slim body."

"Well," I said, somewhat embarrassed, "I have to admit there is some resemblance, though I've never worn my hair quite that long."

"And you didn't rise from the sea on a shell." Marina turned to me with a twinkle in her eye. "Unless you did, and that's why you named me Marina, as some sort of secret reference to your real identity."

"You're in an unusually fanciful mood."

"I know. How did that happen?"

"I have no idea, but it's cute."

"Cute? I'm not sure I like being called cute."

"All right then," I conceded. "Let's just say it's 'nice' to see you being—silly."

"Silly? Nice?" Marina rolled her eyes. "Now I'm sorry I said anything."

26

Dear Answer Lady:

What degree of loyalty and service do I owe my mother? I mean, she's healthy now, but when she gets older and frail, do I have to have her live with me and my husband and children just because she's my mother? Is it okay if I establish her in a nice apartment close by, or a really good nursing home if need be? Do I have to disrupt my children's daily life and risk destroying my marriage by adding my mother to our household? Not to mention overtaxing my own energy and patience. Can you offer some advice, please? The guilt is already beginning to nag me, and my mother is only fifty-five.

Dear Dutiful Daughter:

Perusing my well-worn copy of a collected works of the poet Robert Browning the other evening, I happened upon the following lines: "Lovers grow cold, men learn to hate their wives / And only parents' love can last our lives." Nice sentiment, Bobby. That said, no, you are in no way obligated to bring your mother (or father) into your home, where, as popular anecdote proves, no doubt disaster will ensue. Better to be a good daughter (or son) from a block or two away than

to attempt to force an unnatural extended fam-
ily. This is life, honey, not The King of Queens.

We had lunch that afternoon in a pizzeria which little re-
sembled the chains back home but which was close in spirit
and offerings to a pizzeria Rob and I frequented in the North
End. Marina ordered a panini *parmigiana di melanzane,* a
southern specialty, we were told, a delicious combination of
fried eggplant, melting cheese, and tomatoes. I chose a panini
tonno e carciofini, tuna with hearts of artichoke.

"The food in this city is amazing," Marina said, wiping
her mouth in the delicate way she had, the way that had so
annoyed me the night of our big fight.

"You should have tried the *cinghiale* the other night," I
teased.

"Have you noticed that almost no one is fat?"

"Have you noticed the portion size? Every plate we've
been served has had far less food on it than you'd get in the
States."

"That's true," she said. "I mean, my panini was about half
the size of a so-called panini at Bagel-O-Rama. Sometimes
even Jotham can't finish one."

"They must be enormous. I've never seen Jotham unable
to finish anything on his plate."

Marina laughed. "Yeah, well, if he keeps it up, he's going
to have a weight problem by the time he's forty."

"His parents aren't overweight," I said.

"That's because they work at it. They have a home gym,
you know. Mrs. Grandin thinks gyms are unsanitary."

More to the point, I thought, her dignity wouldn't allow
her to be seen sweating and prone in unflattering positions.

"You haven't seen Jotham's uncle," Marina was saying.
"His dad's brother. He's only fifty, and already he's had two
bypasses."

Rob was fifty. I determined to remind him to get his annual checkup. On occasion he'd been known to "forget."

"Well, for Jotham's sake—and for yours," I said, "I hope he starts taking care of himself before it's too late."

"Yeah. Hey, Mom, remember that guy you dated for a while when I was in junior year of high school? The one who wore those weird reflective sunglasses with the red frames?"

"Of course. Tony." The other man who had asked me to marry him. Marina was not ever to know that. "What made you think of him?"

"Talking about weight."

Oh, I thought. Right. Tony had been a health fanatic. His body was a temple and all that. He spent two hours every day at the gym, and any time Marina or I ate an Oreo, his face got tight with disapproval.

"He was an idiot," Marina said then. "I never understood what you saw in him."

"He was not an idiot," I said automatically. Except for the reflective sunglasses with the red frames. "I don't date idiots." Except when I do and they get me pregnant and leave me.

"Whatever. All I'm saying is that you could have saved yourself a lot of trouble if you'd just married Rob when he asked you—and for the second time!"

"What you're really saying," I corrected, "is that I could have saved you a lot of trouble if I'd married Rob."

"Well," she said, "not so much trouble, but it would have been nice to have him around for the senior father/daughter dance."

I was stunned. "I didn't know that bothered you. You never said a word to me."

"I didn't want to be a pain. But I definitely would have taken Rob if you guys had been together."

I'd tell Rob this bit of news, of course. It would please him, though it would remind us of the fact that he would have been there for the dance if I had been able to make a further commitment to him. My weakness had been everybody's loss.

After lunch we happened upon the Church of St. Jan of the North, Martyr. I couldn't find a mention of it in any of my guidebooks. Apparently, St. Jan of the North, Martyr wasn't considered worthy tourist material. I, however, thought his church both charming and moving.

Marina and I walked from the nave along the far left aisle toward the main altar. Along the way were minichapels and small shrines to local saints; many of these were adorned with small vases of dusty-looking plastic flowers and strewn with burnt-out votive candles. Unlike many churches, this one hadn't turned to the more modern and safe practice of electric candles. The smell of incense lingered in the close air.

"There sure are a lot of Madonna and Child paintings," Marina whispered when we stopped before a tiny alcove in which an old, somewhat stained-looking canvas was propped on a makeshift easel. The artist had depicted an anemic-looking Madonna holding up an even more anemic-looking baby Jesus as if to boast of her prized possession. "They're everywhere, even on the street. Have you seen those little shrines in stone niches?"

"Well," I whispered back, "it is a Catholic country."

The next tiny chapel was dedicated to St. Margaret of Cortona. Marina pointed to the painting to the left of the small altar. A golden-haired shepherd boy played a lute while his older companion, a burly, dark-haired, bearded man, staff in hand, gazed down on the baby Jesus.

"Some of the babies in these paintings look really—strange. Look at that one. He's downright ugly."

"Yes, well," I said, "every artist has a unique ability, and every age has a dominant style and—"

Marina put her hand on my arm. "You don't have to lecture, Mom. I know all that. I'm just saying that some of these kids could not be used to sell baby food. I mean, can you picture that baby in a Gerber ad?"

No, indeed, I couldn't. The poor thing's face was gray, pinched, and wizened like that of a very old man. The baby in another image we'd seen looked so otherworldly, you'd think he'd been fed a bottle of LSD disguised as baby formula.

Suddenly, I recalled a Mother's Day card Marina had given me when she was about ten. Ironically, I'd bought the same card for my mother that year. I'd given the choice of a card a lot of thought; at the time, I wondered how much thought Marina had given her own choice.

I still had Marina's card; my mother threw out mine a few days after Mother's Day. I guess it hadn't struck her as strongly as it had me. The card quoted Amos Bronson Alcott, father of Louisa May Alcott, as saying "Where there is a mother in the home, matters go well."

It was food for thought, and though I knew only that the man was an abolitionist and a forward-thinking educator, I thought his words and sentiment a great compliment to the far-reaching power of women—because children and husbands take their experience of home out into the world and thereby affect the world through their actions.

I described the card to Marina as we walked on to the next chapel and asked if she remembered it. She didn't.

"So you don't remember my telling you that I gave Grandma the same card that year?"

"You're kidding," she said. "No, I don't remember that at all."

"So you have no recollection of choosing the card because of the quote?"

Marina laughed quietly. "I probably picked it out because there was a pretty picture on the front. I'm not really into poetry."

"I don't think it's a line from a poem, though I don't know that for sure."

"What made you think of that card now?"

I shrugged. "You know how things just pop into your head."

After a moment, Marina stopped and turned to me. "Oh no! I forgot Mother's Day!"

"Shhh," I said, mindful of the few people kneeling in afternoon prayer. "That's not why I brought it up."

"I'm sorry, Mom," she said in a softer voice. "I guess I was all wrapped up in graduation and everything."

"Oh, I wasn't upset," I told her truthfully. "By the way, here's an interesting fact about old Amos Alcott. For the last years of his life, he was cared for by his daughter, Louisa May."

Marina shot me a look of concern. "What are you saying?"

"Nothing." I shrugged. "Just reciting a fact of history."

"Mom, you're only in your forties. Why are thinking about 'last years'? You're not sick or something, are you?"

I smiled. Marina was really becoming a drama queen. "Don't worry, I'm perfectly fine. And I'm not planning on being a burden to anyone, ever, least of all my child."

"It's not that, it's—"

She was interrupted by the ringing of her cell phone. Marina scrabbled madly through her gargantuan bag to find it—why she didn't keep it in the little pouch sewn inside for that purpose, I don't know—while I mouthed apologies to an old woman in black who had been lighting candles when we'd rudely interrupted her.

"You're supposed to turn those things off in a church," I said unhelpfully.

"Got it." Marina looked at the display screen and frowned slightly. "I suppose I should call him back."

"Can't it wait? We haven't even seen the main altar up close."

"I suppose. Okay."

We wandered through the rest of the church, Marina always a few steps ahead of me, a quick glance at each chapel seeming to suffice. And I wondered how much of my daughter's mind was focused on the small religious masterpieces, on the marble saints and the beautifully carved woodwork, and how much was focused on the guy back in Boston waiting for her call.

27

In Victorian England, all those from the doctor to the women he attended agreed that childbirth was in fact an illness. After giving birth, women were expected to spend several weeks in bed regaining their strength, i.e., being catered to in a way they would never be catered to otherwise. In this writer's mind, spending a few weeks in bed alone (no pawing husband!), with someone bringing meals, books, and other amusements, as well as taking care of the squalling baby you have just pushed out of your swollen, exhausted body, sounds like heaven. Ladies, it's time to revel in weakness, even if it is only feigned. (And who's gonna know if you don't tell?)
  —The Beauty of Being an Invalid, or Reclaiming
   Our Right to Be Sick

That night Marina and I ate at another small but wonderful family run restaurant suggested by the foodie couple staying at our hotel. We shared a bottle of superb Chianti with our meal, which included a very satisfying *zuppa di funghi*, or mushroom soup, and an incredibly tasty *tortellini rinascimentali*, which our waiter, one of the owner's sons, explained meant tortellini with pork filling.

"You know, Mom," Marina said at one point during the meal, "your new ring really is amazing."

"Thanks," I said, inordinately pleased that Marina approved of my purchase. "I've never had anything eighteen karat before. It's already developing a bit of a patina, but that's to be expected. It'll only give the ring character."

"You're leaving it to me in your will, right?"

The look on my face must have been really odd, because Marina burst out laughing.

"I'm kidding, Mom! Sheesh! You know I'm not one of those awful, grasping children who can't wait to get her hands on her parents' estate."

"It's not that," I explained. "You just took me by surprise. I don't think we've ever talked about—you know, a will and what that implies." Although, of course, I had made a will; any responsible parent has made a will.

"And we're not going to talk about it now."

"Fine by me." And then, tentatively, I said, "While we're sort of on the topic of jewelry, does your ring still feel tight?"

Marina held out her left hand and frowned. "Well, to be perfectly honest—this is probably the wine making me say this—it's not what I had in mind. I mean, it's a perfectly fine ring and everything, but—"

"But it isn't you."

Marina looked up at me, surprised. "Yeah. Do you think so, too?"

"It doesn't matter what I think about it."

"But I'm asking."

"Well, to be perfectly honest back at you," I said, "I don't think it suits you. It's too—"

"Yes. I know. It's too—something. Too—fussy. But Jotham gave it to me, and I accepted it, so there's nothing I can do about it now. Maybe when I get my wedding ring I'll put this away and wear it only on special occasions. Weddings, anniversary parties, that sort of thing."

"Won't Jotham wonder about that?" Being the sort, I was sure, who wanted to impress everyone around him with his beautiful wife wearing the beautiful—and expensive—jewelry he'd bought her.

Marina shrugged. "I don't know. Probably not. He's not very observant. He doesn't usually notice when I'm wearing something new or when I get my hair cut."

"That describes a lot of men," I noted. "Which doesn't make it any less annoying."

"Well, it's better than being with someone who scrutinizes everything about you, like Allison's fiancé. Jordan gets on her if she's gained a pound. He's such a perfectionist."

I'd met the guy once or twice. He wasn't a perfectionist; he was a royal pain in the ass, even more critical and manipulative than Jotham. No wonder they'd been buddies for years. "Well, that does sound worse than being ignored," I said carefully.

"Sometimes . . ." Marina looked hard at her ring; her face wore a frown.

"Sometimes what?" I prodded. Sometimes I'd like Jotham to pay more attention to me. Sometimes I wonder what it would be like to date other men. Sometimes I just want to walk away.

As if waking from a daydream, Marina shook her head and looked away from her hand. "Oh, nothing. I'm having another glass of wine. This is our holiday, right?"

"Right. Eat, drink, and be merry, for tomorrow you—"

"Mom! Don't say it. Can we keep things light for once?"

"All I was going to say is 'tomorrow you diet.' "

"That's so lame." Marina pointed at the tempting arrangement of tortellini on her plate. "Anyway, I don't want to think about dieting while I'm in Italy."

"I don't want to think about dieting, ever."

"You don't need to diet. I told you, you just need to tone up. You should start an exercise program when we get home."

It was an old argument, and I knew Marina was right. "Here's another rule," I said instead. "No talk of exercise on our holiday."

"I can live with that."

"Good, because it's a rule I'm going to strictly enforce. Especially since I am planning to have dessert."

Marina sighed and put down her fork. "Okay, this is probably the wine talking again—what's that phrase, *in vino veritas?*—because I swore I wouldn't tell you this, at least not yet."

"What?" I asked. "You're having a sex-change operation? You're going off to Tibet to become a Sherpa? You're thinking of taking up bungee jumping?"

"Uh, Mom?"

"Sorry," I said. "Just trying to be amusing. What were you going to say?"

"Well, I told you about Hawaii, right? About how Jotham thinks we should go there for our honeymoon."

"And about how you'd rather not."

"Yeah, well, what I didn't tell you is that he's already made the reservations. Actually, his parents have already made the reservations. The Grandins," she said, leaning in, almost whispering, "are paying for the whole thing."

"Oh," I said. "How—nice of them."

"Hawaii might even have been their idea in the first place."

"Really."

"Mom, don't you find the whole thing kind of, I don't know, odd?"

Yes, I thought, it was kind of odd. But not all that surprising.

"I don't know," she went on. "I told Jotham I wasn't comfortable with their paying, but he said that I was being ungrateful. He said that his parents were giving us a gift and that if we didn't accept it they'd be hurt."

Jotham, I thought, is a bullying creep. And as for his parents . . .

I knew I shouldn't feel jealous or resentful of the Grandins' generosity. Really, it was nice that they wanted to spend such money on my daughter at such an important time of her life.

Besides, money wasn't what counted in the end; I knew that, and Marina did, too. The Grandins couldn't buy my daughter; she wasn't for sale at any price.

"You can still talk to Jotham about it, you know," I said finally. "Maybe—"

"Yeah, maybe. But honestly, Mom? I'm not sure it's worth it."

"You pick your battles with him is what you mean."

Marina shrugged. "Sure. Don't you do that with Rob, let some things go?"

"Yes, of course," I said. "But not things that really matter to me. That wouldn't be fair to me, or, in the end, to the relationship. Sorry for sounding like a therapist."

"No, you're right. I know that. It's just that . . ."

"Just that what?"

Marina waved her hand in dismissal. "Oh, nothing. I'm having dessert tonight, too. I saw the tray when we came in. There was this creamy chocolate thing that looked amazing."

28

Dear Answer Lady:

Lately I find myself obsessed with thoughts of how I'll be remembered by my children when they're grown and have families of their own. I try so hard to be a wonderful mother; I read every parenting magazine I can get, and I belong to a parenting workshop in which we discuss and critique our responses to each situation we encounter as mothers and fathers. I shower my children with love and support while at the same time I never neglect to discipline fairly. But what if it's not enough? What if in spite of all my efforts my children remember me as a terrible mother? Help!

Dear Worrywart:

I believe it was the insuperable Jacqueline Kennedy Onassis who said, and I am not quoting directly here, that nothing else you do well can make up for your having screwed up your children. The problem here is in perspective. I've known plenty of mothers who rest comfortably in the belief that they have done a magnificent job in raising their sons and daughters, while those very same sons and daughters beg, some quite loudly, to differ. And I've known other mothers who lie awake at night regretting their every parenting decision while their sons and daughters

recall their childhood with great fondness. Fi-
nally, might I suggest the radical notion that ex-
haustive efforts to be a good mother should be
undertaken solely for the health and welfare of
the children, and not for your own remembered
glory. Stop thinking about YOU and your future
reputation and start focusing on what really
matters—the CHILDREN.

Friday, June 9

"Shall we see the Giotto works next?" my mother suggested.

Once again we were in the Uffizi Gallery, having spent several hours that morning viewing works by Leonardo da Vinci, Raphael, Michelangelo, and Perugino. Thanks to my mother and her guidebooks, I now knew more than I ever had about each of these great artists. How long that information would stay in my head, I'd no idea.

"Sure," I said.

"Okay, but first I have to use the ladies' room. Wait here?"

My mother hurried off down the marble corridor. Unlike my grandmother, who had to run off to find a ladies' room every half hour, my mother was usually able to hold out for about an hour and a half. Still, I thought, if this was the future I faced, maybe I should look into a bladder transplant or something.

I shifted my bag on my shoulder, sighed, turned to my left—and there he was, a few yards away, looking at me intently. When our eyes met, he smiled. I smiled back. And then he came over to me.

"Hello," he said.

"Hello."

He carried a sketchbook and over his chest was slung a battered leather bag, like an old-fashioned satchel. A pair of sunglasses was pushed up onto his head. I figured he was in his mid to late twenties, definitely older than me. He was not very tall, not as tall as Jotham at six-one, but beautifully proportioned; not gangly but not muscle-bound and bulky like our friend Jason, who had to buy his clothes at one of those shops for big and tall men. His hair was a dark and glossy brown; it was thick and sort of floppy, like Al Pacino's in *Dog Day Afternoon*. His eyes were unusual, a sort of mix of brown and green, a color like olive but not exactly olive. He wore jeans like very few American guys can wear them—certainly not like Jotham and our friends—with a white cotton shirt rolled up at the sleeves.

But what really compelled me to talk with him, when I should have just excused myself and joined my mother in line for the ladies' room, was his smile. I know it sounds ridiculous, to be captivated by the curve of a lip or the whiteness of teeth, by the way the skin around a pair of thick-lashed eyes crinkled just a bit.

Jotham had teeth and lips and eyes. Every man did. But they weren't like this man's.

"You are from the States, yes?" he asked.

"Yes," I said. "Boston. That's in Massachusetts."

I wondered if I'd been insulting. Maybe everyone knew that Boston was in Massachusetts. Or did they?

"Where are you from?" I blurted. "I mean, I know you're from Italy. I mean, I think you are. I—"

He laughed. "Yes, you're right. I'm from right here in Florence."

"Oh."

"Are you traveling alone?" he asked then. "Or maybe with friends?"

"I'm here with my mother," I told him, gesturing vaguely in the direction she'd gone.

"Ah, it's nice for family to be together. Right now—" he laughed sheepishly—"I should be with my father. I work for him, but I sneak out sometimes to come here or to go to the other museums and galleries. Oh," he said then, "forgive me for being rude. My name is Luca."

"Oh," I said, thinking that he hadn't been rude at all. "My name is Marina."

"A beautiful name. It suits you."

"Uh, thanks." I wondered if he knew that in English it meant the place where boats were docked.

"And is your father traveling with you as well?" he asked.

"I don't really have a father," I blurted, utterly surprising myself with the blunt honesty of my reply.

"I am sorry," he said simply.

I twittered nervously. Mortified, I nodded at the sketchpad he held in his right hand; I now saw that the hand was smudged with charcoal. "May I see your sketches?" I asked.

"It is bad. I'm not skilled," he said. "But I wish I were."

His reluctance charmed me. "Please?"

He seemed to consider. Finally, he smiled again and shrugged. "Why not? I admit I am not an artist, though I have a great appreciation for beauty. You must be kind, okay?"

I smiled back and said, "Yes, I'll be kind." I thought: what else could I be to this totally handsome, totally nice guy?

Luca handed me his sketchpad. I opened it carefully. "What were you drawing today?" I asked.

Luca leaned toward me and turned a page. I felt tingly from my head to my feet though he hadn't touched me. I looked up, and our eyes met. For a moment, neither of us said a word.

"This," he said, finally. I looked down at a drawing of a sculpture I'd seen earlier that morning, what my mother had called a "marble group." It depicted Niobe and her children, characters from Greek mythology. I vaguely remembered her story, involving the murder of the children; Niobe had done something to offend the gods.

My mother had pointed out that the statue was a Roman copy of an original Greek statue. From what I remembered of the sculpture, which even I had thought pretty powerful, Luca had captured it beautifully.

"I think it's very good," I said honestly. "I certainly can't draw like this. I'm not very artistic."

"Really? I would have thought otherwise."

He would have? What would make him think that I was artistic? I was just matter-of-fact, unromantic, utterly respectable Marina Caldwell from Boston.

"Why?" I asked.

"I don't know, exactly," he admitted. "Just . . ." And then he waved his hand lightly in the air. "It is something about you. I can usually tell such things about people." And then: "I hope I didn't upset you."

His expression was so earnest. "Oh, no," I said, and unbelievably, my hand was resting—just for a moment—on his arm. "Not at all."

I held out the pad for him; he took it, and there was another moment of silence as we just looked at each other.

"Maybe," he said, finally, "maybe you would meet me for a coffee tomorrow?"

"Yes," I said. "I will."

He gave me his cell-phone number. We arranged a meeting place for the following morning at ten. He took his leave, saying that his father would be angry if he wasn't back at his desk in time for their scheduled meeting. I watched him walk off toward the entrance; he turned once and waved. And then he was gone. And before I could breathe, before I could fully realize what had just happened, I heard my mother's voice.

"I'm sorry I took so long," she was saying. "That line was interminable! When is an architect going to design a public bathroom for women that doesn't require standing around breathing foul odors for what seems like a lifetime?"

"What? Oh, that's okay. No problem. No big deal," I babbled.

"Are you okay?" my mother asked, peering at me closely.

"You look kind of flushed. It is awfully hot in here. Do you feel faint?"

"No, no," I protested. "I'm fine." How could I tell my mother that I was not fine, that something extraordinary had just happened to me?

"Okay. Well, let's get out of here anyway. I could use some fresh air. We'll come back after lunch to see the Giottos."

"Yes," I said. "Sure."

I followed my mother to a trattoria close by the museum. As soon as we'd taken seats, my phone rang. It was Jotham, of course. I took the call automatically, but suddenly, feeling strangely uncomfortable talking to him in front of my mother, I got up and walked a few steps away.

"So what are you doing?" he asked.

"What am I doing? Um, we're just about to get something to eat."

"Yeah, and?"

"And then we'll, I don't know, I'm sure my mother has something planned."

Jotham laughed. "Something boring, I'm sure. Like yet another museum, right?"

"Some of the museums are great," I said in defense of my mother and me. In defense of Luca and his sketch of Niobe.

"Yeah, well, better you than me."

I hurried Jotham off the phone, citing the arrival of our lunch as an excuse. It was a lie; we hadn't yet ordered. I rejoined my mother at the table.

"Sorry," I said, aware that I rarely retreated to talk to Jotham. After all our years together, it wasn't as if we had anything particularly intimate to say to each other.

"What did he have to say?" my mother asked, more out of politeness, I'm sure, than any real interest.

"What?" I said. "Oh, nothing. You know, the usual."

"Is he nervous about his first day at work? It is today, isn't it?"

"Oh," I said, ashamed. "I forgot to ask. He—he wanted to talk, but I said that we were having lunch and . . ."

My mother shot me an inquisitive glance and looked back to her menu. Since when had I hurried Jotham off the phone because of lunch, because of anything? Never. Jotham had always come first.

"I'll call him back when we're finished," I promised her—and myself. Poor Jotham, I thought. His first day clerking at the law office where he hoped to practice someday and I hadn't even wished him luck.

I suddenly felt very uncomfortable. One brief conversation with a handsome stranger and I had neglected my fiancé and, in essence, lied both to him and to my mother. It was an unhappy realization—a shock, really. I'd always thought my character was unimpeachable; it was something of which I was proud.

My mother put her menu aside. "Tell him I said 'break a leg.' "

"Sure," I said. And right then I determined to cancel my date with Luca for the following day.

29

*Where was Goldilocks' mother when her daughter
slipped out of sight to break into the home of strangers?
Why was Mary quite contrary? When did Little Miss
Muffet's mother last clean her insect-infested house?
What possessed Little Red Riding Hood's mother to
dress her daughter in such a way as to attract the
criminal intentions of a predatory male?*
—The Neglectful Mother: The Source of All Deviant
   and Erratic Behavior

After lunch, which had included a flavorful plate of *spinaci
alle accinghe,* or spinach with anchovies (Marina carefully
extracted the anchovies and put them on my plate), and before going back to the gallery, we strolled around the Piazzale
degli Uffizi. Though Marina and I had grown comfortable
with each other in the past days, we hadn't yet adopted the
European custom of strolling arm in arm. Frankly, I wasn't
sure we ever would.

Marina nodded. "Look over there, Mom. See that woman?"

"The one with her mother in the wheelchair? Well, it could
be her grandmother. She's so old and tiny, it's hard to see if
there's any family resemblance."

"No, not them," she said. "The young woman with the
baby, to the left. See, she's wearing one of those slings instead
of a more traditional baby carrier; you know the ones I

mean. I like the slings better. They seem more natural some-how."

"Really?" I said. "The slings seem kind of awkward to me. And the baby doesn't get to look around much. Although if he's in a traditional carrier and he's facing his mother—"

"I'm really looking forward to having children," Marina said, interrupting my babble. "It's too bad that Jotham and I have to wait until we're thirty to start a family."

"You don't have to wait that long, Marina."

"Yes," she said—resignedly?—"we do. We won't have as much money as we need before that. Jotham wants to build a certain financial base before we start a family."

"Well, that is rational of him."

"Jotham is very responsible."

And he's very selfish. What Jotham wants, Jotham gets.

We strolled on in silence, which allowed me to think about motherhood, Marina, and me.

When I was a child, I was what people now call a "girly girl"—my favorite color was pink, my favorite fairy tale was *Cinderella*, I collected ceramic unicorns, and my go-to toy was a baby doll. If it was covered in glitter, I loved it. And yet, I never wanted to grow up and be a mommy.

In fact, by the time I was about nineteen, I'd decided that motherhood was something best left to other women. It seemed like too much power to have over a person; one care-less word from a mother could virtually destroy her child. One careless or one deliberate word, because some women were just not suited for motherhood. What if I was one of those women and only realized it too late? No, I decided, motherhood presented too many chances to go horribly wrong, too many opportunities for abuse.

But then life had interfered, and here I was, a mother of al-most twenty-two years, talking with my daughter about the children she hoped to have one day. Actually, Marina had been talking about having children since she was fifteen—

right after she met Jotham, in fact—as if she'd already given the topic all the thought it required and had come to the definite conclusion that she was mother material.

And when Marina had children, I'd be a grandmother and my mother a great-grandmother. How proud that would make us both, though of course my mother would be happier if Marina and Jotham were securely married before a baby made its appearance.

I turned to my daughter. She was looking around as if she hoped—or feared?—to spot someone. There was a look of wistfulness in her expression but also something else I couldn't name. Apprehension?

"Are you sure you're okay?" I said. "You don't seem—yourself."

"Mom, I'm fine. Please stop asking me."

"I'm sorry. Just being a mother."

Marina smiled. "Well, if constant worrying is what I have to look forward to, maybe I'm not in such a hurry to reproduce after all."

30

Dear Answer Lady:

My mother is always commenting on my appearance. Okay, nothing unusual there, I suppose, except that unlike a lot of mothers (so I hear), my mother piles lavish compliments on me every time she sees me, which is often—my clothes, my hair, my skin. I feel objectified by this constant scrutiny and attention. I mean, it's so over the top, it just can't be real. I can't help but feel there's something almost aggressive or punishing about her behavior. Am I nuts? Should I just feel lucky she's not insulting me outright?

Dear Co-Opted Daughter:

Here's the bitter truth: there's never any point in talking to mothers about behavior that hurts you; they'll turn the tables in a heartbeat, and you'll be left feeling like the spiteful one in the duo. So I'm not even going to suggest you sit your mother down and express your discomfort with her excessive praise. I am going to suggest that you ignore her comments as best you can; try, also, changing the subject immediately—world hunger is always a good way to go. And no, I don't think you're nuts. Whatever your mother's bizarre motives for her behavior, the fact is that it's disturbing you—which, I suspect, is exactly what she wants, even if her desire is unconscious. In my humble *opinion, no one should ever comment on another person's appearance to his or her face. If a person must open her big mouth, she should compliment the person's shoes or handbag, never the person's body. Our bodies, after all, are ourselves. Unfortunately, mothers believe they own their children's bodies/selves, and any form of comment—positive or negative—is a way of asserting their (assumed) right to your life. Welcome to the human race, honey.*

I don't remember much about dinner that night: where we went, what we ate, or what we talked about. In spite of my resolution to break my date with Luca, I couldn't stop thinking about him.

After my mother went to bed, after she fell almost immediately into her usual enviably deep sleep, I sat in my bed, propped against the pillows, a magazine unopened on my lap. Jotham had texted me again.

"Only eleven days to go," I read.

Yes. Only eleven days away from home and Jotham. Only eleven days until my real life returned, or, rather, until I returned to it.

But from a different perspective, a whole eleven days to enjoy, explore, and experience.

I closed my phone.

The piece of paper with Luca's cell-phone number printed on it was folded carefully in my wallet, behind my library card, where it couldn't be seen. I reached for my bag—I'd dropped it on the floor by my bed—and dug it out. All I had to do was call and tell him I couldn't meet him after all. Simple. But not so simple.

I looked down at my engagement ring. Luca had to have seen it; it was too big to be missed. Still, I thought, maybe like a lot of men he wasn't all that observant. But would someone who could make such an exact sketch of a sculpture be someone unskilled in close observation? I didn't think so.

There was another possibility: that Luca simply hadn't recognized the ring for what it was. Maybe, I thought, in Italy engagement rings were—different—than they were in the U.S.

Or maybe Luca had recognized the ring for what it was, but it just didn't matter to him that I was "taken." Maybe he just wanted a one-night stand with an easy American girl. Or maybe he had no romantic interest in me at all, and I had completely misread our brief encounter.

It was certainly possible. I was suddenly aware of being very ignorant in the ways of men—in the ways of the world.

The realization of my ignorance produced a strange result. Suddenly, I was overcome with anger. I was angry with myself for agreeing to meet Luca, whatever his intentions. I was angry with myself for neglecting Jotham, the man to whom I'd committed my life. And I was angry with myself for keeping the secret of my brief encounter from my mother.

I looked over at her sleeping form and wondered what she would do in my situation. I tried, but I just couldn't imagine her response. I also tried to imagine what she would counsel if I woke her right then and asked for her advice. Oddly, the answer to that question eluded me, too.

Right then, I decided to call Jotham. I hadn't talked to him since I'd hurried off the phone earlier. Though I'd called his cell after lunch, he hadn't answered. Probably busy with work, I'd thought, and left a cheerful message.

Now I needed to hear his familiar voice—his slight Boston accent, his laconic, almost bored-sounding laugh. I knew that just hearing it would so fill me with love and appreciation I'd once again feel safe and secure and immune to a stranger's beautiful smile. I knew that I'd no longer feel so angry and lost.

I pulled a light sweater over my nightgown and slipped into the hallway. Again I felt the need for privacy, though it was unlikely my mother would be conscious again until morning.

As soon as Jotham answered, I asked about his first day at the law firm. Everything, he said, had gone just great. His boss was awesome. He was sure he'd made a solid first impression. His voice exuded even more confidence than it usually did.

"I'm glad things went well," I said sincerely. "I knew they would." Things always went well for Jotham. Sometimes I wondered if he was charmed, one of those extremely lucky people. Jotham would have laughed at such "nonsense." People made their own success, he'd say. Maybe he was right. Either way, Jotham's habit of success would make him the ideal husband and father.

"Oh, before I forget," he said, "Jason invited us to a private party one of his father's colleagues is having at the Ritz in Boston. Everyone important is going to be there, politicians, the big names in finance." Jotham laughed. "Jason even said Tom Brady might come by, but I think he's just fantasizing."

"When is it?" I asked, not entirely sure I'd feel comfortable hobnobbing with Tom Brady and positive that I'd need a new dress for such a swanky occasion. A swanky-occasion dress wasn't in my budget; this would require some very canny bargain hunting. Marshall's, T.J. Maxx, Loehmann's Online, Bluefly.com—I'd have to start the moment I got back to Boston.

"I've got the date written down here somewhere, a Saturday in August. It doesn't matter. I said yes for us."

"What?" I said after a moment. "But we're supposed to talk to each other before accepting an invitation. That's one of our rules."

"Yeah," Jotham said, his tone dismissive, "but I knew you'd want to go."

"That's beside the point, my wanting to go. You should have asked me first."

"Well, I didn't."

"What if I have something else to do that afternoon?" I argued.

"You don't."

"What?" I realized I was staring blindly at the hall's overhead light and that my head was beginning to hurt. I blinked and looked away.

"I know your schedule," he said. "You would have already told me if you had plans."

"But—"

Jotham sighed heavily. "Look, do you want me to tell them we can't make it?"

I felt confused; angry, yes, but also chastened. I felt backed against a wall. "No," I said. "I'm not sure. Look, you can always go without me if I decide I don't want to."

"What? I'm not going to a party without you!" He sounded absolutely horrified at the prospect.

"Jotham, come on," I said. "We're not attached at the hip. You can go if you want, and I—"

"No," he said firmly. "We're either going together or we're not going at all. So what should I say to Jason and his father? What's your excuse for not wanting to be at a private party being catered by the top caterer in Boston? Guys from the Philharmonic are going to be performing. Jason swears the gift bags are going to include something from Louis Boston. Oh, and the attorney general of Massachusetts will be there. Meeting him could be excellent for my career. But hey, if you—"

"No, no, no," I cried, unable to bear the sound of his voice beating me down, implying that I was being ridiculous, that I didn't know what was good for me. "Fine, we'll go, we'll go."

"You'll have a great time," he said, and I heard the smug self-satisfaction in his voice. "I promise."

It wasn't his to promise, whether or not I'd have a great

time. But Jotham was always assuring me of things over which he had no control, presuming I'd feel a certain way, swearing to me that I'd see he'd been right all along.

"Marina?"

"Look," I said, "I have to go. It's late and—bye, Jotham."

"Wait, Marina, one more thing I—"

I snapped the phone shut.

31

Remember, not everyone considers your child of the utmost interest. Be prepared to ask your child-free friends about their lives—careers, homes, travel plans, etc.—before you launch into a detailed account of how your precious Pomegranate ate all of her creamed peas at dinner the night before and how your adorable Bismarck outperformed every other kid in gymnastics class that morning.
—Mothers Are the Biggest Bores: How Not to Alienate Your Non-Mother Friends

Saturday, June 10

"Why aren't you dressed?"

My mother's expression was one of surprise, not alarm or suspicion. Still, I felt my cheeks flush as if I'd already been caught out in the lie.

"I'm sorry, Mom," I said. "I—I just don't feel very well. I think I should go back to bed for a while."

"What's wrong?" she asked, dropping her bag onto her unmade bed. "You look okay, a bit flushed maybe. Do you want me to check if you have a fever? I brought a thermometer."

My mother turned to go back into the bathroom. "No, no," I said. "I don't have a fever. It's my stomach. It feels a little queasy. I just think I should stay here in case."

"Are you sure you don't want me to stay with you?"

"I'm sure, Mom," I said, slipping back under the covers and pulling them up to my chin. "How boring would that be?"

"Can I at least bring you some tea or soda water?" she asked. "I have some antacid tablets, too."

"No, nothing." I said. "I'm fine. I'm sure all I need is some sleep."

With obvious reluctance, my mother retrieved her bag stuffed full of guidebooks. "All right, if you're sure. But promise to call the front desk if you need anything. Now I feel stupid for not having brought a phone of my own. I can't even be in touch with you, and what if you need me? Maybe—"

"Mom, really," I implored, on the verge of losing my nerve and abandoning the secret rendezvous. "I'll be okay. It's just a queasy stomach. I'm sure I'll be fine—later."

Looking miserable, my mother came over to kiss my forehead.

"I love you," she said. "I'll be back before lunch. Maybe you'll feel better by then. I hate to see you sick on our special vacation."

I only nodded. I couldn't speak as tears of guilt and shame threatened to swamp me. Finally, my mother left. And when she did, I lay there in bed, letting the tears come.

I was certain that she suspected nothing; I'd never been the sort of person to fake an illness. I felt terrible about worrying her, I did, but how could I have told her about my date with Luca, a person I'd talked to for all of ten minutes, a person I should not, as an engaged woman, have been meeting?

And then, when the tears had dried, I got up, took a shower, got dressed, and left the hotel. I'm embarrassed to admit that not for one moment did I consider the possible danger of meeting a stranger in a strange land. Not for one moment did it occur to me that I should tell someone, my mother or the hotel concierge, where I was going and who I would be with. Smart women, foolish choices. In that moment, I was entirely a cliché.

He was waiting for me as promised at an outdoor table at a little café called Lorenzo's a few blocks from the Hotel Francesca. He got up as I approached the table.

"Hi," I said, barely able to croak out the word.

"Hello." That magnificent smile again. "I am glad to see you this morning."

He gestured to the seat across from him, and I sat, careful not to get a sandal strap caught on a chair rung or do anything else clumsy or stupid. I couldn't remember when I'd felt so nervous. Once I was seated, Luca sat back in his own chair.

"Well," he said.

"Well," I said.

We both laughed.

"I can't say much for our conversational skills this morning. Maybe we haven't had enough coffee yet?"

"Yes," I said, relieved. "That must be it."

Luca ordered for us. I felt excited hearing him speak his native language. Italian had never sounded so beautiful.

"So, how is your mother today?" he asked then.

"She's fine," I said, hating myself anew. "Thank you. She went to a museum. Or something. Um, how's your father?"

Luca shrugged. "Wondering where his son is this morning."

"Oh, are you supposed to be at the office?"

"It's okay. I have some freedom. It is not bad to be the son of the owner of the company."

Luca grinned, and while I couldn't imagine ever taking advantage of my employer, no matter who he was, I found myself grinning back.

"Would you like to walk?" he asked, our tiny coffee cups empty.

I said yes. Luca paid, and we left the café. Only steps later my cell phone rang.

"I'm sorry," I said, frantically digging through my bag. "I forgot to turn this thing off."

I finally grabbed the phone and looked quickly at the screen before turning it off. A new message from Jotham. I stuffed the phone back into my bag and wished he would just leave me alone. I was still mad at him for forcing me to give in about the party and for not apologizing for having broken one of our relationship rules. It was as if a veil had been lifted with that conversation, and I'd suddenly realized that I never, ever got my way in our relationship.

"I hate the cell phone," Luca said as we walked on. "It might be necessary for us, how we live today, for business, but it is also very annoying. And rude. Two people walk together, and yet each is talking to someone else! The cell phone has destroyed intimacy."

I'd never really given it any thought and felt embarrassed by that—as well as oddly embarrassed by my attachment to the person on the other end of that "line."

"Yes," I said, keeping those uncomfortable thoughts to myself. "My mother refused to get an international cell phone for our trip. She says the cell phone has destroyed freedom and autonomy. Or something like that."

Luca laughed. "I think I would like your mother."

I smiled, but I wasn't so sure my mother would like Luca. At least, not given the situation.

"There is a saint in my church with your name, St. Marina," he said suddenly.

"Oh?" I said. "I don't really know much about saints. I'm not Catholic."

"I will tell you what I know about her. But it's not much. She lived in the eighth century. When she died, her relics were sent from Constantinople to Venice. Some, too, are in a church in Paris. Her feast day is June eighteenth, very soon."

"How do you know about her?" I asked. The eighth century?

Luca shrugged and laughed. "Odd bits of things stay in my head from school. Plus, I have been to Venice. You must come to Venice some time. It is a strange and beautiful city."

"Yes. I mean, I've seen pictures, of course. You know," I said, surprising myself yet again, "I've never really liked my name."

"No? Why?"

"Um, I don't know, it doesn't really—feel like me. It feels like the name of a character in a story or a poem more than a real name. I can't really explain it."

"But you are a character in a story and a poem. The story of your life, no? The poem that is your life."

"Oh," I said, not entirely sure I understood. "I guess. I never thought of it that way."

"You are a character, but also you are the author of your life. Like I am the author of mine." Here Luca smiled. "Though I admit that sometimes I have trouble finding the next step in the plot."

"I hate not knowing what's going to happen next," I admitted. And to myself I added: which is why I try so hard to make plans and stick with them—though being here with you isn't a part of any plan I've ever made.

"I find it exciting," he was saying, "not knowing. Sometimes scary, too. But what can you do?"

What can you do? Life is full of the unexpected. Wasn't that what my mother was always saying?

We walked along in silence for a bit. Luca's arm brushed mine when he moved aside to let two older men, arms entwined, free hands gesticulating as they spoke, pass us. As if the light and accidental touch had inspired me, I said, "What I told you yesterday, about not really having a father?"

"Yes?"

"I do have a father, of course. Everybody has a father."

"Yes, I suppose that is true. But yours?"

"Mine has never lived with us. Mine's never even seen me."

Luca took my arm and steered us to the curb. He let go of me, and I wished he hadn't.

"I'm sorry," he said quietly. "I feel bad for this man. He doesn't know what he has lost."

I thought of Jotham's standard remark concerning my father and compared it to Luca's careful, even kind, words: "The guy's a creep, and if I ever run across him someday, he'd better watch out."

That sort of macho response, one that entirely ignored all the subtleties of the situation, had never comforted me. Luca's words, a stranger's words, had given me a sort of solace.

"Thank you," I said.

Luca just smiled, and we walked on again.

"What did you study in college?" I asked.

"Something very useful. I am kidding. My father teases me. I studied European history, medieval and Renaissance, mostly. He wanted me to become an economist, but that wasn't for me."

I thought about Jotham and his father, how Mr. Grandin had planned for his son to go to law school from the time Jotham could walk, maybe before. As far as I knew, Jotham had never questioned the decision that was made for him long before he could argue back.

"My degree is in accounting," I said. "I've always been good with numbers. I guess that's kind of boring."

"Not at all," Luca replied promptly. "My sister Arianna, she is with an international bank. And my sister Margharita, she is a lawyer." Luca laughed. "I'm the dumb one in the family."

"You're not dumb!"

"My teachers would argue with you. They always said I was a dreamer. That my 'head was in the clouds.' It didn't bother me. Clouds are very beautiful."

And I so wanted to say "You are very beautiful," but what came out of my mouth was entirely different.

"Luca," I said, this time taking his arm and forcing us both to stop. "I—I'm engaged." My left hand fluttered as if to prove this assertion. "I'm going to be married next year."

"Yes," he said. "I thought so."

I took off my sunglasses though the sun was very strong. I wanted him to see how sorry I was. "I shouldn't even be here with you. I don't know why I said I would meet you."

That was a lie, and we both knew it. I was there because I wanted to be, because I had to be.

"We are only talking. There is nothing—"

"No," I said firmly. "We're not only talking. If this were—okay—I could tell him. My fiancé. But—"

"I should not have asked you for coffee." Luca shook his head. "I'm sorry."

"No, no, it's not your fault. It's all mine. I'm the one who should be sorry. I am sorry. I didn't mean—I didn't mean to lead you on. Do you know that expression?"

"Yes, of course." Luca smiled; it seemed kindly. "But don't apologize, Marina. I am not a child. And I have been enjoying this morning very much."

"Me, too," I admitted. I'd been enjoying it far more than I should have been. "I should be getting back to the hotel. My mother . . . She's expecting me."

"And I must get to the office or my father will scold me." He smiled again. "Well, I am too old to scold, but he will not be happy."

"Oh, I hope you aren't in big trouble!"

Luca laughed. "I am not worried about that, and you should not be, either. Marina, you are a serious person, aren't you?"

"I guess. Yes. Anyway, thank you for such a lovely morning. I'm sorry—"

Luca took my hand. "No more apologies, okay?" And then he leaned in and kissed me. And I felt more excited by that one gentle kiss than I had ever felt in all my years with Jotham.

"Luca, I—" His eyes on me were so dark and so deep.

"If you would like us to meet tonight," he said softly, "I will be at the café Lorenzo's again. I will wait for you. But you must only come if you truly want to."

"Yes," I said. "I will."

32

Dear Answer Lady:

What are the allowable limits to which a mother can go to punish the despicable little shit who is bullying her own blameless child? I mean, it's acceptable for a mother, whose job it is to protect her child from all dangers, to do whatever it is she feels she needs to do to ensure that, say, that lard-ass creep Mike Warner stops shoving her delicately built son into the bushes outside their school every morning—right? Even if what the mother feels she needs to do is technically not within the law. In my opinion (but not in my husband's, which is why I'm writing to you), I have a perfectly valid right to have this Warner creature's legs broken (and I know just the people to do it, too). That'll teach him a lesson he won't soon forget! What do you think?

Dear Angry Woman:

First, have you taken your high-blood-pressure medication today? Good. You don't want to stroke out, thus depriving your delicately built son of the care of his doting mother. Now, though I understand and sympathize with your desire for retribution (bullies are the lowest of the low), I am sorry to say that you are in no way allowed—by law as well as by common sense—to cause harm, physical or otherwise, to this bully you call

Mike Warner. There are several acceptable and intelligent ways to deal with this matter, starting with a discussion with your son's principal and a request for a mediated meeting with young Warner's parents or guardians. So calm down and start thinking long-term—like, what would life in prison be like and how would your son feel about visiting Mom in the clink? Finally, if you have not used a pseudonym, there's a good chance young Warner's parents or guardians are now apprised of their son's misbehavior and, if they are at all the right sort of people, will begin steps to correct the deviant's behavior. (Note: genetics being what they are, you might want to apologize for the use of the descriptive term "lard-ass" when you all sit down to find a solution to this problem.)

"Marina? It's me."

I closed the door of our hotel room behind me. Marina was half sitting, half reclining in her bed, covers pulled up to her chin. Her massive bag, which when I'd left the hotel that morning had been in the closet, was thrown on a chair. Her cheeks were flushed. I wondered if she'd gone out, but I said nothing. Maybe she'd only gone to get something to drink or to buy some aspirin.

"How do you feel?" I asked.

"I still don't feel so great," she said. "I think I'd better skip lunch, Mom."

For a sick person, her voice was almost robust. Her eyes were clear, not glittering with fever or dulled by congestion.

"I'll stay with you if you want," I offered, suddenly feeling as if I was somehow—intruding.

"No, no, go ahead," she said, inching the covers up to her

ears. "Keep the reservation. You've been looking forward to eating at Matteo's."

"So have you. I could call and try to reschedule."

"No, really, Mom," she urged. "Go ahead; I'll be fine. Tell me all about it when you get back. As soon as I feel better, maybe we can go again. Together, I mean."

Marina, I thought, can't get rid of me fast enough. Still, I proceeded with caution, having nothing solid on which to base a suspicion that her illness was feigned. "Well, all right," I said, "but I'm not thrilled about going without you. Can I bring you something to eat? Maybe some soup?"

"Nothing, Mom. But thanks."

At the door I turned, my hand on the knob. "Oh," I said, preparing to lie, "I just remembered. I saw something this morning that Jotham might like, in a cute little shop on Via Donato. You'll have to come see it."

"Yeah, okay," she said without interest.

"You're sure you're going to be okay alone?"

"Yes, Mom, I'll be fine."

I left the hotel. Earlier that morning I'd had no doubt that my daughter felt ill. But now I wasn't at all sure. Something was up with Marina, and it wasn't a rumbling stomach. For a brief moment I was tempted to watch for her outside the hotel, but I rejected the idea as ridiculous and unworthy of me. A supposedly trusting mother doesn't spy on her daughter.

Besides, Marina was twenty-one, legally an adult. I wasn't technically responsible for her any longer. Not that this fact was at all comforting.

I walked on toward the restaurant and a solitary lunch. What good would it have done if I had followed her? I'd learned long ago that no matter how hard you try, you simply couldn't prevent fate from having her say.

33

You think marriage is a prison? Think again, sweetheart. These days it's almost as simple to divorce as it is to get married in the first place. You think signing a job contract with a corporation is going to keep you employed for the time specified in its legalese-ridden content? Think again, buddy. These days any halfway competent corporate lawyer can get and keep you canned without breaking a sweat. No, my friends, the only "relationship" that truly is permanent is the parent/child relationship. Like it or not, that's one bond that simply cannot be broken.
—Mom, Dad, and Me: Yoked Together Forever

Marina claimed she was well enough to join me for dinner, though she wasn't much of a companion. Before we'd left the hotel, she'd been full of an odd sort of energy, fidgety, flushed, distracted. She'd let me feel her forehead; she didn't have a fever, at least of the physical kind.

Now, at dinner, she seemed almost listless, unfocused. I wanted to know why, though my motives for wanting to know the truth of Marina's secret weren't entirely clear. Was I trying to trap her in a lie? Force an admission of guilt? Was I trying—hoping—to help or to punish my daughter? Or did my need to know her secret come down to the embarrassing fact that I felt somewhat abandoned, like the girl everyone decides to slowly freeze out of the clique by withholding the usual chatty gossip?

"Are you still thinking of having both Allison and Jessica as your maids of honor?" I asked with a deliberately casual tone.

"What?" she said, dropping the spoon she'd been twirling. "Oh, probably."

When nothing more seemed forthcoming, I said, "You know, back in the day, a married maid of honor was called a matron of honor. By the time you and Jotham get married, both Allison and Jessica will be married, won't they?"

"Uh-huh." Marina poked at a small bowl of olive oil with a slice of bread.

"Of course, I don't know who I would ask to be my witness, if I were ever to get married."

"Yes." Marina looked in my general direction as if reluctant to meet my eye. "I mean, sorry, Mom, what did you say?"

Whatever bug Marina claimed to have caught had certainly decimated her conversational skills. Her mind, wherever it was, was not at the table with me.

"Oh," I said, "nothing important."

Marina took another sip of red wine. Her cheeks were hectic with color.

"You've hardly touched your dinner," I pointed out.

Marina looked down at the plate of food as if surprised it was there. "I guess I'm just not that hungry. My stomach. I mean, maybe it's not one hundred percent yet."

"Too bad," I said. By then I didn't believe the upset-stomach story at all. "The *bistecca alla Fiorentina* is wonderful. Try to eat just a little."

Obediently, Marina cut a small piece of her steak.

Something was going on with my daughter, all right, and if I knew anything about life, that something was a man. When do women stop eating? When they're newly in love. Maternal concern battled fiercely with the desire to remain calm and supportive in the likely case that Marina would need a shoulder to cry on if—

If I was right, and a man had caught my daughter's attention. If I was right, and passion had taken her unaware. If I was right, and Marina's life was about to get messy.

"Should I get a check, or do you want something sweet?" I asked.

Marina jumped a bit in her chair. "Oh, the check, please."

We walked back to the hotel in silence. Marina immediately undressed and got into her bed with a magazine. I slipped under the sheets in my own bed with one of my guidebooks. I was determined not to fall asleep as I usually did—rapidly and soundly. Guiltily, I wondered if I was being unfair to my daughter, suspecting her of a secret midnight rendezvous. Maybe, I thought, Marina's distraction had nothing to do with a romance. Maybe, but I doubted it.

Concern was not enough to keep me awake. Before I'd read a chapter, I was fast asleep.

34

Dear Answer Lady:

I hope you can help me talk some sense into my daughter. Just the other day she up and announced that she was no longer coming to Mass with her father and me. (We're Catholic, and my daughter is twenty, by the way.) Not only that, she told us she'd left the Church all together! Well, I can assure you I was furious, and I demanded she come with us to Mass. But all she did was say "No, after long and careful thought I've made up my mind." Her mind? Who does she think she is! I'm her mother, and I know what's best for my daughter!

Dear Deluded:

No matter what you have convinced yourself is the "truth," your daughter is not an extension of you. She is not your Mini-Me; she is not your possession. Instead, she is an entirely separate, individual being over whom you have no power or influence other than that which she chooses to grant you. "Mother knows best" is a dangerous cliché, and like most clichés should be studiously avoided. Here's what you need to do: back off from your daughter and find your own life. Yeah, it's hard. But hey, everyone's got to do it.

Sneaking out of the hotel without waking my mother was easy, though the actual process—getting redressed, tiptoeing into and out of the bathroom, closing the door of our room behind me—left me a bundle of nerves.

Luca was waiting for me at Lorenzo's as promised, but we didn't stay. Instead, we got on his Vespa—I'd never been on one before but found myself tossing a leg across as if I rode one every day—and drove to his apartment. It was in an old building whose interior had been renovated massively. Even the elevator was sleek and impressive, though how I managed to notice my surroundings puzzles me. My hand in Luca's was trembling; the other hand clutched the strap of my bag as if for life. A part of me was keenly in the moment, aware of where I was, whom I was with, and what I was about to do. Another part of me was numb, disbelieving, and oddly unafraid.

"This is it," Luca said, opening the door to his apartment. He let go of my hand. "I'll get us something to drink."

While he was gone to the kitchen, I stood just inside the door, and suddenly, it hit. Panic. Because I couldn't tell Luca that, aside from a quick and inexpert peck on the lips from a boy in seventh grade, I'd never been kissed by anyone but Jotham. And, of course, I'd never had sex with anyone but Jotham.

I was scared. What if I was so awkward that Luca laughed or, worse, threw me out of his apartment to find my own way back to the Hotel Francesca? What if everything I thought about him was wrong? What if he wasn't kind and humble but evil and selfish?

My experience was limited—I knew that much from magazines and movies and books. And there had never been a possibility of broadening my sex life with Jotham to include—other things. There simply wasn't. I would never suggest a change; frankly, I wasn't sure I wanted to, not with Jotham, anyway. And Jotham would never suggest a change, either. No. What I knew firsthand of sex between a man and a woman was never going to be more than what it had been since I was seventeen.

Unless I had sex with Luca; unless Luca was kind and loving and patient and . . .

Luca came back into the living room with a bottle of wine and two long-stemmed glasses. He put those on a glass-and-marble coffee table and came to me. He smiled and kissed me. I felt my bag slip off my shoulder and to the floor, and suddenly all thoughts of Jotham simply vanished, and with them all connection to my life back home. I was no longer Jotham's fiancée; I was no longer anyone's daughter or granddaughter or best friend. I was no longer serious, worried Marina. I was someone else entirely—and yet, never more absolutely me. That's the best way I can put it, though it made no rational sense.

I was barely aware of Luca's lips leaving mine, of his taking my hand and leading me to his bedroom at the back of the apartment. But I was intensely aware of my own unexpected but absolutely natural movements, of my pulling his mouth back to mine, of my forcing him back onto the bed with my body. I felt an urge—entirely new, incomprehensible—a need to abandon my self, to become part of Luca, and stranger still, a part of something other than the two of us. Luca responded to my—to my ferocity—with an equal ferocity of his own. And yet, in spite of the intensity of his desire he was gentle as well.

The sex we had that night was revelatory and entirely without shame. It's not too extreme to say that in those few hours I became a different Marina, a truer person than I'd been before. Though it would take some time for me to fully realize that there was no going back to who and what I'd been before that night, my life was, indeed, irrevocably changed.

Afterward, after the most passionate and true experience I'd ever had, we curled together on the black leather couch and sipped the wine.

"I can't stop—looking at you," I said, awkward with what was to me an entirely new language of simple, naked truths.

Luca laughed. "That is good, because if you were looking all the time at the table or the chair I would think you don't like me!"

"I do like you."

"I know. And I like you, Marina."

I felt myself blushing and so then did look at the shining black dining table and the upholstered red armchair and all the other pieces that conspired to make Luca's apartment look like something featured in *Architectural Digest*.

"Your apartment is beautiful," I said. "Everything seems so—I don't know how to put it. Everything seems so—right."

"Ah, you have to thank my mother for that. She chose everything here, from the tables and chairs to the pots and pans. Everything but for the art. The paintings and sculptures, I chose each one."

"Is she a professional decorator?"

Luca laughed. "She thinks she is. She has decorated my sisters' apartments, too. Her taste is very good. Better than mine, though mine is not so very bad."

"Didn't you even have any choice in the matter of curtains?" I asked, trying to hide a smile.

"Not at all! What Mama wants to do, she will do! My poor father, he must put up with the bills for new this and new that all the time."

Suddenly I checked my watch. It was almost three in the morning.

"I want to stay," I said, "more than anything. But my mother . . . I should get back before she wakes up."

"Yes," he said. But in spite of my good intentions, I didn't make it back to the Hotel Francesca until almost five.

We kissed, Luca on his Vespa, me standing next to him on the pavement, when he dropped me off.

"Until tomorrow?" he murmured.

"Yes."

Luca waited until I was in the hotel's lobby before he drove away. I nodded at the concierge, though avoided making eye contact. I was embarrassed, sure he knew what I'd been doing out on my own all night. I hurried up the three flights of stairs to our room, all the while determining never to tell a soul about what had happened between Luca and me that night. I'd always hated those ads for the Las Vegas tourism industry, the ones that condoned, even celebrated, bad behavior, and now I was in possession of a secret that if revealed would destroy my world back home in a spectacular way.

What happened in Florence would stay in Florence.

I snuck back into the room I shared with my mother. She lay in the same position as when I'd left so many hours earlier. Quietly, I undressed and got into my bed. Sleep would be near to impossible, but for once that was okay because I had my thoughts and memories of Luca.

I was sublimely happy.

I was sublimely miserable.

35

Have you always dreamed of a mother who resem-
bled the ample-bosomed, kitchen-bound, softhearted
Aunt Bea of Andy Griffith *fame? Have you always*
regretted that fate instead chose to inflict upon you
an exercise-obsessed, forever-dieting, cold and criti-
cal mater who wouldn't know an apple pie if it hit
her in her Botoxed face? Don't despair! There is help
for such tragic cases as yours, and you don't have to
go to jail as a consequence.
　　—When Mother Is Nothing Like Your Fantasy:
　　How to Adopt a Mom

Sunday, June 11

"Maybe Jotham would like a nice dress shirt," I said, more
to fill a silence that was becoming increasingly awkward than
for any other reason. Whatever was bothering or distracting
or preoccupying my daughter was really putting a damper on
our Tuscan holiday. So much, I thought, for mother/daughter
bonding. Why did I continue to harbor such fantasies?

"Hmm," she said, continuing to tap her coffee spoon on
the table. It was uncharacteristic of her to be so fidgety—and
now her generally odd behavior had been going on since . . .
since when? Since the afternoon we'd visited the Uffizi
Gallery and we'd been apart while I waited on that interminable line for the ladies' room.

Marina's phone rang. I assumed it was Jotham. Did that boy never sleep?

Marina barely glanced at the display screen before returning the phone to her bag.

"If you want to take the call—" I began.

"No. That's okay."

"Jotham?"

"Yeah."

I drained my cup of Americano coffee. "Well," I said, "shall we get going?"

Marina shot out of her chair as if she'd been fired from the proverbial cannon. It wasn't caffeine that was fueling her; the nervous energy was coming from someplace else entirely.

"I thought we could visit the Galleria dell'Accademia this morning. Across the Arno. How does that sound?"

"Sure," she said without enthusiasm. "Wherever you want to go."

In spite of the magnificence of Michelangelo's *David*—the original, not one of the many reproductions—I was almost certain that Marina was barely conscious of being in its presence. In a hushed voice that befitted the museum setting, I read from one of my guidebooks.

"The Accademia contains paintings and sculptures executed from the thirteenth through the sixteenth centuries. It's amazing, don't you think," I said, "to be surrounded by objects crafted all those years ago by human beings so long gone. I find it very moving."

"Mmm," Marina said. Her head was tilted back, but her eyes, I noted, seemed to be looking at the middle distance, not at the *David*.

"There's also a collection of musical instruments, started by the Medici family. We could come back to see that after lunch."

No response. With a gentle tug on her arm, I suggested we leave the museum and get something to eat.

Once outside, Marina seemed ready to explode with anxiety. When from the depths of her bag her phone rang, she jumped as if someone had pinched her. She didn't answer. Instead, she stopped dead and reached for my arm.

"Mom," she said, "I have to talk to you."

My heart thudded in my chest; my hands felt tingly. I tried to keep the alarming symptoms of panic from Marina. I was certain that fainting or having a heart attack would not help her.

"It's about time," I said as calmly as I could manage and without a trace of the annoyance I'd also been feeling. "You've been—not yourself these past two days."

"No."

"Here, let's sit." I led us to the closest café, where we took a table *à deux* as far away from the other customers as possible. When the waiter had taken our order—a Pelligrino for both of us—I said, "Tell me. But first, turn off that phone."

Marina lowered her eyes; she looked unbearably young just then. "I did a horrible thing, Mom."

I reached for her hand. She let me clasp it, but her hand was limp in mine. "Just tell me you're okay. Are you in some kind of trouble?"

"No," she said. "I'm okay. I mean, I'm not hurt or anything, but . . . oh, Mom"—here she looked up, her eyes darker than ever with emotion—"I can't believe this happened to me!"

"You met someone," I said, withdrawing my hand. "A man."

Marina's mouth hung open in shock, a silent film heroine. "How did you know?" she croaked. "Did you see us? Did—"

"Marina, calm down. It's okay. I didn't know for sure, but it felt like a very good guess."

"Yes." She exhaled deeply with the word. Confession must have brought some small relief, if only for a moment.

"Where?"

"At the Uffizi, on Friday. While you were on that endless line for the ladies' room."

Yes, I thought, of course.

The waiter brought our drinks. When he'd gone off, I said, "Who is he?" I didn't have to ask if Marina had slept with him yet. The truth was all over her face. Of course she had. There was no way she couldn't have. And yes, I understood that.

"Oh, Mom," she said almost pleadingly, "he's perfectly respectable. He's not some kind of creep, really. He told me all about himself on our first date. His name is Luca Sarna and he's twenty-seven and he works for his father's textile company and he—"

"Does he know you're engaged?"

Marina nodded and then lowered her eyes again. "Yes. But Mom, we both feel—we both feel really bad about what's happened, honestly. It's just that . . ."

"Yes. I know."

"I can't believe I've been so horrible to Jotham." Here Marina shook her head. "I just never, ever thought something like this would happen. Not in a million years. It wasn't supposed to happen, Mom. Meeting another man wasn't in the plan."

What could I say that would be of comfort—and that wouldn't sound suspiciously like "I told you so"? Yes, Marina, life is unpredictable. Yes, Marina, you can count on nothing definite but death. It's something you just have to accept.

In the end, I said nothing.

Marina's next words burst from her; she clenched her fists and brought them down on her thighs. "If I hadn't come to Italy, this never would have happened!"

I heard the implied blame. What Marina was really saying was: if my mother hadn't dragged me to Italy, my life wouldn't have exploded so spectacularly. Of course Marina needed to blame someone for an act she could barely comprehend having committed. Of course I would be the one to blame. Rejection and blame are a mother's old companions.

"Of course it would have," I said, thinking that maybe I should be keeping my mouth shut. "I mean, it could have happened anywhere." Anywhere, I thought, out of Jotham's sight.

Marina didn't protest, at least not aloud. And while she stared blindly at the tall bottle of sparkling water on the little table, I ashamedly admitted to myself that I resented Marina's having kept this secret from me, though it had only been for two days. It implied a certain amount of distance between us, and I naïvely had wanted our Tuscan holiday to be all about closeness.

But I also knew this wasn't a time for the indulgence of selfish thoughts and feelings. Marina needed me—but God only knew what I could do to help her.

"Oh Mom!" Marina cried suddenly, oblivious to the stares of two older women at the nearest occupied table. "What must Luca think of me? He knows that I'm cheating on my fiancé. He must think I'm a horrible person! But I'm not, Mom. I swear I've never done anything like this before, but—"

"Yes?" I said when the silence had gone on for some time.

"Why can't I just walk away from Luca?" Her voice was low, tortured. "I can't bear the thought of never seeing him, of never touching him again."

I waited. What was there to say to such passion?

"Mom," she said after another tortured moment, "how can Luca say that he loves me when he knows that by being with him I'm betraying another man?"

Oh, I thought, because love knows no reason.

I didn't want this person, this stranger named Luca, to be in love with my daughter; I was pleased to see her struggle with the morality of her situation; I wanted Marina to be happy and to experience passion; I wanted to turn back the clock, give my ticket to Jotham, and prevent Marina from ever meeting Luca.

"The rules of passion," I began, loathing myself for every empty word, "such as they are, are very different from the rules of reason. When you're in love, you don't judge the person the way you would someone you don't know very well, someone dispensable. Luca is in—love—with you, and he sees everything through that love. He sees perfection. He finds reasons and excuses for behavior he otherwise might condemn."

Marina nodded glumly. I wasn't sure how much of my little speech she'd actually heard. And I remembered our fight over dessert on Tuesday night; it was almost as if I'd been predicting this crisis for Marina, as if I'd known that very soon something was going to happen that would violently disrupt the careful world she'd thought she'd made for herself.

Of course, I hadn't known anything for sure, least of all that the catalyst for change would take the form of a handsome, urbane, twenty-seven-year-old man with a beautiful smile.

"You can't tell anyone, Mom," Marina pleaded then. "Not even Rob, okay? Please, promise me! I'm so embarrassed."

"All right," I said reluctantly; I'd thought immediately of turning to Rob for solace and advice. "I promise."

"Thank you."

"Are you seeing him later today?"

"Yes." Marina barely whispered the word.

"When?" So that I can plan the rest of my day, which it seems I'll be spending alone.

Marina looked at her watch. "In a few minutes, actually. Mom, I'm sorry. I have to go."

The look in her eyes broke my heart. It was so familiar. She did, indeed, have to meet this man.

"It's okay," I said.

She stood, grabbed her bag, and with the assurance of a native walked into the busy street.

"Marina," I called after her.

She looked back, her sunglasses now obscuring her eyes.

I shook my head. "Nothing."

And Marina hurried off.

I stopped back at the hotel before heading on to a day of solitary roaming and called Rob, cursing my stupidity in not having brought along an international cell and fully intending to break Marina's confidence. I didn't want to bear this burden alone; I wasn't sure that I could.

The connection was beyond bad. Shouting didn't help; I could barely hear a syllable, and before anything at all could be communicated, the call was cut off.

Standing by the still-unmade bed in that small hotel room, I felt frustrated, isolated, terribly alone. I was frightened for Marina—so many terrible things could happen to her because of this man, this stranger—and frightened for myself as well, though I couldn't quite understand why.

I went into the bathroom for some ibuprofen. As I lifted the glass of water to my mouth, I caught my image in the mirror over the sink and was shocked by the look of misery I saw there. Suddenly that smug old adage came to mind: be careful what you wish for, because you just might get it.

36

Dear Answer Lady:

My mother is turning sixty-five in a few months.
All her friends were given big parties by their
kids when they turned sixty-five. (Not the kids,
the mothers.) The thing is, organizing and paying for a big party is going to be a real pain. My
sister is an idiot, so I know she won't be of any
help, and my brother is the cheapest person ever,
so forget about his forking out some cash. What
the hell am I going to do? And don't tell me that
maybe my mother doesn't want a big party. She's
been dropping hints for the past six months, like
leaving advertisements for caterers and function
halls in my house every time she's over. I'm
going nuts over here!

Dear Self-Centered Swine:

Question for you: have you ever heard of the
Ten Commandments? In particular, Command-
ment Number Four? It goes like this: "Honor
thy father and thy mother." It's in the freakin'
Bible, which, even if you aren't a practicing Chris-
tian or Jew, you should have some passing acquaintance with as a decently educated person.
(Wait, there's my mistake, the assumption that you
can read beyond a second-grade level. My bad.)
Slap some sense into your idiot sister and use ex-
tortion if necessary to get some money from your

cheap-ass brother and give your mother the best damn party ever. Go!

Luca led me to a charming garden atop the roof of his building. It was for the use of all the tenants, he explained, but since everyone in the building worked at an office, it generally went unused until evenings, at least during the week.

"Except that today I am 'playing hooky' with you. Do you still use that expression, 'playing hooky'?"

I laughed. "I guess. I was never the type to skip school. I think it's also called truancy. You're being truant if you skip school."

"Good. I will remember that the next time I am being truant and not going to the office!"

The disturbing thought that I was in some way being truant by leaving my mother on her own tapped at the back of my conscience, but I ignored it. At the moment, it wasn't hard to do.

"You did this all?" I asked. There was a round table covered with a white cloth and laid out with china and silverware and glasses. In the center stood a small vase with a thick cluster of some blowsy pink flower I thought might be a type of rose.

"Yes," he said. "But the best is in here." Luca indicated a picnic basket like the kind I'd seen at home: wicker, with big handles that dropped down on either side. "I carried it all the way to the roof for us. Aren't you impressed?"

"Um, you live on the top floor," I said, smiling.

Luca pretended to pout. "Ah, yes, that is true. Well, I will just have to impress you with what's inside!"

From the depths of the picnic basket (complete with a checked cloth interior), Luca withdrew three cheeses; a variety of salami and prosciutto; several kinds of olives, some dark and shiny, some wrinkled and brown, others large and bright green. A loaf of bread accompanied our meal, as well as a plate of fresh figs (figs were something I'd never tasted outside a Fig Newton, but I didn't tell him that) and small oranges that were bright red inside.

"Blood oranges," he told me. "These are called Tarocco, from Sicily. I think you can get them in the States, but I am not sure."

"Oh, I hope so," I said, thinking that an orange had never tasted so good.

Our feast certainly wasn't lunch at the Cherry Pit. I couldn't even begin to imagine bringing Luca there, not after experiencing this lovely rooftop meal. Jalapeño poppers; mozzarella sticks; French fries smothered in bright yellow cheese spread. And I realized even then that my old stomping ground was never going to hold the same attraction for me it once had.

Luca turned back to the picnic basket and pulled out a tall, slim bottle of a clear liquid. There was no label on the bottle, but it was stamped with an image of curling vines.

"Have you ever tasted grappa?" he asked.

"No. What is it?"

"It is made from the skins of grapes that have been pressed to make the wine. It must be very clear to be good. And it should be chilled, which is why there is a bag of melting ice in the basket. Don't tell my mother I am such a mess!"

"I won't," I said, wondering if I'd ever have the chance to meet Luca's mother.

Luca poured a small amount of the clear liquid from the bottle into a glass.

"This is made by my uncle. His grandfather taught him. He is very proud of his grappa. You take little sips, like this." Luca demonstrated with his own glass.

I raised my glass to my lips. The clear liquid smelled vaguely acrid. It didn't seem to have much of a taste at all. In some ways, it reminded me of my first reaction to vodka. I knew that I'd tasted something, but I couldn't say what it was.

"Well," I said, "it's not a Bellini."

Luca laughed. "Don't drink it if you don't like it. It's okay. I won't tell my uncle."

"No," I said. "Actually, I do like it. It's very—surprising."

After our lunch on the roof, we went back down to Luca's apartment and made love. If possible, the experience was more powerful than that of the night before. Our intimacy had deepened.

"Do you believe in fate?" I asked afterward, lying in his arms, tracing his beautiful cheek with my fingertip.

"Yes," he said promptly. "I do. I am a romantic. I believe there is much that reason cannot explain. And I do not believe that some things are random. I do not believe that we, you and me, are random."

"Before I met you, I thought it was all—a joke. A lie. Love at first sight, two people meant to be together, soul mates."

"And now?"

"Now—now everything is changed."

"Are you glad that it has changed?" he whispered, kissing me gently.

"Yes," I sighed. "I am."

And at that moment, I was glad.

37

Every human being on this big blue ball we call planet Earth has two things in common: birth and death. Death can and does come in a variety of forms, some relatively painless if not pleasant and others prolonged and rife with suffering. Birth, however, is universally acknowledged to be traumatic for all involved—witnesses, assistants, mother, and, of course, child. Is it, then, any wonder that the role of "mother" has been, is, and most likely always will be associated with agony?
—The Inevitability of Hatred: Or, What to Expect When You Choose Motherhood

I had lunch in the heart of the historic district at a café in the Piazza della Signoria, Florence's most famous square and home to Ammanati's *Fountain of Neptune*. My father had been right. The piazza was swarming with tourists, many of them American, even though my guidebooks had informed me that July and August, not June, were the most popular months for visitation.

I ordered *risotto di frutti di mare*, or risotto with shellfish, accompanied by a glass of Prosecco and followed by a small plate of sliced fresh figs. I bought figs rarely when home. They were hard to find, expensive, and Marina didn't care for them. In fact, I'd never been able to entice her to try one—outside of a Fig Newton, that is.

Marina. Since she'd met Luca, I'd found myself with an awful lot of time for reflection, something I hadn't counted on when planning our Tuscan holiday, something I resented. I hadn't wanted this trip to be about solitary contemplation—I could get enough of that at home. I'd wanted it to be about my daughter and me.

But being a parent is sort of like being an open wound, constantly subject to irritation, with only the dim hope of healing—which implies scarring—to keep you going. Everything and anything can hurt you; you're sensitive beyond reason. At least, I was at that moment, and not for the first time since becoming a mother.

This particular example has stayed with me. Almost a year after Marina's birth—she was born on October 25, at the height of fall; everything was in brilliant color that year, and the weather was of the idyllic autumn kind—I was reading a novel by an obscure Russian writer who at one point quoted Aristotle, of all people, as saying that—in the philosopher's illustrious opinion—mothers are fonder (that was the word chosen as translation; I don't know if it's the best word for the translator to have chosen) of their children than fathers because mothers are certain the children are their own.

That line depressed me for such a long time and for so many reasons. The most obvious one, of course, was its piercingly personal relevance. Hadn't the father of my child accused me of cheating on him with another man? Hadn't he denied paternity and refused to cooperate in my efforts to prove to him that he was, in fact, Marina's father?

Women, Great Men had long ago declared, are by nature untrustworthy, sexually insincere, capricious. They are various, mutable, prone to changing their minds on a whim, careless, and unstable, ever coming and going like the tide, ever waxing and waning like the phases of the moon. Given their flexible natures and unstable characters, it's only natural that women betray their men with rivals. Of course, it follows logically from the unshakable premise.

Except when it doesn't follow. Except when the premise is

flawed, because I am not untrustworthy or unstable, and I never was. I remember how shocked I was when Peter accused me of sleeping around. The charge was so outrageous, so out of the blue, so, I thought, unworthy of Peter, the man I loved so deeply. But then again, I hadn't really known Peter. I'd only thought I'd known him. The real Peter was a stranger, and how blindly in love had I been to follow him around like a cowed dog follows his commanding master?

Enough, I told myself, summoning the waiter. I vowed not to let negative thoughts ruin the rest of my vacation.

That afternoon I visited the Church of San Lorenzo, a place I was certain Marina would have little interest in, especially now that she was preoccupied with Luca. A guidebook informed me that it was probably the oldest religious building in Florence, possibly erected before the year 400.

I tried to focus on the church's interior. I tried to give the works of art the attention they deserved, but I was just too distracted. I was looking at works by Donatello and Bronzino. But I was seeing my suddenly mutable, untrustworthy, and capricious daughter in the arms of a stranger.

38

Dear Answer Lady:

I'm a sixteen-year-old girl and a sophomore in high school. I get okay grades and am on the junior varsity basketball team and sing with my church choir. Everything in my life is awesome except for the fact that the other kids at my school think I'm weird because my mom is my best friend. We do everything together, like go clothes shopping, see movies, and just hang out. What's so wrong with spending time with your mom?

Dear Stepford Daughter:

Unless you want to turn out like the Grey Gardens *gals (look it up if you don't get this reference, either), you need to break away from your mother pronto. It's simply not normal for a mother and teenage daughter to be "best friends." I might even go so far as to suggest it's against the very laws of Nature. Rebel now; throw your dirty underwear at her, contradict everything she says, and try some stomping around and slamming doors. There's plenty of time later for getting along with your mater. (Note to the mother: I have to wonder if you have any friends your own age; if you do, I'm willing to bet they view your relationship with your daughter with some*

*trepidation as well. What the hell are you think-
ing, keeping her in your greedy clutches? Set her
free and get a life already.)*

Monday, June 12

I came out of the bathroom that Monday morning to find
Marina sitting on the edge of her bed, frowning down at the
phone in her hand.

"Jotham?" I asked.

She nodded and snapped the phone closed.

I pulled my robe closer around me and sat on the edge of
my bed, facing her. "Do you want to talk more about—about
what's going on?"

"No." Marina shot to her feet; she looked miserable. "I
never should have said anything. I wish everyone would just
leave me alone. This stupid phone—"

Marina tossed it onto the bed behind her, grabbed her bag,
and headed for the door.

"Where are you going?" I asked, alarmed.

She shook her head, hand already on the doorknob. "I
don't know. Just—out."

"I thought we were going to that cute little pastry place for
breakfast."

"I'm not hungry."

I rose from the bed and took a step toward her. "Will you
be coming back soon?" I asked. "Should I wait for you?"

"I don't know, okay? Just—" And she almost ran from the
room, leaving the door to slam shut behind her.

I didn't like that Marina had run off. I didn't like that she
was without her phone; how could I reach her if she stayed
gone for too long? Short of following her, there was nothing
I could do. Anyway, by the time I dressed, she'd be long gone
from the Via Cavalcanti.

Without enthusiasm I made my way to the pastry shop.

Without appetite, I ate an almond-flavored bun and drank an espresso. All I could think about was my daughter.

A mother can read her child like the proverbial book, but closer than anyone can read and understand words on a page. This can be a real annoyance for the child. I hated when my mother would look at me with "that look," the one that I'd learned to interpret as saying "I know exactly what's bothering you."

True, for a long time my mother could tell what was bothering me. But some years before my Tuscan holiday, her ability to read me so closely had begun to fail. She'd say, "You're worried about such and such, aren't you?" or she'd tell my father, and he'd say, "Your mother says you're worried about such and such," and in 99 percent of the cases, she'd be wrong.

Maybe I had changed; maybe she had; maybe time had just worn thinner the groove between us. Whatever the case, I was glad for the privacy. I didn't miss her close scrutiny even though I knew that most times it was done out of love. I simply didn't need my mother knowing me so intimately.

And until Florence, I'd been sure that Marina didn't need me to know her so intimately, either. When she was only just twelve she'd made it clear in no uncertain terms that I was not the boss of her (never mind that I was, of course, until she was eighteen) and that as much as I thought I could, I could not, in fact, read her mind. Since then I'd learned to wait for Marina to come to me when she needed to talk about a problem.

But now there was Luca, and though Marina was reluctant to talk, I knew that she was deeply troubled and that she needed me. Maybe it was finally time for me to make an approach. The worst that could happen was that she'd reject my overture. And a mother is no stranger to rejection.

39

Stop taking her calls. Move out of town and leave no forwarding address. Legally change your name. Undergo extensive plastic surgery on the off chance that you'll run into her while living incognito on the beaches of Borneo. Trust me: save yourself the time, money, and bother. None of it is going to work. Your mother will find you, either in the flesh or by haunting your memory until you once again acknowledge her perpetual and absolute presence in your life.

    —There's No Running Away from the Facts: A
      Mother is Forever

Marina returned to the hotel after about an hour to find me waiting for her.

"I'm sorry," she said immediately. "I just had to walk. I felt like I was going to explode."

"You forgot your phone," I said. "There was no way I could find you. Please don't forget it again."

Marina smiled tentatively. "You've changed your mind about that phone, haven't you?"

I smiled back. "Somewhat. Look, I have an idea. You're not meeting Luca until later, right?"

She nodded. Luca had told Marina he had to be at his father's office all that morning for a very important meeting. Silently I prayed that his "important meeting" didn't involve another unsuspecting young woman from abroad.

"Then let's go somewhere and just sit and stare and do nothing for a while. No sightseeing. No guidebooks. Okay?"

"Sure," she said. "That's pretty much all I have the energy to do now, anyway."

A half hour later found us sitting on the steps of a decidedly unspectacular old church in a decidedly unfashionable piazza. And in my bag was the one and only photo ever taken of Peter and me.

Marina tilted her face to the sun; her bag was lumped on her lap like a sleeping cat. And in the welcome quiet I thought back to the time just after Peter's exodus.

In those first few unimaginably difficult weeks, I couldn't bear to look at the artifacts of our relationship—not that there was much to look at. Peter hadn't been a gift-giving sort of person; maybe that should have alerted me to something about his real nature.

About two months after Peter had left for California, I finally asked my mother to put the things I'd collected during my relationship with Peter in a box, which my father then brought up to the attic. "Just throw it all away," my mother had urged. "Just get it all out of here. What do you need with memories of that man?"

Well, doing away with a cardboard box of mementos wasn't going to do away with the memories. Besides, I thought that maybe I needed the memories to linger because the fact was that Peter and I were going to have a child, and maybe, someday, I would owe it to that child to remember her father for her.

Then, after a particularly bad phone call, there followed a raging impulse to burn the meager contents of that stupid box. It was about five months into the pregnancy, and I was feeling very low one evening. Against every bit of good judgment, I called Peter at his dorm. It hadn't been hard to track him that far; I knew what law school he was attending, and I simply called information for the town. I knew he'd have his own phone. He wasn't the type to share a hall phone.

He picked up on the second ring, enough time for me to regret having called. Maybe I should have just hung up the moment I heard his voice. But I didn't. Instead, I started to cry, a pitiful, whimpering noise. "Oh, shit," Peter had said wearily. "Look, I told you I don't need this. I want nothing to do with you. Stop calling me. Do you hear me?" I couldn't answer. Peter hung up. Clearly out of my mind, I dialed again, and of course he didn't pick up. When I tried again the following day, I got a recording saying the number had been changed to a new and unlisted one.

The neutral, mechanized voice informing me that Peter had gotten an unlisted number to avoid me got through in a way that his own harsh words hadn't been able to. I didn't try to contact him again until after Marina's birth.

When Marina was approaching her first birthday, I started to think about what she might want to know when she was old enough to ask about her father. I thought about what I had of Peter's that I might want to show her. I thought about what might help her to know a little bit about the man who was her biological father, if not her father in practice.

The mix tape Peter had given me a week into our relationship would reveal nothing of importance about him. It was made up of the current popular hits; there was nothing remotely soulful, poetic, or individual about it.

Love letters might illuminate a person's character. The problem was, Peter had never written me a love letter. In that lopsided cardboard box, the only evidence of Peter's own words—of his handwriting—was the title he'd given to the mix tape: "Cool Club Mix."

The only truth the contents of that box proved was that I'd been a typical romantic girl: a box of matches from the Jamaica Plain pub where Peter and I had first met; the program from a play we saw at the American Repertory Theatre in Harvard Square; a few lines of bad poetry I'd scribbled when Peter had gone to visit a friend in New York one weekend and I'd sat home miserable and lonely.

The cardboard box, the repository of our relationship, did, however, contain two items of potential interest—two photos, one of Peter and one of us together. I'd taken the one of Peter on the bridge in the Public Garden. He hadn't suggested taking a picture of me, and I hadn't asked him to. But that was typical of both our relationship and my infatuated, deeply uncritical state of mind.

A friend of Peter's had taken the photo of the two of us together. The friend, whose name I've forgotten, and his girlfriend, whose name I strangely do remember—Sally—had suggested a picnic at the Esplanade. I spent a lot of time and too much money putting together a picnic lunch for the four of us—a round of good Brie, a bunch of shiny black grapes, two fresh baguettes, a selection of fancy mustards, a jar of cornichons. Sally brought a bottle of wine. Her boyfriend, Peter's friend, brought a bag of pretzels. Peter brought nothing.

I'd showed Marina the photo of Peter on the bridge when she asked to see a picture of her father and not before. She was about ten, maybe eleven. I remember her staring hard at the photo, saying nothing.

"You look a lot like him," I said finally, quietly.

Marina had only nodded.

"Do you want to keep the photo, or should I?"

"No," she said, her eyes still glued to the image of her father. "I'll keep it."

Later, I'd found the photo in Marina's jewelry box; I wasn't snooping, just returning a bracelet to its proper place while dusting the bureau. For all I knew, the photo was still there; I never opened the box again.

The picture of Peter and me together I'd held back. It was, I felt, too personal, too revelatory, and the memories it evoked were for a long time too raw. But just days before our departure from Boston I'd made the decision to bring the photo to Italy, hoping that the time had finally come for Marina to see and acknowledge the look of adoration in her mother's eyes as she gazed up at a laughing Peter, who, not surprisingly, was directing his attention entirely at the camera. I hoped that by seeing the photo Marina would better understand why I had done what I'd done—first chosen to go through with the pregnancy and then tried again and again to persuade her father to acknowledge her.

What I hadn't counted on when considering this moment of (hopeful) bonding was Luca. But as I thought about sharing the photo with my daughter, I came to think that Marina's understanding of my past might actually be deepened by the experience of her current romantic situation.

"This was a good idea, Mom," Marina said, recalling me to the moment. "I feel a bit better than I did this morning. Less—frantic. Less like a crazy person."

"Good." I checked my watch. In less than an hour, Marina would be off to meet Luca. "So, I want to show you something," I said.

"Okay."

I didn't hear much interest in my daughter's tone, but for all she knew I was going to break my promise, drag out one of my guidebooks and lecture on yet another portrait of yet another power-corrupt Medici.

I took the small, padded envelope from my bag and handed it to Marina.

"What's this?" she asked.

"Open it. You'll see."

Carefully, Marina opened the gummy flap, peered inside, and withdrew a three-by-five inch photo.

"It's your father and me," I said unnecessarily, nervously.

Marina stared down at the photo for what seemed like ages before turning back to me.

"My God, Mom, I can't believe you never showed this to me."

"I wasn't sure ... I wasn't sure I could," I said. "Until now. I wasn't sure you'd even want to see it."

"Of course I'd want to see it," she said, staring back down

at the photo. "It's a picture of my parents, maybe the only picture of you two together. Unless, of course, Peter has one."

"No," I said definitely. "He doesn't."

Marina continued to study the photo intensely. "You look—you look like you're one hundred percent totally in love. You look so happy."

"Yes," I said carefully, responding only to her first comment. "I was in love."

Marina murmured something; I didn't ask her to repeat it.

"Does it help," I said, "seeing this? I mean, does it explain a bit about why I tried for so long to get him to acknowledge you?"

She didn't answer for a moment, and then said, "I don't know. I think so."

Marina handed the photo back to me.

"Do you want to keep it?" I asked her.

"No," she said promptly. "You should. Thank you for showing it to me, Mom."

"You're welcome."

Marina checked her watch. It had been a gift from my parents for her birthday the previous autumn. Then she looked at me, and I thought I saw something like sadness in her eyes. She touched my arm briefly.

"I've got to go," she said. "I'm sorry, Mom. I—"

"It's all right," I said. "Really."

Watching my daughter hurry off to meet her lover, I wondered if by showing her the photo of her mother in love—not happy necessarily, but in love—I'd inadvertently pushed her even closer to Luca. Maybe showing her the photo had been a very stupid thing. But it was too late to do anything about it.

I took one last, lingering look at the photograph of Peter and me. Yes, it had lost its power. I slid it back into the envelope.

Later that afternoon, I visited the Basilica di Santa Croce in the Piazza Santa Croce. I didn't feel guilty about sightseeing without Marina; I wasn't about to wait at the hotel for her *affaire de coeur* to run its course. I might have been waiting a very long time.

My guidebook informed me that Santa Croce is the largest Franciscan church in all of Italy. I saw for myself that its vast interior contained beautiful examples of stained-glass windows and frescoes.

One of Brunelleschi's most important works is also at Santa Croce, a chapel called Cappella dei Piazzi that, according to the guidebooks, is geometrically perfect. Designed in the 1430s and worked on by Brunelleschi from 1442 to 1446, the Cappella wasn't completed until after this death.

I paid a visit to the tombs of Michelangelo, Machiavelli, and Galileo, and then moved on to visit the memorial tomb of Dante Alighieri, one of the places I'd most wanted to witness on my Tuscan holiday.

I slipped one of my guidebooks from my bag—which by now was showing serious signs of wear at the sewn seams— and opened it to a marked page. Yes, the poet had died in 1321 and was buried in Ravenna, his native city of Florence still at the time of his death unwilling to grant the return of its most famous political exile. But eventually Florence relented, and though it several times requested the return of Dante's remains, the city of Ravenna refused. So in 1829, this memorial tomb was erected in the Basilica di Santa Croce.

I looked back up at the tomb, familiar from my reading with the line carved across its front. Onorate l'altissimo poeta. Roughly translated, it reads "Honor the most exalted poet." It's a line taken from the fourth canto of Dante's own *L'Inferno*, spoken in reference to the great Roman poet, Virgil.

I looked back down to my book to read the second half of the poet's line, interestingly absent from his tomb. This translation rendered the line as follows: "His spirit, which had left us, returns."

I closed the book and looked back up at the memorial. I wondered what it must be like to be exiled from the home you love, from the very land, the people, the sights and sounds and smells that have informed your life since birth. It made me very sad to imagine a life lived in that sort of reverse prison, all the world open before you except the one small corner in which your body and your soul crave to reside.

I was deeply moved by Dante's plight. It made me think of other sorts of exile, too—like how Peter had exiled Marina, banished her from his life, set her adrift without a father— and suddenly, I felt adrift myself, in need of a deep connection with another human being. And the only person I knew who would understand just how I was feeling was Rob.

I fervently wished I had Marina's phone, though of course I wouldn't have used it in the church. Instead, I reached into my bag for the post card I'd begun to write that first afternoon in Florence.

"I wish you were here with me," I wrote. "I wish we were sharing this place together."

I mailed the post card from the hotel later that afternoon, wishing futilely it could reach him by nightfall.

40

Dear Answer Lady:

My mother is always co-opting my friends! It's been going on for years now, ever since I made the mistake of introducing her to a friend from the office. Before I knew it, my mother was calling this woman and making plans, and suddenly my friend didn't have time for me because she was spending so much time with my mother! It's happened every time my mother meets someone important in my life. And the worse part is that now I have no one to complain to about my mother because all my so-called friends think she's great! Help!

Dear Dumb Daughter:

One: stop introducing your friends to your mother. Clearly, she has a need to poach from your life (some sort of convoluted need to "inhabit" you or to keep you from truly moving on and away from her) and isn't going to change. Two: be thankful she hasn't started to steal your boyfriends.

Luca had called to say that he was running late. He apologized profusely. Honestly, I barely heard him, so focused were my thoughts on the photograph my mother had just showed me.

I waited for him at Lorenzo's, at the table where he'd waited for me that first day. And while sipping a coffee, I thought about what I'd experienced that morning on the steps of a crumbling church.

The photo of my mother and my father had affected me deeply. I remembered the look on my mother's young face and knew for a certainty that I'd never gazed at my fiancé with that look of love and adoration. And until then, I'd always thought that was a good thing. That look, that feeling of complete devotion, could only get you in trouble, and I was living proof of that.

Still . . . sitting at Lorenzo's, waiting for Luca, I found myself wondering for the very first time if I could spend the rest of my life with someone I didn't feel passionately about. And I never had felt passionately about Jotham, not even in the beginning. Our relationship had always been more like that between friends, which I knew was supposed to be a good thing, especially for the long run.

Still . . . There was Luca. Though I'd known him only a few short days, when I looked into his eyes, it was with love, with adoration, with devotion. I could feel the emotion on my face. I couldn't hide my love from him or from the world, and I didn't want to hide it.

For the first time in my life I recognized my mother in me and was scared. We had more in common after all than our bad eyesight and the fact that we each looked hideous in orange.

Suddenly, I hardly recognized myself. Only days earlier I'd been Marina Caldwell, engaged to her long-time boyfriend, busily planning a contented suburban future. And now, in another country, in another city, waiting for another man, I felt I was almost another woman entirely.

And how could I reconcile those two women? Was it even possible?

I'd always hated feeling confused about anything, from little things like what to have for lunch at Friendly's (though in the end I always got the same thing, the tuna melt) to big things like which college to go to. But that decision hadn't been hard to make in the end. Jotham was going to Graham, so I'd gone, too. Just like whether or not to go to France that summer. Jotham had made that decision for me as well.

But this was different. Any decision about Luca and Jotham—any decision about me—was going to have to be my own. The problem was that my head, split in two as it was, wasn't being very helpful, and my heart had totally betrayed me. And I realized that for the first time in my life I was very much alone—and that it was all my doing.

I couldn't talk to my friends for advice or consolation. Allison and Jessica would go straight to Jordan and Jason, and they in turn would go straight to Jotham. They were our best friends. We were going to be in each other's wedding parties. There was simply no way Allison or Jessica would (no way that they could?) understand what I was going through, and there was simply no way they'd keep a secret like this from Jotham.

Grandpa was entirely out of the question, as was Rob. I could never talk about my feelings for a man to another man. And Grandma wasn't a possibility, either. I knew she'd be keenly disappointed in me for "straying" and wasn't sure I could live with her disappointment.

And then an idea struck me. My mother had shown me the photo for a reason. She'd wanted me to see, to really see, the truth about my father and mother. She'd hoped that by providing evidence of a sort, she could prove that her feelings had been real and valid and undeniable.

Now, I would show her Luca, because maybe then she would understand, as I had understood. I needed her to see us together, to prove to her—and maybe, just maybe, to me?—that what Luca and I had was also real and valid—and above all, undeniable.

I spotted Luca approaching on his Vespa and jumped to my feet, very, very glad to see him. I threw my arms around his neck and kissed him.

"Oh," he said with a grin, "so you have missed me? That is good. I have missed you, too."

"Yes," I said, "I've missed you. And, Luca, I have a favor to ask of you. And it's very, very important."

41

You thought you were teaching your child how to eat healthily. He remembers being mocked by classmates for eating "weird" food like yogurt and "wimpy" food like salad. You thought you were protecting your child by not allowing her to see the R-rated movie all of her friends were seeing. She remembers the humiliation of being called a "baby" and worse. Face it: no matter what you do in the name of good parenting will be interpreted by your child as a failure.
—Motherhood: The Impossible Profession

Tuesday, June 13

It's safe to say that meeting my daughter's lover constituted one of the most uncomfortable thirty minutes of my life. To be fair, I think it was awkward for him, too, if his knocking over his espresso cup twice was any indication of discomfort. I'm sure the café and the street on which it sat was bustling with morning travelers, but my attention was entirely on our dramatic trio.

"Mrs. Caldwell," he said, clearing his throat (more nerves?), "what do you think of our city?"

"It's very interesting," I said, sticking to my plan of being polite but restrained, determined not to upset Marina but equally as determined not to give this man an inch. I didn't want him thinking for one moment that I approved of this affair—as if my approval mattered to either of them.

"I think Florence is a beautiful city," Marina said. She smiled up at Luca reassuringly and squeezed his arm. I felt uncomfortable seeing her touch a man other than Jotham with such familiarity. I'd often wondered what it must have been like for Marina to see me with Tony or any other man after Rob. Now I knew for sure what my daughter had felt; I sent her a silent apology.

"I have never been to Boston. I hear it is also a very interesting and beautiful city."

Poor young man, I thought. He could have been sulky and aloof, he could have paraded his unconcern, but he was trying very hard to make a decent impression. "Yes," I said. "Boston is a fine town."

"Luca's father sometimes has business in New York," Marina said. "Luca's been there, too. And all over Europe."

Luca smiled down fondly (was it real or feigned?) at my daughter. "Well," he said, "not to every place. Yet. Someday I hope to say I have been to every truly important city in Europe."

"My mother's been to Paris and London."

Luca looked to me eagerly. "Ah, yes, Mrs. Caldwell? And did you enjoy your visits?"

Could I just run away, I wondered. Could I just abandon this excruciatingly boring and awkward and absurd conversation? "Yes," I said. "I enjoyed the visits very much."

Marina put her napkin on the table and rose. "I'll be right back," she said. "I need to go to the ladies' room."

I begged with my eyes not to be left alone with Luca, but Marina ignored my plea and went off.

I wondered what Luca and I were going to talk about now. The weather? Crop rotation? The addition of Lycra spandex to women's jeans? Some other blandly safe topic?

"Mrs. Caldwell, I—"

"Yes?" I said. It would be a lie to say I wasn't enjoying his discomfort. He should sweat. He should work. When he wasn't making my daughter ecstatic, he was making her miserable. Let alone what he was doing to her mother.

"Your daughter, she is very special to me."

All right. It would also be a lie to say that I didn't approve of his seeming sensitivity.

"And to me," I said.

"Of course. Please understand I will do nothing to harm her."

Too late for that, I thought. But maybe fate was to blame, not the lovers. Anyway, Peter certainly had never promised as much to my parents. The few times he'd met them he was downright insolent. Of course, at the time, infatuated as I was, his boorish behavior escaped my notice.

I nodded.

"Marina, she says that you like the paintings most, yes? In the museums and the galleries."

"Yes," I said. "I enjoy art, especially painting."

"She tells me she would like to learn more from you. She says you are always reading to know more."

Marina wanted to learn more from me? Then what about all the wisecracks regarding my guidebooks?

"Yes," I said. "I like to read."

Luca smiled. "Me, too. I am always reading. When I was a child, my mother, she would take the books away and tell me to go outside and play."

Marina was right. He did have a spectacular smile—and I wondered how many unsuspecting women he'd lured to his no-doubt well-appointed apartment using that smile alone. It was an unfair thought; I really knew nothing of his character, only that he claimed to feel badly about seducing another man's fiancé.

"A balance of intellectual and physical endeavor is important," I said neutrally. Though try telling that to Jotham, who proudly (I thought) professed to read only what was absolutely required of him for school and no more. Oh, yes, I thought,

Jotham will make a wonderful lawyer someday, just brimming with wit and wisdom.

Marina returned then, glancing from me to Luca as if to ascertain no blood had been drawn. I was glad for her return; it distracted me from the sudden notion of tossing both of her lovers off a very high building.

"Are we ready to go?" she asked.

I stood abruptly. "Yes," I said. "I—" I what? Had an appointment with my hair stylist? A lunch date with a client? A meeting with my lawyer?

Luca spoke to the waiter and left a few coins on the table.

Marina hugged me—it was uncharacteristic of her to be so demonstrative with me, particularly in public—and whispered, "Thanks, Mom."

I didn't know what to say, so I simply hugged her back.

Luca shook my hand while looking directly in my eyes. His initial self-consciousness had worn off, and the fact that I hadn't threatened him with bodily harm seemed to have given him a degree of confidence.

I watched as Luca and Marina got on his Vespa. With a honk of the horn and a wave, they drove off, leaving me staring after them until they were safely out of sight.

As I left the small outdoor café, I couldn't help but think about Jotham—who had never, I was sure, been on a motor scooter. And though I'd never been a huge fan, I fervently hoped that whatever happened, Marina was careful with him. It's so terribly easy to be careless with a person's heart; even with the best of intentions we hurt each other all the time.

On my own once again, I decided to visit the Giardini di Boboli, a large park on a hill in the middle of Florence, behind the Pitti Palace. And while I came prepared to enjoy the green expanse, the Fontana del Bacco, boasting a particularly fat and happy god of wine, and the Neptune fountain, among other interesting features, my attention insisted on returning to the conversation I'd had with Marina the night before, when she'd come to me with the extraordinary request that I meet her lover.

My first instinct had been to reject the notion. I felt sure that nothing but extreme discomfort, even ugliness, could come of such a meeting. But after Marina had explained her need for the get-together and the way in which the idea had come to her—it was that photo of her father and me, after all—I agreed.

Even after that she'd gone on about how she would never get over Luca, and I'd let her talk. There'd been no point in trying to comfort her, to assure her with words that would surely sound like platitudes. In the depth of despair, despair is certain.

I sat on a bench in sight of three teenaged boys playing with a soccer ball. I wondered if they were allowed to play in the gardens; I wondered if they cared; I wondered if years from now, when they were middle-aged, married fathers, they would remember this carefree morning in June. Who was it that said that without forgetting it's impossible to live at all? Whoever said it was right.

But that lesson is one you don't learn for some time. When you're young, you're absolutely convinced that you're going to remember forever, and in vivid detail, every moment of joy or heartbreak, whether it be of your own making or caused by some outside force. You're absolutely convinced that the moment will utterly define the rest of your life.

And then, over time, you start to forget, not every detail, but a lot of them, and some time after that, the emotional impact starts to dull, and after that there come days when you don't consciously think about the moment of joy or heartbreak you were so certain would actively pursue you to the grave.

I'm no brain surgeon, but I'm pretty sure the memory isn't really gone. It's somewhere deep in your brain, but you find yourself living quite well in spite of it. Some people get scared when they reach this stage, scared of what they see as a void in their lives, and they search for that memory and drag it back to the foreground of consciousness, and once again they become miserable—safe in what they know. Some people are afraid to abandon the bad because they've allowed it to define them. And when you're in recovery from a negative experience, you've got a wonderful excuse for not having a life.

A fat tabby cat paraded imperially by, pausing only to rub its sun-warmed body against my calves before parading on. The teenaged soccer players flung themselves to the green grass for a break, oblivious to the middle-aged woman analyzing her life.

It had, of course, occurred to me from time to time that I might be guilty of clinging to the past as a way to block my progress in the future. It was possible that I'd avoided marrying Rob because I hadn't entirely let go of my identity as Abandoned Woman. But for the first time, sitting in the beautiful Giardini di Boboli, I felt a bit sick to think that I might have allowed myself to take refuge from my life in a stereotype.

A very old couple strolled by very slowly, arm in arm, the man with a cane, a scarf covering the woman's head. I watched them until they'd settled on the bench a few yards from mine, their worn faces turned up to the sun. Would that be Rob and me someday, I wondered. Or would I be walking painfully alone, my arm entwined with no one's?

I got up from the bench and found the Viale dei Cipressi, the Avenue of Cypresses. With its sun-dappled path and its random display of marble statues, it was even more beautiful than the pictures in the guidebooks had led me to expect.

And as I walked, I shook off thoughts of my past as well as those of my future (not easy) and turned once again to Marina's predicament. As for her absolute conviction that she'd never forget Luca, that she'd never survive his memory, well, there was no point in arguing with her about that. It was true enough, anyway; she probably would never forget him, not entirely. But someday she'd be surprised to realize that what was once so overwhelmingly important had become just another part of the backdrop of her life. And she'd feel, as everyone does, a strange mixture of sadness, disappointment, and melancholy. But most of all, she would feel relief.

42

Dear Answer Lady:

I have no children of my own, for reasons no more glamorous than that I haven't yet met a man I want to marry and I don't want to accept the challenge of single parenthood. I do, however, have a niece of whom I'm very fond. She's a joy to be with, and I love every moment we spend together. In some ways I feel as if she is my daughter. But every once in a while, someone, sometimes a colleague or even a stranger I meet at a party, will make what I feel is a terribly rude and thoughtless comment about nieces, nephews, godchildren and the like not being "as good as" one's own children. I feel as if people just don't value the relationships between adults and children not their biological offspring. Am I being overly sensitive?

Dear Adoring Aunt:

I think it was Oprah Winfrey (and no doubt countless others) who said that "biology is the least of what makes someone a mother," and in my humble opinion, no truer words were ever spoken. No, you are not being overly sensitive. Those rude and thoughtless commentators are being terribly insensitive and blind to the astonishing range of human emotional experience. Go ahead and love your niece as "your own." I just

*hope she's smart enough to know how lucky she
is to have you as her aunt.*

I returned to the Piazza della Signoria for lunch but chose a
café new to me, one from where I could clearly see on the
Loggia della Signoria the reproduction of Michelangelo's *David*.

I ordered a plate of *crostino*, toasted bread with chicken
livers (cholesterol be damned), and a bowl of *cozzi al vino
bianco,* or mussels in white wine.

Sitting at the table directly to my left was another woman
dining alone. She could have been anywhere from mid forties
to late fifties. I've never been able to pin the age of people in
middle life; it seems to me that people begin to show signs of
aging at a remarkably different rate.

We finished our meals at about the same time, though she'd
been seated when I arrived. When the waiter had brought us
each a coffee, the woman smiled over at me.

"How was your lunch?" she asked in a decidedly Mid-
western accent.

"Great. And yours?"

"Fantastic." She leaned over and extended her hand. "I'm
Lydia Dunbar, from Chicago."

"Elizabeth Caldwell," I said, extending my own hand,
"from Boston. Nice to meet you. Are you here with—" Suddenly I realized what an awkward question I'd been about to
ask. "I'm sorry," I said hurriedly. "It's none of my business."

"I'm traveling on my own, actually," she said, seemingly
not offended. "I've taken a leave of absence from my job. Believe me, it was long overdue. I've got two months to travel
through Italy and France."

"That sounds amazing. And a bit daunting."

Lydia laughed. "Oh, yes, it's both. Especially since it's the
first time I've traveled alone since college. Thirty years ago. I
wasn't sure I still had it in me."

"The energy?"

"That, and the courage," she said. "The ability to take each adventure as it comes and not to panic. The ability to break my routine. The ability to think on my feet outside of my secure boundaries."

"Yes. Travel can be a serious undertaking, and a life-changing one. I hope you're enjoying it."

Lydia laughed. "I'm loving every minute of it, including the bumps in the road."

Yes, bumps could be managed. Hurdles could be—well, hurdled.

"In case you're wondering," Lydia said then, "I'm divorced. Ten years now. No kids. You?"

Her straightforward manner charmed me. "Never married, actually," I told her. "One daughter. She's here with me. Well, obviously not at the moment."

"How old?"

"Twenty-one. She just graduated from college. The trip is her present from me."

Lydia eyed me shrewdly. "So, where is she?"

I hesitated, then realized there was no point in lying. "Well," I said, "if you must know, she's off with her Florentine lover."

"Huh. And how do you feel about that?"

"Abandoned," I admitted. "How's that for honesty?"

"The young don't understand loyalty the way we do."

"I know. And the funny thing is, I was the one who wanted her to live life a little. To see other men before settling down. She's engaged, you see. To her first and only boyfriend."

"Wow," Lydia said with an impressive whistle. "She's going to remember this trip all her life, that's for sure."

"I just hope the memories are good ones. Though I can't believe they won't be mixed up with—sadness."

Lydia was silent. I wondered if she was remembering a pivotal moment in her own life, a moment in which the world around her flipped over and she suddenly found herself facing an entirely new direction.

"So," she asked abruptly, "if you don't mind my asking, where's her father?"

"Darned if I know. Well, last I heard, California. He didn't stick around for long when he found out I was pregnant."

"How manly of him."

"Yes, well . . ."

"And good for you for having the child. What's her name, by the way?"

"Marina. I liked the sound of it."

"Beautiful name," she said. "So, this fiancé, is he a father substitute?"

"Hard to say. He's only twenty-two, but he is rather—paternal, in the not-so-nice ways. He can be bossy. And overprotective. And controlling."

Lydia pretended to shudder. "Yikes. Let's hope she's having a rollicking good time with this Florentine lover. Sounds like she deserves it."

"What about you?" I asked, emboldened by her forward nature. "Anyone after the husband?"

"Here and there. But I wouldn't tie the knot again. Didn't, actually, until I was thirty-five. Things weren't bad at first, but they got bad over time. It's just not worth it to me, to go through all that again. Maybe if the marriage had ended on a better note. But the nastiness put me off."

"Oh. I'm sorry."

"Don't be. But what about you?" she asked. "Someone special?"

I gave her the outlines of my long relationship with Rob, and I discovered, at the ripe old age of forty-two, the pleasure of telling one's story to a stranger. It's a relief to be totally honest without the "repercussion" of friendships. Which is not to deny the glory of friendship. But this stranger would hear my story and take it away with her, in a small way relieving me of the burden that is my particular life. Friends, while essential, remind you of your story by their very presence, and there are times when you'd just like to forget—and to be forgotten.

"You're lucky," Lydia said plainly. "Oh, I'm not saying I think your life is a bed of roses. No one's is. But if you're being straight with me, it sounds like you and this Rob person have something good going."

"Yes. I'm being straight, and, yes, I am lucky. It took me a while to realize just how lucky."

"We never know what we have until it's threatened or lost. We're a sorry lot, human beings."

I laughed. "Aren't we though!"

Lydia sighed, stretched, and began to gather her belongings. "Well," she said, "I must be off. Can't spend every moment of my sabbatical sitting on my butt in a café, though the temptation is huge."

"It was very nice meeting you," I said sincerely, offering her my hand.

We shook heartily, and she was off, camera slung over her chest, sun hat at a jaunty angle, seemingly unencumbered by the past, both the good and the bad memories. Unencumbered. Yes, I thought, maybe it was time for me to further shed some of the proverbial baggage I'd been lugging around for so long.

Like the fact that I believed that Peter's abandoning of Marina and me had largely defined our lives to date and colored—tainted?—our mother/daughter relationship. He was the absence that haunted us, in some ways more powerful an influence than if he'd stuck around and done the right thing.

Suddenly I remembered an incident that took place when Marina was about four. I'd heard through the grapevine that the Duncans had moved away, retired to someplace in the south. So when I came upon them in the produce section of the local grocery store, I was surprised.

It was a strange moment, one of those moments when you feel more like you're part of a movie or a play, one of those big, dramatic, well-scripted moments you rarely enjoy, even if the outcome is innocuous. There we stood, my daughter and me, only a few yards from the family that had disowned us. The woman frowning at the peach in her hand was Marina's grandmother. The man staring up at the ceiling, obviously bored, was Marina's grandfather.

A crazy idea came to me. I'd go up to the Duncans and introduce Marina. Let them see for themselves that their son had lied when he'd sworn he wasn't my daughter's father. I'd throw Marina in their faces, so to speak, and let them live with the shame.

But it wasn't in me to do something so soap-operatic. Besides, I thought with a growing sense of panic, what if, after realizing that Marina was in fact their flesh and blood, they tried to wrest her away from me? Stranger things had happened; you read about bizarre custody cases in *People* magazine all the time. And maybe the Duncans would cite my aggressive behavior as one reason Marina should be taken from me, because wouldn't approaching them be in some way an act of aggression?

It quickly became clear that the best thing for me to do was to get us out of there. Being a good mother meant protecting my daughter at any cost, even at the cost of her never meeting her paternal grandparents—not that she'd know who it was she was meeting, not that she would recognize in their features herself or the father she'd never known.

I grabbed Marina's hand and hurried out of the produce section. Marina protested, more because that's what a child does when mom changes course than for any outstanding love of vegetables, and as we scurried away I wondered if Peter's parents had heard Marina's voice and turned curiously to watch the young mother dragging her child away from the pyramid of oranges. And if they had seen me, had they recognized me? I thought it unlikely. After all, they'd only met me once years before and briefly at that. Peter and I had stopped by their house one Saturday afternoon for a reason I now forget. Mr. and Mrs. Duncan had been eating lunch in the well-appointed kitchen and hadn't seemed pleased to be interrupted.

Still, afterward, I couldn't let go of the feeling that the Duncans had seen and recognized me. For weeks I lived in an alarming state of nervousness, half expecting a call from the Duncans' lawyer, but I heard nothing from them and saw them no more around town. After about a month, the anxiety was finally gone.

Peter Duncan had been the cause of a lot of unhappiness in the lives of my family.

But no more. Sitting in Florence's most famous piazza, I determined not to allow the man to influence my life for one minute more. Easier said than done, of course, but I imagined Lydia Dunbar of Chicago saying "Well, Elizabeth, every journey begins with a first step. Enjoy the trip!"

43

Everybody's mother makes a few mistakes. Look at Hamlet's mother, Gertrude, for example. Could she have made a worse choice of a second husband? (Okay, Gertrude is a character created by a man, but you get my drift.) I mean, she marries the man who killed her beloved husband—a man who is her husband's own brother? Hellooooo! Let's everyone cut our mothers some slack here, okay? Everyone makes mistakes. Why should mothers be held to a higher standard than anyone else?
   —The Burden of Meeting an Impossible Standard:
      Or, It Sucks Being a Mom

"Luca's birthday is only three days before mine. Isn't that interesting?"

"No," I said. "Not really."

Marina didn't seem to have noticed the rudeness of my response. "I mean, it's a coincidence," she said. "Maybe it helps explain why we're so drawn to each other. We're the same sun sign."

We were having an early dinner; no long, lingering courses that night, as Marina was off again that evening to meet her lover. I'm sure the food was fine, but my notes from that night reveal nothing more than the names of the dishes we ordered.

"Since when do you go in for astrology?" I said. "I thought

you considered all of that stuff a waste of time. Numerology, palm reading, channeling. Mystical nonsense, you've always said. Just schemes for charlatans out to make money."

"Well, I did consider it all nonsense," Marina admitted, "but Luca's been telling me some really amazing stories about this psychic friend of his, and, I don't know, it makes you wonder."

I conquered a nasty urge to ask what Jotham would think about her change of mind. I wondered briefly if my sudden foul mood was due to my having drunk a glass of wine too quickly on an empty stomach or to something else entirely. I didn't really care.

Marina seemed not to notice my lack of response; either that or she hadn't really been expecting one, so wrapped up was she in her lover's hobbies and interests.

"Anyway," she went on, "he's going to have his friend do a full reading for my birthday this October. I just have to give him the basic information, as much as I know, like exactly where and when I was born, and he'll do the rest."

And how, I thought, is Jotham going to feel about his fiancée receiving a special birthday package from her Florentine fling?

"Did I ever tell you how I spent my twenty-second birthday?" I asked, aware of but choosing to ignore a sneaking suspicion that my motivation for telling the story was less than mature. It was entirely possible that I was trying to make Marina feel guilty for leaving me alone every night since having met Luca. Shameful behavior on my part, a pitiful bid for attention.

"Uh, no," she said. "At least, I don't think so."

"Well, I was seven months' pregnant, and I remember August fourth fell on a Friday that year. I hadn't seen my three closest college friends since just after graduation—everyone had jobs or was traveling—so I thought it would be fun to have them over that evening. I wasn't much into going out, you see. The weather was terrible that summer, seriously hot and humid, and it really bothered me."

"Mmm."

It was impossible to know if she'd been listening. Marina's thoughts were so easily distracted since she'd met Luca. I understood it. I resented it.

"Are you listening to me?" I asked.

"Yes, yes, the weather was terrible, the humidity bothered you. Go on."

"Anyway, I called Heather and Christine and Maura, my three closest friends from college, and invited them for dinner. I couldn't drink, and I didn't have much of an appetite because of the heat, but I promised beer and wine and pizza, fun stuff, nothing fancy. Everyone said yes, great, they'd love to come, it'd been so long since we'd all hung out together."

"Uh-huh?"

"Well, I got all the supplies, and since it turned out to be oddly cool that day, I set everything up in the backyard—Grandma and Grandpa were at the Jacksons' summer camp that week. My friends were due to arrive at seven. Then, about four, Heather called, saying she didn't feel well and didn't think she should come and make me sick. Because of the baby, of course."

"That was nice of her," Marina said.

"Yes, well, about an hour later, Maura called. Seems she, too, didn't feel good and couldn't make it."

Marina shrugged. "Maybe something was going around. Some sort of bug. People can get really nasty summer colds."

"Well, the thought certainly occurred to me. And I thought, okay, I'm disappointed, but they were just being responsible, not wanting me to catch any germs. And then Christine called with the exact same excuse. It just seemed strange that all three would get sick at the same time and wait until a few hours before the party before letting me know they couldn't make it."

"I can see why you were disappointed," Marina said. "No one likes to spend her birthday alone."

"Especially when she's pregnant." And the father of her child has run off. And her parents aren't even home.

"I guess. So what did you do with all the food?" Marina asked.

"It was too late to cancel the pizza order, so it all went into the fridge. And I was so depressed I just left everything out in the yard, tablecloth, place settings, glasses, everything, and went to bed. The real kicker is that it rained heavily that night. You can imagine the mess I found in the morning."

Where, I thought, were the violins? Where was the keening chorus, the wailing women?

Marina leaned over and patted my hand. "I'm sorry, Mom," she said with the voice you use when consoling a child who's overly saddened by the fact that the grocery store is out of chocolate-chip ice cream. "What a bummer. Did you reschedule?"

Ah, the moment I'd been waiting for. "No," I said, "I didn't. Because in the library a few days later, I overheard Maura talking to someone about the concert she'd gone to on Friday night. Seems she and 'some friends' had scored last minute tickets to see some band of the moment in town."

Marina's eyes widened. "Ow. Did you confront her?"

"I most certainly did not. I started to cry and got out of there as quickly as I could."

"So they never knew you'd found out the truth?"

"Not for sure," I said. "Christine did call just before you were due, maybe out of guilt, I don't know. I was polite but cold. She had to know I'd found out about the concert. In short, that was the end of the friendships."

"What a bunch of losers. I can't believe your so-called friends ditched you for some stupid concert. You were better off without them, Mom."

Had I been better off? I really didn't know. Since Marina was born, I hadn't made an effort to make another close friend. Occasionally I went out for drinks with a few of the women from the office. Once a year we went to the theatre and had dinner afterward. Otherwise, my life included—revolved around, was dedicated to—my daughter, my parents, and Rob.

"This year," Marina was saying, "we should make up for it and do something really spectacular for your birthday. I'll plan something with Rob."

I felt maudlin tears threaten. I'd got what I wanted from my daughter—a show of kindness, a few caring words—and I felt ashamed.

"No, no," I said hurriedly, "don't be silly, it's fine. I'm totally over it. Just that when you mentioned your birthday . . ."

Marina checked her watch and then grabbed her giant bag. "I'm sorry, Mom, I've got to go." She got up from the table and peered down at me. "Are you going to be okay?"

"Of course!" I protested. "I'm fine."

"Okay then. Goodnight, Mom. I'll be home late. Don't worry."

I had the perverse desire to say, brightly, "Give Luca my love!" but didn't. What could I say that wouldn't sound too—personal? Have a good time! Well, of course she would have a good time. She'd be having sex with her lover. Be careful! In other words, be sure to use a condom.

"Okay," I said lamely, safely. And Marina was off.

Extending the orgy of self-pity, I poured another glass of wine and allowed myself to think back on my final attempt to make contact with Marina's father, the attempt that killed any lingering desire for his acknowledgment.

Marina had just graduated from middle school. Earlier that year I'd ordered the requisite school portraits—just a few, as they were ridiculously expensive—and decided to send one to the last address I had for Peter. Admittedly, it was a long shot, his still living in the same place. In my mind, Peter had become a man who never stayed in one place or with one person for too long. This was my prejudice. Anyway, I mailed off the photo; with it I enclosed a short note, something to the effect of "Thought you might want to see this." At first I planned to send the photo via regular mail, but finally I sent it via FedEx, signature required. If Peter no longer lived at that address, fine, I'd learn soon enough. And if he did live there, but refused the package . . .

He refused the package. The FedEx employee I spoke with was very apologetic. She explained that, of course, they couldn't compel anyone to accept delivery. The package was returned, I tore up the note, and stuck the extra photo on the fridge with a magnet Marina had made for me in art class. It was a papier-mâché flower, painted fluorescent orange. The magnet is still there, though now it holds the current phone bill. One of its petals broke off long ago, but it's still one of my favorite things, a precious artifact of my relationship with my daughter.

The wonderful daughter who wanted to take away an old hurt by giving me the birthday party I'd never had.

44

Dear Answer Lady:

Here's my situation. I'm a gay woman in a long-term relationship—is there any other kind of lesbian? (joke)—and my partner and I have been talking about having a kid of our own. Every time I thought about this kind of thing in the past, I felt sure I wouldn't want to be the one to be impregnated. But now that my partner and I have made the decision to go ahead and have a kid, I kind of think I might want to be the one to get pregnant. I'm not 100 percent sure, but I kind of think so. The big problem is that my partner just assumes she'll be the birth mother. I haven't said anything to her because I don't want to start a fight or freak her out or anything. She's got an appointment next week to be, you know, impregnated, so I'm kind of panicking over here. What should I do?

Dear Tongue-Tied:

I commend your decision to start a family under the pressures of a society still inclined to favor heterosexual couples over homosexual couples. On the other hand, I suspect you have some personal issues you need to work out and pronto. I strongly suggest you TALK TO YOUR PART-NER about your feelings before dragging an un-

suspecting fetus into what can only become an unhappy home. Remember: communication is the key. Silence only breeds resentment.

Wednesday, June 14

With Marina off to meet Luca yet again, I spent the morning wandering aimlessly, plagued by thoughts of my behavior the previous night. Little registered in my mind—not the hurrying people I passed; not the shop windows filled with rounds of white and yellow and blue-veined and marbled cheeses; not the honking of car and scooter horns—but the ugly truth that I was jealous of a twenty-seven-year-old man.

But with reason, I argued, stepping carefully over someone's spilled coffee outside a café. After all, Marina and I had come to Italy to spend quality time together—hadn't we? Oh, I knew I was being selfish, wanting to monopolize my daughter's time. And yes, I saw the inconsistencies in my attitude. On the one hand, I wanted my daughter to explore, to open up her world. Hadn't I been hoping that Marina would cool things with Jotham? But on the other hand, now that Marina was "exploring," I resented her lack of attention.

Jotham. Luca. It didn't matter. No matter how much you come to like, even to love, your child's significant other, you always prefer to have your child all to yourself, and it can make for misery.

A particularly insistent horn broke through my thoughts, and I realized that I was the object of the driver's annoyance. Without being aware, I'd wandered off the narrow sidewalk and onto the cobbled street. Hastily, I stepped back onto the sidewalk; while I managed to avoid being hit by his car, I didn't manage to avoid the glare of the driver as he whizzed by.

The brief encounter left me feeling rattled and urged my thoughts back to more unhappy realizations—like the notion that maybe, just maybe, I'd been living too much through my daughter, or for her, or because of her, and that maybe, just maybe, it was time I broke away and let her live her own life—and let myself live mine.

I was coming to see that I'd been unfairly—if unconsciously—relying on Marina to create meaning for my life. As a mother, I had a role and a purpose, but as Marina grew to need me less and less, I would have to redefine my role and purpose in the world. It was a scary thought. Exciting, too—but oh, yes, pretty scary. Still, it wasn't as if countless other women hadn't gone through what I was just beginning to recognize as "empty-nest syndrome." There was some comfort in the fact that I wasn't alone on this journey.

I stopped at a café to treat myself to a glass of *vin santo,* a delicious drink I'd read was sometimes called "meditation wine." Well, I thought, if that wasn't appropriate for the occasion, what was?

A woman I took to be a Florentine was sitting to the right of the one empty stool at the little bar. She was about my age and dressed in a beautifully tailored gray skirt suit with a silvery, silky blouse opened to reveal enviable cleavage. On her feet—I had to look—were pointy-toed, skinny-heeled pumps in a dusty lilac. I found myself hoping she didn't look at my own serviceable but decidedly unfeminine walking shoes.

I nodded and smiled as I sat; she nodded back without the smile. But no sooner had I'd taken a sip of wine and she'd stubbed out what looked to be her eighth or ninth cigarette in an already-brimming ashtray than she pointed at my right hand around the wine glass: specifically, at the chunky gold ring on the middle finger.

"Married?" she asked.

"No," I said, "not married. But I'm beginning to think I'd like to be." Now where had that come from, I wondered?

The woman, whose name I never learned, made a face that suggested I was a fool for wanting to take on such a nuisance as a husband.

"Men," she said, lighting another cigarette, "they are all

trouble. I am married for twenty-two years to the same man. I cook, I clean, I have my own business so I help with the money, and what do I get? He complains about this, complains about that. It never stops." The woman shrugged elaborately; her perfectly coiffed, shoulder-length, highlighted hair barely moved. "But divorce, it is not an option for me. It would kill my mother. But of course," she added, making the sign of the cross, "she is already dead, may she rest in peace."

"I see," I said helplessly, fortifying myself with another sip of wine.

"Of course, I have a lover, so my life isn't all so boring."

Frankly, I had a hard time imagining that this woman's life was boring in any way, shape, or form. Her personality alone, I imagined, aside from her seemingly effortless sensuality, must surely prevent the slightest trace of boredom from approaching. She seemed the sort of person able to make a dramatic event out of the most mundane bits of life, from peeling an orange to wiping the kitchen counter.

"I see," I said. "That's—nice."

"They never grow up, these men," the woman said suddenly, with forceful scorn. "It is impossible to have a mature relationship with a man, because he is never mature. He is always his mama's little boy. It is disgusting."

I don't know how I dared, but I asked her if she had a son.

The woman shrugged. "Of course. He is a good boy, the only one who really loves me. He is devoted to his mother. It is the way it should be."

I fought to contain a smile. Of course, I couldn't be sure if my new acquaintance was exaggerating about the extent of an Italian man's devotion to his mother, but I did wonder about Marina's new amour. What if Marina did leave Jotham for Luca? What would Luca's mother have to say about her son's American girlfriend?

But that would be Marina's problem, not mine, not if I were no longer "the single mother supporting a dependent

child" but an independent woman with a life—and a man—
of her own to manage.

The woman stubbed out her cigarette. "Don't be in such a
rush to get a husband," she advised—warned, rather—her
black eyes intent on my face. "Choose with care. Make sure
he can support you. But first, make sure he is good to his
mother."

When she'd gone, I allowed myself an exuberant laugh,
not at the woman's expense but at the glorious inconsistency
of her world—and at the glorious inconsistency of mine.

45

*You swore you'd never force your child to eat every
last bite of dinner before leaving the table. You promised you'd never compare your older daughter to
the younger. You roundly declared you'd never, ever
repeat the mistakes your mother made when raising
you and your siblings. And yet, you find your mother's
words coming out of your own mouth; you catch
yourself copying her every poor choice of behavior.
Face it: every generation is doomed to failure in parenting. The sooner you make peace with that sorry fact,
the better you'll sleep at night. (And maybe you'll avoid
falling into the sleeping pill addiction your mother
suffered for most of your teen years.)*
—The Apple Doesn't Fall Far from the Tree

Luca took me to the Giardini di Boboli. I wondered if my
mother had been there yet and realized I'd neglected to ask
her what she'd been doing with all the time she spent alone. I
felt guilty for abandoning her; at the same time, I felt absolutely helpless to do anything about the situation. To say to
Luca, "I can't spend the afternoon with you" seemed utterly
impossible.

That afternoon we sat perched on a low rise of thick
green grass, Luca's arm around my shoulder, our heads
touching lightly. Before us was an expanse of manicured
lawn, surrounded by masses of cypress. In the distance was

the Kaffehaus, built, Luca told me, in 1776. Healthy-looking, well-groomed cats seemed everywhere, rolling around on the grass, approaching strangers for back rubs, nibbling tasty plants.

"I would like to make a drawing of you, okay?" Luca said after some time had passed peacefully.

"Of me?" I pulled away from him a bit. "Oh, Luca, I don't know . . ." To be honest, I didn't even like having my picture taken. The thought of posing for someone was—disturbing.

Luca smiled and rose. "You don't have to do anything. Just be relaxed. Don't worry about sitting still. Just let me look at you breathing, enjoying the beautiful day."

Well, that was easier said than done. Luca and I had shared great physical intimacy, but something about this was different, almost frightening. It wasn't that I felt objectified; I'd half expected the experience to be isolating, but it wasn't; it was more that I felt—exposed. I felt under Luca's scrutiny.

I watched him sit on the low stone bench a few yards away and open his sketchpad. I wanted to tell him what I was feeling, but I didn't think I had the nerve to speak so honestly. Had I ever had the nerve to speak honestly?

The question seemed to come from nowhere, and I actually shivered in spite of the warm sun. Had I, for all these years, been hiding my real self?

With nothing else to do but to sit and look and think, I let my mind puzzle out that question. The truth was that since meeting Luca, I'd found myself wondering if Jotham knew me at all. Time and again he'd proven that he seemed not to, or, worse, that he didn't care to know me, that his own likes and dislikes should be good enough for me to share. This reality had come brutally clear only once I was a continent away from him.

But posing for Luca that morning—a word he rejected but one I couldn't help but use—a newfound honesty compelled me to ask myself if maybe it wasn't my fault that Jotham didn't know me.

Maybe, just maybe, I hadn't let him know me because I hadn't really known myself. I wondered if all along I'd been putting up a front, living behind a façade. I'd never meant to lie to anyone; it's not as if I'd set out to pretend I was one person when I was really, secretly, another. It was just . . . just that I hadn't known any better.

Maybe, I thought, I just hadn't come into my own—until now, until this time with Luca. Or maybe the process of becoming me was only just beginning. How could I know for sure?

I heard a sigh and a rustle: Luca turning a new page in his sketchpad, maybe frustrated with his attempt to capture me on paper. And I wondered if he would actually be able to capture the real me on paper. Only, I thought, if I let myself be seen.

If I let myself be seen.

If I went back to Jotham as the person I really was, or as the person I thought I might be becoming—would that be fair to him? In a way I'd be breaking a deal we'd made years before: This is me, Marina. This is the person I am and the person I will be until death do us part.

If I let myself remain hidden.

If I went back to Jotham and tried to sustain the act I'd unwittingly begun, would that be fair to Jotham? Would it be fair to me?

The answer was clear. Deception is never fair.

"What are you thinking?" Luca's voice startled me. I turned toward him. "Your expression, it is different now from when I started to work."

"I'm thinking about how you seem to know me so well," I said, wishing we sat close enough to touch but wondering if he wanted me to stay where I was. Marina Caldwell, artist's model.

"It's easy."

"What do you mean?" I asked.

"I listen."

"But it's more than that," I said. "I can't explain it. I can't find the words."

"Yes. We seem to have known each other forever. We make the connection in here."

Luca pointed to his stomach.

"You mean, like an instinct?"

"Yes. It is something there are no words for."

It was then I got to my feet and came to sit beside him on the bench. He took my hand and held it in his lap.

"Luca," I said. "I have to tell you something. While you were sketching me and looking at me so—intently—I felt . . . It was difficult."

"I'm sorry."

"No, it's okay. I wasn't going to tell you. I felt—exposed."

"Not bad, I hope."

I laughed. "Yes, at first. But then—it was okay."

"Thank you," he said, kissing my cheek, "for telling me how you felt."

I kissed his cheek in return and smiled. "You're welcome."

"Looking, seeing, is an intimate thing. More than talking, I think." And then he jumped to his feet and pulled me up after him. "Come, I want to show you the most fun thing here, the Grotta del Buontalenti."

Hand in hand we walked to the grotto, near the entrance to the gardens.

"It's so pretty," I said. "And we haven't even been inside."

"At the top, that is the Medici family's coat of arms, with the red balls on a gold shield."

"Oh, I've seen that all over town," I said. "I'm sure my mother told me what it meant, but I guess I just didn't listen."

"Everyone should listen to his mother."

"Or her mother."

"Yes. Mothers, they know best."

"I'm beginning to think you're right, Luca. At least about mine."

Luca took my hand. "Come on, let's go inside."

The grotto, chock-full of stalactites and stalagmites, was a sort of fanciful cave with three chambers, one after the other. In the first chamber the walls and ceiling were covered with stucco decorations of pastoral scenes, sheep cavorting with their shepherds.

"It's like a fairy world. Like something in a storybook I had when I was a child," I said.

Hand in hand we moved on to the second chamber.

"These marble statues," Luca said, "they show Paris kidnapping Helen."

"Ah, the love affair that started the Trojan War. See? I remember odd bits from school, too."

"See, you know more than just numbers."

"Maybe. Isn't Helen known as 'the face that launched a thousand ships'?"

"Yes. But what the poets talk about is more than what is on the outside. They talk about love. Love can be very powerful. It can create or destroy. It can change everything."

Suddenly Luca turned, pulled me to him, and began to kiss me. I pushed hard against his chest; he didn't fight me, but he continued to hold my arms.

"What's wrong?" he asked.

"What are you doing! We can't kiss here!"

"Oh. Why not?"

"What if someone sees us?"

Luca smiled, and his hips pressed into me. "They'll think we are in love. Maybe they will be jealous."

"But Luca," I said weakly, "it's not right."

"Why?"

"Because . . . I don't know, because—"

But Luca's mouth was on mine again.

Jotham had never, ever kissed me in public. He wasn't a

fan of public displays of affection. Once, I'd attempted to kiss his cheek at a lawn party given by a friend of his father's, and he'd been furious with me for hours, later lecturing about inappropriate behavior damning a person's reputation. I supposed he'd learned this from his parents, who might as well be living in parallel universes.

Only the sound of voices—German—in the first chamber ended our passionate embrace. I could feel my cheeks flaming, but this time my shame only made me laugh, and I pulled Luca on to the third chamber.

Later, after Luca had dropped me back at the hotel, I turned my phone back on to find a new text message from Jotham.

"Worried. What's up?"

There were two new voice messages from Jotham also. And one from Allison, who said she'd seen "the gang" the night before and that Jotham was concerned because he hadn't heard from me in a while.

"Are you okay?" she said, her voice echoing itself across the Atlantic. "I told him your phone is probably just not working. Right?"

I sank onto my bed, overcome with guilt and dread. I knew I had to send Jotham a message. "Just do it," I whispered into the empty room.

My fingers trembled as I pressed keys. Mistake, correct, another mistake. The measly message took almost a full two minutes to get right.

"Phone weird. Having fun. See you soon."

And then, how to sign off? With the usual "Love, Me" or simply with an initial?

"Love, Me" felt like a lie. "M" would give away my secret;

it would indicate the end of something I wasn't at all sure I wanted to end. Rather, an ending I wasn't sure I was strong enough to survive.

I typed "Marina" and shut the phone off once again.

It was the last message—electronic or otherwise—I could bring myself to write to Jotham during that two-week vacation, though I had promised to be in touch all the time, every day, every night. Another promise broken.

46

Dear Answer Lady:

I love my mother but have had a troubled relationship with her for as long as I can remember. My husband and I just learned that we're pregnant and are overjoyed. When I told my mother, she reacted in her usual cold and indifferent manner. In spite of my expecting nothing else, I was hurt by her response. The other day I read an article that talked about how a baby can bring its mother and her mother closer, even sometimes heal a major rift in the relationship between the two women. I would love to believe that my baby might bring my mother and me closer. Do you think this is true?

Dear Hopelessness Is Your Only Hope:

It's said that hope springs eternal in the human breast. You, my poor, dear girl, are just such an example of this unfortunate truth. It is my advice—and I speak from experience—that you immediately dash all hope and/or expectation of improvement in your relationship with your mother and focus instead on your new relationship with your baby. If it turns out to be a girl, you'll have quite the task ahead of you to avoid making the mistakes your mother made with her own daughter. In fact, I suggest you start praying to the god of your choice for the safe delivery of a boy.

Marina and I had dinner together at a restaurant Luca had recommended as one of his parents' favorites. The stand-out dish that evening was a large, shallow bowl of incredibly flavorful *funghi misti,* or mushroom ragout, accompanied, once again, by a bottle of good Chianti.

Marina's appetite had returned; being with Luca seemed to have energized her. She ate heartily though refused dessert, as Luca was taking her to one of his favorite haunts for that.

"I can't help but wonder," Marina said about midway through our meal, "if my father ever thought, even once, that maybe he'd been wrong and that maybe I really was his daughter."

"I don't know," I said. "I wish I could answer that question definitively, but I can't. The last I heard about him, about your father, was when you were in fifth grade. I ran into an old college acquaintance at the Marshall's on Boylston Street, and she mentioned she'd seen Peter in Los Angeles when she'd been out there on business. I'm not sure she even knew about you. Anyway, after that, nothing."

I didn't tell her about the time I'd sent Peter the package containing Marina's middle school graduation picture and he'd returned it unopened. I couldn't.

"He could find me easily enough," Marina said. "If he wanted to."

"Yes. He could." But, I thought, he won't.

I don't like to think of myself as a liar. Still, I'd never told and never will tell my daughter the entire truth about Peter's rejection, the nasty things he said to me, the time he threatened me with a restraining order if I didn't stop calling him. (The shame of that is still with me.) That information would be far too hurtful to impart, and it would serve no good purpose.

How do you tell your child that her father wanted—wants—nothing to do with her? That he refused to believe or acknowledge that he was, in fact, her father? That he has so little regard for me, her mother, that he was such a coward, he preferred to believe me a cheating whore (those were his exact words) who was trying to entrap him into raising another man's child?

Those are rhetorical questions, of course. You don't tell your child any of those things, not straight out, anyway. The information comes out of you in carefully considered and edited increments, and you're never sure if you're giving out too much or too little, never sure if the time is right or wrong, always grappling with the question of truth—is it, in the end, better revealed or kept hidden.

But then, I wondered, did Marina's "coming of age"—her affair with Luca—demand that the entire truth be told? Resulting, possibly, in fury or terrible sadness or, maybe, a long-awaited sense of relief?

It was strange that I should think of my daughter's infidelity as her coming of age, as the first truly defining experience of her adulthood. Strange that it wasn't her fidelity to the boy she'd loved since high school that struck me as defining her maturity.

"Marina?" I said. "Are you thinking of contacting your father?"

"Maybe." She paused for a moment, and then: "Mom, when you told him—my father—that you were pregnant, did he suggest you get an abortion?"

And there it was, the worst question possible, the one I'd been most dreading for twenty-one years, the one I still wasn't sure I could or wanted to answer. The question I wasn't sure I should answer—truthfully, that is.

Marina waited while I scrambled to work through the turbulent emotions and to make a decision, one that would be right at least at that moment in time.

I didn't think Marina would accept "I forget" as an answer. It was not the sort of thing you forget, your boyfriend asking you to abort his child.

My confused silence had gone on too long.

"That's okay, Mom. You don't have to say anything."

Marina seemed to be studying the remains of soup in her bowl, so I couldn't read the expression in her eyes. Her hands in her lap were still.

"But—"

"Mom. Really. It's okay."

She knew. My idiotic hesitation had told Marina more than she'd wanted to know and more than I'd wanted to tell her. It was one of those horrible moments, knowing you've inflicted pain on the one person you want most to protect. It was one of those horrible moments when you wish you'd been born a glib, bold-faced liar. "Of course he didn't suggest an abortion," I might have said. But I hadn't.

47

Far too many women, deeply disappointed in the direction their own lives have taken, attempt to mold—and in some cases, to force—their daughters into careers and relationships that are not in fact appropriate for the young women, that reflect, rather, the thwarted desires of the mothers themselves. This is a shameful situation, and such utterly self-focused mothers should be identified and roundly punished. This writer suggests various methods of torture standard in such admired government-sponsored institutions as Guantanamo Bay, etc.
—Tough Talk for a Tough Situation: Or, Giving
Mothers What They Really Deserve

My mother went back to the hotel after dinner. And I thought about our conversation while I waited for Luca at Lorenzo's.

I don't know why I'd felt compelled to ask the question, but I had been compelled. And my mother's silence, the look of dread on her face, dread and confusion and struggle, were all enough to give me the answer. It wasn't the answer I'd been hoping to hear, but it was the one I'd expected to hear.

My father had suggested that my mother abort me. Maybe he'd done more than suggest. Maybe he'd demanded; maybe he'd given her an ultimatum—get rid of the kid, and I'll stay.

Keep the kid, and I'm out of here. And when my mother had said I'm keeping her, my father had skipped out.

Lovely. And that was my heritage, too, not only my mother, a person who accepted responsibility, but my father, a person who rejected it completely.

I was startled out of my thoughts by a man about my mother's age—about my father's age—suddenly at my side.

"Good evening," he said, in heavily accented English. "May I join you, do you think?"

His hand was already on the chair across from me when I blurted "No, you can't!" I grabbed my bag and dashed from the café, feeling unaccountably upset, unsafe. I looked over my shoulder, but the man had gone. I peered down the street, hoping that the force of my desire would make Luca appear.

It did. At least, a moment later Luca drove up on his Vespa. I was hugely relieved.

I climbed on behind him and hugged him tight. "I'm so glad you're here," I whispered in his ear.

Back at his apartment, while I sat curled on the leather sofa, sipping a glass of wine, Luca slipped a CD into the stereo.

"You like opera?" I asked, as the first notes poured forth from the speakers.

He shrugged. "I try to like it more. My father, he is passionate about opera. He gives me these recordings to try to teach me."

I couldn't imagine Jotham and his father bonding over opera. Golf, yes. The stock pages, yes. But the arts? Never.

"I've never been to an opera," I said. "I've never even heard one all the way through. I guess that's pretty sad. What's this one we're listening to?"

"Something new to me. I borrowed it from my father today. It's called *Paride ed Elena,* Paris and Helen. Like the statues in the grotto."

"Ah."

"It was written by a man named Gluck in 1770. I know

we're supposed to pay close attention, but tonight, I'll keep it low, okay? So we can talk."

"Thanks. Is my mood that obvious?"

"To me, yes. What's wrong, Marina? You seem—troubled."

Luca sat beside me on the big, comfortable sofa; the look of genuine interest on his face allowed me to speak.

"Sometimes," I said, "I think I'm okay with my father, with what he did to my mother and me. And sometimes . . ."

Luca took my hand and gently stroked it.

"And sometimes I feel so angry with him. I don't like feeling so angry."

Luca nodded encouragingly, waited patiently. And I realized how long it had been since I'd stopped trying to talk to Jotham about my feelings concerning my father. He didn't seem capable of listening carefully enough to understand; subtleties were beyond him. Life was black or white for Jotham, and he believed it should be that way for others, too.

"And yet," I said finally, "sometimes I still wish my father would show up and apologize for abandoning me. Sometimes I still want him to—to care."

Luca squeezed my hand gently. "Yes," he said.

"I know I'm being ridiculous—"

"No, no. Why do you say that?"

"Because what's done is done, right?" I heard the bitterness in my voice. "What's in the past is in the past, and there's no point in remembering it."

Luca shook his head. "I'm sorry, Marina, I think you are wrong. What this man did, it—what is the word—it—defined— your life, even up until today. The past does not go away. I think maybe you need to mourn for your loss. But I am not saying you should throw a black shawl over your head and roam the wilderness weeping and wailing."

I laughed. "I hope not! Because I don't think I would like the wilderness."

"And I would not like to see you there." Luca held my

eyes with his. "Seriously, Marina. Maybe you need to—to make peace with this man, in your heart. No?"

I couldn't reply. I honestly didn't know if making peace with my father was possible. But maybe, I thought, after all those years of waiting for my father to come to me, maybe I should consider going to him. It was a startling thought, completely new.

"Now," Luca said after a moment or two. "Should I turn off the opera and put on something lighter, something to help make you happy?"

I nodded; the tears welling in my eyes prevented me from speaking.

48

Dear Answer Lady:

I'm having a huge problem with my mother. One afternoon a week she watches my kids after school until I come home from work at about seven. Okay, that's nice of her. The problem is that no matter how many times I tell her that my kids are NOT allowed to eat junk food (and I've provided a detailed list of what I consider junk food, so ignorance isn't an excuse), she shows up with McDonald's fries, or Dunkin' Donuts, or some other absolutely worthless "food." I mean, I come home and there's an empty box of Oreos in the trash! She doesn't even try to hide the fact that she's giving her grandchildren—my kids!— the crap that I expressly forbid her to give them! When I confront her, she just smiles and says that I worry too much, "a little fun food won't kill them." Uh, hello! Yes, it will, but not until they've lost a limb to diabetes! Needless to say, my kids— aged six to ten—just love it when Grandma picks them up from school bearing ice-cream drinks larded with Reeses Pieces! What can I do?

Dear Health-Conscious Mom:

Two words: Lighten. Up. If your kids are eating healthy the rest of the week, your mother is indeed correct in thinking that a little "fun food" isn't going to kill them. Balance, my dear, is key. If you label too many foods as "bad," human na-

ture dictates that your kids will specifically seek out and abuse these very same foods. Allow your kids the sheer fun of the occasional sugary or greasy treat, allow your mother the pleasure she gets from making her grandchildren smile—and allow yourself that Hershey's bar you know you've been craving.

Thursday, June 15

With my wild child and her lover off on their own for the day, I decided to visit San Gimignano, known since medieval times as "The City of Fine Towers." The helpful hotel concierge had recommended this particular excursion into the Tuscan countryside as suitable for a "lady of my circumstances." Not quite sure what that meant but charmed by his gracious manner, I booked a seat on the tour bus.

My circumstances turned out to be "woman traveling without a man," as one quick look at my fellow passengers showed me. There were about twenty of us, none younger than forty, the oldest a well-preserved (I use that word purposefully) sixty. (How do I know the ages of these women when I've already admitted to having trouble guessing age? I know because age was a great topic of their conversation as we drove. "Can you believe I'm fifty-four? Look at my skin, look. That new laser treatment is fantastic!")

The drive of about thirty-three miles took less than an hour. Risking being thought of as rude, I kept my attention on the landscape—terraced hills, groves of olive trees, dark green umbrella pines—and tried to ignore the exuberant chatting and frantic boasts of my fellow passengers.

Once the bus had parked and the driver had instructed us to be back in two hours, I slipped away from the group, sure my presence would not be missed. Alone on the cobbled streets, I opened one of the guidebooks I'd brought with me and read a bit about the fine old city of San Gimignano. While once there were seventy-two defensive towers, now there remained only fourteen. Still, they were impressive and, in their own way, beautiful.

I spent over an hour wandering through the city. The day was fine, and the air was fresh with the scent of rosemary and thyme from small private gardens. I stopped to pet a fat, one-eyed tabby cat perched atop a stone wall. I rested under a stand of cypresses and stumbled upon a tiny thirteenth-century church dedicated to St. Augustine. In spite of being unexpectedly alone, I felt peaceful, almost happy.

When I finally returned to the central piazza, there was still a half hour to spend before we were to load the bus. I thought that I would peek into a few of the shops, maybe find some small, poignant reminder of the afternoon, something that might help me to recall, even years ahead, the scent of lilacs, the peculiar color of the stone towers.

Coming out of one shop—my search thus far fruitless—I spotted a vaguely familiar figure across the piazza. I blinked, lowered my sunglasses for a better look. Yes, it was him, Jim Olberman, the one man I hadn't told Rob about after our reunion. The one man I'd almost succeeded in forgetting entirely.

Jim Olberman was the one man in my life with whom I'd had an entirely physical, nonemotional relationship. Never mind how I met him; it's unimportant. I kept his existence from Marina—and from my parents—by seeing him at odd hours, like on my lunch break, and by meeting him at his apartment, never our own.

The fact of the relationship surprised me. I didn't think I had anything to "get out of my system," but clearly I did, my youthful, carefree life having been cut unexpectedly short by the arrival of a baby.

Anyway, the relationship—if it could be called that—ran

its course as these things will, fizzling out after a few months and leaving the both of us bored, and me not a little embarrassed. Jim looked a lot like Peter—the olive complexion, the slim build—and it wasn't lost on me that in some ways I had been using him as a replacement, a substitute for someone I couldn't actually have. I didn't like the fact that I could consider—even unconsciously—another human being in such a casual, careless way; hence my embarrassment.

And now, all these years later, there he was, an unwelcome reminder of a strange bit of my past. He'd be about fifty, I thought, Rob's age—though, noting Jim's prominent belly, in much worse shape. Still, age hadn't stopped him from convincing the much younger woman with him from joining him on an Italian jaunt. Jim's arm was slung around the bony shoulders of a platinum blonde in need of a decent meal.

I was pretty sure he hadn't seen me. Or, if he had, I was pretty sure he was as determined as I was to avoid a meeting. The last thing I wanted was the past to interfere with the enjoyment of the present moment. Imagine my surprise when he suddenly called out to me.

"Hey, is that Elizabeth Caldwell!"

I gave a half-hearted wave, which seemed to give Jim permission to walk briskly toward me, Trophy Gal in tow.

"Oh, hi," I said as they approached. Trophy Gal's eyes—and half of her tiny face—were covered by gigantic black sunglasses. Her mouth was glossily made-up and grim. Thankfully, Jim made no attempt to touch me. I was pretty sure Trophy Gal could bite.

"Hey, what's it been," Jim said, "a few years now, right?"

"Right."

Suddenly Jim seemed to remember that he came with an accessory. "Oh, hey, let me introduce you to my wife. Elizabeth, this is Marissa. Marissa, this is Elizabeth, an old friend."

Marissa barely managed a smile and turned ostentatiously to look toward the row of shops to our right. This little meet and greet, I thought, was going to cost Jim a substantial sum. At the very least, Marissa would be going home with a new and very pricey bauble.

"So, what've you been up to?" Jim asked, oblivious to his wife's boredom or discomfort or mounting wrath.

"Oh," I said, mustering a false, polite smile, "lots of things." And before he could ask "Like what?" which I had no doubt he would have, I added, "But no time to talk now. I have to rejoin my group. Enjoy your vacation."

As I walked resolutely away, I heard Jim call, "Honeymoon. It's our honeymoon."

Jerk. There had been no reason at all for Jim to approach me except to show off his beautiful young wife. And he'd lied. We weren't friends; we'd never been friends.

I ducked into another small shop though my thoughts were far from retail. The unfortunate meeting with my former lover and his obviously incompatible wife sent my thoughts rocketing in the opposite direction, toward the solid, thoroughly compatible relationship I had back home with Rob.

I needed our relationship; I wanted Rob in my life, and at that moment, standing in that small, crowded shop, facing a shelf of mini reproductions of San Gimignano itself and calendars featuring photographs of Italian cats and hand-painted, glazed pottery, I realized quite forcefully that I never, ever wanted to lose him again, that maybe I couldn't stand to lose him again.

I was already in my forties. My daughter was raised. What was holding me back from making an ultimate commitment to Rob, what further proof did I need of Rob's love and devotion—of my own love and devotion? Things could go on as they had been, and that would be all right. But things could be made even better. It was at that decidedly unglamorous moment I determined that the moment I got back to the States, I'd ask Rob to marry me.

I left the store empty-handed of souvenirs but possessing a

new determination. My fellow day-trippers had begun to gather at the bus. I joined them. No one spoke to me, but I listened to the conversations around me. Certain words seemed to arise with frequency: "divorce," "alimony," "custody," and "bimbo." Even on vacation these women weren't free of the ugly words that described their world back home—the often unfair world of the middle-aged single woman.

I'm sure now that my grim mood was resposible for my conviction that many if not all of my temporary traveling companions were trying desperately to pretend that they were happy and fulfilled—and failing miserably. Maybe it was the three who seemed determined to leer at every passing young man; maybe it was the almost hysterical comparison of Botox results; maybe it was the desperate boasting about weight loss; or maybe it was the large number of them who were wearing outfits far more appropriate to women in their twenties, outfits that emphasized the inevitable bulge of a middle-aged tummy, the unavoidable sagginess of a middle-aged derriere, the certain strain apparent on a middle-aged neck.

Their lives, as I glimpsed them that afternoon through the prejudice of my own discontent, seemed not only sad but also exhausting, as if every one of them was forced to make a strenuous effort simply to survive another birthday or Christmas or summer vacation without a partner.

I spotted Jim and Marissa across the cobbled street. (How she managed the stones in those outrageously high heels, I couldn't imagine.) He opened the door of a shop, allowing her to pass inside. Then he followed, his wallet, I was sure, already feeling lighter. (Another uncharitable thought, but there it was.)

Yes, time was too precious to be wasted, as was opportunity. I reconfirmed the decision to give Rob, myself, and our relationship the respect it deserved.

I got back to the hotel around five that afternoon, hoping that Marina had returned, needing to be greeted by a friendly face and longing for some easy company. But at the desk there was a message from her telling me that she and Luca had decided to extend their day trip and would therefore be back in Florence quite late.

Keenly disappointed, and facing another dinner alone, I called Rob and got only his voice mail.

"It's me," I said. "I miss you and I love you and I wish we were together right now."

49

Is it, then, inevitable that we women morph into our mothers, in essence "become" the women who gave birth to and attempted to raise us in their image? No, no, and a thousand times no!
    —Claiming Our Lives as Our Own: A Daughter's Revolution

While my mother had decided to take a one-day trip to San Gimignano, Luca and I visited the Castello Banfi, a famous winery started in 1978 in the Brunello region, almost an eighty-mile drive from Florence. We took Luca's car, a minuscule thing painted electric blue. I tried to imagine Jotham or Jason or Justin squeezing into its driver's seat and smiled to myself.

Castello Banfi—the building itself—was once a medieval fortress, Luca explained, but it had been restored as a hospitality center. Inside was a museum of old glass; many pieces dated from Roman times, and I couldn't help but think that my mother should have been there with us to enjoy the exhibits. There was also an *enoteca*, which was sort of a wine bar and wine shop combined, as well as two restaurants. We had a delicious lunch at the more casual one, called the Taverna Banfi, and afterward strolled around the grounds surrounding the old fortress.

It was very hot, so hot that the gravel drive leading to the Castello seemed to shimmer, but I didn't mind. I was so happy to be in that peaceful spot with Luca, gazing down at what seemed like miles of grape vines, beautiful in their orchestrated symmetry. In the not-so-great distance stood the tall, slim, dark green cypresses I'd seen so often since coming to Florence in paintings of the Holy Family and saints and martyrs, people of the ancient world transported to medieval and Renaissance Italy in the artist's imagination. Off to our left was a grove of olive trees, the silvery green leaves almost sparkling in the intense sunlight. Frankly, I'd never given olives much thought until those two weeks in Tuscany, when I developed, unaware, a real appreciation for their flavor and appearance.

Luca walked off a bit to take some pictures with what he called a "real" camera—not digital, but film. I perched on the stone wall overlooking the vineyard, feeling peaceful and content, and watched him work, a camera bag at his feet filled with various lenses and flash attachments and extra rolls of film.

So unlike the man I was to marry. Jotham wasn't much for taking pictures, but he was very into expensive gadgets, what he called "life equipment." He had what he boasted was the top-of-the-line, most up-to-date automatic digital camera, a sleek little silver box that took pictures and video and for all I knew or cared brushed Jotham's teeth at night. Not for Jotham Luca's do-it-yourself picture-taking machine, one that required thought and the making of decisions. No, there was something lazy about Jotham. What was I doing planning to marry a man who preferred letting others do the work for him?

Suddenly, I didn't feel so peaceful and content. The critical, traitorous thoughts about my fiancé had intruded rudely, smashing the fantasy of uncomplicated summertime happiness in which I'd lost myself.

The first time the thought of breaking my engagement had flickered across my mind, late one sleepless night only days earlier, I was stunned. It was such a rebellious notion and seemed utterly impossible to pull off. How did you go about ending a relationship that was so firmly established? How did you pull away from another life that was so intertwined with

your own that for years you'd hardly been aware of owning
an individual self?

But as the thought of leaving Jotham began to occur more
frequently—not only in the middle of the night but while
drinking morning coffee with my mother, while on the back
of Luca's Vespa, while considering a statue in a museum—it
began to seem possible. If the actual process remained foggy,
the result seemed within reach.

Still, that afternoon at Castello Banfi I had no idea if the
result was something I truly wanted. I was in love with Luca,
yes, but not so far gone that I couldn't see the unfairness of
comparing him to my fiancé, not so far gone that I believed
one man could be so easily exchanged for another.

And I was scared. I was scared that by breaking my engagement for no more significant reason than a passion for
another man, I'd be exhibiting my father's cowardice, his inability to accept responsibility for his actions. I had said yes
to Jotham's proposal, and in doing so I'd made a promise.
Weren't all promises binding in some way, even if you didn't
sign a legal document?

What would life be like if people just walked out on promises all the time? It would be insufferable; you wouldn't be
able to count on anything. You wouldn't be able to count on
your professor showing up for the one class you really needed
to graduate. You wouldn't be able to count on your boyfriend or girlfriend not cheating on you. You wouldn't be
able to count on your friend driving you to the airport when
your car was in the shop, and you wouldn't be able to count
on your mother taking you shopping for a dress when the
guy you really liked had finally asked you to go to the prom.
In fact, if everyone broke his promises all the time, you certainly wouldn't even be able to count on the guy showing up,
corsage in hand.

The uncertainty would be maddening. And I so didn't
want to be one of those untrustworthy types who gradually
lost all meaningful relationships because of their inability to

be true to their word. I so didn't want to be like my father. Not for the first time, I wondered if he had continued to live a life of irresponsibility, or if he had matured, made a commitment to a woman, gotten married and had a family.

I wondered if he cheated on his wife.

Luca knelt on the dry ground, the camera aimed at something I couldn't see. The curve of his back, the way his hair fell forward—he had become so familiar in such a short time. So familiar, and so precious, so exciting.

I willed myself to imagine Jotham—and felt nothing. I realized with a start that it had been days since I'd thought of searching for his special gift. I realized that I no longer cared about finding it.

How, I wondered, did you know when changing your mind was the right thing to do and not just a symptom of laziness or cowardice?

It certainly had been cowardly of me not to return Jotham's calls or his text messages promptly. And no lame excuse could account for cowardice. "Oh, my stupid cell phone just died, and do you know how much the hotel was charging for international calls? We just can't afford to be spending that kind of money with a wedding coming up."

A wedding. A budget. We'd even talked about life insurance! I had a life with Jotham, and he had one with me. Was that life worth throwing away for—for what I thought was love? What was I thinking, that I wanted to stay in Italy and spend the rest of my life with Luca?

"Marina! Come here!"

Luca called to me from a yard or two away. I was glad for the distraction from my thoughts, even though Luca was himself the source of so much of my newly realized uncertainty.

I smiled as I joined him; the knees of his jeans were dusty from where he'd knelt.

"Smell this."

He held out a small bunch of vivid green leaves.

"It smells like mint!"

"It is mint. Growing here wild." Luca crushed the leaves between his palms and held them out for me to smell. "You see?" he said. "You never know what beauty is right under your feet unless you look."

Yes, I thought. And sometimes that unsuspected beauty is terribly disturbing.

When I got back to the hotel that night, my mother was already asleep. I was glad; I didn't want to compare notes on our days. I was disappointed; I felt the need to be comforted.

Quietly, I got ready for bed—washed my face, brushed my teeth, applied moisturizer to my face, neck, and hands. All as usual. And, as usual, I took off my engagement ring and put it safely into a small red silk pouch I'd bought just for that purpose.

I stood holding the pouch, feeling the weight of the ring inside. And I made a decision I didn't know I'd been considering. I crept into the room and over to where I'd placed my bag by my bed, feeling oddly like a criminal sneaking through his sleeping victim's house. In one of the interior, zippered pockets of my bag was my passport. Into that pocket I put the pouch, where it would stay, with me but unseen.

50

Dear Answer Lady:

My fifteen-year-old daughter has her father's nose, and let me tell you, it's a big one. I'm not breaking any confidences here; anyone can tell from a mile away that her nose is way too big for her face. I've been trying to convince her to get a nose job this summer so that when she returns to school in September she'll be a whole new person. The problem is that my daughter doesn't think she needs plastic surgery. She swears she's fine with the way she looks and points out that she has friends and a boyfriend (who, in my opinion, isn't exactly George Clooney) and that she gets good grades and is on the JV softball team. (Just wait until she gets hit in the nose by a fly ball. I know it's going to happen.) To make matters worse, my jackass of an ex-husband supports her decision and has warned me that if I don't stop "nagging" our daughter he's going to file for sole custody. I just know that my ex is taking our daughter's side to punish me; he knows how important appearances are to me!

Dear Totally Self-Focused Mother:

Do you by any chance recall the tragic story of Dr. Frankenstein's monster? Are you familiar with the ancient Greek concept of hubris?

Are you at all troubled by the fact that those who "play God" by manipulating Nature are treading on dangerous ground, the results of which can be the bloody destruction of all ethical tenets? No, you probably flunked out of college in the first semester. So let me address you in a way you might understand. You are a shallow person, an irresponsible parent, and a bitter ex-wife who is determined to undermine her daughter's self-esteem in a twisted attempt to punish the girl's father, the man who had the wisdom to leave you. Leave the girl ALONE. Clearly, in this case father knows best, and you would be wise to take his threat seriously. On second thought, keep nagging your daughter. She'll be far better off living with a person who knows the value of character over appearance.

Friday, June 16

"The message said he'd call back in a few minutes. He sounded worried."

Marina and I were at a café, two glasses of *vin santo* on the table before us. We'd been enjoying the moment until Jotham's call. It had acted like the proverbial thunderbolt, startling us out of our calm. In the blink of an eye, Marina went from looking relaxed and happy to looking absolutely miserable.

"I think you should call him back now," I said, risking her anger. "When was the last time you talked to him?"

Marina laughed unhappily. "First you tell me I'm spending too much time on the phone with Jotham, and then you tell me I'm ignoring him."

"Well, you are ignoring him. And he's not going to disappear just because you don't want to take his calls."

"It's not that I don't want to, Mom. It's more like I can't."

I reached out and squeezed her hand. "I do understand, really."

After a moment of heavy silence, Marina sighed. "Okay, I'll call him."

"Do you want me to give you some privacy?" I asked.

"No, that's okay. I'm not going to say anything—important."

I opened one of my guidebooks, knowing the words and pictures wouldn't register, knowing that no matter how hard I tried to ignore the one-sided conversation at the table, I would fail.

"Jotham? It's me." Marina's voice was unnaturally high.

"Of course not, everything's just fine. Florence is—great."

"No, something must be wrong with the ringer. And sometimes I can't get any reception."

"No, I'll just throw it away when I get home. It didn't cost much anyway. Besides, I have the new iPhone Rob gave me for graduation."

"Of course I have the warranty, but—"

"No, Jotham, really, you don't have to—"

"But it really doesn't matter so—"

"Fine."

And there was the too common note of resignation, of defeat. I fought down a surge of pointless anger; what was I going to do, grab the phone and remind Jotham that no means no?

"Don't be silly," Marina was saying, with some annoyance. "Of course not. That's ridiculous."

I guessed that Jotham had asked her—teasingly, jokingly— if she'd met someone else, if that's why she'd been so elusive. It would be like Jotham to ask.

"Yes. No, I'm not angry."

"I have to go now, Jotham."

"Okay. Good luck with work."

"Jotham, I really have to go. Mom is waiting." Marina shot me a look of apology; I nodded, the pretense of reading long abandoned.

"Yes, me too. Good-bye."

Marina clicked the phone closed and tossed it into her bag.

"Well, I don't know what that accomplished," she said with a bitter laugh. "At least he knows I'm alive."

Marina put both hands to her forehead and rubbed gently, as if she had a headache. And it was then that I noticed she wasn't wearing her engagement ring. I didn't comment on its absence.

"The guilt is killing me, Mom." She dropped her hands into her lap. "When I get home, I think I should tell Jotham about—about what happened with Luca."

"I'm not sure that's the best thing to do," I said carefully. What I really wanted to do was throttle my daughter and shout "Are you insane?"

"Are you saying I should lie to my fiancé? After what I've already done to him?"

"No," I said. "Not exactly. But I do think you should ask yourself what you want to hear from Jotham if you tell him about Luca."

Marina looked puzzled. "What do you mean?"

"I mean, what do you hope to accomplish by telling him about Luca? Do you want Jotham to forgive you? Do you want things to go back to being just the way they were before you left for Italy? Which, of course, they can't, not really, whether you tell Jotham about Luca or not."

Here, I paused; what I was about to suggest might meet with some extreme emotion.

"Or," I said, "are you hoping that Jotham will break up with you?"

Marina's eyes widened. Before she could say anything, I

rushed on. "Now, don't get upset with me for suggesting this, it's just a possibility, but it seems to me that Jotham's ending the relationship would save you the trouble of having to end it yourself."

"I don't know," she said after some time.

It was a more honest and mature answer than what I'd expected to hear. It made me bold enough to say, "Marina, do you want to hurt Jotham?"

"Of course not!" she cried. "That's the last thing I want!"

"All right. But do you really think telling Jotham about Luca won't be hurtful? Do you really think Jotham will feel nothing when he learns that his fiancée fell in love with another man?"

"No, of course not. I just . . ." Marina frowned down at her lap.

In spite of Marina's denial, I couldn't help but wonder if she did want to hurt her fiancé, though the desire was sure to be unconscious. I couldn't help but wonder if a part of her wasn't sick and tired and bored with Jotham and wanted to blame him for her own sudden and disconcerting discontent. It seemed a likely possibility.

"I've certainly gotten myself into trouble, haven't I," she said softly.

"You've gotten yourself into a difficulty, yes."

"Mom?" Marina shoved her sunglasses onto her head and looked at me. "Do you think I'll be able to find my way out of this mess?"

"Of course you will."

"I mean, without destroying everything?"

She looked so young and so vulnerable it almost broke my heart. No matter how old one's child, it's a terrible thing to know she's in any sort of danger. And my daughter wanted something of me then, something I couldn't truthfully give—an assurance of the future. That hurt, too.

"No matter what you do," I said carefully, "something will end. And something else will begin. I'm afraid there's no getting around that."

Marina sighed and lowered her sunglasses. "Yes. That's what I thought you'd say."

51

You can never do anything right. You host Thanksgiving dinner at your home for your entire extended family, and your mother complains that she had to travel on a holiday. You go to the grocery store and spend almost an hour searching for the brand of soap your mother prefers, and she complains that, while you've brought her the correct brand, it's not the scent she wanted. You pay off your mother's mortgage at no small sacrifice to you, and your mother complains that you've made her feel like a pauper. There's no doubt that the demanding, perpetually discontent parent is an enormous drain on the adult child unfortunate enough to still care. But don't lose heart. A week or two without a phone call from you will have this chronic complainer at your door with a box of expensive pastries and an unusually meek manner. (Note: repeat this procedure as needed; the exacting parent will always revert to her thankless ways.)
—It's Never Enough: Surviving the Exacting Parent

That afternoon Luca took me to visit the Cattedrale de Santa Maria del Fiore. And instead of groaning (inwardly) about having to spend time in yet another church filled with images of macabre martyrs and odd-looking babies, I was genuinely interested in exploring the old buildings and their contents. I borrowed one of my mother's guidebooks—which she handed over without so much as a smirk—and now, hand in hand, Luca and I made our way to the Piazza del Duomo.

The cathedral, I learned, was also called the Basilica. " 'It was begun in 1296, consecrated in 1436, and holds twenty thousand people,' " I read from the guidebook. "Wow. This is the biggest church I've ever seen. I don't think there's anything like it back home."

"Nothing as old, that much I know."

"No. The U.S. is a teenager to Italy's adult."

Luca smiled. "Does the book say that everyone must cover arms and legs to go inside?"

"I don't know, why?"

"For modesty."

"Ah, so that's why you suggested I bring a sweater. Back home I see people coming out of the local Catholic church, St. Anne, I think, wearing shorts and T-shirts."

Luca shrugged. "To me, it's not what is outside that matters. So, long or short-sleeves, either is fine if you are a good person."

"I suppose," I said, though I wasn't ready to abandon all sense of decorum.

The cathedral was magnificent, its exterior a combination of green, pink, and white marble.

"It looks like candy," I said. "Like a confection."

"Except for the dirt and the pigeons. Nothing in a city is ever clean, that is the reality."

"Oh, I don't want to see the reality. I don't want to see the dirt and the pigeons. For once I'd much rather see just the beauty."

"Romance over reality." Luca grinned. "That is okay with me. Do you want to take the stairs to the top?"

"There's no elevator?"

"No."

"Um, how many stairs are there?"

"Oh, only four hundred and sixty-three."

"What!" And then I thought: I might never get back to Florence. This might be my only chance to visit the top of the Duomo. "Okay," I said, "why not? It'll be good for my legs."

"Your legs are perfect."

"Luca! Are you supposed to be saying things like that in a church?"

"No. I am certain to be going to hell."

"You don't seem very upset by that."

Luca shrugged. "I accept my fate. What else can I do?"

In the end I was spared the hike; the stairs were closed for repairs of some sort. After a brief journey around the interior—marred, I have to admit, by the crowds; though supervised, the mass of tourists made me nervous—Luca and I walked to the Piazza San Giovanni, just off the Piazza del Duomo. In the center of that plaza was the Baptistery of St. John.

"The Baptistery was built in the eleventh through thirteenth centuries," I said, summarizing a detailed account of the building. "It's particularly famous for the three bronze doors. Inside there's a marble mosaic of the zodiac. That's strange."

"What is?"

"I didn't think Catholics were supposed to believe in astrology."

"The medieval and Renaissance church was a very exciting thing," Luca said. "There were many strange beliefs, many contradictions, many heresies. Nothing surprises me about my religion's history."

We pushed our way near the front of the crowd of people gathered to see what Luca told me was the most famous of the three bronze gilded doors. Called the "Gates of Paradise" by Michelangelo (he thought them beautiful enough to be the very gates of Heaven) and designed by Lorenzo Ghiberti, it depicted in high-and low-relief images from the Old Testament. The door gleamed golden in the strong afternoon sun.

As I stood there, I found myself wondering what it would be like to belong to a church from birth, to be born into a religion like Luca had been. It must, I thought, allow for a level of cultural inclusion or membership that could, if you wanted, have a little or a lot to do with faith. I picked out on the grand door the creation of Adam and Eve, and figures Luca told me were Old Testament prophets, Solomon and the Queen of Sheba. And for the first time in my life I felt a bit bereft, as if I lacked a heritage. Bad enough I lived with the absence of family history and belonging, but to also feel untethered in the larger world was unpleasant.

I pushed aside the strange thoughts and turned to Luca. "Let's go back to see the Bell Tower again. It's so pretty."

We walked back to the Piazza del Duomo, which was still thronged with visitors and would be, Luca told me, all summer.

"The first story of the Bell Tower was designed by the artist Giotto, and so we know it also as Giotto's Campanile."

"How many stairs to the top of that?" I asked.

"Only four hundred and fourteen. And there is a lovely view."

"Oh. Uh . . ."

"We have had enough talk of stairs for one day?"

I laughed. "Yes! I confess to being lazy."

"I can't believe you are lazy."

"No. I guess I'm not. Just hungry!"

"We will go to Lorenzo's and have something to eat."

The café called Lorenzo's had become "our place." It amazed me how quickly our relationship had slipped into a sort of domesticity; we enjoyed shared habits and the return to familiar haunts as if we'd been together for months.

"My father and mother used to come here when they were dating," he told me when we'd been seated at "our table."

"It is nothing special, as you can see. There are lots of other cafés that have better food and prettier tablecloths! But I like it here because of the memories."

"Because of your parents' memories."

"Yes, that is right. But now I like it even more because of our memories, you and me."

And would all I had of Luca next week, next year, be memories? Would he become just another absent presence in my life, something powerful and determining but unseen, untouchable?

"You know," I said suddenly, "when I was about eight or nine I used to wonder if my mother was lying about my father."

"What do you mean?"

"Well, that maybe instead of just being some guy she used to date in college, he was someone rich and powerful, like a king or a prince. I used to think that maybe my father was someone glamorous, not just some guy who'd gone to law school after college. Not just some businessman."

"Ah, yes," Luca said. "A man who is probably balding and who wears boring suits and who has a paunch from spending so many hours at his desk."

I laughed. "Right. I wanted him to be someone totally unlike all the other fathers who came to pick up their kids from school or who cheered them on at Little League games."

"But if he was just like those other fathers, he would be with you. It must have been difficult, and very confusing, trying to understand."

"Yes," I admitted. "It was. Then when I was a little older, I guess around twelve, I went through this phase when I thought that maybe my mother was lying about my father's rejecting me. Maybe she'd never even told him she was pregnant."

"Why wouldn't she tell him that she was going to have his baby?"

I shrugged. "Oh, I imagined a lot of reasons. Stupid ones,

of course, most of which reflected badly on her. Like I said, it was a phase. I was rebelling."

"Yes. I, too, have had a phase of rebellion. There was a time when I thought that bathing was bourgeois. I think I didn't take a bath for a month before my father dragged me into the bathroom and forced me into the tub."

"Oh, Luca! That's disgusting!"

"Yes," he said, smiling. "And very smelly. But tell me your story, Marina."

I hesitated. My story. I'd never told anyone—not Jotham, not my mother—what I was telling Luca.

"Well," I said, "I know it sounds ridiculous, but I thought that maybe all those years my father had been living in ignorance of me. And I'd fantasize that somehow he'd see me and recognize me instantly and whisk me off to live a charmed life with beautiful clothes and expensive gifts. We'd spend every day together doing fun things, and everything would be just—perfect."

"I don't think that is so unusual. I think I can understand why you would hope for such a thing to happen. A rescue, maybe."

I thought about that. A rescue. Had I wanted to be saved from—from what? From my life? Was I still looking to be saved? The thought disturbed me.

"Marina? Did I say the wrong thing?"

"No, no. I'm sorry. I was just thinking about being so young and stupid."

"Not stupid."

I laughed. "That's debatable. I even wrote stories about that fantasy father and daughter. I even illustrated them with drawings of me in a ball gown and my father with a crown on his head." I put my hands to my forehead, as if trying to hide. "I can't believe I'm telling you this. I'm so embarrassed even thinking about those stupid stories!"

Because what good had those stupid stories done me?

Only this: I'd learned to confuse wishful thinking with true creativity. Telling stories achieved nothing. Acknowledging reality and careful planning were what got you through life. Or so I'd been convinced.

Luca took my hands from my forehead and held them. "Don't be embarrassed, Marina. Please. You are so hard with yourself, unforgiving."

I didn't know how to answer that. "Let's walk a bit, okay?" I said suddenly.

We left Lorenzo's hand in hand. I felt they fit perfectly together, our hands. And suddenly, I was overcome by a feeling of loss.

"We have so little time left, Luca," I said, leaning into his arm, into the reality of him.

"It makes me sad to think you are going home."

"It makes me sad, too. I don't know—I don't know how I can handle it."

Luca replied by stopping in the middle of the sidewalk and drawing me close to him. I laid my head against his chest and wrapped my arms around him.

"We will make the best of it we can, Marina, until—"

I squeezed him even more tightly. "Oh, please," I begged, "let's not talk about it anymore! Please. I can't stand it!"

Tears ran down my face, wetting his shirt, staining it with mascara.

"I'm sorry. I hate to cry."

"Crying is good for you," he said softly. "As long as it is not so much."

"Lately, I feel like all I want to do is cry."

"I'm sorry. I think I am part of what is making you so sad."

"No, no, it's not you. It's . . ."

It was that everything had changed. It was that there was no going back. And I no longer felt as good about that as I once had.

"It's nothing," I said, stepping abruptly away from him, rummaging in my bag for a tissue, unable to meet his eye. "Do you want to go to that new gallery you told me about? The one where your friend has a show?"

Luca looked unhappy, but he shrugged. "Sure," he said.

I took his hand again. At least I could give him that much.

52

Dear Answer Lady:
I'm so confused. I just can't decide if I want to have a baby! My husband isn't pressuring me; in fact, he's admitted he could go either way, have kids or not. I'm the one who's all muddled inside. I just wish there'd be a sign, something to point me in one direction or the other, no confusion. Maybe you could help?

Dear Muddled:
The other afternoon I happened upon the following quote from Honoré de Balzac, noted nineteenth-century French writer. "A mother who is really a mother is never free." Admittedly, the quote lacked a context, but I'm going to go out on a limb here and say that Monsieur Balzac got things right when you consider that mothers are an almost universally put-upon lot, enslaved to the desires and well-being of their offspring. Sign enough for you?

Marina and I had dinner together that night; at least Luca allowed us that little time together. To be fair, the choice was as much Marina's as his.

We each had a bowl of delicious *zuppa di fagioli alla Toscana*, or Tuscan white bean soup. For me, there followed *spaghetti all'aglio e olio*, or spaghetti with garlic and oil, and for Marina, tortellini stuffed with prosciutto.

"Luca had to put in some serious hours at work today," Marina said. "His father wasn't happy about his taking so much time off this week."

"Yes. I can imagine." I wondered if Mr. Sarna knew how his son was spending his time and figured that, yes, he probably had a very good idea.

"You did like him, Mom, right?"

"Marina, how often have we had this conversation? Yes, I liked him, the little I saw of him. But that's not saying much. I really don't know the man at all." And neither, I added silently, do you. I wondered if Luca had told Marina anything about his past loves, and, if he had, had he been truthful. Was there, for instance, a child somewhere out there in Florence with Luca's particular smile? There was no way she or I could know.

"He said you were very kind to him."

"I know," I said, trying to hide my impatience. "You told me."

"And that you were beautiful. He said your hair is the color of 'a pomegranate at dusk.' Isn't that poetic?"

Well, I thought, to give the guy his due, he could sling a phrase. "Yes, I suppose it is poetic."

"I had the strangest dream last night," Marina said suddenly. "I hardly ever remember my dreams, but I remember this one so clearly. Do you want to hear it?"

"If you want to tell me, sure."

"Okay. I'm with a man on a hilltop. It's very windy and isolated. The man and I are in love, and we're holding each other very close, but at the same time, I'm aware that I'm also another woman. That I'm married to another man and that I love that other man as that woman. It's like I'm two people, with commitments to two men, but I don't want to be two people, I want to be one person. Do you understand at all, Mom?"

"Yes," I said. "I think I do."

"Okay. So I try to tell the man I'm with on the hilltop that to be with him forever I have to go back to my husband and—somehow detach myself from my other self, while at the same time leaving that other self in place so that my husband isn't alone. I have to somehow—finish—that other relationship so that my husband is okay and happy—and only then can I come back to the man on the hilltop. But he isn't happy about letting me go back, and he doesn't want to accept the fact that I—that I love my husband, but that my husband has nothing to do with my love for the man on the hilltop." Marina made a dismissive gesture with her hand. "Well, it makes no sense saying it out loud, but it did make sense when I was dreaming it. It was really troubling. I felt like I was going to lose both men no matter what I did, but that if I didn't do anything . . . I don't know."

Did Marina really not see how clearly her dream illustrated—enacted—the particulars of her waking life? In the supreme illogic of dreams, there is always truth.

"Interesting," I said. I wasn't about to do the interpretation for her.

"Yes. You know, it's funny, but now, talking about it, I feel like the dream me might really have wanted to—to just run away from both men. But the idea was too strange, too disturbing. I mean, she cared for the husband, and she was in love with the man on the hilltop, but she was so unhappy."

"Yes."

Marina shook her head as if shaking off the memories of the night. "Well, it was only a dream."

"Allan."

"What?"

"I just this moment remembered your father's middle name. Allan, with two L's."

"Huh," she said. "I never liked that name. Did he tell you where it came from? I mean, was he named after someone in his family?"

"I don't really know. Honestly, I don't think I ever asked. And Peter didn't talk much about his family. I got the feeling that maybe he and his parents weren't very close."

Marina looked at me keenly. "But they were loyal to each other, weren't they?"

I knew what Marina meant. That Mr. and Mrs. Duncan had chosen to believe their son innocent of having fathered a child with his girlfriend, that they'd taken their son at his word.

"Well, his parents were loyal to Peter," I said. "I don't know if he was loyal to them."

"Luca is very close to his two sisters. He says they're his best friends. He talks to them every day."

If it wasn't a lie calculated to make him sound all warm and fuzzy, Luca's relationship with his sisters counted in his favor. "Do you miss not having a sibling?" I asked.

Marina shrugged. "You don't miss what you've never had. Isn't that supposed to be true?"

"I don't believe that for a second," I said. "I think that longing and desire and ambition are often about wanting what you've never had, what you've read about or dreamed about but haven't yet experienced."

"Maybe. I guess it would have been nice to have a brother or a sister. But it's not something I think a lot about."

"Well, I'm glad. It's a little late to do anything about it now."

"It's not too late, Mom," she said. "Plenty of women in their forties are having babies."

"Yes, but this woman in her forties is not one of them. Besides, it's not easy to get pregnant at my age. Even if I wanted to, I'm not sure I could afford the expense of fertility treatments."

"That's why I'm starting my family when I'm thirty. I'd like to have at least two or three children. I mean, Jotham and I have planned to—"

The stricken look on Marina's face as she realized what she was saying almost broke my heart.

"Oh, Mom," she whispered desperately, "what am I going to do?"

I reached across the table and took her hand. "I really don't know," I said. "I'm sorry."

53

You swore you'd feed your six-year-old only fresh, healthy food, and now you're packing his lunch box with Uncrustables and Pringles. You vowed you'd limit TV time to one hour per week, and now your ten-year-old son is addicted to nighttime reality shows. You swore you'd impose strict rules as to what sort of clothing your twelve-year-old daughter could wear, and now she's baring her belly and talking about a pair of four-inch Jessica Simpson heels. Relax. Let go of the guilt. Being a parent in the U.S. in this day and age is a losing battle. The sooner you admit defeat, the lower your blood pressure will drop.

—Parenting in the Twenty-First Century: Just Give Up

Saturday, June 17

As soon as it was late enough back home not to rouse Rob from sleep, I placed a call to him from the hotel.

I'd missed him twice, and once the connection had been so bad nothing could be understood. I so wanted to hear his voice; I missed our daily conversations, the ones about something but also more importantly, the ones about nothing.

"Rob," I shouted. "It's me, Elizabeth."

"There's no need to shout; I can hear you just fine. And hello!"

I laughed. "Hello! I'm glad I got you."

"Me, too."

"How are the parents?" I asked.

"The usual," Rob said. "Your mother is obsessively scanning the headlines for news of disaster in Florence."

"We never should have gotten her set up with that computer. Maybe I should cancel her subscriptions to the *Globe* and the *Times*. How's Dad?"

"Good. I took him out to that imitation English-style pub he likes the other night. Boys night out. He needed the break. No offense to your mother."

"Thank you, Rob. That was really nice of you."

"Yeah, and then he totally destroyed me in pool."

"You didn't let him win, did you?" I asked, knowing it would be entirely in Rob's character to stage a defeat for the benefit of my father.

"Are you kidding? The guy is good, Elizabeth. He could have made a living at pool."

"I don't think that would have gone over very well with my mother."

"No," he said with a laugh, "I don't think it would have. So, are you and Marina having a good time?"

"Oh, sure. You know, we're seeing the sights, eating good food." I heard the false cheer in my own voice; it wasn't surprising that Rob, the person who knew me best, heard it, too.

"Is everything okay, Elizabeth?" he said. "I'm sensing there's something you're not telling me."

"No," I lied, getting up from the bed, as if pacing would make evasion easier. "Everything's fine. Things have been—interesting."

"Interesting? That's all I'm getting? Should I be concerned?"

"No, no," I said hurriedly, eager to reassure him, "don't

be concerned. It's just stuff with Marina, you know, typical mother-daughter stuff. We'll talk when I get home."

"Promise?"

I promised, though I wasn't sure how much I would be able to share once Marina and I were back in Boston. Marina's decisions would determine what Rob could and could not know. If she returned to Jotham as if nothing at all had happened in Florence, then Rob would never know about Luca. Though I'd been tempted to, I wouldn't break that promise to my daughter.

"Okay," I said, "I should go. Lots to see and do for this dedicated tourist."

"Same plan for the Logan pickup?" Rob asked.

"Same plan." And then I remembered we were all to meet at Logan, the four of us, Rob and me, Jotham and Marina. I was very sure I did not want to witness the first minutes of my daughter's reunion with her fiancé. It was bound to be tense. "No, wait," I said. "Meet me at the taxi stand instead, okay?"

"Sure. Any particular reason?"

"Uh, no. I just think it will be easier."

If Rob questioned my reasoning, he didn't let on. We ended the call after the usual exchange—"I love you, Rob" and "I love you, too, Elizabeth."

In spite of my promise to Marina, I did feel bad about keeping a secret from Rob. And I wanted his thoughts, his perspective. I'd become so used to sharing my troubles or concerns with him; as with any strong couple, we routinely shared each other's burdens.

But all that talk of loyalty to one's family had led me to decide that loyalty to my daughter must prevail over loyalty to my partner.

I headed back out to the Piazza del Duomo to visit the Cattedrale de Santa Maria del Fiore, and the Campanile; to see the impressive bronze doors of the Baptistery of St. John—

the doors on the east side by Andrea Pisano; the second pair by Lorenzo Ghiberti, who won a competition against Filippo Brunelleschi for the commission.

The lines for admission to the cathedral were long, and the sun beat down without mercy. Never a fan of hats, I looked with envy at women under broad brims and silently cursed my prejudice.

Once inside, I was particularly interested in seeing a painting of Dante by Domenico di Michelino done in 1465; it portrayed Dante in a landscape he could not have known while alive, a Florence almost one hundred and fifty years after his death. A bust of Giotto, and one of Brunelleschi. Forty-four stained glass windows depicting saints from the Old and New Testaments, the Virgin Mary and her son. The cathedral was both a museum and a place of worship. Did the art distract from prayer or heighten it? Depending on the depth and nature of one's spirituality, I supposed it could do either.

I reemerged into the bright June sun. On a series of low steps, a group of Australians gathered around their tour guide, who held aloft a bright orange umbrella. One of the group, a man about my age and sporting an ill-fitting baseball cap that read FIRENZE, winked at me. I frowned back. His poor wife stood with him, clutching his arm and listening intently to the guide, oblivious to her husband's antics.

As I walked off, I remembered how horrified Marina had been when the young man had flirted with me in the café, and how nervous she'd been when the older gentleman had sent us a bottle of wine. I remembered thinking how narrow her point of view, how little her experience of the world, of men and romance.

How much had changed for her in two weeks! Her world had been revolutionized, and even if the revolution would lead to a better state of affairs, it had inevitably caused a degree of pain and suffering. Marina was experiencing her own renaissance, her own time of incredible growth and creativ-ity—her own time of risk and danger.

And I was a mere witness to it, someone to verify events, to record changes, more a member of Marina's audience at this point than an active character in her drama. I walked back to the Hotel Francesca, sending out a prayer for my daughter to whoever would receive it. Let her triumph, I asked. Let her be well.

54

Dear Answer Lady:

My father cheated on my mother all the time—
everyone knew—she had to have known! Why
did she put up with it? It still haunts me, and I
really want to confront her about it. I mean, no
wonder I have such serious self-esteem issues.
No wonder every one of my relationships with a
man has been a disaster. Don't I have a right to
some answers? Don't I have a right to an apology for her messing up my life?

Dear Woman Who Wants Permission to Pass the
Buck:

Listen carefully: you are responsible for messing up your life, no one else, not your mother,
not your father, not your strange third-grade
teacher. That said, I don't know if you have a
right to answers about your mother's choices in
her marriage, but I do think it's okay for you to
open a dialogue with her, if, of course, she agrees
to participate. If, however, she refuses to discuss
her marriage with you, let it go. Everyone has a
right to privacy, even mothers (surprise!). Get over
the need to blame (it's a sign of a weak character),
get past the need to make assumptions (it's a sign
of a narrow imagination), and get into some sort
of therapy before you're too old to make a significant change in your life. Have a nice day!

"The view from here is really spectacular."

"Maybe not as good as the view from an apartment in New York though."

I turned from the living room window and smiled at Luca. "Oh, who needs New York when you have Florence?"

"The way to my heart is through my city. How did you know?"

I laughed and settled onto the cushiony leather couch. I'd become comfortable in Luca's apartment. I'd miss not only the view, but also the odd and interesting assortment of paintings and sculptures, and the sleek and simple kitchen, and the bookshelves sagging under the weight of fat volumes of art history. Even the evidence of his mother—of his life apart from me—was welcome.

Luca opened a bottle of Prosecco and poured us each a glass. Then he joined me on the couch.

"There is something I want to say to you," he said.

I nodded, suddenly nervous, almost shy under his gaze.

"I have given this much thought, Marina. I don't want you to go home. I want you to stay here in Florence, with me."

It was what I'd wanted to hear. It was what I'd dreaded to hear.

"What?" I said stupidly. "Luca, I—"

Luca grabbed my hand and held it tightly. "Please, let me speak. These days together, they have been very special to me. I don't want our time together to end."

"Oh, Luca, I know, neither do I. It's just—"

"Just that you are frightened?"

"Yes," I said. "I'm very frightened. Everything's happened so fast. I—I'm very confused."

"But I am not frightened or confused. I know we are meant to be together."

"But—"

Luca lightly touched my lips with his finger.

"Try to trust me in this," he said. "My heart is never wrong. I know inside of me what is true."

What is true for you? Or what is true for me?

"I love you, Marina."

"I know," I said. "And I love you, too, I really do. And that's part of the muddle. Luca, how can this be real? We've only known each other since last week. How—"

"This is why you must stay here with me. So you can be sure. So that I can prove to you I am right about us."

I looked down at my lap, needing respite from his dark and imploring eyes.

"Marina," he said, softly and yet urgently, "we talked about fate. You said that when you met me you learned to believe that fate is real. You said that everything has changed for you. You must believe that now. You must continue to believe that we are soul mates, that we are meant to be together."

When my silence had gone on for some time, he said, "It is the only way, Marina. The only way I can convince you that our future is together. You must stay."

What he said made sense. But what he said was also madness. To stop from having to think, I kissed him. My sudden passion surprised me; it was as if I could burn away all the uncertainty facing me by lighting a fire between Luca and me. Looking back, I realize that we made love that night as if out of desperation. At least, desperation was my motive.

After, lying together in his bed, Luca asked me—implored me—to spend the night with him, something I hadn't allowed myself to do, as if that additional intimacy—that almost domestic act—was simply one betrayal too far of my life with Jotham.

"We can call your mother so she won't worry," he said. "Please, Marina, stay here with me tonight. In the morning everything will be clear."

Looking into his eyes, my hand on his chest, I was sorely tempted to give in to his desire, but in the end I simply couldn't.

"No, I have to go back to the hotel," I said. "Please try to understand."

He wasn't happy, but he accepted my decision. Silently, we dressed and, Luca's Vespa in the repair shop, took a cab back to Via Cavalcanti.

When the driver pulled up outside the Hotel Francesca, Luca asked him to wait a moment, and he got out along with me.

"Remember, Marina," he said, lightly stroking my cheek with the back of his hand, "in this life, feelings are all that matter. Feelings are all we have."

"Yes," I said, though I wasn't at all sure I agreed. I wasn't at all sure I even knew what he meant.

"Promise me that you will think about staying in Florence with me, yes?"

"Yes," I said. "I promise."

Once in the lobby I looked back over my shoulder to find Luca still standing on the sidewalk, watching me.

55

Being a Mother is much like being constantly at war with an enemy who simply refuses to acknowledge the tenets of the Geneva Convention. However, all is not lost. The best weapon God has bestowed on Mothers in their ceaseless struggle with their children is Guilt. Yes, initially Guilt produces resentment in those toward whom it is directed, but eventually, over time, the recipients become so badly worn down their every ounce of resistance fails and they are compelled to play by Mother's rules.
—Guilt and Motherhood: A Match Made in Heaven

Sunday, June 18

"Mom, I need to talk to you about something."

We were still in our hotel room. Marina had been up before me, which was a bit unusual and made me wonder if she'd slept at all.

"Okay," I said.

I should have known what was to come. Our time in Italy was running out; I knew that the situation with Marina and Luca would have to come to some sort of dramatic conclusion. And yet when she told me that Luca had asked her to stay on with him in Florence, I was stunned.

"It's so we can get to know each other better," she explained unnecessarily when I'd failed to respond.

My heart started to race and my hands to shake. Was this what I had wanted for my daughter when I had dreamed about her experiencing life? To have her move in with a man she'd known for little over a week? A man I knew virtually nothing about?

"I need," I said, sitting heavily on my bed, "some water."

Marina hurried off to the bathroom and returned with a glass, into which she poured water from a bottle on the dresser.

"Are you okay, Mom?" She knelt on the floor by my side. "You're not going to faint are you?"

I managed a little croaklike laugh. "No, I'm not going to faint. And please get up. I can't talk to you like that."

Marina retreated to her bed and sat on the edge, facing me. Where, I thought, do I begin? And how do I not screw this up?

"What about Jotham?" I said finally.

Marina looked down at her hands, folded in her lap. "What about him?"

"Don't be evasive, Marina. Or stupid." I heard the anger in my voice, but I couldn't hide it. "Do you still love him? Are you ready to break off the engagement?"

"I don't know. I don't know anything for sure right now except that I love Luca."

"How can you know that you love him?" I demanded. "You've only known him for a few days!"

"That's why he wants me to stay on," she argued. "So we can see how we work as a real couple."

Until, I thought, he gets bored. Until he's had his fill of the pretty young American girl and sends her off home, her heart shattered, her bank account considerably lightened. I took a deep breath before responding.

"And while he's figuring out if he likes your being a 'real' couple, his life goes on as usual. He goes to work for his father and spends time with his friends and talks every day to his sisters, and what do you do? Your entire life will be disrupted, all your plans put on hold. What about your job? You were so proud of getting that job. And you'll be thousands of miles away from your family and your friends, from your home."

Marina had no easy comeback to this, so I pressed my advantage.

"You have no friends here, Marina. You don't know the language. It's not as if I can easily take more time off work to visit you. I can't help but think you'd be terribly, terribly lonely. I can't help but think that you'd feel isolated."

"I'd have Luca," she said, with touching and utterly ridiculous conviction.

And we'll live on love, I added silently. Well, at least the guy had a job; at least he could afford to buy them food. But how was I to know he wouldn't want Marina to pay his rent?

"And like you said the other day, Mom, I know some Spanish. How hard can it be to learn enough Italian to get by?"

Again, I didn't respond. Think, Elizabeth, I told myself. Just think before saying another word.

Marina's attraction to Luca was enormous; I knew that. And clearly she thought the attraction just might be worth pursuing at the risk of losing her fiancé, who only a week earlier she had claimed was the most important person in her life. It wasn't hard to guess what Marina was thinking. If she let go of Luca and went back home to Jotham to dutifully fulfill her promise of marriage, she might never again experience true passion. And that, too, would be a great loss. I didn't envy my daughter one little bit. She was in a horrible, horrible position.

"I know," I said finally, in as neutral a tone as I could manage, "that you don't want to hear what I have to say—"

"So then don't say it."

"—but I have no choice."

Marina sighed softly. "Go ahead."

I held her eyes as I spoke. "I can't help but feel that in

some way Luca is acting as demandingly as Jotham. Asking you to stay on with him in Florence is a huge request, Marina, you must realize that."

"I do, Mom, really."

"Please," I said, "think carefully about your tendency to do whatever it is a man asks you to do."

There was no need to list the most obvious or most recent examples: Marina's decision not to go to Paris, her decision to let Jotham have his way regarding their honeymoon, her acceptance of an engagement ring she didn't even like.

"I do not have a tendency to do whatever a man asks!" she cried. "That's ridiculous."

"I'm sorry," I said quickly, afraid I'd destroyed what new and fragile bond we'd established. "I shouldn't have used that word. I was wrong. I'm a bit—overwhelmed."

"It's okay," she mumbled.

"Marina, I know I can't force you to come home with me. Honestly, I don't want to force you to do anything, ever. Believe me. But please, please think very carefully for a moment. What is Luca sacrificing by asking you to stay here with him? Nothing. And what is he asking you to sacrifice?"

I wanted to answer my own question aloud: everything. He was asking my daughter to sacrifice everything, and for what? Not for a commitment, but for a dream.

Marina was quiet for what seemed like a long time. "I didn't say I'd already decided," she said finally. "I know I have to think about it. I know this is a really big decision."

That was progress, I thought. Wasn't it?

"If he's worth it in the long run, Marina, he'll understand if you decide to go back home and—and take care of things first. If he's worth it, he won't try to make you feel bad or guilty for taking more time to make a decision. My God, Marina, we're supposed to leave on Tuesday morning. This is too much pressure on you."

And on me, I thought. I don't know if I can handle this.

Heart disease is the number one killer of women, Elizabeth. Take a deep breath.

As if she'd read my mind, Marina said, "I'm sorry, Mom. I didn't mean to put you through all this."

I patted the place next to me on the bed. Marina crossed the room and sat. I put my arm around her shoulder and squeezed. "Don't say that, Marina. Don't apologize. You have nothing to be sorry about, nothing."

She had no answer. And we sat there, still and silent, for some time.

56

Dear Answer Lady:

Here's my problem. I'm deathly afraid of relationships. I mean, I am the definition of a commitment-phobe. The longest I've ever gone out with a guy was two weeks, and I swear, by the tenth day I was having major anxiety attacks. I've gone to therapy about this, but it didn't take or whatever, so I've been racking my brain trying to figure out why being close to someone is so horrifying. Anyway, I think I've found the answer, but I wanted to run it by you. (I really love your column; you're so smart!) When I was a little kid, I wanted a dog, but my mother wouldn't let me have one. What I figure is that growing up without a dog, I never had the opportunity to really bond with someone, you know? I mean, dogs are supposed to be a human's best friend, am I right? So isn't my fear of bonding with a guy all because my mother refused to let me have a dog? I would feel so much better if I could point to my mother as the cause of my being single at the age of thirty-five.

Dear Freak:

Where to begin? Seriously, I'm having trouble here. Your idiocy runs so deep I am at a loss for words that can actually go the distance to find what tiny, infinitesimal grain of intelligence you might possess. To hell with it. I give up. Sure, *yeah, your mother is to blame, why the hell not? Feel better? Not that I give a crap. Oh—please don't ever write to me again. Thanks.*

I waited for Luca at Lorenzo's. He was running late again; he said that his watch had stopped and that he was going to get a new battery on the way to the café. I fought against a sliver of annoyance, the first tiny critical thought about my lover I'd ever entertained. It made me unhappy, and it also made me think.

I didn't want my mother to be right, but I was beginning to think that maybe she was on to something about my tendency to submit to men. Maybe somewhere along the line I'd confused submission with loyalty, gotten compliance mixed up with support. I didn't think I'd learned the behavior from my mother, who was—or who had become—resolutely her own person.

So maybe, I thought, the confusion was the result of my father's desertion; maybe the desertion had given birth to an odd and unconscious desire to prove that I could be the kind of person he couldn't or wouldn't be.

It all made no sense, and yet—in some way, it all made perfect sense. Because now, anything and everything seemed possible. Why couldn't I be as mixed up as any other twenty-one-year-old? As any other woman who suddenly, unexpectedly found herself at one point in a romantic triangle?

Marina Caldwell is involved in a ménage à trois. She is having an affair. She has taken a lover. She is running around on her fiancée. She is cheating. In a very short amount of time I had become someone alien to myself. Only days earlier I'd believed that if Jotham—if anyone—cheated on me, it would mean the absolute end of the relationship. I'd believed there could be no forgiveness. I simply hadn't understood.

Now I had betrayed someone, and as much as I hated myself for doing it, I also understood why it had happened. Maybe not entirely, but I did see that I was—that I had been for some time—unhappy with the way things were between Jotham and me. I hadn't set out to betray Jotham's trust in me, but something—something larger, something more powerful, than my commitment to him—had just slammed into me and thrown me off my feet. Now I had finally begun to understand all the talk about passion and romantic love, all the talk I'd always dismissed as phony, something writers and filmmakers indulged in to sell their products. Passion, I'd thought, romantic love, would ruin your life if you took it seriously, if you believed in it, if you succumbed to it.

Well, I was discovering that maybe passion did ruin your life, but in the process it also created your life. In those final days of our Tuscan holiday, I was finally beginning to understand that passion was real, not a fantasy, and that it was as much an enemy as it was a savior.

And I wondered. If Jotham and I did get married, and he cheated on me someday, and if it happened for him and his lover in the way it had for me and Luca—would I be so quick to judge and condemn him? Would I let him go graciously, or, if he wanted to stay in the marriage, would I welcome him back with understanding? Could I?

One thing I was sure about. My mother was right. If Jotham and I were to stay together, he could never know about Luca, ever. That much I'd decided. That, and only that.

I spotted Luca walking toward me along the narrow sidewalk and remembered how he'd told me he'd crashed his Vespa four times in the past year. When I'd asked him if his insurance rates had gone up terribly, he'd laughed.

"I always forget to buy insurance. I know it is irresponsible of me. My father is always telling me that someday something very bad will happen, and I will have no money for hospital, and I always tell him, what will happen will happen."

I'd opened my mouth to argue and then shut it. Luca was—Luca. Not me. Not Jotham.

And then suddenly, strangely, I heard Jotham's voice in my head. "You'll have a great time," he was saying. "I promise. Trust me. You'll see I was right. I don't want you to go to Paris. I think you should go to Graham College with me."

And then the voice became Luca's. "So that I can prove to you I am right about us. Try to trust me in this. I know inside of me what is true."

Jotham had had his say. Luca had had his say. Fate or Romance had had hers. When, I thought, would I get mine?

For a split second I had the urge to dash away into the crowds, to lose myself, to hide away, to save myself.

But I didn't.

"Marina!" Luca flashed that incredible smile, and I couldn't help but smile back.

57

Warm, soft-hearted, indulgent, merciful—these are adjectives traditionally used to describe the Mother. I say: poppycock. Short of the Virgin Mary and maybe, in the realm of non-fiction, the now-deceased Beverly Sills, the majority of real-life mothers are cold, hard-hearted, withholding, and unforgiving. Deal with it. And deal with the fact that chances are good you'll repeat the same toxic behavior in your dealings with your own children as your mother exhibited in her dealings with you.

—No Way Out: The Grim Pit That Is Motherhood

I had vowed to try a piece of *panforte*—literally, "strong bread"—before leaving Florence. A specialty, I'd read, of Siena, it was a dense, spiced bread made with a combination of nuts such as hazelnuts and almonds; spices such as cinnamon, ginger spice, and cocoa; candied lemon and orange peel; honey, flour, and sugar, dusted all over with a thin layer of confectioner's sugar. Comfort food, if ever there was.

So that day, while Marina once again met with Luca and tried to puzzle out her future, I took myself to a small, family-owned café suggested by the hotel concierge as serving a delicious *panforte*.

The slim wedge of cake—made, I was told, by the proprietor's aunt—was vastly superior to any fruitcake I'd ever tasted, delicious to the point of sinfulness, but my request—my pleas—

for the recipe were in vain. Even the waiter seemed proud to serve this specialty and with or without the consent of his manager gave me another thin wedge "on the house."

But delicious—and as comforting—as the cake was, it couldn't entirely keep out thoughts of my daughter and the enormous decisions she was facing.

I remembered what I'd said to Marina when she'd told me that Luca had asked her to stay on in Florence with him— about her tendency to please the men in her life at the cost of her own happiness. And not for the first time I thought that maybe this tendency was related to or maybe even caused by the absence of a father. There was little I could do about it at that point except feel guilty in retrospect. Maybe I should have provided my daughter with a constant paternal presence other than her grandfather. Maybe my mother had been right; maybe for Marina's sake I should have married Rob when he first asked.

But I hadn't. And all I could do now was to help Marina understand her choices and why she was making them. All I could do now was to help her make decisions based on her own wants and needs and not on those of another person. And that was a tall order. Marina was technically an adult; just how much was a mother allowed to "interfere"? I certainly didn't want to do any more damage than I might already have done.

Parenting is exhausting, and it doesn't seem to get any less exhausting as your children age. It's hard if not impossible to break the habit—the instinct, or the learned behavior—of caring and worry.

But even the most devoted parent needs a break, and sitting in that small café with a second wedge of *panforte* on my plate, I realized that for the first time since Marina had met Luca, I was actually enjoying being on my own. Being left to my own devices had forced me to think about my life, the direction it had taken thus far and the direction it might take in the future.

An old movie poster was tacked to the wall by my table, its edges a bit grimy, one corner torn. *Roman Holiday*. I wondered if Marina had ever seen it and somehow doubted she had. It had been years since I'd last watched the movie, on AMC, but facing the drawing of a wasp-waisted Audrey Hepburn, the plot came back to me. And it occurred to me that while I wasn't exactly Hepburn's character, a woman running away from a life of large and demanding duty to my country, there was some similarity between the princess and me, Elizabeth Caldwell from a suburb of Boston. Except that what I'd found in what I already had—my relationship with Rob—brought me pleasure; what Princess Anne had found in what she already had—duty to her country—brought not exactly pleasure, not of the kind I knew, but some satisfaction with self.

A more obvious relationship could be found between Hepburn's character and my daughter. Though Marina's dereliction of duty—her abandoning the role of devoted fiancée—wasn't undertaken with the same daring and purpose as Princess Anne's, she was in fact trying to come to terms with a future that was (or that seemed) predetermined, ordained, and inescapable.

I finally left the café (a good pound or two heavier) and wandered until I found myself at the old, dilapidated church on whose steps Marina and I had contemplated the photograph of her father and me. I sat once again on the broken stone steps, a well-worn guidebook for company. In it I found a few pages about Dante's *The Divine Comedy*. Not having read *L'Inferno* since college, and fresh from a visit to Dante's memorial tomb, empty of his exiled bones, I was struck anew by the universally powerful opening lines.

> In the middle of the journey of our life I came
> To myself in a dark wood where the straight
> Way was lost.

On the streets where Dante walked until he was exiled from Florence in 1302, I had begun to find my way anew— while on those same streets Marina had begun to realize that everything she thought she had known was, if not entirely wrong, then only partially right.

I flipped ahead a page or two to where the author spoke about Dante's doomed lovers Paolo and Francesca, to where he commented on how unfair it was that great love, the kind that absolutely won't be denied, the kind that absolutely won't be avoided, must be checked by willpower and reason. To where the author lamented that great love is most often punished.

And again, I thought of my daughter, committed to one man and madly in love with another and, if I was any judge of these things, terribly unhappy.

It might very well be that Marina survived this experience as the greatest casualty. My daughter was facing a decision that could—that would—affect her entire future. And, by extension, my future, too.

I closed the book, got up, and continued to wander.

58

Dear Answer Lady:

I recently found out that my mother had an affair with another man while she was married to my father. My mother's best friend mentioned it to me about a month after my mother died. She said she thought I knew, and then, when I freaked out, she tried to make it all sound okay by saying the other guy was the love of my mother's life. (Like that makes it any better for me, to know my father wasn't the love of my mother's life?) This changes everything! Everything I thought I knew about my mother has been thrown into question. How many other things was she hiding from me? What else did she lie about? What other crimes did she commit? My mother's friend is begging me to "try to understand" and to forgive my mother, but I just can't let go of the anger. Am I wrong?

Dear Disappointed:

Newsflash: Mothers are people. Parents aren't perfect. Good fathers aren't always great husbands. And adultery isn't a crime, at least one punishable in a court of law. Unless you know every little detail of why your mother did what she did, and unless you have a fully empathetic understanding of her emotional state at the time, you have no right to judge her for having an affair. Okay, you're disappointed; your fantasy of your parents' marriage has collapsed. Big deal. Get over it. Like you're so perfect? Besides, the past is the past; you can't change it. What you can change is how you deal with its repercussions in the present. I'm making myself gag over here with this pseudotherapeutic lingo, so pay attention to my final words on the matter: Let. It. Go.

Monday, June 19

It was our last full day in Florence. Our Tuscan holiday was drawing to a close, and a time of reckoning was drawing near.

While waiting for Marina to finish showering and dressing, I thought back to the day we'd visited the flea market, early in our visit. I remembered watching the lovers, and I remembered hoping that Marina and I would have a big, exciting, life-altering experience while in Italy, something we could remember for years, something that would change our lives in a profound way, something we could someday share with Marina's children.

Well, my wish made in all innocence (one might also say ignorance) had come true for Marina, and in some ways for me. That morning I vowed to try not to obsess over Marina's impending decision and to simply enjoy this time with her—with the daughter I might be leaving behind.

Together we set out from the Hotel Francesca. The humidity had dropped, making it a perfect warm and pleasant June day. Before we'd gone far, I stopped outside a bookshop I hadn't noticed on our previous jaunts.

"I need to go inside for a moment," I said. "There's something I've been thinking about."

Inside the wonderfully cluttered and musty old bookshop I

found a perfect gift for Rob, a nineteenth-century leather-bound volume of architectural drawings. It cost a small fortune, but I didn't care. Rob, of all people, was worth the expenditure. The book was incredibly heavy, but in spite of the proprietor's offer to ship it via Federal Express International, I insisted on carrying it home with me.

"I thought you said you didn't need to get Rob anything special," Marina teased after a quick stop back at the hotel, where I asked the concierge to put the book in the hotel's safe. "I thought you guys were beyond gift giving. I thought you guys were too mature for material tokens of affection."

"Yeah," I said, cringing as my words came back to bite me, "well, sometimes I say stupid things."

"You! I think I've become the master at saying stupid things. At doing them, too."

I looked fondly at my daughter. She'd grown so much in the past two weeks. "Don't be unnecessarily hard on yourself, Marina," I said.

She smiled. "Only be as hard as it's necessary to be?"

"Well, yes. If we're not at all hard on ourselves, we'll run amok."

"Guilt acts as a check on our behavior, right?"

"Yes," I said. "Some degree of guilt is productive. But no more talk of unpleasant things. It's our last day in Florence. I don't want to waste one minute of it."

We continued our stroll through the city we had both come to admire. If I'd been somewhat remiss before then in taking photos, I now wanted to notice and capture everything, every stone fountain, every shop window, every passing Florentine face, so that I could take home with me vivid memories and powerful impressions that would last a lifetime. Or at least until Rob and I came to Florence together, which suddenly seemed like a very good idea indeed.

I smiled down at Marina, walking by my side. She smiled back. I'd hesitated to tell her about my decision concerning my relationship with Rob. Marina had so much on her mind. I didn't want to bother her with the news of something that might not even come to pass. But she had shared so much of herself with me in the past two weeks; maybe, I thought, it would be a good thing if I shared some of myself with her.

"So, here's something I think you'll find interesting," I said. "I've decided to bring up the topic of marriage with Rob. I feel it's time."

"Mom, that's fantastic," she cried, grabbing my arm and forcing me to a halt. "It was time ages ago!"

"No," I said. "I think I needed to put some things aside first, let go of some other things, be in the right emotional place, feel—"

"Stop! You sound like some goofy self-help manual. Next thing you'll be saying that you're 'in the zone' for marriage."

I laughed. "I know," I said, continuing our stroll. "I'm making myself sick, actually. But I'm glad you approve of my decision."

"You don't need my approval, Mom," Marina said. "You're an adult, remember?"

"Maybe I technically don't need your approval, but—let's just say I'm glad to have it."

"Grandma is going to be so happy. She's wanted this for years."

"Yes," I said dryly. "You'll remember that I'm aware of Grandma's desires concerning my life."

"Grandpa will be happy, too. I mean, he considers Rob already part of the family; we all do. But I'm sure he'd like to call Rob a son-in-law."

Yes, I thought. My father would like that very much. It could be a sort of gift to him, though it wasn't one he'd ever ask for, or, like my mother, demand.

"If you had one word to describe the Tuscan countryside," I said suddenly, "what would it be?"

"Talk about a change in topic. Only one word?"

"Yes."

"Okay. I guess I'd say yellow. There's lots of yellow. Now, your turn."

"I'd say the Tuscan countryside, what I saw of it anyway, is gold. Most everything is gold, and what isn't gold is deep, dark green."

"What about Florence?" Marina asked. "What one word would you use to describe Florence?"

"I'd still say gold, but a different gold than the gold of the countryside. What would you say?"

"Gray."

"A depressing gray?"

Marina shrugged. "No, not really. I mean, it's a city, so it's going to be ugly in parts. But I like Florence. I think it's beautiful—in a kind of harsh and gritty and frantic way."

"Interesting," I said, pleased with my daughter's attraction to urban life. "Okay, what was your favorite meal?"

"That's hard. I don't think I can say."

"Do you remember hoping there was a McDonald's in Florence?"

Marina frowned. "I never said I hoped there was one. I said I wondered if there was one."

"Sorry. Anyway, I know what my favorite meal was. Hands down, the *cinghiale*."

Marina laughed. "I knew you'd say that."

"I just hope I can find it at home. I bet it would make a fantastic hamburger."

"Yes, I suppose you can make a hamburger out of any kind of ground meat, not just beef. Funny how . . . Never mind."

"No, what were you going to say?" I asked, truly curious.

"Just that it's funny how so many little things, really simple things, never occurred to me before. Like making hamburgers out of pork or, I don't know, eating flowers, or Catholics believing in astrology." Marina shrugged. "All sorts of things."

I smiled. It made me glad to be a witness to the rebirth of

creative thinking. Marina had been only half alive until our Tuscan holiday, and if there's bliss in ignorance, there's also danger and waste.

We spent the remainder of the morning doing nothing in particular, though I remembered reading somewhere that doing "nothing" in Italy is doing very much indeed.

And not once did I mention the topic uppermost on my mind.

59

*Back in the good old days, pregnancy was considered
a condition to be concealed for as long and as much
as possible. Today, and much to this writer's disgust,
pregnancy seems a condition to be flaunted. The unsuspecting public is regularly victimized by the presence of bared bulbous bellies, unsightly stretch marks,
hideous blue veins straining under skin ready to burst,
absurdly swollen ankles, and ridiculously dimpled
knees. It's time to reconsider the tentlike garments
that tactfully hid the more disgusting traits of pregnancy from the world.*

—Stop the Madness! Putting Pregnancy Back Into
the Closet

We ate lunch at my mother's favorite café in the Piazza della
Signoria, a place where she'd met a woman from Chicago
and had what she'd called an inspiring conversation. But that
afternoon, neither of us seemed inclined to talk. My mother
read while she ate *insalata di frutti di mare*, or shellfish salad,
and while I picked at a panini of tuna and egg, I tried to keep
pace with my thoughts.

My mother. I had begun to realize there was so much about
her I didn't know. This—this ignorance—had never bothered
me before. Honestly, it had rarely if ever occurred to me that
my mother was someone other than "my mother." I suppose

that's normal thinking on the part of a child. But now, since coming to Italy, I'd begun to feel curious about her.

Who was Elizabeth Caldwell apart from the mother of Marina Caldwell—if there was such a person? And if there was—there had to be—would I ever know her? Would she let me know her, and if so, was I capable of seeing past my prejudices and assumptions about "my mother" to see the whole person?

I wondered then, and to some degree I still wonder now. Maybe it's an impossible thing for a daughter to do. And maybe it's impossible for a mother to acknowledge that she doesn't entirely know her daughter. She can't know her. No one can know anyone but themselves entirely, and it was becoming clear to me that summer after college that lots of people, maybe most people, don't even know themselves completely, because that degree of knowledge is just too scary.

My mother gestured for the waiter and ordered another glass of Vernaccia. "It's our last day," she said. "Girls gone wild."

I rolled my eyes at her and laughed. Only weeks ago I would have criticized her for being silly. Now I found it—cute.

Everything in my life seemed to be exploding like fireworks in a night sky, spectacular but also a bit frightening because one of those brilliant sparks could fall onto your upturned face and scorch you.

What I thought I knew, I realized I'd only assumed. What I thought was fact was turning out to be fiction or foggy fact, if there is such a thing, something that's sometimes true and sometimes not true depending on a whole bunch of factors you just couldn't keep an account of.

It all came down to perception. For example, I'd realized that for a long time I'd seen my mother as a victim. And I'd also realized that I needed to reassess that notion, to ask myself why I'd assigned my mother such a passive role when in actuality she was an independent and successful person.

Not merely a victim of love.

As I was not merely a victim of love. I accepted responsibility for the relationship with Luca. I'd gladly risked everything; no one had forced me to love him, not even Luca himself.

That photo of my parents.

Slightly faded, the edges dulled, it had given me valuable insight into my mother's relationship with my father; it had helped me to understand how passion is bigger and stronger than reason, and how, with a few exceptions, people aren't really victims to passion—they're participants, even celebrants.

And celebrations come to an end.

So much had happened so quickly. Too much. Too quickly.

The dream in which I had been two women in one, hoping to satisfy the very different needs of two men, thinking, in the very back of my mind, that I might be better and happier on my own.

Sitting with my mother in her favorite Florentine café, aided by the comfortable, even supportive silence she offered me, I made my decision.

I simply wasn't brave enough to stay on with Luca. And I simply wasn't cruel enough. I knew I had to face Jotham, and I knew it was going to be terribly hard; I even doubted I had courage enough to be totally honest with the man with whom I had promised to spend the rest of my life. Because maybe I'd never been totally honest with him. Because maybe I'd never been totally honest with myself.

Two young girls dashed by, about ten years old, long hair flipping up and down on their narrow shoulders. I had a vision of myself at that age of innocence, before love, before duty, before passion. It seemed so very, very long ago.

I would return Jotham's ring. I would tell him I needed time. I would make no promises, though I knew deep down that there would never be a wedding, not to Jotham Grandin.

I knew it would it be kinder to cut all ties with Jotham right out, to leave him with no lingering hope, to say "The wedding is off" rather than "The wedding is postponed indefinitely." Maybe at the very last moment I'd find the guts to speak definitively, but I wasn't counting on it.

The young girls came by again, this time strolling arm in arm, each with an ice cream, one pistachio, the other chocolate. I envied them their simple joy. I wished that youth didn't have to be wasted on the young. I wanted those girls to know and appreciate the years of freedom and blamelessness.

Blame. Guilt. Responsibility.

I knew that staying with Jotham and trying to pretend that nothing had happened was wrong. I didn't know if turning my back on Luca was right, but the thought of staying on with him terrified me. Maybe, I thought, the best thing for me to do right now is to be by myself until my heart stops racing.

"Are you okay?" my mother asked, the first words she'd spoken in a while.

Not really, I thought. It might have helped to give voice to my decision, but I couldn't bring myself to do so, not yet.

"Yeah, Mom," I said, mustering a smile. "I'm fine."

60

Dear Answer Lady:

Everything that has ever gone wrong in my life, from losing out to Kathy Curry in second grade (I deserved the role of Mary in the Christmas pageant, not that cow!) to getting kicked out of college for cheating, is totally my mother's fault. Don't ask me how, just trust me on this. Now, my father, on the other hand, is perfect! No daughter could ever want a better father; he's always treated me just like a princess. The trouble is that my mother has him so cowed he just can't stand up to her. And this time it's really causing a big problem for me because I need a few thousand dollars to make rent and buy this absolutely fabulous dress. I asked my dad for the money, and he said sure, but then my mother caught him writing a check and she tore it right out of his hands and shredded it! I mean, isn't that spousal abuse? Anyway, back to me: Any ideas of how to deal with my horror of a mother? And to get the money from my father, of course.

Dear Ungrateful Pig:

Here's an idea: drop dead. If you can't muster the courage to apologize to your mother for being a self-centered bitch and the decency to withdraw

your request for money from your father, at least
have the courtesy to leave them in peace to re-
pair the marriage your presence has so severely
strained. (Don't worry; they won't miss you.)

We stopped midafternoon for some refreshment. Marina
had had ice cream on her mind since seeing two young girls
earlier that afternoon eating ice-cream cones.

"This was a good idea," I said when we were seated at a
gelateria. "I love this *semi-freddo.* It's so wonderfully rich."

Frozen dessert was a safe and neutral topic. I'd worked
hard all day at providing some balance between conversation
and quiet, to preserve my own precarious piece of mind as
well as Marina's.

"You like anything fattening," she said with a smile.

"Guilty as charged."

"Mom?"

"Mmm?"

"I've decided to get in touch with my father when I get
home. Whenever that is," she added hastily.

I put the cup of *semi-freddo* on the table, unfinished. With
my thoughts focused on Luca and Jotham, I'd momentarily
forgotten the other key man in my daughter's life. I tried hard
to hide the dread I felt at hearing those words, all of them.
"Get in touch with my father." "Whenever" I get home.

"Are you sure?" I finally managed to say, wondering why I
was surprised. Hadn't I expected this moment for some time?
Hadn't I seen it as inevitable?

"Yes. I'm absolutely sure. I've been giving it a lot of thought
in the past few days. I guess it's always been at the back of
my mind."

"Okay. Do you—um, do you want any help?"

"No. I don't think so," she said. "But thanks."

"Okay."

Marina eyed me. "You don't look very happy about this, Mom."

"I don't?" I laughed. "Well, I guess I'm not. I'm—I'm afraid for you."

"Why?"

"I'm afraid he'll reject you." Again. I'm afraid he'll hurt you beyond repair.

"How," Marina asked, "can he reject me if I show up on his doorstep? He has to at least listen to me."

Oh, my poor girl, I thought. She really didn't know who she was up against, my having kept the worst of Peter's behavior from her.

"Not necessarily," I said. "You have to be prepared for him to slam the door in your face. You have to be prepared for him to call the police and report you as a trespasser. You have to be prepared for any sort of reaction. Your appearance will be a big shock. You can't predict his response."

Marina seemed to ponder the possibility of an extreme rejection. Finally, she said, "It'll be all right. I'm not going to scream and shout. I'm going to appeal to him as an adult. I'm going to tell him that I don't want any money. I don't even want to be friends. I just want to know why he refused to acknowledge me."

"He might not give you an answer. He might still refuse to acknowledge you."

"Then I'll get a lawyer and demand a paternity test. And when it's proved he's my father beyond all doubt, I'll get a copy of the family medical records or whatever I can get legally, and then I'll walk away."

It was a nice and neat little plan, but one I seriously doubted would go off without a hitch. "It might not be that easy to walk away after seeing him," I cautioned. "Just be aware of that."

"I can handle it. I'll be able to walk away."

And then, I realized. "You want to shame him, don't you?"

"Yes," she said. "I do."

We were silent for a few moments. I thought about the fact that if Marina succeeded in locating her father, he'd once again be in my own life—at least tangentially. Marina would relate her experiences to me, and it wouldn't be right to refuse to hear them. If she took Peter to court, I might be asked to give testimony. I dreaded the prospect, but I wasn't sure I had the right to ask my daughter not to go ahead with her search.

"You realize," I said finally, breaking the silence, "that by confronting your father you'll be disturbing whatever life he's made for himself. He might very well be married, with children. I can't imagine his wife is going to take kindly to learning her husband fathered a child he abandoned before she was even born."

"Then he should have thought twice about abandoning us," Marina said firmly.

"Be that as it may, your father might be an important man in his community. His career might be irrevocably damaged if he acknowledges you. For all I know, he could be in the ministry." For political purposes only, I added silently. In spite of my attempt to imagine him otherwise, Peter was the most profoundly unspiritual person I'd ever known.

"All the more reason for him to admit the truth straight up and avoid negative publicity," Marina argued. "Anyway, why are you taking his side?"

"I'm not taking anyone's side," I said honestly. "I don't even want to think of this as a confrontation or a battle, but I guess in a way it's going to be. I just want you to be fully prepared before you go ahead with this search. I want you to really think things through."

"I have thought things through," she replied stubbornly.

"Have you considered the fact that he might have other children? Are you ready to learn you have a brother or a sister you might never get to know? Are you ready to be responsible for possibly destroying their family as they know it?"

Marina hesitated. Clearly, there were aspects of her decision she hadn't fully considered—or maybe she had considered them, and in spite of her determination, they still gave her pause.

"Yes," she said finally, but without the conviction of a moment ago. "I've considered all that."

I sighed. I hadn't meant to; I hadn't meant to show Marina just how exhausted even the idea of her confronting her father made me feel.

"These past two weeks, Marina," I said, "have been—well, they've been revolutionary. Once you're home, you might find that you feel very differently about pursuing your father."

"No," she said, shaking her head, all hesitation gone again. "I won't. Being here has—it's given me courage. You have, too, Mom."

"Well," I said with a resigned laugh, "either you got courage or you got insanity."

Marina smiled. "Insanity is a possibility. But I guess everyone has to go crazy at one point in her life. It might as well be now, when I'm still young enough to recover."

"While you're busy being brave or insane," I said carefully, "you might also want to consider forgiving your father."

"I don't know if I can do that, Mom," she admitted. "Maybe later, when I've met him. Depending on how he reacts, depending on how he treats me. I don't know. What about you? Have you forgiven him?"

It was a tough question, and a fair one. I thought for a moment before answering. "I'm not sure I ever actively forgave him. I'm not sure I ever made a conscious decision to forgive him. But I think that on some level it just sort of—happened. I think that maybe time made me sort of—sort of forget the intensity, or no longer feel the enormity—of his leaving us."

"Time heals all wounds?"

"Yes," I said. "But I'm not sure that's really forgiveness. I think forgiveness is something you have to consciously choose."

"I never thought about it that way."

I had. I had thought in all ways about forgiveness. Things had worked out well for Marina and me. Maybe if we'd had a harder time, maybe if our lives really had been destroyed by Peter's abandonment, I would still feel angry and hurt. In that case, I doubt I would have been able to forgive the man I'd once thought I loved.

And maybe now, by confronting her father, Marina would succeed in putting our shared ghost to rest. Maybe the specter of Peter Duncan would finally stop haunting us. Maybe, I thought, Marina would turn out to be our family hero.

We left the *gelateria*. According to local custom, Marina slipped her arm through mine.

"Thank you," I said.

"For what?"

"For—for this."

"For linking arms?"

"Yes."

Marina laughed. "Whatever, Mom."

61

The main theme of the first years of every marriage is the struggle over who gets to be the whacky one, i.e., who gets to be the puppet master, the one pulling the strings while seeming not to be capable of such a feat. In this writer's experience, women invariably win this struggle for ultimate control, and if for some reason they don't, if for some reason they allow their husbands to control the marriage, something must have been wrong with their mothers. If a mother doesn't teach her daughter, both by example and by verbal lesson, how to be the woman—i.e., the boss—behind the ostensibly great man, she is seriously failing in her duties.

—What a Mother Needs to Teach Her Daughters

Marina and I shared our final dinner in Florence at the restaurant we'd gone to the very first night, the night the older gentleman had sent a good bottle of wine to the table. I had the *sogliole al marsala,* or sole with Marsala wine, and Marina ordered the *pollo alla diavola,* a local grilled chicken specialty.

Although the food was wonderful, my attention was largely occupied by the big decisions my daughter must have been struggling with all day. Somehow, I'd managed to hold my tongue. Marina's announcement that she was going to find her father had given me hope that she'd decided to come home with me. But I was wary of making an assumption.

Finally, I simply had to ask her. Marina was to meet Luca later that night; time was running out, and my patience had long since fled.

"What have you," I began. "I mean, have you decided what to do about—"

"Yes," she said. "I've decided to go home with you, Mom. And I've decided to break off my engagement with Jotham."

Oh, thank God, I thought, she's coming home with me. And then: Oh, my poor girl, her life has really begun. And finally: Oh, poor Jotham.

"Okay," I said, hoping the relief—the elation—I felt wasn't annoyingly obvious. "You know I'll be there for you if you need my support."

Marina gave a slight smile. "Thanks, Mom. Frankly, I'm frightened to death about telling Jotham it's over. At least," she amended, "over until I can think things through. I know I said that this trip has given me courage, but . . . I don't know how long that courage will last."

"Yes, I can see why you're not looking forward to talking to Jotham," I replied carefully. Badgering, bullying, stubborn Jotham. Marina's defection was going to be a terrible shock for him. No one had ever said no to him. He was going to fight it all the way.

"The thought of hurting him . . . And, well, you know how he has a habit of getting his own way."

"Only because other people are in the habit of giving it to him."

"Yes, yes, I know. But I can't let it happen this time, Mom. I can't let him talk me into staying with him. I have to be strong. I need—I need some time on my own."

"I'll be happy to remind you of that," I said. "If necessary, of course."

"Thanks."

"What are you going to tell Luca? How do you feel about seeing him tonight?"

"I'm scared as well," Marina admitted, and I imagined that her voice already had the melancholic note of remembrance. "But scared in a different way, not like how I feel about talking to Jotham."

"Yes."

"I'll tell Luca that I love him and that I'd like us to stay in touch. I know long distance relationships are ridiculous, but . . ." Marina's eyes pleaded with me to understand. "I don't really want to leave him, Mom. But I just can't stay, not with Jotham waiting for me. I can't just end things with Jotham without talking to him face to face. I owe him that, at least. I—I did love him once. I must have."

"I'm very proud of you, Marina."

Marina shook her head. "Why would you be proud of me? Look at the mess I've made. Jotham's going to be miserable. Luca's going to be miserable. There's a good chance I'm going to be miserable, at least for a while. And all because—"

"All because you're human. Get used to it, Marina. Mess comes with the territory." And, I thought, people recover from mess, mostly.

"I guess," she said, but she didn't sound entirely convinced. "I just thought . . . I just thought that nothing—complicated—would ever happen to me. How could I have been so stupid?"

"Not stupid," I corrected. "Just learning. Just growing up. We're always surprising ourselves, no matter how old we are."

"Yeah, well, thanks for not saying 'I told you so.'"

"I would never say that," I lied. Hadn't I said as much the night of our big fight? I was embarrassed by the memory.

"I just hope Luca understands," Marina said, her voice wistful, as if she'd already left him behind.

He'd better understand, I thought. Or I'll have to have a

harsh word with him before we get on that plane tomorrow morning.

"He will," I said. "If he's the good person he claims to be." And I wondered if Marina had really known Luca, if she had understood him, seen to his core. I'd never know—and maybe, neither would she.

"So, Mom, on a much happier topic, now that you and Rob are getting married—"

The change of subject to something less weighty was a kindness she offered and one I gratefully accepted.

"Hopefully," I corrected. "I haven't even asked him yet."

"Anyway, assuming he says yes, and of course he will, are you going to have another baby?"

"What?" Life with my daughter had become a series of uncomfortable questions, startling revelations, and embarrassing confessions.

Marina laughed. "Oh, come on, Mom, I'm sure you and Rob have talked about having children. You've been together forever."

"I already told you I'm not interested in spending a fortune on fertility treatments. And besides," I said, "the baby question is kind of personal. It's kind of between Rob and me."

"I told you about Luca," she argued. "And back when Jotham and I first started sleeping together, didn't I come to you for advice about birth control?"

"Yes," I said patiently, "but that's different. You're the child, and I'm the parent. There are some aspects of my life my daughter doesn't need to be burdened with."

"Well, if you did decide to have a baby, I'd be more than just a sister, really. I'd be like an aunt. I mean, who better to babysit than flesh and blood? You're going to trust some silly high-school girl more than you're going to trust your own daughter?"

I laughed. "Wait a minute. You're only just out of college.

I am not going to expect a young woman just starting her life to be shackled to a crib while I'm out on the town with my new husband. Especially—"

"What?"

"Nothing," I lied.

"Especially if I'm newly single. Isn't that what you were going to say?"

"Well, yes. I want you to enjoy your life, Marina. I want you to meet new people and have new experiences."

"I will enjoy life, Mom," she said. "At least, I hope I will. But I'm not the sort to abandon my family. Plus, you know I want to have children of my own some day. I can think of your baby as practice. And you won't even have to pay me."

"We are so jumping the gun here, Marina." Poor Rob. He didn't know what he was in for, Marina on a campaign for a baby brother or sister!

"I know," she said. "I'm just happy for you."

I reached across the table for her hand. "I know. Thank you."

Marina grinned a bit of a wobbly grin. "I bet you wish you could say the same for me."

"Yes," I said with a wobbly grin of my own. "I most certainly do."

62

Dear Answer Lady:

For years now I've been reading your column and listening—as it were—to you give advice regarding parenting in general and motherhood specifically. And it finally occurred to me to ask: do you have kids? Because if you don't, I'm not sure you have any right to be doling out advice on how to raise children and what to expect from motherhood, etc. I mean, only those of us blessed with kids of our own—the real kind, the ones we gave birth to, not the pseudo kind, like stepkids— really know what it's all about. So—what's the answer? Are you a mother?

Dear Insufferable, Self-Righteous Bitch:

If you're not a professional Answer Lady, I'm not sure you have any right to be doling out advice on what topics I am or am not qualified to discuss or on which topics I may or may not offer a considered opinion. P.S. You might want to read up on the notion of the sympathetic imagination. Then again, I'm betting you're probably too ignorant to comprehend the term. And that's my professional opinion as an Answer Lady.

I slipped back into our hotel room just after midnight. The lights were off; I assumed my mother was deeply asleep. But from the dark came her voice, heavy with exhaustion.

"You okay?"

"Yeah," I said quietly. "Go to sleep, Mom. We'll talk in the morning."

I knew how hard it must have been for my mother not to fall asleep long before I returned, and I appreciated her effort, but I just wasn't ready to talk, not yet. A few moments later I heard her breathing change and knew she was fast asleep.

I moved the desk chair to face the window; my mother, not bothered by street lamps and broken illuminated signs, had left the curtains open. I sat gratefully, suddenly terribly tired. It had been a long and difficult night, more difficult than I had expected it to be, and yet my resolve had held. For that, I felt proud.

But mostly, I felt weary. And relieved. And melancholy. And strangely excited.

I think Luca had known what my answer to his request would be long before I arrived at his apartment. I think he suspected it the night I'd refused to stay with him until morning. I think he was certain when I'd told him earlier that afternoon that I'd find my way to his apartment on my own. No ride on the back of his oft-repaired Vespa; no cab generously paid for by his father's salary.

"I need to go home," I'd said, almost immediately after entering his apartment. I couldn't bear the thought of prolonging what very well might be a heartbreaking moment.

"Don't let someone else tell you what to do, Marina," he said, misunderstanding.

I put my bag on the floor just inside the door and took his hand in mine. "No, Luca. I want to go home."

His beautiful dark eyes expressed his unhappiness; Luca could be eloquent with his body as well as with his words. I felt my resolve waver but held on.

"I'm sorry," I said. "Really I am. It doesn't mean that I don't love you."

Luca smiled feebly. "There is nothing I can say, nothing I can do to change your mind, Marina? Please tell me what it is, and I will say it and do it gladly. Anything."

Those lovely eyes. His dark hair tousled over his forehead. I would be lying if I were to say his plea didn't move me at all. His hand that fit so well with mine. Of course it moved me. I was in love with this man. I was in love with him, but I was unable and unwilling to abandon my life for him.

"No," I said after a moment. "There's nothing."

We walked to the couch, our hands still clasped, and sat, knees just barely touching.

He asked me what I was going to tell my fiancé. I realized I'd never told Luca his name, and it remained unspoken.

"I'm going to tell him that I need some time to think." It was only a partial lie, or, depending on your perspective, the partial truth. I'd realized I didn't owe either man the intimacy of all my troubled thoughts and emotions.

"Will you tell him about me?" Luca asked.

I'd tried to read his eyes, the tone of his question, but couldn't. Did he want my fiancé to know I'd had an affair with another man; did he want him to know I'd told another man that I loved him?

"No," I said, "I'm not. It would be too hurtful."

"But it is the truth, Marina," Luca insisted, squeezing my hand and leaning closer. "He should know what has happened."

So Luca harbored a degree of machismo as well. He wanted his rival to know of his presence. It disappointed me, but I thought I understood.

"No," I'd said firmly. "I've made up my mind."

We agreed to e-mail and to call; Luca promised to come to Boston any time I wanted him to. There was business he could conduct for his father in New York, and afterward he could fly up to Logan. We could rent a car and drive to Maine, he said. He'd heard interesting things about the New England coast. He wanted, he said, to see a moose. He wanted to eat a whole lobster.

I made no promises; I answered carefully, vaguely. I'd realized the hard way that I had so little experience with men, with relationships. I'd come to Florence knowing nothing other than how things were with Jotham. Now I knew a little more, but it still wasn't enough to keep me safe, to keep me true to myself. I didn't want to make a commitment to someone else—I couldn't—before I knew more about Marina Caldwell and what she needed for a good life.

Even then, still in his apartment, still on his couch, knees touching, I had a sense that long-distance communication with Luca could interfere with my trying to figure out my life on my own. I figured I'd have to be vigilant. I figured I'd have to learn how to speak my own mind, and to do that I'd first have to know my own mind.

We'd made love, of course, and I cried the entire time, tears of sadness and also, I suspected only much later, tears of joy, of liberation.

My mother shifted slightly in her bed, bringing me back to the moment. I glanced over to where she lay and was overcome by a rush of love for her. Even if I never saw Luca again, even if Jotham's anger soured the months ahead, I would always have my mother on my side. There was great comfort in that, and I promised myself never again to take her love for granted.

I looked back again to the open window and noticed for the first time that the broken neon advertising sign had been repaired, the light bulbs replaced. Now the completed sign read *rustichella d'abruzzo* and not *rustichel d'abr*. When, I wondered, had that happened? Had it been fixed days ago, and I'd simply failed to notice, to see?

Was my noticing it now some kind of omen? I couldn't say. Yes, my eyes had been opened since coming to Italy a little over two weeks earlier. But really seeing things outside of myself, really seeing things inside of myself—paying attention and learning anew—those were skills I'd need to further develop, especially if I was determined not to let anyone rescue me from the responsibility of my life. Jotham couldn't rescue me. Neither could Luca. Not even my mother could be allowed the role of savior.

I stared out at that neon sign, whole once more, and wondered what would happen to me. I'd come to expect the unexpected. I was beginning to make peace with, to accept the reality of, uncertainty. But still, I was anxious to know. I was impatient to learn who and where I would be tomorrow, the next month, the next year, and the year after that.

My mother would have said something like "Only time will tell," and she'd have been right—but it wasn't the sort of thing I wanted to hear.

I went to bed that night fully expecting to lie awake until dawn. Instead, I fell immediately into a deep and dreamless sleep. Maybe, I thought later, that sleep had been a gift from my mother.

63

It is the firmly held belief of some professionals in the field of psychology and family dynamics that the state of one's relationship with one's mother is an unfailing indicator of the state of one's well-being in general. Setting aside the complications of stepmothers, adoptive mothers, and other variations on the maternal theme (for example, households comprised of two parents of the same sex), this writer is inclined to agree. For example, it is an undisputed fact that when her own mother acts out in a way that is destructive to the emotional health of this writer, said writer's marital relationship takes quite a beating.

—Making Peace with Your Mother: How to Preserve Your Sanity and Every Relationship in Your Life

Tuesday, June 20

Marina made a mad dash to the duty-free shop, me in tow, Rob's chunky book of architectural drawings wrapped in brown paper and strapped to the top of my wheelie bag.

Soon after meeting Luca, Marina had given up her search for a perfect gift for Jotham. I'd noted this, of course, but hadn't said anything to her about it. What could I have said? But now, at the last minute, and against all logic, she was determined to buy him something. Not something special, just—something.

After ten minutes of frantic searching, she bought a silk, navy blue tie. But when the cashier handed her the slim package, she turned to me as if waking from a dream.

"What am I doing, Mom?" she said, bewildered. "I can't give this to Jotham. I can't give him anything. Just imagine. 'Jotham, I'm returning your ring. I can't marry you, at least not yet. Oh, and by the way, here's a tie I got you in Italy.' That's not going to go over well."

"Give the tie to Grandpa," I suggested. "Grandma will make sure he wears it to church."

"But I already got him that hand-knit sweater. That makes two gifts for him, and I only got Grandma the silk scarf! She'll feel ignored."

She was right. My mother would notice and take offense. "Okay, then, give the tie to Rob."

"Do you think he'll like it?" she asked. "It's kind of—bland."

"If it's from you, he'll like it." This was true, and we both knew it.

We left the duty-free shop, and with almost an hour until boarding time, we found seats at the gate and prepared to wait.

"Do you think Grandma is going to be disappointed in me when she finds out I'm breaking off my engagement?" Marina asked. "You know how much she likes Jotham."

I did know. And at times I'd wondered if my mother's fierce support of Jotham was partly a reaction against my own lukewarm feelings for the guy.

"Look," I said, "I can't honestly say what Grandma will feel, except that she won't be happy about it. But you can't let her feelings determine your decisions, okay? Promise?"

"Oh, I won't let her influence me. I just hate to upset her, or Grandpa."

"Let me tell you, your grandmother is a pretty tough cookie. And Grandpa pretty much rolls with life's punches, or haven't you noticed?"

Marina laughed. "Yeah. I remember when the neighbor, that really old man, Mr. Nettleton, totaled Grandpa's car, he didn't even get mad. Even when the insurance company took forever to pay up."

"Even when we found out that Mr. Nettleton was driving without a license because he'd been declared legally incompetent!"

"Yeah. Mom? I'm really sorry again for forgetting Mother's Day. I promise to get you a great present when we get home."

"Save your money," I said. "You've got a lot going on, and—" I stopped, realizing that I was doing to Marina exactly what my mother was in the habit of doing to me.

"Mom," she said, "don't be a martyr. I'm taking you shopping, and you're going to pick out something special, and I'm going to pay for it, so there."

So maybe Marina really needed to do this for me. And I could give her the gift of gracious acceptance.

"Well," I said, "if you insist."

"And it had better not be something that costs, like, five dollars. We're not going to Wal-Mart."

"You might regret this," I teased.

"No. I won't regret it."

"And my birthday's coming up, too. . . ."

"I told you, Rob and I will take care of everything. We'll give you that birthday party you never had, but it will be a million times better than pizza and beer."

"You're in a very generous mood this morning," I observed.

Marina laughed. "Nervous energy. I feel as if I could fly up to the ceiling or burst apart into a million pieces."

"No more coffee for you."

"I'm going to miss Italian coffee. I'm going to have to rethink my breakfast strategy. I'm not sure I can go back to drinking Dunkin' Donuts coffee."

"I like Dunkin' Donuts coffee," I said. "But I know what you mean. Maybe I'll get rid of our old drip machine and get a press pot. I'm sure I can't afford a cappuccino and espresso maker."

"You could check eBay. Didn't Rob get that old-fashioned toaster he loves on eBay?"

Coffee. Online auctions. Car insurance. There we were chatting about nothing of substance when in only a few hours Marina would face one of the most difficult moments of her life thus far.

I wanted the confrontation with Jotham to be over (and it would be a confrontation); I wanted to protect her from any further pain. I wanted to grasp for Marina these final moments of peace, the calm before the storm, and make them last forever.

"He does love that toaster," I said. "Do you know he polishes it once a week?"

"Rob can be a bit of a nerd, can't he?"

I laughed. "Oh, yes. He certainly can be."

"Well, at least he's our nerd. I, for one, wouldn't trade him for the world."

"No," I said. "Neither would I."

64

Dear Answer Lady:

My friend and I each have a twelve-year-old daughter in the same class at our local middle school. Both girls have been invited to a coed sleepover. I have no problem letting Heather attend, but my friend is outraged about the whole idea and won't allow Melinda to go. I just don't see what the big deal is; coed sleepovers are totally common in our suburban town. But my friend goes on and on about how ridiculous it is to encourage boys and girls to spend the night together in the family basement or in a hotel, largely without chaperones. She says all sorts of things can go wrong, but I say come on! They're only kids! What could possibly happen? The disagreement is really putting a strain on our friendship. So, who do you think is right?

Dear Woman Just Asking for Trouble:

With people like you raising children, is it any wonder that teenage pregnancy is on the rise, that the spread of STDs is raging, that the rate of cervical cancer is soaring, and that respect for women in this society is seriously disintegrating? Your friend is the one with a brain, my dear, not you. The Answer Lady strongly suggests that parents *keep boys away from girls until the boys can control their hormones—say, until they're about thirty-five. Remember, separation of the sexes is a healthy and a sane option.*

Our flight left on time. Almost immediately my mother took out the notebook in which she'd been writing down her observations of Florence as well as her impression of almost every meal she ate while there. Watching her furiously write, I regretted not having kept a notebook or journal of my own on our Tuscan holiday. The thought had never even occurred to me.

Next time, I promised myself. Next time I'll do many things differently.

I lay my head against the pillow the steward had kindly provided and looked out at the featureless sky. It had been quite a day thus far, what with final packing and futile, last-minute gift buying. And the day had started out on a dramatic note with my telling my mother over coffee and pastry about the parting with Luca. Not the details, of course, but the fact that overall Luca had been kind. Unhappy but kind, which, given my "tendency" to cave under pressure from men, had made it easier for me to stay strong and say what I'd needed to say. For his kindness, my mother, too, had been grateful.

Finally, I'd thanked her for having remained awake until I came home.

"Oh," she said, "no problem. I just propped up my eyelids with toothpicks. It's a foolproof method."

Now, well on my way home to Boston, I turned my thoughts to the man I'd just left behind and realized with a shock that I couldn't recall his face clearly. The impression was there, but the details refused to come. The tiny mole—

was it on the right or the left of his nose? His hair—was there a glint of gold in it when the sun was at a certain angle? His fingernails—what was their exact shape?

It was disconcerting. What did it mean when memory abandoned you so quickly? Was it a self-protective mechanism, instinctual maybe, or maybe something learned?

I reached for my bag. I could easily bring back the memory of Luca's face. He'd given me a photo of himself, one taken by his sister Margharita at a recent family gathering. But I sat back, letting my bag remain under the seat in front of me. Instead, I tried to puzzle out my feelings.

I was disconcerted, yes. I felt sad, too, and disappointed in myself. Also . . . I felt a little bit relieved.

I was horrified. How could I feel relieved? I'd said I loved this man. Was my inability to recall the details of his face yet another sign of an inherited genetic failure, a sign of my father's aversion to responsibility? Was it a sign of an inherent moral weakness? Or was my faulty memory instead simply evidence that I was finally growing up—and away—from a person I might have allowed to keep me from becoming myself?

I was stepping away from Luca. I was stepping away from Jotham. I was frightened. I was glad. I hadn't known I was suffocating, until I wasn't suffocating any longer.

I didn't look at the photo of Luca on that flight. Instead, when my mother got up to visit the ladies' room, I took from my bag the sketch of me he'd made the day we visited the Giardini di Boboli, and I remembered how uncomfortable I'd felt when he'd suggested I pose for him.

I looked at that sketch for a long time and wondered. Had Luca captured the essential me, or only his view of me? It's true we're a different person to everyone who knows us, and I was finally beginning to realize that the real difficulty in identity lay in finding the essential Marina and not allowing her to be lost in other people's perspectives and interpretations.

Eventually, I put the sketch back into my bag, having come to no conclusion about whom it was that Luca had drawn.

The photograph of Luca. The sketch he'd made of me. I imagined I would always keep both images. I imagined I would want to. They were tokens of the moment when my life had taken its first radical turn.

My mother returned from the bathroom, explaining her long absence as due to a woman with three small children on line in front of her.

"She had to take them in one by one. Poor thing. I assured her I'd watch the other two while she was inside with the third. And then she had to use the bathroom herself!"

"Where was her husband?" I asked.

My mother shrugged. "I have no idea."

Two weeks earlier I had been expecting to have a husband within a year, to be Mrs. Grandin, Jotham's helpmate and partner in life.

I touched my family's heirloom locket against my chest and wondered if I should return it to my grandmother now that my wedding was being postponed indefinitely. But then I had a better idea. I was sure Grandma wouldn't mind. And if she did, well, the locket was now mine to give. Gifts, my mother had taught me, should have no strings attached.

I resolutely unclasped the chain and held it out to my mother. "This rightfully belongs to you, Mom."

"Why?" she said, hesitating to take it. "Because Rob and I might be getting married? Maybe you should wait until things are definite."

"No. I don't want to wait. I want you to have it now. For your wedding day or for no reason at all," I said. "Don't worry. I took Jotham's picture out last night."

She finally took the locket and fastened the chain around her neck. "Thank you, Marina. This means an awful lot to me."

"You're welcome," I said. "So, when you and Rob get married—"

"If we get married."

"Humor me, Mom. When you and Rob get married, I don't have to wear some disgusting shiny dress, do I?"

"Have you met me? Do you really think I'd be so cruel? Or so tasteless."

"Good. So what's your color scheme?"

"My color scheme?" My mother laughed. "Marina, I don't know. I don't even know if Rob's going to want to go through with a wedding after all this time."

"Oh, come on! You can't seriously think he isn't going to be thrilled. Mom, really, sometimes you are just so dense."

"Okay," she said, relenting. "Let's see. Maybe peach and mint green. I always thought a spring wedding would be lovely."

"Spring? That's like nine months away! Mom, the poor guy's been waiting around long enough. Just do it, already. No later than early fall. Late September, maybe."

"What about October?" she said. "Chances are the weather will be nicer."

"Only the first two weeks. I don't want your wedding overshadowing my birthday."

"Of course not!"

My mother lifted the locket from her chest and looked down at it. "I have to admit," she said, "that I was horrified when you told me you were thinking of changing the locket to make it look more contemporary."

"When did I say that?" I asked, thoroughly surprised.

"On the plane over."

"I don't remember that at all. Isn't that strange? Why would I have wanted to change it? Grandma would be so upset."

If my mother had an opinion, she didn't share it. "Well, thanks again for giving it to me. I really appreciate the gesture."

"I'm glad you like it," I said. "Now, when am I getting your gorgeous new ring?"

She pretended to be appalled. "And to think I was just about to ask you to be my maid of honor!"

"Really, Mom?" I felt tears come to my eyes.

"Really," she said. "So? What do you say?"

I leaned over and kissed her cheek. "Thank you," I said. "It will be my pleasure."

65

The most interesting heroines in literature are often motherless. Consider, for example, Jane Eyre, the heroine of the eponymous novel by Charlotte Bronte. I propose that this is a bit of wish fulfillment on the part of the female authors of such heroines. Could it be that without a mother's constant criticism and endless undermining, a woman—be she fictional or real—is simply freer to live an exciting and challenging life?
—A Woman On Her Own: Life Without the Mater

The pilot announced that we were approximately thirty minutes from landing.

"Are you really as okay as you're acting?" I asked Marina. Considering that my daughter's life had been rattled to the core, she was behaving quite normally.

"I don't know if I'm okay," she said quietly, turning away from the window to face me. "I think I am, but maybe when I see Jotham I'll fall apart. Maybe I won't be able to go through with it. I hope not. But I just don't know."

"I do." I took her hand, a hand empty of Jotham's inappropriate engagement ring. "I know. You won't lose courage, not now. You've come too far—and in a remarkably short time—to turn back. You'll be fine."

Marina's smile was faint. She squeezed my hand and then let go. "Thanks, Mom. That means a lot."

But then, as the plane began its final descent, Marina turned to me again.

"Mom," she said, her voice ragged, "I'm afraid. How can I do this? How can I hurt Jotham? What if I ruin his life? What if he's never able to trust anyone ever again?"

I thought either possibility highly unlikely but kept that opinion to myself. "It would be more hurtful," I said, "to the both of you, to lie to him and pretend that nothing's changed. You know that. We've talked this through."

"Yes," she said, "I know. But I'm afraid. I feel like such a coward, Mom."

"You're not a coward. You're a brave young woman. You'll be strong, and you'll say what you know you have to say." And as the words left my mouth, I willed them to be true.

"I'm pretty sure I won't be able to count on Allison and Jessica for support," Marina said after a moment. She sounded so sad, so resigned. It hurt me.

"Yes," I said carefully. "They'll be in a tough spot."

"I mean, the guys will definitely side with Jotham; they've been friends forever. And I just know Jordan and Jason will tell Allison and Jessica to have nothing to do with me. How can I stay friends with them if they have to see me behind the guys' backs?"

"You can't," I agreed.

I wished I could argue that it would be otherwise, but I'd seen too much evidence that proved Marina's prediction. A couple breaks up, and the scramble to lay blame and take sides is fast and furious. And it wasn't as if Marina, Allison, and Jessica had developed much of a friendship on their own; inevitably, everything had come down to the priority of the couples. Marina was facing potential loss from many quarters. I just hoped the gain would be worth it.

Marina looked at me with a wry smile. "You know what, Mom?"

"What?"

"Suddenly you've become my only friend."

"Your BFF?"

"That phrase is so over," she said, complete with eye roll.

"Sorry."

"But yeah, maybe. I guess we'll just have to see how things go."

"Sounds good to me," I said. It sounded very good.

66

Dear Answer Lady:
I'm really upset. The weirdest thing has hap-
pened. Suddenly, it's like my mother likes her
dogs better than she likes me—it's like the minute
I moved out, she forgot I existed! Seriously, I got
my own apartment about six weeks ago, and
since then it's like every time I call my mom and
suggest we get together, she makes some excuse
like Fifi doesn't feel well and needs peace and
quiet or that Nigel has a massage appointment
she just can't cancel. And she never asks me
what's going on in my life! It's like, hello, I'm
your child, not those four-legged ratty-looking
things you let sleep in your bed every night! How
can I get her to pay attention to me again?

Dear Idiot:
It's like, hello, those four-legged ratty-looking
things sound a lot less annoying than you do. No
wonder your mother prefers their company to
yours. Stop calling her, and let her live her life in
the company of creatures who are grateful for
her love and concern—and who actually give her
something in return.

The plane landed at Logan Airport exactly on time. Marina and I waited together at the baggage carousel. There

was so much still to say, in spite of our having talked though most of the intercontinental flight. But both of us were silent.

When our bags were yanked off the circling belt, we hugged.

"Good luck," I whispered. "Are you sure you don't want Rob and me to wait in case you need a ride home?"

"No, Mom, but thanks," she whispered back. "I'll see you at home later tonight."

I watched as Marina walked away and felt as nervous for her—and as proud of her—as I ever had since the day she was born almost twenty-two years earlier.

Rob was waiting where we'd planned to meet, at the taxi stand, an entirely different location from where I knew Jotham would be waiting for Marina. My instinct had been right. My daughter didn't need witnesses to the reunion that wasn't going to be a reunion.

Rob. There he stood, wearing his usual, open-necked, rolled-up-sleeve shirt with a pair of well-worn chinos. And he was holding a bouquet of yellow and purple flowers. My heart swelled with happiness at the sight of him.

"Rob!" I called unnecessarily, for he'd seen me and was striding toward me with a big grin.

I launched myself into his embrace, almost knocking him over in the process.

"Ooof!" he said into my hair.

"Sorry."

"I've smashed your flowers."

"And I've crunched your gift," I said.

"You brought me a gift?"

"You deserve one."

"Well, I don't know about—"

"Rob, let's get married," I whispered into his neck, suddenly shy, almost embarrassed to look him in the eye, afraid I might not see what I wanted to see.

"How about this weekend?" Rob whispered back. "If we're recovered from this backbreaking hug."

I pulled away enough to look into his smiling face. "You mean it?"

"I've meant it all along, Elizabeth."

I laughed. "We're having a big romantic airport moment, you realize that don't you? Like in a movie."

"But no violins. And no applauding crowds. Rats."

"Champagne? This is a special occasion; I think we deserve it."

"There's a Fresh From the Sea inside," Rob said. "I'm not sure it's open, but—"

I grabbed Rob's free hand. "Let's go find out. And let's get some bluefish pate and some shrimp cocktail while we're at it. Marina is right: airplane food is awful."

My baggage, a crushed bouquet, and a bulky old book in tow, we made our way back inside the terminal building. I looked across at Rob; he couldn't seem to wipe the grin off his face. It made me very happy to see.

"You know your mother's going to be out of her mind with excitement," he said.

"I know," I said, pretending to shudder. "Mother-of-the-Bride-zilla. Well, you know what I mean."

"Yeah. I'll try to keep your father—and me—out of the way. Poor guy."

"My parents will have something else to think about soon, in addition to our wedding."

"What?" he asked.

"Marina's breaking up with Jotham."

Rob came to a dead stop, and because we were holding hands, I did, too. I'm sure it was only a slight case of whiplash. My neck had stopped hurting by the next morning.

"You're kidding me," he said.

"No, I'm not. And there's more. She's decided to hunt down her father and confront him."

Rob eyed me closely. "What happened to you two over there?" he asked. "Did you each have a major epiphany? Did you receive divine inspiration? Did you get religion?"

"Something like that," I said. "Look! Fresh From the Sea is open! Let's go!"

67

Women are like beautifully appointed boutiques,
redolent with the scent of lilacs and freshly baked
scones. Men are like Wal-Mart—harsh lighting, wide
aisles, and piles of mass-produced crapola. Just where
do you go when you need some tea and sympathy?
Mom, that's where.
   —Learning to Appreciate Your Mother: It's Not as
     Hard as You Think

I stood in the lobby of the parking garage, partly hidden
from general view, and watched Jotham. He was standing, as
planned, by the bank of elevators. He was checking his watch
and scanning passengers straggling toward him and then
checking his watch again. I continued to stand there, clutching the strap of my bag in one fist, gripping the handle of my
wheelie bag in the other. I stood there gathering my courage.

And with each second that passed, I felt stronger. Yes, I
told myself, you've made the right decision. Your life does
not abide with this man. Your future is elsewhere, and someday, you'll find out where.

From where I stood, I could see Jotham's frown of impatience deepen.

It was time. I took a deep breath, whispered "Wish me
luck, Mom," and walked determinedly toward him.

And then I walked on into the rest of my life.

TUSCAN HOLIDAY

Holly Chamberlin

ABOUT THIS GUIDE

The suggested questions are included to enhance
your group's reading of Holly Chamberlin's
Tuscan Holiday.

DISCUSSION QUESTIONS

1. The question of honesty is raised several times during the course of the story. With the notion of honesty in mind, do you think that Marina's decision not to tell Jotham about her affair with Luca was the right one? When is it kinder to keep silent? What does Marina owe Jotham in the end?

2. The question of loyalty is also raised throughout. For example, Elizabeth decides to keep Marina's affair with Luca a secret from Rob; she feels that her loyalty to her daughter supersedes her loyalty to her longtime partner. Do you agree with her choice? Does loyalty to one person before another depend on the circumstance in question? Do you think that Jane (Elizabeth's mother) should have told Marina about Elizabeth's extensive efforts to reach Peter, Marina's father? (Is Elizabeth's assessment of her mother's motives in this regard reasonable?)

3. In Chapter 3, Marina thinks about the absoluteness of a mother's love. What do you think? Is a mother's absolute love a myth or an achievable possibility? Are there times when it's right or justifiable for a mother to abandon her love for her child? Might there be moral reasons for such an act? Might a mother consider the abandonment of her child an act of self-preservation, or one that might ultimately benefit the child?

4. While spending the day with Luca, Marina finds herself wondering: when is changing your mind an act of

salvation, and when is it an act of cowardice? How, she wonders, can one tell? What do you think?

5. What do you consider Elizabeth's greatest strength as a mother? Greatest weakness?

6. Do you agree with Elizabeth that Marina latched on to Jotham in direct (though perhaps unconscious) response to the end of her mother's relationship with Rob?

7. In relation to Peter's abandonment, Elizabeth ponders the notion of forgiveness. Is it, as Elizabeth has come to think, a deliberate act, or is it an accident of the passing of time? Is forgetfulness or the dimming of memory/feelings the same as forgiveness? What do you think are the benefits of forgiveness?

8. What do you think Marina means when, late in the book, she says that she was coming to realize that passion acts as both savior and destroyer? Do you agree?

9. Do you, like Marina, think there is such a thing as love at first sight? Do you think certain people are fated to be together, as soul mates? In the case of Marina and Luca, do you think she fell in love with him immediately, or do you think that her growing dissatisfaction with Jotham had primed her to seize upon another man as a way out of her stifling engagement? Might Marina's relationship with Luca have been the result of both physical attraction and personal boredom?

10. Is maternal feeling an instinct, a learned habit and skill, or a combination of both? Compare Elizabeth's adolescent thoughts/feelings regarding motherhood (largely negative) with Marina's (largely positive).

11. How has Marina's view of her mother as a victim colored her own life and helped determine her own choices? How could she have come to have this view, given the fact that her mother is by all social standards a successful person? Do you think a daughter can ever really know her mother as a person apart from her own daughterly prejudices?

12. Elizabeth is disturbed by the fact that she sees her daughter's infidelity, rather than her engagement to Jotham, as her coming of age. Can you understand why she sees the affair as a point of maturation?

13. In Chapter 11, Marina reacts with fear and distrust when the elderly "gentleman at the end of the bar" sends a bottle of wine to the table where she and her mother are having dinner. Why do you think Marina has this negative response? Might there be other reasons besides, as Elizabeth says, she's "been with a rather jealous boyfriend from age fifteen"? Do you think that Marina sees Jotham as "a man" or as the boyfriend she plans to marry?

14. Elizabeth studies a painting of the Holy Family and, reflecting on Mary's humanness, thinks of all the traits that she, Elizabeth, has passed on to her daughter. She says, "I automatically condemned my child to be the recipient of any number of weaknesses and difficulties." Is Elizabeth being realistic or too harsh on herself? Later Elizabeth wonders "where a mother's responsibility ends." Do you think a mother's responsibility for her child ever ends?

15. Marina is spending much time calling Jotham, and her mother suggests she might spend more time seeing Flo-

rence. Marina responds, "You just don't know what it's like to be getting married." Elizabeth says, "I felt as though I'd been slapped" but knows that her daughter didn't intend to hurt her. What is the author telling us about Elizabeth as a mother?

16. In Chapter 39, Marina sees the photo of Elizabeth and Peter for the first time and says to her mother, "You look like you're one hundred percent totally in love. You look so happy." Elizabeth responds that, yes, she was in love. Pointedly she avoids the second comment. Do you think Marina, in love with Luca, can understand that being in love doesn't necessarily mean being happy?

17. In Chapter 46, Elizabeth ponders what she has told and what she has not told Marina about her father and wonders if there's ever a right time and a right way to tell a truth that might be hurtful. Is Elizabeth more concerned with the right time for her daughter or for herself? Is there a difference?

18. Luca asks Marina to stay in Florence with him; he says that "in this life, feelings are all that matter. Feelings are all we have." Marina agrees but is not even sure what he means. What is the author telling us here about this new man in Marina's life? Is Luca being fair in asking Marina to stay in Italy with him?